SMOKE AND DAEMONS

CAUGHT BETWEEN WORLDS

CANDICE BUNDY

LUSIOS PUBLISHING

Smoke and Daemons
Copyright © 2012
by Candice Bundy

Previously published as The Daemon Whisperer.

Editor: Zippy Wizard Redaction

Identifiers: ISBN-13: 978-0-9854185-8-8 (paperback)

Published by Lusios Publishing, Denver, CO.
Second Edition, 2021.

Manufactured in the United States of America.

CONTENTS

CHAPTER 1

*M*eri coughed as the summoner heaped yet another handful of cinquefoil onto the brazier. She pulled her cowl lower and tucked a stray lock of her long, chestnut-brown hair back underneath, not wanting to be recognized. Her employer had hired her to oversee two daemon invocations this week. At the first one, she had been a mere bystander to an uneventful and failed attempt. Would this be yet another waste of her time?

Reverend George coughed and mumbled in low tones through the required chants, and she shook her head, rubbing her fingers along her brow. She recognized the words for the spells meant to cleanse and ward the space, but without the proper consistency of intonation -- which he lacked -- they held little force. He continued chanting away as he picked up a bowl from the small altar and then walked clockwise, laying out a line of mostly even sea salt along the ground around the outer perimeter. The attendees' faces she could make out through the shadowy fog held undeniable tension and fear --

not exactly a show of faith in the summoner's skills, or perhaps they rightly feared the ritual's intended product.

"Amateur," Meri whispered under her breath. Reverend George was an abject example of 'you get what you pay for.' In daemon-infested Denver, this was just another empty hovel permeated with mold and filled with rats as the backdrop to yet another summoning. The internal walls of the building had been stripped of any burnable wood for nightly cook fires for the city's homeless, and anti-Corporate graffiti decorated what remained.

In the economically depressed city, it never surprised her how many desperate souls were willing to risk a career as a summoner for the promise of the cash payoff. The Reverend was a middle-aged man of mixed heritage, his hair and long beard held equal parts buzzard feathers and blackened mud. His flamboyant, long-sleeved, velvet purple jacket and alligator boots lent him an air of eccentricity, enhanced by the speckles of grime scattered upon them. Would the people, maybe the same ones who crowded this room, mistake the ritual elements as signs of power? Plus, she'd heard the newcomer worked for reasonable prices. What a deal.

Not exactly a selling point when the summoned creature might end up eating you for dinner. But heck, The Reverend had made it this far, right? So let's fire up that brazier! A few words mentioned on the street guaranteed you an audience of casual onlookers, all the better to spread your reputation. Assuming, of course, you lived through the night.

She itched to step in and show the Reverend each of his mistakes before anyone got hurt. However, she wasn't being paid to be a Good Samaritan, so she held her ground and waited, as much as watching such poor techniques chafed her.

Reverend George finished warding the space using a bowl of sanctified water, repeating a similar pattern as he had with the salt. He held up his hands to those in attendance. "If you have doubts or fear that your mind can't handle what you're about to see, then leave now!" Everyone stood still, waiting to see if anyone else would bolt. No one did.

She watched him face the crowd, arms stretched out wide, inviting challengers. He walked into the center of the ring of salt and knelt. Dramatically, he tore open his shirt and picked up a consecrated ceremonial blade from the altar before him. Not a speck of daemon ink was in evidence on his skin. What a novice.

"Engetheus, daemon of rage and retribution, I invoke thee!" Reverend George took the blade and sliced across his abdomen above the liver. A trickle of blood ran freely across his otherwise unmarked skin.

He doesn't even know the right offering? This summoning was going to end predictably.

"I present my flesh offering in kind, and command you to rise and take form!"

Meri waited and listened to the Reverend repeat the chant, over and over, until a familiar tingle in her liver crept under her skin, building into fingers of flaring heat and ice, tracing patterns across her nerves. A swirling vapor cloud wafted from the floor. The familiar colors of green, gray, and black were visible even in the dim light; contrasting against the sigils the reverend had drawn earlier on the floor. She smiled then, knowing things were about to get interesting. Her employer's fee would be well spent.

The chanting Reverend George kept his eyes closed, so he missed the emergence of Engetheus. Gasps and shrieks erupted from the onlookers as they beheld the daemon's bright red, muscular body, all seven feet of him -- not counting the jet black horns which rose another foot. His coal-black eyes and long, sharp fangs matched his gleaming horns. If the crowd expected rage personified to look like a bunny rabbit, they'd just gotten an education. Only the bravest resisted fleeing the hovel, and everyone but Meri took a few steps back.

Reverend George stopped his chanting and gazed up at the beast, eyes wide with fright, fixated on the daemon's horns. She sighed and watched him stand up in front of the rage daemon. His awkward movements to stand up reminded Meri why she never knelt at a summoning. Even after standing, the daemon still towered over the reverend, emphasizing the inherent lack of power balance. Being only five-foot-eight and weighing about one fifty-something, she'd long ago gotten used to looking up to the often tall daemons. The important part was never showing them a hint of fear.

"I am summoned, Reverend George," Engetheus rumbled, "but to what end?" By the glint in his eyes, she imagined he had a long list of his vengeance targets.

At least one gasp went up from the crowd, and Meri guessed the witness just put two and two together and figured out daemons could identify humans by scent alone, even if it was the first time they'd met you.

"I have called you forth to exact retribution upon Harold E. Fields." He pulled from his jacket pocket a small bag and held it out with a shaking hand. "This contains his hair and will guide you to him."

Engetheus snatched the bag and took a long whiff and then tossed the bag aside. "Yes, I have met this one. Finding him again is no challenge."

Meri lifted her chin and narrowed her gaze on Engetheus while running her hand over his marking over her liver. The daemon's eyes flashed to hers for a moment, no more.

"What form of retribution?" Engetheus asked the Reverend.

"Death to him and any kin abiding with him. The form is of your choosing."

"That is to my liking, summoner. But first, payment is required." A smile spread across Engetheus' face, revealing even more sharp, black teeth. His thick, black tongue snaked across his teeth; he was eager for his due.

Reverend George took a small bowl from the altar and made a light cut above his abdomen again, taking care to collect the blood in the bowl. He held the bowl out to the daemon. "Accept this blood from my liver, to satiate your hunger."

At this, Engetheus chuckled, and Meri sighed. Reverend George hadn't done his homework.

Engetheus slapped the bowl from the Reverend's hands. "That is not a suitable payment. You will give me what I require." The daemon moved with lightning speed, knocking the man to the floor. Engetheus crouched over him and raised his fangs over his liver. The few remaining onlookers fled, not wanting to watch or be next in line for the daemon's appetite.

"Engetheus, hold!" Meri commanded. She dropped the cowl from her cloak and stepped forward, again tracing her hand over the pattern of Engetheus daemon-ink under her clothes. An answering fire lit in the daemon's eyes, his ink a living fire across her flesh.

Engetheus roared, now unable to move any closer to the errant reverend. His black eyes turned to stare her down, but he didn't back off from his intended prey. Her liver burned with a reflection of the daemon's emotions, a visceral reminder of their prior engagements.

"I saw you, summoner Meri. I assumed you were just here for the show." The daemon flashed her a wide, toothy grin, which held no mirth.

"Bound once, bound always, rage-bearer. I'm here to modify your orders."

"No, you can't do that!" said Reverend George. "I summoned him!"

"Yes, and you were doing so well, sport," Meri said. "Unfortunately for you, Engetheus and I go way back. If you were a pro, you'd know not to invite anyone else to your summoning to avoid just this potential conflict of interest for the daemon. Daemons will respond to whoever displays the more dominant hand. It's called the A Priori Rule, not that it helps you now."

"There's no conflict for me." Drool dripped down onto Reverend George's chest, drawing a whimper out of him. The daemon deferred to Meri. "Command me."

"First, you are to ignore the previous command to inflict retribution on Mr. Fields and his kin."

"For what length of time?" Engetheus asked.

"Until I, and only I, lift the restriction. Now, tell me who hired this summoner."

Engetheus sniffed deeply, and then returned his watchful gaze to her. "Mr. Sam Hodge."

"Well done. You will hunt Hodge down, tear him limb from limb, and then feast upon him, as you will. You will leave his kin unharmed."

Engetheus frowned, no doubt disappointed at having fewer targets to kill. "Done."

"Third, when this task is complete, you will exit this dimension and return to your own, harming no others in your wake."

"As you command. Anything else?"

"One last thing. I feel this client would like some trophies. Bring me the standard ones when you're done."

Engetheus' muscles rippled across his torso, and his inky tongue darted out. Meri steeled her nerves and wondered what range of emotions the daemon tasted in the air right now. "'This pleases me," he replied.

Her gaze drifted from the tips of Engetheus' ebony horns, his cruelly curved fangs, his broad and stout red-skinned bulk, all the way to his black-clawed hands and feet.

"'This isn't about your amusement or mine. I simply wish to make a statement to a sub-standard and puny human, should he challenge me. Surely you can appreciate this?"

Engetheus bared his full complement of fang. Meri supposed it was a smile. "I like your style, summoner. As you command."

Their agreement bound, she steeled herself. "As to your payment."

She picked up the bloodied bowl and gave it a quick rinse with the handily available sanctified water from the altar. Without a second thought, she shoved two fingers down her throat and then, on cue, vomited into the bowl. She swished some water through her mouth and spat it out into the bowl as well. She turned to see a disgusted human gaze from Reverend George and a worshipful daemonic one.

"You see, Reverend, rage daemons hunger for our hate, and energetically we store hate in our liver. As our bodies cleanse, we secrete this negative energy as bile." She handed the bowl to the still crouching daemon. "All debts are paid?" she asked, still holding the bowl.

"Paid in full," Engetheus replied with a greedy gaze. "All shall be as you command."

"Thank you for the lesson, Miss Meri," Reverend George said.

She looked him in the eye, yet managed no remorse. Engetheus noisily consumed her offering, engrossed in his momentary delicacy.

"I guess I'll be going now," Reverend George said. She watched him try to back his way out from under the massive daemon.

"There's still the matter of your payment." Engetheus pinned him down with a clawed foot while he finished the offering from Meri.

"But you're not taking commands from me anymore. I don't owe you anything!"

The daemon's laughter reminded her of rocks scraping together. "You summoned, you pay. Her payment doesn't apply to our arrangement."

"But, but, I can't throw up as easy as she can! Just give me a moment!"

"I'm not the patient type."

Meri watched as Reverend George's skin was torn asunder, his tortured cries echoing through the exposed rafters of the dilapidated building. He was no match for the powerful daemon he'd summoned and failed to bind. It was a risk each summoner faced at every summoning. She stood and watched, unable to walk away, the grotesque reminder of her potential future staring her in the face. Instead, she witnessed Engetheus eat the man's liver bite by bloody bite. The Reverend refused to die quickly. He continued to whine while he tried to fight off the daemon.

With every mouthful, Engetheus' marking upon Meri's flesh pulsed with invigorating life force. The connection wasn't lost on her: this creature was rooted under her skin. When the daemon swung his head in her direction and met her eyes, his dark eyes blazing with hidden knowledge, she knew without words he reveled in their bond.

She finally left the building when the Reverend ceased flailing, the pool of blood around his body hauntingly familiar. She walked on, despite the growing awareness in her liver as more daemon ink bubbled up onto her skin, intensifying her connection with the rage daemon. And deeper, as only summoners understood, under her skin, her bile churned and her mood inflamed. She could have bargained with the daemon for the man's life. However, there was only so high a payment she was willing to take on to any daemon. She had to preserve every inch of remaining bare skin and every ounce of sanity she had left.

eri walked a few blocks, hoping for a taxi, when the air turned sultry, perfumed with

vanilla and sandalwood. Soothing warmth heated her blood, easing the pain in her belly and traveling like an electric current from the top of her head to the tips of her toes.

Meri stopped and scanned the area around her. She'd had daemons sent after her before, but one who curled her toes? That was original. "Reveal yourself!"

The daemon appeared a few paces in front of her. He towered over six feet tall and could pass for human, that is, if humans could ever be mistaken to look so perfect, or to manifest out of thin air. He was lanky yet muscular. Silvery blond hair framed his angular face and was cropped close to the nape of his neck. His clothes appeared like a typical human's: black pants, boots, and an expensive-looking button-down white shirt.

The intensity of his ice-blue eyes riveted her, and Meri couldn't help but notice his full lips and imagine what his skin might feel like pressed against hers. Would it be cool in contrast to hers, as it appeared in color, or deceptively warm? The texture could be silky smooth, as it looked, or rough as sandpaper. You never knew with daemons. Things were always different from what they first appeared.

Wait a second, Meriwether Storm, daemon summoner extraordinaire, mesmerized by a daemon? She focused on the pain in her abdomen, a stark reminder of recent, and true nature of the daemons she'd come to know. This one was likely no different, regardless of his charms. Meri sighed deeply. Why couldn't she have better taste in men? Could Meri at least be interested in a *human* male? She put her best game face forward.

"State your name, daemon," Meri demanded.

"Azimuth."

"Why have you sought me out?" And, more importantly, who had summoned this creature to her? She doubted his arrival meant anything fortuitous.

"You look unwell, and this is not the best place for a private conversation." His concerned gaze struck her as either entirely genuine or cunningly calculated.

Yeah, a *private conversation* was the last thing she needed to have with this temptation. "My present health is not up for discussion," she replied, knowing it would take days for her liver and mood to recover from the encounter with Engetheus. "My schedule doesn't presently permit time for a private meeting with the most impressive Azimuth."

The faintest hint of a smile curled his lips. "Perhaps you would feel more comfortable closer to home?"

He moved towards her, his steps fluid and graceful as a cat, and she fought the instinct to back away. She was determined to concede no ground and show no sign of reacting to him.

He reached out towards her, and it took all of Meri's willpower to resist flinching when his hand rested lightly on her arm. Azimuth's teleportation was instantaneous and had no sense of movement and the next moment they stood on her front porch. He stepped away from her, breaking their near-electric connection.

"I'm not paying for that. I'd intended to catch a cab."

"Consider it a simple gesture of my goodwill. Besides, that neighborhood is a slum. I wouldn't trust the taxi drivers there."

"And yet I should trust you, daemon?" She took a seat in

one of the wicker chairs on her front porch, a welcome relief for the pain in her belly. Azimuth smiled broadly, and Meri warmed under the focus of his attention. *Damn him.*

"That's entirely up to you, Meri. I'm sure in time you will judge me as you see fit."

He took a seat across from her on the porch, and she gave him the once-over again. His fine linen white shirt was spotless and draped his form yet held a crease. Meri had no doubt he'd had it tailored. Did daemon tailors exist? His black leather pants molded to his thighs in all the right places. His black leather boots didn't have a single scuff mark on them. Was this daemon a master of illusion or very well compensated by his master? What did he mean, 'in time'? How long could this job take, after all?

"What business, pray tell, does your summoner have you on tonight?"

"My employer wishes to hire you, due to your impressive reputation."

His flattery stroked her pride, and in turn flamed her temper, which echoed the burning in her liver. She knew what daemon flattery was worth: nothing. However, she'd never had a daemon present a job offer before, and she couldn't help but be curious.

"Your employer sent a daemon instead of contacting me directly?"

"I can be suitably persuasive."

"Oh, I bet you can," She replied under her breath. He raised an eyebrow, and Meri sucked in her breath and focused on the pain in her liver. If she didn't watch herself, he'd catch on that her interest was more than professional. "You've piqued my curiosity. What's the job?"

Azimuth's lips curled in a self-satisfied smug. "Rest tonight, and I'll be in touch tomorrow."

Before Meri could speak another word, he was gone, and to her distaste, she discovered she wished he wasn't.

CHAPTER 2

The buttery fragrance of blueberry pancakes roused a smile on Meri's lips, waking her like a beloved alarm clock. The muscles of her slight teenage form protested a thorough under-the-covers full-body stretch, and then her feet hit the floorboards running towards the kitchen. Golden shafts of morning light filtered through the white cotton eyelet drapes covering the windows, bathing the entire family room in a warm, sunny glow. When Meri's body slid into the seat of the chair at the small kitchenette table, the legs groaned, and the feet danced a noisy jig.

"Hungry?" her mother, Bethany, asked, casting a grin over her shoulder while she flipped another pancake.

"You know I love blueberry pancakes!" Meri rested her head on laced fingers to contain her excitement while her feet wound around the chair legs below the table. Her mother was already dressed for the day, as usual. Meri sat up, her back ramrod straight, hands gripping the table. The low-slung neck, cap sleeves, and above-the-knee dark red dress exposed her mother's daemon ink, which complimented her olive skin tone, although she wore an apron over it while she cooked. She'd even pinned her long, raven tresses up atop her head. "Big summoning today?"

Her mother gave her 'the look' and placed a plate of pancakes and bacon in front of her. Meri's stomach kicked into gear, and she dug in, forgetting her question for a moment.

"You know your father, and I don't like to discuss specific clients with you, sweetie. Summoning techniques, yes. Daemons and their attributes, we'll drill you on rigorously. It's the least we can do in case the worse happens, and those damned daemons find a way to run rampant on Earth. But until you're out of high school, we won't have you involved with any of our jobs, no matter how impressed we are with your attempts to date."

Meri pointed with her fork. "I'm not a child, mother. I'm fifteen, and I've been summoning for four years now. That's more than many adults in the trade."

Bethany ran her fingers down the side of her daughter's face and sighed. She held out her arms. "Look at my ink, and then look at yours. I still have some advice to give you, no?"

Meri surveyed her mother's skin, a patchwork of daemon ink and testament to many, many successful summonings. She smiled sheepishly in response.

Her mother placed a glass of orange juice next to her, and Meri took a long drink. "Wait, this is fresh orange juice!"

Her mother drew herself up to her full height, which wasn't much considering her Spanish ancestry, yet her imperious gaze knew no bounds. "We are not poor, Meri, and I will not act a pauper solely to try and blend in! Now finish eating, you've got to get ready for school."

She groaned but resumed eating. Bethany turned and cleaned up the kitchen.

Her father, Gary, wandered in through the living room, around the simple brown couch framed by the pair of armchairs. His attention focused on the shoe box of family photos he was rifling through. He was similarly dressed in a crisply pressed short-sleeved shirt, black slacks, and black shoes, his short hair carefully groomed.

"So, what's wrong with school?" he asked, catching on to his daughter's mood.

"Jerry's telling kids I cheated on my report using my summoning skills. He's told a teacher I used daemons to research society before the Fall."

Her mother turned to her, wiped her hands dry on a dish-towel, and laughed. "You know, that's a bright idea. If you did, your grades would certainly improve. Not that we'd allow it, of course."

Meri nodded. "I pointed out my unimpressive grade to my teacher, and she agreed. Then she said if I spent as much time studying math, Corporate history, and English as I did summoning, I'd be a much better student."

"You're a wonderful student. But if you study what they want, you'll grow up poised to make a pauper's income in the post-Fall economy," her father replied. He placed a handful of photographs on the table and then served himself up some breakfast.

"The preferred term is *Corporate*, Gary." Bethany's lips pursed, her eyes were drawn to the photos.

"Aren't you going to eat?" Gary asked Bethany. Her fingertips lingered on one of the images he'd placed on the table, and her complexion paled slightly. Without a word, she put the picture back in the box. Meri's heart hammered in her chest as she tilted her head, trying to get a glimpse of that picture, but the image was just beyond her line of sight.

"I don't have much of an appetite this morning."

Gary caught Bethany's hand and squeezed it tight. Meri looked back and forth between the two of them, caught up in the gravity of their caress. She opened her mouth to speak, but the words stuck like glue to the back of her throat.

"Go get ready for school, Meri," her mother prompted. "You're going to be late."

The tension on her mother's face shifted and wavered, the scene changing, fading away with the light. Meri tried to hold onto the image, to her mother, but it was stolen away, and she stood in the front door of her house, a backpack full of books slung heavy over her shoulder as the smell of death filled her nostrils. The early afternoon light filtered through the curtains, making the usually cheerful home drab and the oppressive silence muffled her ears.

Where were her parents?

The hairs on the back of her neck stood on end, alerting her to a fresh daemon presence and the tapestry of spell wards hanging thick in the air. She dropped her backpack to the floor, knowing her father would chastise her for it later, but Meri knew something was off. Why would they leave the summoning space without clearing out the wards?

"Mom? Dad?" Her call echoed through the home, fear building in her throat, spreading downward through her chest.

Meri stepped into the open living space, eyes scanning the mahogany desk next to the front window for clues on the summoning, but it held the barest of tools, the bowl of pristine water, consecrated knives, thick charcoal pencils, and a collection of unlabeled oils.

On the corner sat the shoe box of pictures, filled with family memories.

She backed away from the desk, fear gripping her gut, lancing through her fingertips. Where were they? Meri's sneakered foot slipped on the floor, and she caught herself, spun around, and fell forward onto her hands and knees.

Face first into a pool of blood.

Sitting back on her heels, she freed her hands of the viscous substance as a sob bubbled up from the depths of her soul. Although she'd smelled the stench, the blood hadn't stood out against the dark hardwood floors. However, now it was all she could see through her welling tears, the outline of a blood stain covering the living room floor.

So much blood littered with scraps of clothing she recognized all too well from this morning.

*M*eri sat bolt upright in bed covered in a layer of cold sweat. The otherwise empty house was hushed, standing in silent effigy these past thirteen years. She ran a hand through her damp hair, pulling it out of her face and threw her daemon-ink covered legs out of bed, automatically checking the clock. Despite the dim light sneaking in around the thick slatted blinds, it was already 8:15 am. She needed to hurry if she wanted to get this business wrapped up with Mr. Fields before noon.

Meri disabled the alarm on the clock and then pulled the

shoe box of photos out from under the bed, driven by the nightmare of her parent's final day alive.

She picked through the pictures, a swath representing a slice-in-time of her family history starting the day her parents met and ended the day they died. She'd meticulously destroyed all pictures others had created of her after their death. A single person isn't a family; after all, she was an orphan.

Meri shuffled through the pictures, grateful again for her parent's foresight to protect her with the best lawyers. They'd kept things tied up long enough with the court system to have Meri declared emancipated at sixteen. She'd never had to endure the new nightmare of foster care, thank goodness. Now she was financially set for life, yet her heart ached for the one thing Meri could never have back. The daemon had stolen her family from her, and she would find a way to make it pay even if it killed her. She was running out of skin, out of time.

No matter how many times she went through the photographs, Meri couldn't make sense of the meaning. None of them were particular to daemons she'd been able to map, whether by location or emotion. For all she knew she'd already summoned her parent's killer and never knew the difference. It's not as if the creature would have bragged to her.

In the last picture taken of her mother and Meri together, they were strolling through a park on a sunny day and shared broad smiles towards the camera. Her father had taken the shot, and Meri was struck by how much she favored her mother, especially in the eyes. They both had the same dark brown eyes from her mother's touch of Eastern-European heritage.

Meri stared at a picture of her mom and dad, vacationing in Venice, nestled together on a gondola and kissing under a bridge. The lighting was poor, the sky was overcast, and it even appeared to be raining in the shot. Why did they keep a reminder of such a miserable moment?

She put the photo back into the shoe box, shoved it back under her bed, and headed to the shower, frustration mingling with her tears.

CHAPTER 3

*A*fter a quick breakfast and shower, Meri performed the obligatory post-summoning self-exam checking for changes in her daemon ink patterns. Although she'd long ago accepted the changes to her body, her morbid curiosity couldn't help but track every modification to the most minuscule detail. She was content with her body, if not the treatment she'd given it over the years.

For every payment, every offering made to a daemon; a receipt etched itself into her skin. The forms took all shapes and sizes; reminiscent of tattoos, but sometimes they rippled, scarred, spiked up, or even sparkled. There was no faking the source of genuine daemon ink. How the forms manifested depended on the daemon involved. Somehow, through the transaction of wills, they got under your skin, permanently.

Forever linking you with the daemon, until death.

She quickly recognized the new Engetheus marking as it extended from his earlier one located right above her liver. It wrapped in brilliant, dark green tribal cuts around and back over her right hip. How lovely? She gave silent thanks that at least the vengeance daemon markings never sparkled or spiked. Through this psychic tie, Engetheus had found her last night and delivered the requested tokens for Mr. Fields, and then he'd teleported back to Sheol.

Surveying her unmarked skin, she considered gaining some weight. After all, there the matter of her skin's available real estate, and she was seriously dwindling in free space.

Some clients asked for a showing of markings if they were well informed. A summoner's tally of markings indicated their degree of proficiency. Meri was only twenty-eight, but she would be hard-pressed to display a ten-by-ten inch area clear of "daemon ink," as it was commonly called in the trade. The pervasive coverage of ink had led to her reputation, and thus her steady clientele, and thus the continuing daemon ink. In a few places, her markings overlapped slightly, while others had a clear delineation of space around them, but somehow the new daemon ink always surfaced in and around the existing marks. For instance, her light green envy ink on her right forearm got separate space. If she didn't know better, Meri would swear it had staked a claim, jealous of the real estate, but that would be silly, right?

Conversely, her gleaner ink, black as the night itself, wound itself in a thin spider web of lines around and about others from her stomach, down her left leg, and up around her back. Yes, the gleaner ink was downright chummy, assuming you anthropomorphized daemon ink, which she was nowhere near fool enough to do.

Her parents were completely covered in daemon ink by the time she was fourteen. However, the skills they'd gained hadn't kept them alive.

She'd been summoning for over a decade and didn't know of another summoner in Denver who had been in the field as long as she had, despite her youth. It was well known that most summoners died from a botched summoning before they ran out of clear, available skin.

Meri turned from the mirror, shutting those morbid thoughts out of her mind.

Instead, she dressed and turned her thoughts to the enigmatic Azimuth from last night. She rummaged through the grimoires on her mahogany desk, quickly locating the one that she preferred for daemon classifications. She flipped the pages, skipping the sections on the Princes of Sheol, Elders, and Arch-daemons. Assuredly, if Azimuth were in one of those categories, he'd appear more daemonic, and less human. Also, it would take a talented summoner to call forth and bind a daemon of that power, and there were few available, besides herself, who could do such a thing.

Paging through the sections on daemons versus lesser succubi/incubi, Meri weighed what little she knew about the creature. He'd implied an ability to persuade her, and indeed, she'd felt charmed, yet he'd done nothing untoward. No, besides teleporting her, a skill all daemons at every level possessed, Azimuth had revealed nothing about his skills. His cunning alone made her lean towards a fully ranked daemon, but she'd never know until he revealed his powers to her, and by then she might be under his, and thus his employers, control. She'd have to handle things carefully.

But she smiled, looking forward to their next encounter. Azimuth had been fun to spar with, even if he was dangerous.

They were all dangerous. Meri slammed the volume shut. They weren't all stunningly attractive.

She drove downtown to see Mr. Fields with her unusual tote, magically modified to retain scents and liquids, in the seat next to her. Engetheus had returned to her with the trophies not long after Azimuth left the night before. She hadn't even missed her beauty sleep.

Navigating her sedan off the Valley Highway and through the maze of downtown city streets, Meri looped through the heart of LoDo. She had an apartment above the Purple Martini purchased on a whim during her early twenties, small but intended as a crash pad after late nights dancing. That was back when she'd still entertained ideas of some form of social life. Predictably, the intimidation factor of her summoning had always been too high, or those who befriended her always wanted daemonic 'favors' from her. She watched people walk along the street in groups, eating at street cafes, enjoying the sunny day, and looked up to the second-story housing.

She needed to call her lawyer and tell her to sell it. Meri hit the gas and left the hipster district behind, ignoring the lonely ache in her chest.

The office of Fields and Associates was located on an upper floor in an exclusive corporate building in the heart of Denver. The day was humid, and Meri had dressed to impress, wearing a black sheath top and skirt, which exposed her arms and shoulders and her calves just below the knees and comfortable but practical walking shoes, which completed the set.

No one else needed to know she'd sewn extra pockets into the skirt and hidden away certain protective items a summoner never left home without. A vial of sanctified water, a pouch of sea salt blended with saltpeter and kerosene, charcoal pencils, a few varied flasks of incense, oils and mixed blessed waters, and lastly an empty binding container lined her pockets. She'd never had a daemon sent after her in an attack, but Meri had heard of it happening to other summoners. She'd been late to intervene with a client before, and being able to delineate a small but safe space where the daemon couldn't get to, and thus destroy, had saved her life.

She parked at the valet and handed the keys to the attendant, who then dropped them twice in quick succession, his eyes riveted to Meri's ink-covered forearms. Summoners were a rare sight in the city during daytime, despite Denver's reputation for rampant daemon activity. Meri was deliberately displaying a considerable amount of daemon ink.

Despite his fumbling, the doorman was the essence of politeness. "Good Day, Ms. Storm."

Meri offered him a modest smile. He'd put up with whatever it took just to keep a job that paid in actual cash. Mr. Fields was one of the larger players in town, dealing in property management, high-to-mid class rentals, and new construction. Jobs here were at a premium.

A short ride up the elevators and Meri witnessed the receptionist's eyes open wide. The woman checked her schedule book, her scarlet lips forming a pathetic pout. "Ms. Storm! Is Mr. Fields expecting you?"

"I'm most confident he is." He's alive, after all.

Meri was promptly led back to the CEO's posh office, swinging her tote comfortably at her side. All of the paneling in the room was genuine mahogany. No fake paneling, here.

The decorative accents running down the seams of the molding was an actual fine-grained white marble that Fields had probably imported from Italy. Everything here reeked of cold, hard, cash. Of course, Mr. Fields could afford her services. His corporation was stinking rich. Then again, his wasn't the only one in Denver who employed her, either.

"I'm sorry, Ms. Storm," the receptionist apologized. "I keep failing to get your appointments on the schedule book. It won't happen again."

"Look, these meetings can be a bit impromptu. I don't expect you to keep up. Ever." Meri flashed her a fake smile.

Mr. Fields met them at his office doors, waving his receptionist off. "Meri! I don't think you know how good it is to see you today!" He smiled a bit too broadly as he closed the doors behind her.

Meri tried not to take in the flashy abundance of the room. The crystal decanter set. The gemstone-inlaid globe on a silver stand. The wall of collector's edition books, no doubt many first editions and signed. Did he even take the time to read them, or was it simply all a status symbol?

She took a seat in front of his desk and eyed the expansive view. "Oh, I think I might. But how about you show me just how happy you are to see me?"

Fields sat at his teak desk and typed at his computer for a few moments, and then swiveled the monitor around to show her. Meri read the payment amount, $50,000, off his screen and an unwelcome flash of rage roiled through her gut. Just another side effect of the binding, but it was harder to control this time for some reason. She barely squashed the emotion before it flared out.

"And just how happy were you to see your wife and kids

this morning? Mr. Hodge ordered death for any and all under your roof last night."

Fields turned white as a ghost but then stammered out his next words. "I can't believe the gall of that bastard! Sending a daemon after me just because I flirted with his wife at a holiday party."

"Oh, c'mon, you knew better." Meri checked her nails.

Fields nodded agreement, scraping a hand along his jawline.

"On the upside, there no longer is a Mr. Hodge, and the vengeance daemon Engetheus is bound for life not to harm one hair on your head. Nor your kin."

Mr. Fields' lips were set in a grim line, not appreciating Meri's squeeze play. "How do I know you're the one who did the job? For all I know, the other summoner just botched his work and the daemon took it out of the man who'd hired him."

Meri huffed and bent over, unzipping her tote bag. The reek of decomposing flesh suffused the room immediately. Mr. Fields recoiled in terror as Meri unceremoniously cleared his desk and then deposited the bag in the center. Opening it fully, she dropped the sides down to reveal the head of Mr. Hodges, now staring directly at Mr. Fields.

Engetheus had done a clean beheading, but the look of horror on the man's face made Meri think he'd been alive when his heart was ripped out. Meri smirked. That daemon truly took pride in his work.

Mr. Fields, to his credit, didn't vomit, although he paled visibly. Meri reached into the bag and produced a heart for his inspection.

"The heart and head together can be used in a few protective ceremonies." She slid a business card across the table to him. "Here's the number of a voodoo priestess I recommend. You might consider getting your home warded. You know, just in case someone else in the family retaliates. Next time I might not be so lucky in hunting down the summoner."

"Thank you," Fields replied.

Meri leaned forward and tapped the monitor with her clean hand. Mr. Fields took the hint, typed into the keypad, and tripled the original figure. Meri smiled in satisfaction. She placed the heart back in the tote and zipped it back up. She used a tissue from his desk to wipe off her blood-soaked hand.

"I'll take your advice, Meri. I'm in your debt."

"No, you're not. You've paid up." She rose and walked towards the door.

"If I may, can I see the new ink?" Fields asked.

Meri raised an eyebrow and met his gaze. "Seriously?" She fumed inwardly, yet his request was an industry standard. Then why did an image of his belly ripped open keep swimming through her mind? It must be an aftereffect of the summoning. However, it was worse this time, much worse. Every moment she resisted the urge shooting sparks of pain lanced through her Engetheus ink, drowning out other thoughts. She even tasted bile in her mouth.

"I'm just curious. And I've paid well."

Meri hesitated, regaining her composure. She often had to show clients quite a bit of skin in the past to show her street cred before a job. Fields had never asked. She walked around the desk, turned and raised her tight shirt up slightly and pulled the skirt down a little to reveal the area over her liver and right hip.

"Impressive. I had no idea the ink was that extensive, from what I've seen on your arms and legs."

"Only the part past my hip bone is new; the rest is from prior encounters with this daemon." She dropped her shirt.

"Vengeance must be pretty popular," Fields shook his head.

"That it is, Mr. Fields. That it is." She adjusted her clothing back into place and turned to leave.

"Meri, what happens when you run out of skin?" Fields asked.

She met his gaze, her expression blank. She refused to appear weak to a client. It was bad for business. Everyone knew there were no old summoners. Most died summoning a daemon too powerful for their abilities. She had no idea what would happen.

Instead, she held her chin high. "You're assuming I live that long."

She left the office.

---

*H*urrying down the street, Meri paused to appreciate the updated display of trinkets in the front window of Soul Paths on Colfax. Featured prominently near the door was a new hand-painted sign hanging at eye level, just to the left of the door which read:

This establishment under the protection of

SUMMONER MERIWETHER STORM

Other Summoners are to confer with her before shopping here.

Meri opened the door and heard the ubiquitous bell jingle overhead. The haze of incense hung heavy in the air, a potent mixture of the mixed rose and sweetgrass of the new moon, potently spicy dragon's blood resin, and the lavender reminiscent of King Solomon's seal. Meri knew Annamie's incense blends by heart, at least until her friend invented new ones.

The store was filled with a variety of books, herbs, oils, candles, crystals, tarot and rune decks, and cases of jewelry and racks of clothing offered to meet the magical needs of the clientele, and then some. Ornate tapestries and swords hung off the walls. "Meri! Well met!" Drew called from behind the counter. "Your order is waiting right here. Annamie should be right out. She's just finishing up with a reading."

"Well met, Drew." Meri smiled at Annamie's staunchly loyal husband. Drew looked like a biker, covered with tattoos and long hair, but Meri knew he was tender as a kitten in his heart. The t-shirt Drew wore didn't conceal the scars along his arms. Scars he'd suffered fending off a daemon. "The new display looks nice. I never realized you had such a diverse selection of crystal wands."

"Yeah, we redid it last week. Annamie thought they'd catch the light nicely out there, and it's already drawn a few more sales."

"Good call. What's up with the new sign? It's a bit more prominent than the last one. Has a summoner been giving you problems again?"

Meri speared him with her gaze, watching for a hint of anxiety. Drew always kept things close to his vest. He held her look, and then faltered. "There's a new one in from out of town, calls himself Julian. He was gracious, but you hadn't called to let us know he was cleared. When we told him that was our policy, he laughed us off and then left. He didn't appear angry."

Appearances could be deceiving. Meri had been in Soul Paths picking up an order the day nearly seven years ago when the Bloodlust-daemon had arrived, set on killing Annamie and Drew. Meri had intervened, casting an impromptu protective circle around the three of them and preventing their deaths, but not before Drew had been injured. Out of pure self-preservation, she'd summoned the Bloodlust-daemon in return and set it upon the summoner who'd been after Annamie and Drew -- all because she'd felt their prices were too high.

Ever since then Annamie wouldn't do business with summoners unless they dealt with Meri first. In return, Meri had earned Annamie's cautious friendship, a rare but genuine gift.

"Don't worry, I'll call him. If he doesn't like knowing you're under my protection, he can shop somewhere else. There are plenty of other stores, after all," Meri shrugged and smiled amiably, indicating there was nothing to worry about. She'd make sure there wouldn't be.

Drew gave a quick nod and then retrieved a large bag,

and placed it on the counter. "Do you want to look through everything? This is a large order, even for you."

"No worries. Somehow, Annamie always manages to get my orders perfect. It's as if she's charmed!"

It was an old joke of theirs. Annamie was charmed. If Meri was the most notorious daemon summoner in Denver, Annamie was the most well-known spell caster. Too bad talismans only held true for humans and wouldn't protect her from daemons.

"There is one item missing. The dove's blood ink. I'm afraid our supplier has been back-ordered for some time."

She shrugged. "I understand. These things sometimes can't be helped. I'll use a substitution when I have to. Just keep it on my list. I'd like to have it on hand when it does become available."

Meri placed a stack of bills on the counter Drew rung her purchase up on the register. "Thanks, Meri. You know, you've got to be our best customer."

"The best cash customer, you mean."

Drew turned back to her and shrugged. "You've got that right. People save their money for essentials like food, gas, and clothing. Things you can only buy through corporate owned stores. Still, we do fairly well on trades."

"Just be glad the Corporations leave you alone. I do jobs for them all the time. The people who work there, well they have a driven desperation about them rooted in fear and greed."

"You've got the right of it, Meri. Annamie says the same thing."

"Heck, I don't even keep track of who's in charge anymore. The Corporates all make me sick."

Drew frowned. "What? You didn't get your new ident card in the mail last week?"

"I got something. I don't bother with Corporate cards. Their 'security force personnel' never challenge me."

He eyed the daemon ink on her forehead. The sharp lines of the prestige daemon still irked her because it had marred her face. "I bet they don't. But in case you're curious, we're officially living in the Western S-Mart Division now."

Meri rolled her eyes. "And how's that different from IntelleCo SouthWestern?"

Drew shrugged. "I dunno. The security force badges have smiley faces on them now, and a little thunderbolt accent. Paid for with our 'contributions.'"

"Oh, whatever, let them play at politics. They're all the same thing to me. Customers who all want daemons summoned."

Drew sighed. "Sometimes I think the Burners have the right of it -- going off the grid and leaving the cities and Corps behind."

"I don't blame them," Meri smiled, "but I must admit I'm addicted to my creature comforts and classic films."

"I dunno, I keep trying to talk Annamie into it. There's an Enclave up in Firestone, and I like their statement of peaceful coexistence for all members -- it's fairer than what we've got going on here! Plus up there, they raise their livestock, maintain year-round in greenhouses, and even make homemade versions of medical treatments. Annamie would be right at home! Up there we wouldn't live indentured to Corporate greed or rules."

Meri took his hand and gripped it, understanding his

frustration. "Good luck with that. I know she can be stubborn."

He grinned. "You would. You wrote the book on that one."

Just then, Annamie emerged from her office with a teary-eyed teen in tow. "Yes, yes, I have just the thing for you here. Let me see." She went behind the counter and nosed among a number of vials on shelves. Annamie looked like a cross between a faery and a gypsy with her wavy, long, blond hair, diaphanous silk blouse, and layered skirts of every color.

"Here we go. This is an unbinding potion. Spike both your drink and his, and then make sure you both consume them at the same time. Immediately after that, say the words, 'We are nothing together.' At that point, he should forget about you."

"Thank you so much, Annamie!" the teen gushed. She handed over money to Drew who rung her up as she ran out of the store.

"Ah, young love!" Annamie sighed. She fell theatrically into Drew's waiting arms.

"And thus the unbinding spell?" Meri asked.

"Well, the girl was convinced Love needed a little push, so she bound the young man to her."

"That never goes well," Drew said.

Annamie threw up her hands in frustration. "He'd begun to stalk her. Binding spells aren't very predictable. On the contrary, you, my dear, are." She pointed to Meri.

"What, moi?" Meri feigned shock.

"There was some bad juju on the north side with your cleanup mojo all over it, Meri," Annamie said.

"I can neither confirm nor deny your insinuations, my

dear." Meri crossed her arms. Annamie had become a close friend, but they never spoke specifics. It was safer for them both that way.

"Be that as it may, the people are talking. This is both good, and not so good, for particular other people, if you catch my drift. You might want to lay low, stay under the radar. I would hate to have the security forces asking if you might know who hired the daemon who took out that poor gentleman in the abandoned house, or who was involved in a potentially unrelated -- or related -- dealing with a Mr. Hodge."

"Oh please." Meri rolled her eyes. "It was a failed summoning. Idiot children die all the time summoning daemons or spell casting beyond their means. The security forces know most wounds are self-inflicted. And who knows what happened to Mr. Hodge. Corporations feud all the time."

"Uh huh. This is why I hate you being in your line of work. Honestly, I hate all of this summoning nonsense! The world would be better off without daemons as tools in the feuds, and you know it."

Meri frowned. They'd had this argument before, and it never went anywhere productive.

"Sorry, anyway," Annamie replied, her eyes scanning Meri's aura. "How're you feeling, sweetie? Need a gentle, herbal, liver detox? I have them on special, just for you." She smiled sweetly.

Meri opened her mouth for a snappy retort but then thought better of it. Instead, she tapped her shopping bag with a sigh. Annamie fetched the detox while Drew rung her up, again.

"It's said someone is influencing the security forces," Drew said. "I wouldn't be surprised if it's someone with power or daemon-backed. Perhaps the corporations themselves."

"That would be a new way to eliminate the competition," Meri smirked. "Certainly less straightforward. I'll keep my eyes open. Thanks." She grabbed the bag she came for, filled with incense, oils, herbs, and now something to help her recover faster.

"Are you sure there's nothing else, Meri?" Annamie asked. "You're a bit tense today."

Meri shrugged, itching to get out of the store. Her touchiness just wouldn't settle, and being within the calming influence of Annamie and Drew unexpectedly inflamed her further. "It's nothing, just a rough summoning."

Annamie's eyes went distant and out of focus. She frowned. "The next job offer you get, you must take. I know I just complained about your work, but this is different somehow. It's essential."

"Okay. What kind of job?" Meri didn't like it when Annamie had a premonition about her. They were inevitably vague and lacked specific details. She hated to give these mushy predictions much weight.

"It's not clear to me, just that your future hangs in the balance, but it's a journey you must travel. Sorry I can't be of more help."

Annamie's frown worried Meri. Her friend meant every heartfelt word. "Thanks, Annamie. I'll let you know how it works out." Assuming, of course, anything happened.

*O*n her way home, Meri stopped at a street café across from City Park on 17th for a bagel and strong, dark coffee packed with heavy amounts of sugar and laced with a hint of cream. The wait staff knew her and weren't afraid or jittery in her presence, but neither did they chat her up or act friendly. She might be a good customer, but no one wanted to be close to a daemon summoner, and she didn't blame them.

Meri took out her phone and made a few calls to local summoners she knew, and within minutes had Summoner Julian's number.

It was a small, tight-knit community. At least for the ones who were in it for the long haul.

Julian answered his phone on the first ring. "Good afternoon."

"Summoner Julian, this is Meriwether Storm."

"I see it didn't take you long to track me down."

"You're easy to find."

"I'm not trying to hide anything. Sorry, I scared your store owners. Afraid I'm new to town."

My store? No, don't rise to the bait. "Welcome to Colorado. Where did you move here from?"

"Florida. There's a Summoner war going on down there, so I figured I'd head to a more relaxed locale. Tell me things aren't like that up here?"

"Oh no, we're nothing like that. We all like to get along and never take our clients issues personally. I keep Soul Paths under my protection simply because the quality of their supplies is second to none, and I can't afford to waste my time shopping around for a new source every week."

"A wise move, Summoner. May I have your permission to

shop there, as you've recommended it so highly? I swear to treat them fairly and never lash out against them."

"I also request you pay in cash."

He chuckled. "Certainly. I'll pay in cash. Anything else?"

"No, that's it. I'll let them know you're cleared."

"It was a pleasure speaking to you, Summoner Meriwether."

"I hope you enjoy Colorado, Summoner Julian."

Meri hung up and took another sip of her coffee. Julian was new to the state, but not new to Summoning, so he was less likely to fly off the handle over his temper. Still, she'd keep her ears to the street on this new player.

In the park across the street Meri watched children play, couples strolling, and a pair of old men playing chess. If her life had gone another path, she could have lived like them, but it hadn't, and she'd never been like them. Not now. Not ever.

She envied their lives' simplicity. Even if she wanted to stop summoning, she couldn't. Her adversaries wouldn't go away, and neither would the steady clientele. Besides, she had no other job skills. She did one thing, very well and it was very, very dangerous.

Her earliest memories were of her parents drilling her through lessons about what daemons were ruled by and invoked by what. She remembered her mamma's proud eyes and standing with her shoulders set firm when she'd summoned an impressive glamor daemon when she was just twelve. The daemon had required toenail clippings, skin shavings, and a bit of blood too, all so that Meri could appear to be an average child with no daemon markings for summer camp for a month with the regular kids. It had worked, but in the end, it wasn't real. She'd spent the entire time scared to death the spell would wear off early. Now she was left with a permanent, iridescent mark on the instep on her left foot.

Stupid sparklies.

Not exactly something you can put on a resume.

The hair on the back of her neck raised and the ink under her skin prickled, and she looked around for the source, knowing only a daemon would get her ink reactive. Just at that moment, her newest prospective client walked out from among a copse of trees in the park and headed her way. She couldn't help smiling at the trick -- teleporting boldly in broad daylight -- yet none in the crowded park noticed. Damned if he didn't look just as appealing in the sunlight as he did last night. This time he wore a tailored black jacket over a white shirt, black leather pants, and boots. Usually, daemons didn't bother to mix up their wardrobes. Why did this one make an effort?

"May I join you?" asked Azimuth, pointing at a chair.

"You may have a seat at this table." She smiled, unwilling to commit to 'joining' the daemon in his plans by a misguided word choice.

Azimuth sat down, relaxing into the patio chair. Meri could barely take her eyes off him. She picked up her coffee cup, deliberately toying with the empty sugar packet. "I'm not trying to trick you into anything, Meri."

"No one ever is. You're here to offer me a job?"

"Once you're ready to go to a somewhat more discreet location, I can divulge more details," Azimuth replied. A wide-eyed waitress came to take the daemon's order, but he waved her off. His eyes lingered on Meri. "But it can wait. I don't want to interrupt your coffee."

What, a gentleman? She couldn't believe it. A pro negotiator was more like it. She shifted uncomfortably under his powerful gaze. Was he trying to make her squirm?

"You're not used to the company?"

"My habits are not up for discussion," she said and took a sip of her coffee.

Azimuth frowned. "That would be a 'no,' then. I imagine a life, such as yours, would be isolated."

Meri took another sip of her strong brew. Just how much research had his boss done on her? "Just the opposite. I have powerful allies, more clients than I can count, and I'm well recognized. You could say so. Many around town know my name."

"So that's a 'yes' on the isolation."

Meri grimaced. Did daemons feel emotions too? She knew they hungered after their baser natures. Her summoner-trained curiosity wanted to know what made Azimuth tick. "Does it matter? I've bound every daemon I've faced, more than I've bothered to count, or we wouldn't even be having this conversation. Which would be why your boss wants to hire me for my binding skills, yes?"

Azimuth's lip curled in a mocking smile. "You don't even know how many of us you've bound to you?"

Meri drained her cup, stood, and left a twenty on the table, tipping graciously as always. She knew how poorly the wait staff was paid, and the money meant relatively little to her. "I do, but I'm not fool enough to divulge such information to a daemon. Let's go."

Azimuth fell into step beside her. They walked a block, and he turned into the nearest alley and went through a small, private gate of old, beaten up iron fencing. They walked midway down the road before he turned to face her. The corridor was empty, the far end blocked by bricked-off buildings. The way they'd come in was the only entrance. A row of dumpsters lined the alleyway, affording them a surprising amount of privacy.

"Well? Where's your boss?" Meri asked. Pinpricks of fear traveled down her back. They were alone here, and as a daemon, he was much stronger than she was. She'd trusted him about the job offer, but what if it was a ruse? Did she have enough tricks up her pockets?

"I need to know one additional piece of information before I take you to him." Azimuth stepped closer, his expression relaxed and dispassionate. "Show me your ink. I need to see who you've bound previously."

She licked her lips. The prospect of disrobing, even partially, for this daemon in an alley was absurd. Although he worded it professionally, Azimuth's eyes held shadows and a curiosity Meri didn't trust. "Kiss and tell? Not with a daemon, I won't. Your boss, sure thing. But not you."

Azimuth gripped his chin between his thumb and forefinger and raised his right eyebrow. "He won't see you unless I secure certain information first."

"Give me another option." One that didn't involve being naked in an alley with a totally hot daemon. Of course, she wasn't attracted to him. Even if she was, she'd never give him the satisfaction of knowing he'd gotten under her skin. Never.

The iris' of Azimuth eyes flashed to white, and then back to sky blue. Her heart skipped a beat, curiosity over his quirks quickly becoming her newest obsession. After a few moments, he conceded. "I can sense falsehoods if you will allow my contact."

Useful skill. "Wait a moment, Daemon. Explain the terms of this engagement first."

"You're unusually cautious, summoner."

"I've lived a long time. I intend to live a while longer."

Azimuth inclined his head. "I maintain short, discrete, physical contact with you and attune to your energy wavelength while I ask my questions. That is the entirety of the process."

Why did she want to believe him? Was it so that she could learn his secrets and potentially control him later? Was it her curiosity about his boss' job? Or was it the way her stomach clenched at the idea of his hands on her skin?

"That, I can do," Meri replied.

He reached out his hands. "Your wrists, please."

Releasing the tight grip she had on her bag, she wiped off her sweaty palms on her skirt and held out her wrists. "Just get on with it."

Azimuth's long fingers encircled her wrists. His cold skin matched its pale appearance, soft as silk against her own. His thumbs found her pulse points and massaged them gently. The moment he tuned into her energy field, a surge rippled through Meri, giving her the sensation of being pushed outside of her skin. Her pulse quickened in response to the heady awareness.

He leaned in, brushing his cheek and nose along her jugular, breathing her scent in deeply. She closed her eyes and her neck arched toward him as his silver hair whispered across her cheek. She lost herself in the rhythmic sensations he was coaxing out of her skin as her internal temperature rose. Standing this close, it was impossible for her not to be aware of his tense form hovering just above her.

His musky scent of vanilla and sandalwood lulled her. Did his soap contribute to this aroma, or was that just his unique smell? She sighed and leaned against the wall behind her. She hadn't been this relaxed since the last time she got drunk.

She felt cocooned by him. Safe. "Meri?" Azimuth whispered.

"Hmmm?"

"Have you ever summoned an infatuation daemon?"

"Never, I like to think I'm a reputable summoner," Meri slurred.

"Have you ever summoned a lust daemon?"

"No. Can you imagine the ink I'd get?" Meri chuckled. "Where I'd get it?"

"This bothers you?" he asked.

Meri shifted in his grasp, pulling away while ignoring his question, but he held firm. It wasn't just the ink placement with that type of daemon, it was the manner of the binding, and she considered herself above that kind of contact with daemons. "Look. Those clients are never willing to pay what the job is worth, okay? I send them to the witches or the voodoo priestesses instead."

Azimuth didn't ask again. "Meri." He stroked her wrists with increased pressure.

"Azimuth?"

"Have you ever been in love?"

"Nope. I mean wait, what?" Instantly, Meri's anger rose up like a serpent poised to strike. Her eyes opened, and his expression was cool as a cucumber. "I've dated before."

"That wasn't the question, Meri." She continued to struggle, but his touch held her in a vice. He only caught Meri at her wrists, but his body was mere inches away. When she pulled away, it only drew him in closer, forcing their bodies into contact. His touch, deliciously firm against her soft curves, simultaneously sent waves of bliss and panic coursing through her, short-circuiting her brain.

"Release me at once."

"As you wish." He swept his fingers across her wrists one final time, the energy high dissipated, and then he stepped away from her.

Meri swayed, off balance from the encounter. Azimuth was wise enough to keep his distance rather than offering to help. She wanted to punch him in the face but didn't want to look pathetic in the attempt, knowing humans bore a distinct disadvantage in a fight with a daemon. Meri's strength lay in the summoning circle, not outside of it.

"Those were all things your boss needed to know?"

"Yes. You would have been worthless to him otherwise. The job requires a summoner who's never been in love and never summoned an infatuation or lust daemon." Azimuth leaned against the concrete wall next to her, appearing completely at ease. Again, she was inclined to trust him, but she didn't like it one iota. Meri still wanted to hit him.

"And your powers of perception assure you that I was honest?"

Azimuth shrugged. "I suspected the answers before I asked, but I'm required to do the due diligence."

"I really want to hit you right now."

He held up his hands in mock surrender and damned if he wasn't appropriately circumspect. "I know you do. And I adore your honesty. Shall we go and meet my boss now?"

She nodded. "Where are we going?"

Azimuth paused. "Sheol."

Meri laughed nervously, shaking her head. "You're joking?"

He simply met her gaze.

"First, humans can't travel to Sheol, or Hell, or Hades, or whatever you want to call the daemon plane. I've never even heard of such a thing."

"Although you think you're speaking the truth, I can assure you; you're wrong."

Meri was dumbfounded. "And what makes you think that I -- given the opportunity -- would follow a daemon into Sheol? I'd have to be crazy, or have a serious death wish."

"Or," Azimuth interrupted, "you'd have a payment offered you couldn't bear to refuse. We know the name and binding of the daemon who killed your parents."

Tears sprung to her eyes and pain seared her throat and lungs, threatening to render her speechless. Numbness spread down her chest into her arms, flowing down her body until she had to clench her fists. The cutting pressure of her nails returned some measure of feeling. She'd been hunting for this information since she was fifteen when she'd found her parents as nothing more than pools of blood on the living room floor. "All wrapped up in a bow?"

"My boss wants you motivated."

Meri paced, unable to restrain her outward display of anxiety. She wanted to believe him, but crossing over to the daemon plane -- to hear a job offer? Then, what would the job be?

"You could be lying. You're a daemon, after all. Motivate me to trust you."

"You have an empty binding container on you?" Azimuth asked.

"Of course."

Azimuth held out his hand, motioning for her to hand it over.

Meri reached into a hidden pocket in her skirt. She pulled out a flexible, high-density plastic pouch including a blood collection container and handed it over to him.

Azimuth produced a short blade from his belt and sliced off a fingernail and a lock of his hair from his head. Both went into the bag. He then cut his thumb and dripped a few drops of dark black blood into the small vial, and then dropped it into the bag before the cut healed over.

Neat trick.

Satisfied, he sealed it up, replaced the blade at his belt, and held the bag out to her.

"I can't offer you trust, but instead, perhaps, insurance?"

Meri took the bag and zipped it inside the hidden pocket in her skirt. With this and with Azimuth's name, not even knowing his full powers, she could summon and bind him to her will. This was an extreme show of trust on his part, or at least on his boss's behalf. If she lived through Sheol and either the job or the payment didn't work out, she could take it out of his hide. Or better yet, make a preemptive strike on his boss. What consequences had Azimuth faced if he failed in his mission to bring her to Sheol?

"Let's go before I change my mind."

Azimuth stepped close to her and held out his hand. "This will be just like when I took you home yesterday."

"Except we're going to Hell this time."

CHAPTER 4

*T*he teleportation was without sensation. One moment they were in a dark alley, hand in hand, and the next she and Azimuth were in a different place. Meri looked around, and if she didn't know better, she'd swear they were still on Earth, not on some alternate plane of existence. She took in the large but well-lit cave system with rock walls and heavy steel doors leading off to other rooms. The kitchen, on the far end of the main room, had multiple refrigerators and tons of counter space. To their left was an extensive library with walls of books and deep, comfortable couches begging to be sunk into and read in for hours. They stood in front of a large tapestry depicting an elaborate forest scene, which was off to the side of the main room, which held a large television, a game station and set of recliners.

It was nothing like what Meri had expected. Sheol was supposed to reek of fire and brimstone. To be dark, dank, and depressing was as expected. This space was an attractive and well-appointed bachelor pad straight out of a sit-com, except the bookcases lining the walls were littered with arcane artifacts she couldn't begin to name or imagine the purpose for. They were surprisingly dust free too. What in the world? But then, she wasn't in her world anymore, was she? Apparently, in Sheol, people kept things clean and orderly. Who knew?

"Welcome to the burrow, my home within Sheol," Azimuth said.

Shocked back to her senses, Meri disengaged her hand from his. "Thank you, I think."

The sound of a throat clearing reminded Meri that they weren't alone.

Three other daemons entered from the library, and each of them stared at the new arrivals with rapt interest. Two of them were less human looking than Azimuth, and she guessed now why perhaps his boss had sent him to do the recruiting.

"I'd like to introduce you to the members of my cabal."

"Cabal?" Meri asked.

"It's like a team, or working group," answered the tallest of the three daemons. He appeared human, except for his exaggerated, sharp facial features and dark blue skin. He wore loose black robes and held a stack of books as he strode over to greet her. "Our cabal consists of the four of us. My name is Belial, and I am in charge here. It's an honor to meet you."

Meri noted he didn't offer a hand, which was okay. He held many tomes, and his hands had long, sharp claws.

"Belial? Wait. I know that name. Aren't you mentioned in the Apocrypha as one of the crown princes of hell?"

Belial shrugged. "I've found the Apocrypha isn't a very accurate book. Occasionally when your human scribes wrote down details, they got names, numbers, even dates inaccurate. I've done my comparative work on the subject. You'd be surprised how far off the mark things get in some sections."

"Then, you're not a crown prince?"

"I am. I am also what is known as an original, beaten into existence by the frothing magma which created the pits of Sheol itself."

"Sounds impressive."

"I suppose. Sheol and it's inhabitants have existed for millennia. There are a large number of us, and there is a good bit of breeding that goes on. I'm one of many."

She'd never dealt with a daemon Prince before, but her curiosity overrode the encroaching tendrils of anxiety creeping over her skin at the confirmation of his status. "Does your status come with any special perks?"

Belial wrapped the books up in his robes and considered his response. Meri wasn't sure if this was his normal state. She looked to Azimuth, who stood calmly, devoid of expression. She suspected he was hiding a reaction.

"A few," Belial answered.

"Aaaaand moving on!" The shortest of the three daemons stepped in front of her. He was short for a daemon, only about five foot ten. He, too, appeared fully human and reminded her of a football linebacker: stout, muscle-packed, and ready to spring into action. He held out a hand, and despite him being a daemon, she shook it. His broad grin was disarming, and his brown eyes held a genuine mirth beneath his unkempt short, curly brown hair and ivory-colored skin. She let go of his hand and for once wasn't overcome with any energetic daemon residue leaching through her due to the contact. How curious.

He looked at Azimuth, clapping him on the back. "Nicely done, brother. I didn't think you could convince her."

"You cannot fathom the depths of my determination."

Meri and the other daemon both stared at Azimuth and took in the cold, icy fire in his blue eyes. Meri didn't doubt it. She understood her pay off and motivation for this job, but she didn't know what Azimuth and his cabal got out of it. Whatever it was, she doubted they'd disclose their motivations to her. She'd have to remember they had their interests in mind, and she had to watch out for herself, like always. Instead of dealing with Corporates or other high-rolling humans, these beings might break her in half if the deal went bad. She shook off Azimuth's intense stare and turned to face the new daemon.

"Hi Meri, I'm Kobol. It's so nice to meet you. I'm sorry about Belial over there; he can be a bit dry sometimes. He spends most of his time with books and forgets how to interact with others." At this comment, Belial gave a hefty snort.

"Yes, pleased to meet you too. And I should trust you all because you're daemons?" Meri fake-smiled as broadly as possible. She almost liked Kobol. In fact, if she'd met Kobol on the street, she'd have been hard-pressed to know he was a daemon, which set off a warning bell in her summoner's brain. On second glance, the muscle-packed, human-looking warrior struck her as a very effective weapon indeed. Azimuth was very, very still. She bit her lip. Had she offended her potential ally with that outburst? If so, how would she get home?

"I'd offer you a cookie, or something to drink, but I bet you'd turn those down too, wouldn't you?" Kobol joked.

Meri blinked slowly, but then laughed aloud. "I'm not sure. It didn't work out too well for Persephone, did it?"

Kobol laughed heartily, but he was the only one. Meri grinned, unable to help it, and when she smelled the fresh-baked cookies, somehow she knew he was the one who'd gone to the trouble to make them. What kind of place was this burrow, and what kind of daemons were these?

"Of course you won't trust us," said the last daemon, sobering her mood and drawing her focus.

The last of the four daemons drew her eye simply because she'd seen nothing to compare him with, despite her variety of exposure to daemon ilk. He was just over six feet tall, and his skin was oddly dark as if he was walking under a constant shadow. At night, Meri suspected it wouldn't even be noticeable, but with the overhead lights in the burrow, it was a marked effect. His black eyes matched his hair. He looked like a veritable spirit of the night. Did he hold powers of the night as well?

"I'm Orias." He held out his hand, which she shook, and an intense sensation of déjà vu washed over her, and then was gone a moment later. "Right now you despise us all, and that's to be expected. You can't wait to get the hell out of here, pun intended, and get the job done so you can get your payment and your long-sought vengeance. Sadly, vengeance is all that drives you right now."

His words struck home, and her gut wrenched. She didn't want him to be right and know things about her she wouldn't speak to any human soul. She'd been wearing her motives on her sleeve for too long, and they had begun to chafe.

"What you don't know, Meri," Orias continued, "is that we aren't that different, human and daemon. There doesn't need to be such anger between our people. We can work together."

"That's an excellent speech, Orias. But we're not the same. Last time I checked, humans are the result of the evolution of life on Earth. Daemons, on the other hand, began as the summoned creatures called forth from Hell to do the bidding of humans."

"Sheol and the creatures therein existed long before humans evolved into their present state," Belial replied.

Meri blinked. "Is that so?"

"Indeed."

"Then why do so many daemons look humanoid, if they weren't dreamed up by humans?"

"Their evolution has been twisted by contact with the human realm. The more contact daemons have with humans; the more human daemons appear over time."

"But daemons also feed off of the humans. Use them."

"And humans don't use the daemons?" Belial asked. His face was impassive, but his eyes were cold. "Sometimes, transactions are mutually beneficial. Sometimes they are not."

"Aaaaaand again, I think now's a good time to consider that we're here for a common goal, right?" Kobol spoke up, a smile wide across his face. "Yes, we're different species, but we have a mutually beneficial goal right now."

"Right. Now I get why your boss couldn't meet me in Denver. After all, Belial is a little blue to be walking down a city street. One thing -- if no human summoned you, how is it that you're free to teleport back and forth out of hell?"

Azimuth smiled. "That's something of a special arrangement I've had for a while now. The details of which I'll keep to myself if you don't mind."

"Just how common is this? How many daemons are out there walking around with a free pass?"

Azimuth lost his smile. "More than you'd like to know."

Meri's hair stood on end. How were they doing it?

"As Orias said, I'm getting antsy. How about you four pitch me the job so I can get on home?" Meri asked.

"Why don't you have a seat?" Azimuth motioned to the couches in front of the television. Meri debated it for a moment but got the impression Azimuth wanted to make some grand appeal and figured this could take a while. She sat directly in front of him. Kobol and Orias sat on the couch to her left, and Belial dropped off his weighty tomes, and then came and stood to the right of Azimuth. The impact of doing a deal with daemons hit home with Meri and bile crept up her throat, the frustration craved a visceral outlet, preferably by her fist meeting one of their faces. She blew out a long, slow calming breath. She still wasn't healed from the last summoning, and it showed in her temper's need for an outlet.

"First," Azimuth began, "I can confirm that Miss Meriwether Storm, although she's been summoning daemons since the age of twelve, has never summoned a love or lust daemon. There is no scent of them upon her. Secondly, I can confirm she has never been in love." Meri blushed at this, but the daemons took no notice. "Third, if she accepts the job and performs it to our satisfaction, I have offered her the name and binding of the daemon who murdered her parents. Are we all in agreement?" Azimuth looked at his cabal in turn.

"We are," the other three replied in unison.

Azimuth's gaze met hers, and her body felt leaden, dreading the details of the cabal's job yet hanging on his every word. "There is an Arch-daemon named Mahkra. You are to summon him. I will provide you with the list of herbs and oils needed. His binding is lust. Once he is bound, you are to kill him."

"Kill?" she shouted. "How can I kill a daemon?"

The others looked to Belial, who withdrew a small dagger with a black handle from a sheath from within the folds of his robe. The black blade reflected like a mirror.

"This is a tre'jor, a very rare weapon. The blades are something I've invented myself, and they're one of the few things that can kill a daemon," Belial said. He handled the blade with extreme care, sliding it back into the sheath. "Other daemons are unaware these exist, or I should say, once they become aware of them, they don't live long enough to spread the word." Meri eyed the blade, her hands itching to snatch it from his grasp. I could be fearless with that weapon.

"But if he's an Arch-daemon?"

Belial appeared confused. "Yes?"

"Well, won't that make him much harder to kill? Stronger?"

"Yes, a bit. However, no less possible with this weapon. Do not underestimate it because of its size."

"So, if I kill Mahkra, does your cabal get his former, uh, minions? Arch-daemons have minions, right?"

"Yes, and no, we won't," Azimuth answered. "There will be infighting, and whoever fights the hardest, or dirtiest, will win power."

"Then what good does this do you? Settling a personal grudge?" Meri asked.

Meri looked around and was met with blank stares. "Go ahead," Orias said to Belial, who frowned but then nodded after a moment. "There is no harm in explaining our purpose."

"We are at war with Mahkra and his cabal, led by Saleigh and bolstered in strength by Cian. All three are Arch-Daemons," Belial answered. "Taking out Mahkra will weaken the others and expose their vulnerabilities to us."

"Daemons war?" The idea didn't shock her, but the thought of being brought into the machinations of one didn't sound altogether safe or sane.

"Constantly," Kobol answered, a smile crossing his lips. Her eyes lingered on his stocky, muscular frame, and she guessed he liked the action.

Clever devils, they've brought me in to play the role of assassin -- I respect the ingenuity, despite my hatred of their kind. "Can I keep the tre'jor after the job?"

"You wish to kill your parent's murderer and not just punish them?" Azimuth asked.

"It's on my mind." She wouldn't try and hide it.

"I won't be fighting you for it," Azimuth replied.

"Will the cabal?" Meri asked. As she expected, Belial frowned.

"I won't," Kobol replied, but a green light flashed behind his eyes. A sign of his temper, or his honesty?

"Nor I," Orias replied.

After a pause, Belial replied. "After the job, I will wait and see how you use it before I decide if you are fit to keep it."

"Fair enough," Meri answered, recognizing Belial would never let her keep the precious item. She imagined the blue-skinned Prince wouldn't walk Earth in search for it either. Well, she sure wasn't bringing it back to Sheol for his greedy claws. "Once Mahkra's bound, will he be able to fight me after I stab him with the tre'jor? I imagine it could take a while to kill him such a little blade."

"He will be able to fight, but death from the tre'jor is quite swift for a daemon," Orias replied. "You will have the element of surprise. No daemon would expect a mere human to have an immortal-killing blade."

"I suppose you're right."

"Then you accept the job?" Azimuth asked.

"Well, yeah, I mean, it's different, but it's not like you're asking me to kill a person or anything," Meri answered.

The daemons shifted uncomfortably.

"Present company excluded, of course." She pushed her feet against the floor, tensing the muscles of her legs and straightening her back. When the moment passed, and the daemons didn't make an offensive move, she relaxed, letting out a slow breath.

"And all aspects of the job are tolerable?" Azimuth asked.

"I've summoned and bound daemons before," Meri answered.

"But not lust daemons," Azimuth said.

Meri's face flushed under their scrutiny. She knew she'd have to bed the lust daemon to bind it, but having it so frankly discussed with the daemons -- albeit her future employers -- was the last thing she wanted to do.

"You know, Belial, this one's not as interested in the job as her experience led me to assume she'd be," Kobol said. She glared at the daemon and added his face next to Azimuths on her list of ones she'd like to punch.

"Thus why I am cautious to entrust her with an ancient and deadly weapon such as this. If it were to fall into the wrong hands," Belial replied.

Meri's anger rose. This was the closest she'd come to her parent's killer, and she wasn't about to let her inexperience hold her back. Being that vulnerable and exposed with a daemon gave her the chills. Then she remembered Annamie's foresight and her warning. This was the journey she was destined to take. She rose and walked to face Azimuth.

"I accept the job. Give me the tre'jor. Let's go."

Azimuth looked at her for a few moments. "Then we have a deal."

She held out her palm to Belial, who looked a bit horrified. He handed the dagger to Azimuth.

"He will give this to you once you return to the human realm. I prefer for you not to have it here," Belial said.

"Scared of me, Belial? How long have you been alive?"

"Exactly, young one. Good hunting to you." Belial turned and walked into the library.

"Let us know how everything works out," Kobol said.

Orias' stood hidden in his shadows, saying nothing. By the look in his eyes, she had the impression he wanted to say more, yet held his tongue.

What an odd assembly of daemons.

Azimuth rolled his eyes at Kobol, took Meri's arm, and in moments he'd ported them to her home's porch.

"I suppose that went as well as expected." Azimuth sighed.

"I don't think they're all that impressed with me," Meri replied.

"They can be difficult to impress, but so would you if

you'd lived as long as they have," Azimuth studied her. "Are you sure you're comfortable with the job?"

Meri looked up at him, remembering his ability to discern her honesty. "No, I'm not. Can I do it? Yes. Will I do whatever it takes? Yes."

"I hope, for your sake, that it's worth it to you, in the end."

His consideration shocked her. "Thanks, but we're each in this for our own ends, aren't we?"

Azimuth nodded and then handed her an envelope. "Here's the correct spelling, pronunciation, and intonation of his name, along with the required herbs and oils you'll need for the summoning. A tip: Mahkra will do his best to lull you under his spell. His intention will be to keep you complacent once you've bound him. He'll try to distract you, supplant your will with his own. He's famous for keeping summoners so occupied that they forget to take full advantage of having bound him to their will. You must stay clear-headed, for this is when you must strike. Once the blade enters his flesh, do not remove it until he is finished."

He held the tre'jor out to Meri, and she took it. The blade was icy in her hand, and instant revulsion poured through her at a gut-level. Could her daemon-ink be sensing the destructive nature of the artifact? She shook her head. No, surely that was impossible.

"Will he be aware of this in the room?"

"No, but if he sees it, he will sense the power in it. Keep it hidden as long as possible."

"Got it. How long does this take to kill one of you?"

"For an Arch-daemon? A few seconds, perhaps half a minute. Remember; keep it in his flesh the entire time. Just because it can kill daemons, it is still a blade. It can cause damage to humans too. Steer clear of cutting yourself with it."

"I've got it." Meri moved to go inside.

"When will you do the binding?"

She thought a moment. Her liver wasn't fully recovered, and she wasn't about to go into hand-to-hand wrestling with an Arch-daemon when she was still in physical pain. "Two or three days from now. I still need time to heal from my last binding. Tomorrow I'll begin prepping. I have a space I use that's secure. Two days after that I'll do the summoning. I'll report to you that evening or the following morning."

Azimuth put a hand on her shoulder. "Immediately after, Meri. Contact me immediately." He then handed her another envelope. "If calling my name doesn't work, break the seal in here. That will summon me instantly."

"Why Azimuth, it's almost like you care."

He leaned in and notched a finger under her chin. "I care about all of my commitments, Meri. You're not the only one depending on the outcome of this job." He dropped his hands and sighed. "Good luck, and be careful." With that, he disappeared into thin air -- she guessed he returned to his comfortable burrow to await the outcome of this skirmish in their private daemon war.

"Yeah, you're an absolute sweetheart." She gripped the tre'jor. The deadly, icy weight belied its size. An otherworldly chill ran down her spine.

CHAPTER 5

$\mathcal{M}$eri went to her primary summoning space. She owned two locations, both warehouses in low-rent areas of town. The main one was located in the manufacturing and shipping district known as Five Points, in the basement of a building she owned. Railroad lines, interstate hubs, a petroleum refinery, and a dog food plant surrounded the area. The primary warehouse was locked, as was the basement itself. There was a single exit door, with no windows. The basement contained simple necessities, as summonings could take anywhere from ten minutes to several days. A bathroom, efficiency kitchen, and a queen-size bed were all comforts yet ancillary elements to the primary purpose of the room: the large, central ritual space. The floor was painted with glossy black enamel and had a floor drain -- for quick clean up after jobs.

Both were fully equipped this way, just in case one required a lengthy summoning. Then she could still avail herself the use of the alternate location while the other percolated. Likewise, if a particularly messy summoning took place, she'd have the other space in working order until cleanup could be completed.

She had spent an entire day doing the prep work for the summoning and now walked the basement, double-checking every opening to the outside. Each time she'd cast a separate and powerful spell upon each opening, protecting them from not only daemon but also human intrusion. The door had an advanced lock coded to her thumbprint alone, and she'd warded it with powerful spells to prevent magical forms of tampering. Every HVAC vent, drain, and sink -- even the mirror and toilet were warded. The only way in, or out, for Mahkra would be via the sigil Meri would draw out in the center of the floor.

She used chalk made from the compacted ash of the burned bones of sparrows to draw out the initial designs for the sigils and patterns used to name Mahkra. These included the fifth Solomonic sigil for Venus, which looked like two concentric circles with a box in the middle decorated with elaborate symbols. The outer rings contained Hebrew words to 'excite great passion and desire.' Over this pattern, she overlaid the frilly heart-shaped Erzulie Veve. Once satisfied with the work, she redrew over the chalk lines with a mixture containing civet, rose and honeysuckle oils, and a combination of herbs including damiana, kava kava, and ephedra -- all attributed to the lust daemon. Applying the potion shifted the energy in the room line by line, the aromatic blend infusing her senses. Power pulsed along the inscribed surface, occasional flares of glowing light tracing over elements of the immense pattern.

She sneezed at what would have been a pleasant smell in

reasonable quantities, yet this much rose oil in a confined space could only be classified within the realm of 'stench,' let alone the glaring, bright pink colors burning out her eyes. The herbs and oils were targeted to lust, not anger. She was used to calling up vengeance and power-hungry daemons. The room looked bizarre to her in comparison. Normally she'd have a few chickens or a goat sacrificed at this point, simply to have the sigils drawn correctly in blood.

Did Mahkra like the garish pink color, or was that a coincidence? She avoided further stray thoughts, focusing instead on the business at hand. The quicker this job was done, the quicker she'd have her payment -- that was all that mattered.

She tried not to think about the daunting nature of this job. She didn't doubt her abilities, but also couldn't deny she was venturing into unknown territory. Sure, she'd crossed many physical thresholds with daemons. She'd fed them nails, hair, spit, vomit, sweat, blood, tears -- she'd run the gamut past disgusting herself. But having sex with one had been a hard limit.

It'll be worth it at the end when I know who killed my parents.

Finally satisfied with her work, Meri approached her queen-sized bed, meant for the times she spent multiple days during complex summonings and needed to take a rest. She pulled the tre'jor out of her pocket. Where was the best place to hide the weapon? Under a pillow wouldn't work; those could get moved in the heat of passion. Meri considered attaching it behind the headboard with duct tape, but removing it when needed would be noisy and challenging. She needed stealth above all else.

In a moment of inspiration, she lay on the bed and let her

left hand fall to the side and over the edge. She rolled off the bed and used the tre'jor to cut a thin hole in the lining of the mattress where her hand had fallen, slid the dagger into that hole, and hid the sheath separately in her bag. She again lay back upon the bed and tested her reach. Bingo!

The room readied, Meri showered using pure rose oil soaps, towel-dried her hair, and then anointed the pulse points of her body with the flowery and slightly musky mixture of civet, rose, and honeysuckle oils she'd used to draw the sigil. Her skin heated to the oil on contact and then cooled as expected. She put on a pink silk robe over a dusky rose silk chemise and nothing else. When she was done, she dimmed the lights and crossed the room to the brazier. She threw a large handful of incense onto the hot coals. Smoke roiled forth and swept around her ankles as she walked the perimeter of the space, lighting rose-essence candles in her wake.

She walked around to the base of the sigil and stood up straight. Breathing deep from her belly, she began the intonation of Mahkra's name.

"Mahkra, the daemon of lust, I release you from darkness and call you forth into the light. From across the void, hear my plea. Step forth so I may command your actions on this Earth. My words alone call you. My hand alone has drawn the symbol's binding you to this space. My flesh alone will seal the bargain between us. Rise, and fulfill my summons."

She continued for a number of minutes until the sigil began to pulse and glow on the floor. The brightness increased until the room was filled with light. She reached down to touch the sigil. She backed away from the sigil as a whirlwind of a dark maw wrenched it in two, sucking the air

in the room into the depths of hell as the daemon emerged
onto the earth plane. Just as quickly as it'd opened, it snapped
shut again, and she stood face to face with the Arch-daemon
of Lust.

Mahkra was a tall and seemingly of Bedouin heritage
with mid-length dark, curly hair and dark brown eyes. Everything about him oozed sex appeal, from his full lips to his
sculpted, muscular body. He wore only a pair of loose,
billowy, red pants and a number of ornate necklaces and
wide wrist cuffs made of heavy gold. He had a hungry look in
his eyes, and Meri intuited that he met her inspection with a
degree of patience and amusement.

So why, despite his obvious sensuality, was she not drawn
to him? If anything, it was as if he repelled her on an instinc-
tual level.

"I am honored to answer the call of the illustrious
summoner Meriwether Storm," Mahkra said. He bowed low,
took her hand for a chaste kiss, and then his eyes raked up her
body, boring through the thin silk of her chemise. "I can't
begin to express how gratified I am at this turn of events."

Oh please. Meri arched a brow in disbelief over his
pompous delivery and felt slightly nauseous despite her
determination to maintain her composure. Then, what had
she expected? No daemon she'd met had lacked an abundance of ego, why would this one?

"It's a job." She shrugged and flipped her hair over her
shoulder, trying to act natural, feeling anything but. "Some
corporate guy wants a woman. Badly, and forever, and she
couldn't care less about him. Luckily for you, I was offered a
price I couldn't refuse."

Mahkra straightened and released her hand; his intelligent eyes probed her too deeply. She sensed now the strength and self-control, which marked him as an Arch-daemon, and fear crept up her spine while she considered her odds of making it through this binding. "I'd heard you're always a consummate professional. I won't discuss the details of your directives until after the binding."

"Oh? Daemons chat about summoners with each other?"

"Only those who stand out, or should I say 'weather' the years and bear mentioning? You certainly have. There are those of us who have followed your career with interest."

Great, he appeared to admire her. Was this genuine or part of his seductive spiel? She wasn't sure. His scent, reminiscent of patchouli and wine, filled the already rose-bathed air, and Meri fought not to gag as her head spun.

"I'm flattered." She batted her eyelashes and pursed her lips, just as she'd seen women do at clubs while flirting, but her body was wound tight, her thoughts in a jumble.

Mahkra laughed and stepped closer to her. "Are you now?"

She took a step backward. Her distrust of all daemons extended to this Arch-daemon, despite his sweet-talking and her mission d'être. She cursed herself. At this rate, it was going to be a long night.

Mahkra stepped forward again. When Meri didn't back down, he reached forward and ran his palm across her cheek. She tilted her head back. His skin burned against hers, but it wasn't an unpleasant sensation.

He dipped his lips to hers, first for a light, grazing touch and then back for a testing, playful nibble. His hands roamed down her neck, lingering for a moment on the swell of her breasts, and then dropped to the knotted tie of her robe. Meri felt his deft fingers make quick work of the knot. Her robe fell open and slid to the floor at her feet as his unnaturally warm body sizzled into her own. She gasped at the contact and pulled away.

His eyes searched her own.

"You're a smart woman, Meri." Mahkra stroked her arms with his hands. "You wouldn't have called me here without the intent to follow through with the binding. By the rules of this little parley, if you don't bind me, your life is forfeit. That would be a complete waste by my book. I would love to fulfill your every sexual fantasy. Right here. Right now. I also guess the payoff for whatever job you're going to send me on is pretty hefty, so stop holding yourself back."

"Look, can't we just, get this over with real quick?"

A blast wave of scorching heat rolled off Mahkra, blowing Meri's hair back away from her skin, and knocking over a few candles. Meri was amazed she didn't have an instant third degree burn on the soles of her feet. Again, his scent overwhelmed her, and she had to fight back another coughing fit while keeping focused despite her building headache.

"Meri, I need you willing, and fully engaged, during our encounter. What's the human phrase, it takes two to tango?" he smiled indecently.

"I'm trying here. This is not my forte! Why do you require summoners who've never been in love before anyway?"

"Oh, that's an easy one. They aren't usually emotionally tied up with anyone yet. It makes it easier for me to leave a lasting stamp on their soul. You see, Meri, after you have me, no one else will ever measure up."

The unbelievable gall! Meri envisioned slicing the blade across his neck and watching his black blood flow freely. It was almost worth it. Almost. She sighed.

"Perhaps love play is simply of no interest to you?"

She ground her teeth, on the edge of keeping the plan together due to her aching head. "This is not helping your cause."

Mahkra tapped a finger on his bottom lip. "Look. You know how summoners usually send me on jobs to trick mortals into becoming 'in love' with another? I can impersonate someone, and then via my overwhelming aura whomever I target falls for me. Well, they fall for the person I look like, and then they spend the rest of their natural life worshiping them."

The adrenaline spiked through her chest and throat, her lips pursing as she imagined the imprisoned persons he'd described. Killing him today would do the world a great service. Now if only she could turn her anger into a budding passion for a few moments, she'd be able to bind the bastard.

"Yes, I'm fully aware of your abilities. It's the very job I have for you, as I mentioned. But you don't make them fall 'in love,' it's more akin to sexual slavery. It's your specialty."

"Semantics, Meri, semantics." He waved away her words as if he was batting away a fly. "The point is -- I can pull an image out of a mortal's mind. Any mortal's mind. Including yours."

"But I'm not in love with anyone. I'm not even in like."

An intense pain drove through her temples as he invaded her mind, and then it faded, leaving her head throbbing as before.

Mahkra laughed. "Know thyself, summoner. You may not

be in 'like,' but you're in 'want.' It's why you're not responding to me as you should be." Meri wanted to disagree, point out she wasn't responding because he was a royal ass, but she held her tongue. He ran a hand down her arm and gripped her palm in his reassuringly before stepping back a few feet. "All right, this is happening, because otherwise, I have to kill you, and I respect you too much for that. And, besides, I just ate. Consider this a professional courtesy. Don't worry; it's what you desire anyway."

Meri's headache cleared as a layer of disgustingly pink fog rose up around Mahkra, and swirled in all its glory. After a few moments, the fog blew off, leaving Mahkra transformed into Azimuth.

"Oh! Oh, fuck no!" She shook her head vehemently.

"Oh, fuck yes, Meri," Mahkra-turned-Azimuth replied. He smiled just as Azimuth would, with that slight tilt of the head. He sounded just like Azimuth too.

He wasn't dressed quite like Azimuth as he still only wore pants. Except now, he wore black leather pants slung low on his hips and nothing else. Meri couldn't help but stare at his muscular shoulders, tight, rippled abs, and flat stomach.

"I am not attracted to this man." Meri began pacing, unable to stand still.

Amusement glittered in his eyes, and he sauntered towards her. "Oh, my. Has my summoner taken a liking to the forbidden fruit? If it's any consolation, you're not the first. What I don't understand, Meri, is how you ever met this Azimuth? I don't smell his binding upon you." Mahkra's eyes bored into hers.

"Another summoner sent him to me on a job once, relaying a message for his master. I've never summoned him."

Meri deliberately looked away, keeping as much to the truth as possible. She assumed Mahkra knew Azimuth, considering they were at war. Any connection between herself and his enemy might send up a red flag. If he guessed she was in league with Azimuth, well, this night wouldn't end on a high note.

Mahkra let out a guffaw, completely at odds with the impersonation of Azimuth he'd donned. "I see. A one-off meeting and you were star struck?" He continued walking towards her, and Meri backed up, near the bed. "On the upside, he'll never know what happens here today. We can try and get him out of your system."

Meri didn't even have the words to answer. Mahkra-Azimuth stood directly before her, those icy-blue eyes riveting her feet to the ground. A spicy musk filled the air. Her headache was long gone, replaced with a hyper-aware sensation building all along her skin.

Meri licked her lips. Azimuth could be infuriating as hell, and as a daemon -- a terrible idea to fraternize with, but now scenes replayed through her mind. Like when he'd dropped her off after the meeting with the cabal and appeared concerned for her welfare, not just the outcome of the mission. Or the moment he'd tuned into her energy in the alleyway, her entire body lost to his touch, and then her body's shameful response when she tried to pull away, managing to press his body deliciously against her own. Or the various times she'd watched how his clothes fit against his body or cued into his reactions.

For his part, Azimuth treated her as a valuable resource and marginal ally -- nothing more. Why would he? She was a human.

Mahkra-Azimuth was just as attractive now -- more so considering his half-naked state, and this one was less argumentative. He was a daemon she had to sleep with as part of the job. The real Azimuth would never know. What happens in the summoning chamber stays in the summoning chamber?

"You smell spicy. Musky," she said. "He doesn't smell like this."

Mahkra-Azimuth smiled, apparently well aware of the effect he was having on her. "It's my enthrallment, and you're finally under it."

Meri tilted her head, her thoughts tangled. "What does it do? I feel different. Short of breath. Warm. Odd."

A corner of his mouth curled up. "It's a natural aphrodisiac, and you're finally receptive to it."

Wary of Mahkra's compromise, Meri's resistance crumbled away by the second.

She sighed, a throaty sound, which only drew him closer, and gave in to his wiles. Meri reached out and placed a hand on his chest. It was cool to the touch, just like Azimuth, not scorching as Mahkra had been. Mahkra-Azimuth took her hand in his and kissed her palm. He flicked his tongue across her flesh, and heat shot through to her core.

Mahkra-Azimuth pulled her against him with his free hand, and his sizable erection pressed against her through the thin leather of his pants and her chemise. The pressure of his surging hips grinding against her swollen clit made her cry out in pleasure, clinging to his arms like a lifeline.

He took advantage of her open mouth and kissed her fiercely. She twined her arms around his neck, raked her fingers into his silver mane. His hair was soft as silk, just as she had hoped it would be.

He ripped the flimsy-corded straps of her chemise, and it crumpled down between them, exposing her sensitive breasts. His mouth left hers and sought out her nipples, sucking and teasing them with his teeth.

Mahkra-Azimuth lifted her up off the floor, and she straddled his waist, his hands caressing her backside and thighs in the process. He carried her to the bed and laid Meri back onto the sheets, kissing her all the while. He stood up long enough to peel off his leather pants, revealing toned, muscular thighs and a thick, hard manhood that Meri knew was well more than average for a human.

"Does he look like this?" Meri asked. The words slipped out unbidden. Immediately a flush rose to her already heated cheeks, shamed by the wrongness of her interest.

"Close enough." In less than a heartbeat, he was pressed against her, kissing her neck while his erection throbbed against her inner thigh. His hand cupped her breast, rolling the nipple slowly.

"You see, Meri?" he whispered into her ear. "We're faster, stronger, larger, and harder than our weak human counterparts. No wonder you hunger for one of us."

"I don't want to talk about this. Besides, you're killing the mood by reminding me of the immense ego all daemons have. Try being humble for once."

"Why should we be humble? When I look at you, I know. You're built for more. It's written all over you." He ran a hand down her chest, outlining ink with his fingertips, and Meri shivered in response.

Much to her chagrin, Meri warmed to the compliment.

She knew he'd see all of her daemon ink and for him to see her marked as some warrior flattered her, even as she was becoming wary of the chummy dynamic building between them.

"Less talk," Meri said. "More action."

Mahkra-Azimuth eyed her hungrily. His mouth again covered hers and then journeyed down her neck and back to her breasts. He spent a few minutes teasing and nibbling her rosy peaks while Meri whimpered in delight.

A trail of greedy kisses down her belly gave fair warning as Mahkra-Azimuth headed straight for her center. He explored her thoroughly with his tongue, setting a fast pace that soon had her desire peaked and her breath panting.

Mahkra-Azimuth looked up at her. His breath was ragged, his eyes full of need.

"Do you want me, Meri?"

Meri hesitated. His question seemed innocuous, but she'd bet money it was a loaded gun.

"Yes," Meri replied. More than I've ever wanted a human. What's that say about me?

Mahkra-Azimuth smiled triumphantly and resumed lapping at Meri's aching clit. He kept his mouth on her while he inserted first one, then two, fingers into her channel. As he stretched her, the sensation pushed her over the edge. Mahkra-Azimuth growled low in his throat, the sound reverberating through the metal frame of the bed as she took her pleasure. Meri shivered at the sound.

"You've blossomed like a flower for me, haven't you, Meri?" Mahkra-Azimuth asked.

Meri looked up and saw the daemon's eyes washed with crimson. He slowed, spellbound at the moment.

Is that how drug addicts react to a hit? "And now the binding is complete," Meri said, watching him recover.

Mahkra-Azimuth nodded. "Let me show you my appreciation."

He moved back up her body, positioning his taut erection above her swollen core, teasing her with his entry.

"Kiss me first," Meri asked. "I need your lips on mine."

"Gladly." His voracious lips were hot on her own, and Meri was surprised how eagerly her tongue joined in the dance. As determined as he'd been to seal the binding, the daemon was in no rush now to hurry their lovemaking along.

Meri took the opportunity to reach for the tre'jor. His eyes gazed into hers, and Meri held the blade unseen, hidden under the black sheets for a few moments, hesitating. Looking into Azimuth's face, even knowing it wasn't him, made her breath catch in her throat. If it was the true Azimuth with her, would she be able to do it? He was just another daemon, right? Even as she thought it, the answer rang within her: No.

A part of her hated Azimuth for getting under her skin. Another part wanted to wait another hour, perhaps two, before swinging the blade, because now was all she'd ever have, fake though it was. She could never give in to her wanton desire for Azimuth without sanctioning daemons and their realm. One who had killed her parents. No, they had to be used, or, better off, dead.

Meri brought her mind back to the moment and grabbed the blade in an unyielding grip. She reminded herself: this was Mahkra, and he was a slimy, detestable daemon who turned people into sex slaves for the right price. And, when he was dead, she'd have the name of her parent's killer.

Meri reached up with her free hand and pulled Mahkra back down into a kiss. A moment later she sank the tre'jor into his back with her other hand.

He roared and pulled back, but didn't try to fight her off. His eyes changed to jet-black and his face contorted with pain.

"I'd heard rumors of such a weapon. My death will be avenged over your tortured husk!" he choked out.

"It's a job, Mahkra. Don't take it personally."

Mahkra wrapped a hand around her throat, compressing it until it was hard for her to breathe.

"Whoever hired you didn't tell you." His skin began to distend, then darken and wobble, as if fighting an inward force of gravity. He moved his face closer to hers. His hand pressed harder, and Meri winced as she heard something crunch. "Do yourself a favor. Kill them next."

A moment later Mahkra burst apart, ripping into a million tiny pink shards of dust. The wind gusted and swirled out in all directions, building into a tornadic cloud. Her loose hair flew wildly with the force of the unusual air currents, Mahkra's bizarre death throes spinning away with rose-colored abandon.

Meanwhile, her throat ached, and Meri checked it in a bedside mirror, shocked at the red marks and purpling already rising under her skin. Whatever damage Mahkra had done caused her throat to swell, and she was already having trouble breathing. She needed to get to a hospital.

The whirlwind, however, had other plans. It coalesced into a vaporous, pink ball and launched itself at Meri, forcing itself down her already damaged throat. Meri clawed at her neck, unable to breathe past the blockage and crumpled onto her back on the bed, staring up at the pitch-black ceiling.

Heat exploded from her neck, saturating every cell in Meri's body. She fought to suck in air, fought the unknown invader in her body. However, it was of no use. Soon everything faded to black.

⸻

*M*eri awakened with a gasp and shot upright in bed, her hands reflexively grasping for her throat. Disorientation flooded her senses. The pain was blissfully gone, and she could breathe again, but every cell of her body was smoldering at a fever pitch. Next to her on the bed sat Azimuth, or was it a reformed Mahkra wearing his skin? Meri grabbed the thin sheet covering her body, terrified of the answer either way.

"Does your throat feel fully healed?" Azimuth asked. His eyes focused on her and his familiar energy flowed over her, gentle as the tide, seeking her emotional state. This was Azimuth, the real one. She almost threw her arms around him in thanks, or just relief he wasn't Mahkra. Almost.

Meri looked up into those sky-blue eyes, and then she focused on his full lips, remembering what a very similar-looking pair had felt like against her flesh. Breathing in his signature sandalwood and vanilla scent, she wanted to taste his lips, know the feel of his skin against her own. Was it just a trick of Mahkra's prior enchantment not yet worn off? How could she know?

Could he sense the heat coming off her skin? He couldn't

get detailed images from her mind, could he? Meri took a deep breath and tried to calm herself. Why was she so warm?

"Meri? Your throat? Is it improved?"

His look of concern reminded her she'd missed the question. "You healed me? How's that possible? How do healing and scenting falsehoods fit into the same daemon skill set?"

Azimuth smiled enigmatically. "I have many talents, which I'll explain to you at the appropriate time."

"Now, if you're recuperated we should port back to the burrow. There is much to discuss." He rose, retrieved her bag, sat it next to her on the bed, and then stood ready to leave.

"Could you please turn around while I change?"

"Certainly. Let me know if you require assistance." He turned away but didn't move from the spot.

Meri opened her bag, took out a change of clothes and slowly got dressed. Dressing got more challenging by the moment, as alternating chills, sweats racked her body, coming, and going so quickly her limbs jerked in pain. Once finished, she stood and took a few steps. Her body felt downright feverish, and each step she took could have been with someone else's body as they connected with the earth lightly. She barely registered the contact, as if her weight was negligible.

"Azimuth?" She tilted her head. "Did you do anything extra when you healed me?"

"Nothing. But as I said, there is much to discuss, and we are short on time." He held out his hand, his body taut.

Meri crossed her arms. "I think not. How did you manage to get in here, anyway? My wards should have blocked you."

Azimuth dropped her bag and walked to face her; impatience practically oozed from his tense frame. "I came in through the door."

"But it's got a state-of-the art lock keyed to my thumbprint, and I've warded this place to the gills. There was no way for you to enter."

She wanted to slap the imperious grin right off his face the moment it formed. "We assumed you might have complications. By your ink, we knew this was your first time with an Arch-daemon, and killing one is no small task. Take no offense, but we took certain precautions. We knew the location of your warehouse from following you in the past and collected your thumb print during your visit to the burrow. I bypassed the wards with a Doppelgänger spell from Annamie, courtesy one of your hairs. All of this was very easy when planned."

"I can't believe you convinced Annamie to betray me like that!"

"Meri, I can not only sense truth from others, but I can also state it. When she knew you'd die without my assistance, she was eager to help."

Her irritation at Annamie dissipated, but that still left one hole in the puzzle. "How did you know I was injured?"

Azimuth's face darkened. "Orias foresaw you needed help and warned me to move in when I did. We assumed Annamie would assist if you were in danger. She's a genuine friend to you."

Meri spun away from him, feeling like she'd been punched in the gut. If Orias had foreseen her injury, then he had to know the full circumstances -- how Mahkra had been transformed into Azimuth at the time. Her cheeks burned with shame over her exposure.

Azimuth put his hands on her shoulders. "Meri, I know you think poorly of us. Please know Orias handled the matter delicately. He shared the barest details of the vision, knowing you'd be indisposed, but he shared nothing intimate or inappropriate. Trust me; Belial would have had his head if he had."

Meri turned to him and saw his earnest expression. Apparently, Orias hadn't told Azimuth the sordid details, but she guessed he must have seen it in the vision. Just as she knew he'd hold it over her. He was a daemon, after all. It was a valuable bargaining chip.

She'd have to act first before Orias told Azimuth. "I'm going to kill Orias," Meri said. A wave of heat and anxiety rolled off her, blowing Azimuth's hair back and moving the knocked over candles around on the floor. She took a few steps back from him, staring in confusion first at him, and then at her shaking hands. Azimuth didn't appear surprised in the least, confirming he knew what was going on, but he refused to let her in on the secret. "Damn you. What the hell was that, Az? Did I do that? No. How did I do that?"

"As I said, we should be going." Azimuth's stormy expression bordered on anger.

"I don't feel like going to Sheol right now, Az. I'm going home. I'm going to have a nice, long bath. I'm going to watch some silly sci-fi flicks. I'm going to eat some ice cream. And I'm not going to think about daemons for a few days. Just give me my payment, and we'll talk later."

If she didn't know any better, she'd think Azimuth looked panicked.

"That's a bad idea, Meri."

"Why not? What's going to happen if I don't go with you, Az? And are you refusing payment unless I comply?"

"This is not the place." Azimuth squared his shoulders. "We need to get you out of here. It's not safe for you here anymore. You need time to adjust in a safe environment.

Meri cocked her head, itching to goad him into a fight. "Adjust to what, Az?"

His eyes flickered to white for a moment. "As I said, this is not the place to discuss it."

"Fine, we'll talk later, but I'm not coming with you today. I'm likely to gut you or Orias or both of you. You just reneged on a payment, mister! Now you're only willing to discuss the information I want in Sheol? I know when I've been played." Meri walked around him and grabbed her bag off the floor. "You know what Mahkra said while I was killing him? He said I should kill you next for not warning me of the consequences of killing him. You see, I think he'd taken a liking to me, despite the whole assassination thing. I'm standing here wondering, why the hell should I trust you? I mean, your enemy was more honest with me."

Azimuth watched her with a murderous glint in his eyes, but he didn't answer.

Meri thought about staying and demanding her payment, but between Azimuth's mood and her body's odd after effects from the summoning, she needed time to think. Time without his gaze boring into her.

"I'll call you when I'm ready for that talk. I trust you can let yourself out?"

"Don't wait too long," Azimuth replied. "And watch your back."

"Are you threatening me?"

"I'm not a threat to you."

His voice was soft again, and Meri reacted viscerally, heating from the inside out. Meri shut the door between them, reminding herself that underneath his smooth voice were motivations that didn't appear to have anything to do with her best interests.

"Oh yeah, you are. You're driving me out of my mind."

CHAPTER 6

*A*fter a halfway-decent night's sleep, a full scrub down in the shower, and some ridiculously thick coffee, Meri felt more like herself. She was still trying to piece together the meaning of Azimuth's and Mahkra's warnings from yesterday. Meri was not about to humor Azimuth with additional trips to Sheol to get her answers. She wasn't insane.

Images from yesterday kept playing back through her mind. Being lost in Mahkra-Azimuth's kisses and languorous touch while she'd climaxed underneath him. His look of betrayal when she'd impaled him with the tre'jor. Worse, a fevered sweat broke out over her body thinking about the look in Azimuth's eyes as she refused to give into his demands. Haunted by the memory, chills overtook her body.

Meri intended to see Annamie to reason out the meaning behind it all. If she'd been altered in some way, Annamie was sure to know the cause and hopefully also the cure. Or at the least, she'd know who to send her to for help. Meri didn't trust the daemons in that regard.

When she'd searched her body for the new daemon ink, it hadn't been difficult to locate. Curlicues of garish, pink fili-gree now decorated her inner thighs all the way to her knees and over her sex were wisps of color extending almost to her navel. They shimmered silver when she moved. How fetching.

On the upside, Meri no longer felt lighter than air, but the rounds of chills and clammy sweats hadn't stopped, but each round was at least less taxing. At least it was some improvement over how she'd felt after the summoning. Not yet normal, but perhaps it was simply a matter of time?

Meri checked her voicemail messages and Ms. Ride, a wealthy woman and regular customer, needed yet another information scoop. The Gleaner, her go-to daemon for snooping was a quick and easy summoning job, so Meri sent Ms. Ride a quick text with a quote for approval. She asked for more than the last time, as per usual. Her prices always went up; it was the nature of the beast. With each invocation, the pound of flesh and the intimacy with the daemon increased, thus so did the associated cost. Meri smiled when Ms. Ride's reply came before she'd even finished dressing. The offer was satisfactory.

Ms. Ride wanted to know if her daughter's new fiancée had a clean history, and would always have a clean history. That information is worth a pretty penny considering that Ms. Ride had her fortune to think of. Can't have gold-diggers coming after your precious few children.

Meri's first stop of the day was Annamie at Soul Paths. Second: her alternate warehouse where she'd handle the job for Ms. Ride. It was a quick trip, and Meri pulled into the parking lot behind the store. When she stepped out of her car, there was a bee that kept buzzing in her ear. She paid it no mind. As she walked closer to the store, the buzzing grew louder. She tried to wave it off, but there were no insects. How odd. The last few steps to the back door made her skin crawl and itch. Undeterred, Meri reached out to grip the doorknob, but instead, an electrical force ripped through her body and threw her backward onto the pavement. A loud, wailing alarm blared.

"Ow!" Meri rubbed the back of her head. Staff from the store streamed out, braced for an attack. Annamie stepped into the foreground, looking none too amused.

One of the clerks stepped forward to assist her, holding out a hand. "Meri, are you all right? What happened here?"

Annamie's shrewd gaze pierced Meri. "Jesse, Meri can help herself up. Everyone, back inside."

One of the newer staff, Tabby, hesitated. "But she's hurt. Surely we should bring her inside? Get her some tea?"

Meri stood, shivering slightly under Annamie's harsh glare. The buzzing noise hadn't diminished.

"Her welcome at my store and property is hereby rescinded."

To Meri, it was a direct blow to the gut. She feared the reasoning behind Annamie's words.

"Now go," Annamie said to them. "Meri and I must speak in private."

Annamie's staff departed, closing the shop door behind them. She stood with her arms crossed and looking every part the angry mother who'd caught Meri with her hand in the cookie jar. "What have you gone and done to yourself this time, girl?" she shook her head.

"I might have made a questionable deal," Meri answered.

"You think?" Annamie spat on the pavement. "Was it worth it to you?"

"You're the one who insisted my fate required I take the next job." Meri shrugged. "And now I'll have my parents' killer on a platter as payment."

Annamie shook her head. "That's unlike you, girl. Not taking care of payment in a timely fashion. What's holding you up? Oh, let me guess." She ran her eyes up and down Meri's frame. Meri knew Annamie could perceive things well beyond the physical plane, deep into other's spiritual centers, and by the pained expression on her face, Meri feared her friend's insights. Annamie threw her hands up over her eyes. "Summoning daemons has never done well by you, but you've gone much, much too far this time."

"What's it cost me? Be honest." Meri cringed to hear the words, remembering the dire warnings from both daemons.

"I'm no expert on daemons, Meri, but true to rights; you're possessed. Your aura reads it clear enough, and the wards on my store back me up."

Meri trembled, and the telltale heat of daemon possession rolled off her in response to her anxiety. What had Mahkra, and the others, done to her? Or more aptly, in her rush towards retribution, what had she done to herself?

Annamie had only confirmed what she refused to see for herself. "I've heard of summoners, seasoned ones, getting possessed despite years of training. However, I've never heard of a way to undo it. By reports, they've always disappeared within a day or two of their possession. How can I undo this?" Meri held her gaze and didn't miss how Annamie's gaze fell to the ground before rejoining hers.

"As I said, I'm no expert. I don't know how you managed

it in the first place, much less how to undo it. Priests or Voudoun might be able to help you; they're the ones who tout their exorcism skills. I'm out of my element here."

Meri swore under her breath.

"Until you are free of this possession, you can't come back here. Call on my cell if you need something, and we'll ship you any supplies you need, but you can't be here." Annamie sighed, her eyes full of sadness.

"I understand." Hearing the desperation in her voice, Meri swallowed and willed her voice not to break. She couldn't, wouldn't appear weak before anyone. Not even Annamie. "You're a good friend for continuing with that much, considering the circumstances. Heck, Annamie, you're my only friend. You know I don't love daemons. All I've ever done, I've done for revenge against them."

Sadness filled Annamie's eyes. "I'm your friend now, Meri. I always will be. Good luck handling your parent's killer. You deserve it."

Meri shook her head in frustration, her heart in her throat. "You'd advised me to take this job. Look what it did to me! Do you have any idea why the spirits wanted this?"

"No. All I know is, they must have their reasons, but it's beyond my understanding."

They smiled weakly at each other, but there would be no hugs, that much was clear. Annamie entered her shop, and Meri fought back tears as the door shut with a dull click. The new distance between them stung Meri, but she couldn't blame Annamie for fearing what she'd become. Not when Meri was so scared of it herself.

*M*eri left for her alternate warehouse, steeling herself for work despite the shocking news from Annamie. Today she'd do a good, clean, simple summoning, and prove to herself just how able she was to continue life as normal. Afterward, she'd see about getting herself de-possessed and extracting payment from the cabal.

She wiped a line of sweat from her forehead. Yes, this possession was merely a minor hiccup in her plans, never mind the occasional hot flash.

Despite not being able to pick up the dove's blood ink like she'd have liked at Soul Paths, she did have some dragon's blood ink on hand, which was a bit of overkill, but it would have to do. In short order she'd cast the circle, anointed the space, chanted the incantations, and burned the favored heliotrope on the brazier.

Meri took a deep breath, loving this moment. This summoning was proving downright calming. Refreshing, even. She hadn't had a fevered chill hit her for over an hour and credited it to getting back into her routine.

Meri stood at the base of the sigil. She intoned Penethewes' name, and soon the sigil pulsed and glowed. The small room filled with light. Meri cast a handful of celery seeds -- used for their ability to increase mental focus and concentration -- across the sigil, and it erupted with color.

"Penethewes, daemon of gleaning, I release you from darkness and call you forth into the light. From across the void, hear my plea. Step forth so I may command your actions on this Earth. My words alone call you. My hand alone has drawn the symbols binding you to this space. My flesh alone will seal the bargain between us. Rise, and fulfill my summons."

Penethewes sprung forth, a casual sneer plastered across his pasty, unattractive face. Thin to the point of being two dimensional, this twisted daemon barely passed in the human realm. Therefore it was fortuitous people rarely noticed his presence. What clothes he wore hung from him like flags from poles. He'd told Meri once his thin body made it possible for him to maneuver into all possible locations, and that's how he got his information. Was he slender enough to slip into someone's mind? She'd never asked for that level of gory detail and didn't honestly want to know.

"Summoner Meri? Is that you?" he asked.

"Don't be silly, Penethewes. Of course, it's me."

He genuflected. "No offense intended, to be certain. I was simply unaware of the recent changes."

Meri narrowed her eyes. Could he sense the daemonic possession as well? "I have a task for you."

Penethewes genuflected, an honor he'd never before bestowed. "Simply name it."

His odd manners irritated her, but she couldn't justify her reaction, so she shrugged it off. "I have a client, Ms. Ride. Her daughter's new fiancé needs a complete vetting. I need to know if he's out for Ms. Ride's money, his future goals in life, if he's ever tortured a puppy in his youth, his family history, the whole nine yards. Questions?"

"Just a moment," he bowed again and teleported away.

Terrified over his sudden departure, Meri's blood froze like ice in her veins. He'd left the summoning circle before the binding had been completed. Where had she gone wrong? Never before had she lost control of a daemon, especially not one she'd summoned before. She frantically retraced the lines of her casting, reviewed her summoning, and even checked the herbs and oils she'd used. All appeared in order, if anything, she'd been overly cautious. What had gone wrong?

Sweat soaked her shirt and ran down her brow. Unwilling to leave the space and break the ritual bonds, Meri began intoning a general daemonic devocation. She'd never had to use one before, and could only hope it would work on a less powerful daemon. Meri had it on good authority devocations were iffy at best, but better than doing nothing when things went awry. She never thought she'd die at the hands of an insignificant information gatherer daemon. Her parents would be ashamed.

Quiet motion behind her alerted Meri to Penethewes unexpected return. He was on bended knee, eyes downcast, with an envelope extended to her in his hand. Meri couldn't help but gape at his presentation. She took the proffered package without complaint. Without a word.

Penethewes arose. "It is an honor to serve one of your caliber. Feel free to speak my name at any time. None of this," he gestured around at the summoning space, "suits your needs anymore."

Meri kept her face neutral. Could he know she was possessed by the Arch-daemon Mahkra, just as Annamie had? Because the stories of possessed summoners were so scant, she wasn't sure how the daemon/daemon-possessed human dynamic worked. Penethewes acted as if he knew and therefore she might as well roll with it. Perhaps she could glean information off the Gleaner.

She smiled, attempting to mirror his relaxed demeanor. "I

suppose you're correct, Penethewes. I am, however, grateful for your prompt service. Do you desire payment?"

A look of horror crossed his face. "You offend me, Mistress! I would never accept such base payment from one of my own. Unless, of course, you would grace me with your revealed name? Now that, that would be a treasure beyond measure to me on this day. A treasure for me to sing far and wide. For then I would be the first to sing of the turned Meri's true name." A cloying grin passed over his face.

The turned Meri? Other daemons did recognize her possession on sight. Did they smell it on her -- just as they knew humans names, see it, or what? How did they know? Regardless, he kept deferring to her, as if she were his peer, or perhaps his superior? Now she was supposed to have a new name? No wonder Azimuth had wanted to talk to her in private!

Meri schooled her features to her well-developed poker face. "I'm afraid you'll have to wait along with everyone else for the big announcement." She smiled and hoped casting out a daemon wouldn't take more than a week. Maybe two.

"Oh?" He raised a brow. "Will there be a party, and cake, and dancing? I do love a good jig!" He erupted in all manner of contortions. Meri laughed shrilly, startled by his movements.

He continued to dance, mocking a waltz but at an inhuman speed until she was dizzy watching his antics.

"Penethewes! Be still!" Meri demanded.

He obeyed, groveling at her feet. "No offense intended, Mistress."

"It's fine. Thank you for your service, Penethewes. Speak nothing of the work you have done for me here today or anything else you have learned during our time together, or there will be grave consequences. You are dismissed."

He frowned, reminding her of a child who'd just had their lollipop stolen. "You took all the fun out of my day."

When he ported away, Meri was left with a foul taste in her mouth.

She walked over to the basement door, opened it, and waited for her phone to acquire cell signal. Scrolling through her contact list, she selected the hopeful answer to her problems and activated her phone.

It rang numerous times while anxiety snaked through her gut.

"Miss Ria." No titles, spiels, or lengthy intros with Ria. She was all business, all the time. Meri liked that about the old Voudoun priestess.

"It's Meri."

There was a brief pause on the line. "Well now, it's been a while since we've talked. Thank you for the business you keep sending my way. I am most grateful, my dear."

"No problem, Miss Ria. I'm always happy to help out another sister."

"Um hmm. And why are you calling me today?"

"I need a daemonic exorcism done. Do you do those?"

A sharp intake of breath. "Oh my, that's a pickle of a situation. It's been some time, but I'd be willing to try. We need to work quickly, however. Do you know the victim well?"

Meri laughed, but it sounded hollow in her ears. "I'm the one possessed."

She heard movement on the other end of the line. "How soon can you get here?"

"I'm meeting a client now, and then I'll be right over."

"I'll be ready when you get here."

"Thanks, Miss Ria."

"Don't thank me yet, Meri. Be very, very careful. Whatever you do, don't go to Sheol. The possessed don't come back. Ever."

CHAPTER 7

*M*eri stopped by the coffee shop, the designated meeting location for her client, Ms. Ride. Arriving a little early, she ordered a drink to help her relax. The entire encounter with Penethewes fit nothing from her summoner's playbook. A daemon never passed on payment, and rarely would they do a job in a reasonable timeframe, much less ten minutes. While she waited for her iced latte with a shot of vanilla, Meri tried to place the look in Penethewes' eyes during their interaction. At first, she'd thought it was respect, but that wasn't quite right. No, it hadn't been respect at all. He'd looked at her with a healthy dose of fear. Perhaps because she was possessed with an Arch-daemon?

Gleaners were simple daemons, lower ranked but not falling into the succubi/incubi category. If Azimuth were around, she would ask him how Gleaners were perceived among other daemons in Sheol.

At the thought of Azimuth, her body temperature rose a few degrees. Meri gladly accepted the iced latte, but it did little to quench the building heat. She was better off avoiding thoughts of him entirely. It was unfair how a recollection of his ice blue eyes had her clenching her thighs together and looking over her shoulder. Perhaps if she summoned him and agreed to talk, he'd let her run her fingers through his hair?

No.

He'd gotten her into a load of trouble, and she was bound and determined to get herself straightened out on her own. Especially since she couldn't stop craving the very scent of him.

Meri sipped her latte and took a seat at a nearby table, focusing on the envelope she was about to deliver to Ms. Ride. She opened the packet and quickly perused the contents Penethewes had been so quick to offer on Ms. Ride's daughter's fiancée. Jerome Studder was an average college graduate, had some average debt associated with not understanding how to balance a checkbook, but that was a trainable skill. Or, in a household like Ms. Ride's, a job handled by the accountant.

Jerome never tortured animals as a child, had no history of prolonged bedwetting. He called his parents weekly, and they were divorced but amicable with no history of domestic abuse or embezzlement. Jerome himself had once stolen a box of Jell-O from the supermarket, but it was after smoking some weed, he wasn't altogether "with it" at the time. The pot smoking had been a passing phase as well.

Most importantly, he'd never cheated on a woman. Ms. Ride was very particular about that clause for her Julia. No cheaters. Meri sighed. It looked like Jerome and Julia were headed for wedding bells, sanctioned via the power of daemon.

Ms. Ride walked into the café, and Meri slid the papers and pictures back into the envelope, sealing it up tight. She rose to greet Ms. Ride.

"Always a pleasure, ma'am."

"You did quick work this time, Miss Storm."

Meri handed over the packet. "Sometimes it works out that way."

"And how do things look for my daughter?" She took off her sunglasses and toyed with them.

"At a glance? I think you'll feel much relieved. Although I'd recommend some budgeting classes."

Ms. Ride shrugged, as if to say, you can't win them all. "Well, this does make life a bit easier for me, doesn't it?"

"That's my job, Ms. Ride." Meri tilted her head.

"You're due a bonus on this one, Meri. Truly, less than a day. I'm not sure how you did it." Ms. Ride chewed on her sunglasses.

Meri laughed it off. "What, do you think I'm time-traveling now?"

"Oh, don't be silly, darling. It's just you're the best. I almost believe that you're one of them now. It is a fine line, isn't it?"

Meri's lips thinned, and her eyes narrowed -- since when did Ms. Ride talk down to someone of her stature? Meri leaned forward, resting her elbows on her knees. "I'm sure I don't have any idea what you're getting at, Ms. Ride." The air around her increased slightly in temperature. "I'm nothing like the daemon scum I corral on your behalf."

Ms. Ride blanched. "Of course you're not, Miss Storm. I am grateful for your efforts, of course."

"Then you'll make sure your payment, with bonus, is

wired by the end of the day." Meri stood and walked toward the exit at the back of the café where she'd parked, not looking back. Ms. Ride was speechless.

She'd get additional work out of Ms. Ride, despite the abrupt ending. She always did, because Meri's reliability was a standard.

On her way out the back door, a man working on his laptop caught her eye, and she paused. The businessman had dark hair, matching eyes, and a strikingly stern expression. He worked single-mindedly while ignoring his coffee. If not for the faint yellow glow of arcane arrow-shaped sigils on the backs of his hands and a matching shape on his sternum, peeking out from the V of his casually unbuttoned dress shirt, Meri would've thought he was just a typical guy trying to catch up on a deadline away from the office grind.

What did those mean, and why was she seeing them?

Just as she resolved to ask the cabal about this new development, the man caught her staring, and blanched.

"Is there a problem, Summoner?"

"Nothing which concerns you," Meri did her best to show no emotion, lest he assume she was targeting him for a job. She didn't recognize him, so either he was new to town, or worked at a company she'd never done business with. He smiled in solicitous fashion, and then went back to his work.

Meri exited the store and stalked down the street, and quickly cut down between two buildings into the alleyway, wanting to flee the eyes of passersby on her way back to her car. She'd had enough intense scrutiny for one day.

Turning the corner, Meri ran into a group of street thugs caught up in a private conversation. Gangs always gave her a wide berth. Used to being treated as socially untouchable, Meri, lost in her thoughts, ignored them.

Instead of backing off, they blocked her way, leering and leaning provocatively against the walls and dumpsters. The ringleader stood across from her, broad-shouldered arms crossed over his washboard abs, jeans slung low across his hips revealing his underwear. A sheen of sweat shone over his close-clipped head. Everything about him was tight and honed to perfection, and he was planted square in her path. The other four confidently backed him up.

Meri fumed at the display of male machismo. It nauseated her. "What's the meaning of this, boys?"

"We're curious what a beauty like you is doing wandering alone in our hood? You looking to entertain us a while?" He eyed her up and down. His companions hooted and whistled, edging in closer.

Waves of heat and anger rolled off Meri. "You see my ink, yes, boys?" Yeah, her cargo pants covered her legs right now, but the ink on her forehead was always visible, and her short-sleeved, low-neck top revealed her ink-covered arms, upper back, and chest.

"Oh yeah," the leader, unbelievably, took that as an invitation.

"You know, I dance with daemon ilk, not pretty boys like you, get my drift?"

"Oh, you're looking downright edible, daemon ink or no, little lady." They continued to converge.

Meri sighed and muttered under her breath. "Since when am I a sex magnet?" Her hair lifted and clothing swirled as waves of heat emanated from her pores. She dropped the latte, now boiling in its slowly melting plastic cup.

"I didn't quite catch that, sweetheart," the ringleader sidled up to Meri, his eyes fixated on her curves. "But I do know you're the spiciest dance I want to give a whirl."

Meri wasn't afraid of the men or her dramatic temperature increase. The idea of intimacy with them made her ill, but the more they challenged her, the more she ached for a fight.

"You think you can take me? I think I'm a little too hot for you to handle." A heat wave blew off Meri, knocking two of the ringleader's men to the ground. Although they scrambled back up quickly, all of them except the ringleader lost a bit of confidence in their postures.

He grabbed her by the upper arm, thinking to rein her in, but his skin sizzled at the contact. When he tried to pull back, Meri grabbed his wrist.

"I thought you wanted to dance a while?" Meri smelled his skin burn while she stared him down. To his credit, he didn't flinch, apparently not wanting to display weakness in front of his men. When Meri released him, she followed through with a punch to his abs, and to her surprise, he flew back a good eight feet and landed on his ass on the pavement. None of his men moved to challenge her, her point well and truly made.

"I hope that dance met your standards?" Meri asked. She continued down the alley, unobstructed by the men. Behind her, she heard the men dragging their ringleader and fallen friends away, accompanied by much swearing.

Her body temperature quickly cooled, but her temper still simmered underneath. Meri fled the scene, heading towards her car still a few hundred feet away. Thinking back over the altercation, she realized the daemon possession must be the cause of her enhanced physical strength and heat surges. Also, no doubt the unwelcome attraction of men like flies. She wrinkled her nose in disgust.

Half a block down the street Meri fished for her car keys in her pocket and heard the soft sound of a chuckle and a gentle clapping. The hairs on the back of her neck stood up. Turning, Meri saw a petite, curvy woman with thick auburn hair and a sly smile.

"Nicely done." The lady sauntered over to her, slowly circling Meri. Meri had the distinct impression she was being given the once-over.

"Why, thank you," She replied. This woman smelled overly sweet and spicy and looked too perfect in her form-fitting black cami and jeans. Her green eyes flashed with an unholy inner fire, and Meri's breath stilled in her chest. Her hand instinctively went for the tre'jor tucked into the side pocket of her loose camos. She was never going to leave home without it again.

"I go looking for my missing Arch-liege and lover and look what I find. You're not quite what I expected, little girl," the daemon taunted.

"Sorry to disappoint, but I'm afraid I don't know what you're talking about."

The lady let out a deep rumble. "Oh, I think you do. You see, my liege Mahkra -- that name ring a bell? -- Well, he was summoned a few days ago by some human, and he never returned. Someone of his stature doesn't just go missing. I was sent to scent him out. And here I find you, laced with his scent. How do you explain that?" There was a murderous glint in her eyes, despite the enticing smile she continued to aim in Meri's direction.

"I did summon him, and sent him on a mission, which he completed." Meri had the presence of mind to flash some of the daemon ink from Mahkra, right below her belly button, confirming her story. "This must be why I reek of him. I'm not responsible for what he did after he left me. He completed his part of the job, just as I did. The gig's over." Meri shrugged.

The daemon threw her head back and opened her mouth wide, shrieking in a deafening roar. A screeching noise surrounded them, drawn out by the daemon's pain and reflected in the vibration of the hundreds of small and large metal objects slowly warping. Meri took the opportunity to palm the tre'jor. The daemon put her face mere inches from Meri, claws fully extended, her breath full of sweet, intoxicating plums.

"You lie, human filth! I bedded him! I know his essence! The marks you carry are more than a mere conjuring! What have you done?"

In a panic, the damning waves of heat begin to roll off Meri's body, and she knew there were mere seconds to act. This daemon, who claimed to have known Mahkra intimately, would no doubt recognize yet another sign of his presence.

Meri had the tre'jor and a mad-as-Sheol daemon in front of her. Could she survive an all-out assault by the lover of the daemon she'd murdered? Meri knew nothing of this daemon's powers or proclivities, but it didn't matter. Only survival mattered.

Meri held up her empty right hand, a feint to hold her off. "Please don't hurt me."

The daemon's rage wasn't quelled. She grabbed the hand

and pulled Meri close, grabbing Meri by the hair. "I will know the fate of my master."

Body-to-body, Meri slashed upwards with the tre'jor, connecting with the daemon's soft belly. She never even saw the blade enter, but the force was met with a grunt.

"It went something like this," Meri replied, digging the blade deeper, feeling it hit the female's rib bones.

The color in the daemons face bled out, and she released her vice-like grip. "Who knew you had it in you, summoner?" She coughed, and a dark green-gray powder exited her mouth. "My name is Trailian." She dropped to her knees as her form slowly de-solidified, and Meri fell with her, keeping the blade in place throughout the daemon's death throes. "I think my stupidity at underestimating you has earned you that much." Her suddenly solid black eyes fixed on Meri. "Good luck with the other hunters."

Trailian shook, quivered, and collapsed into a pile of greenish-gray smoke. This time, Meri knew what was next. She returned her tre'jor to the sheath in her cargo pants and watched the essence of the daemon's remains reform into a slow-moving ball and swirl in her direction. Meri rose and took a few steps back, but it was hopeless. Should she have let the daemon kill her instead? Now, the mossy-green ball of daemon remnants enveloped her, and soon she was breathing it in, unable to resist its compelling draw.

As the new daemon seeped into her lungs, her blood, her bones, and into her skin, Meri felt it touch her very soul. At first, the pressure was light as butterfly wings, but soon it morphed into a scraping, clawing beast of pressure, fighting for room with Mahkra. Inside her head, Meri let out a scream, wishing for relief, wishing for quiet, hoping for peace.

Azimuth...

A moment later, a hand was on her shoulder, and relaxing waves of pleasure swept through her body. Everything calmed, and the warring internal factions called a truce. Meri opened her eyes and realized she'd balled up on the ground in the alley with Azimuth crouched over her protectively, calming her with his touch. Meri frowned. Damn him and the power he held over her.

"I heard your call, and I see you've gotten yourself into a bit of trouble. Are you ready to come with me to the Cabal for training yet?" His eyes were compassionate.

Meri shrugged off his touch, tried to stand, and then almost lost her footing. Azimuth quickly had her by the arm and hoisted her up with little effort.

"I don't trust your group, or what you want with me."

"That's fair. However, I think you can agree you need us to teach you how to protect yourself. Otherwise, events like this will continue to happen."

"Because of you!" Meri pulled away. Her anger with him brought her mental anguish, or had it been the act of pulling away from him? Meri gripped her hands to her head in a futile attempt to ward off the pain. Had he caused her pain on purpose?

Azimuth shook his head in frustration. "I can't leave you here any longer. You're a smart woman, Meri. Surely you can understand you're in too much danger on your own." He planted his hands on his hips, and his lips were a firm, hard line of displeasure. Azimuth sighed heavily. "I hate to do this, but perhaps the others can talk more sense into you than I can." He reached out and took her hand.

Meri melted under his touch. Her eyes met his, and she wished, for a moment, to be lost in his gaze forever. "Wait, what are you doing?" Meri pulled away. No, she couldn't go with him to Sheol. She'd promised herself she wouldn't. Miss Ria was waiting for her right now. If she could fix one daemon possession, she could fix two, right?

Azimuth rolled his eyes. "See, you're a complete mess. I'm amazed you're able to walk around down here with your new needs." He gripped her firmly by the shoulders. "You're coming with me. Everything's going to be all right. We'll get you trained and able to handle what's going on in your body."

When he said the word "coming" Meri was hit with the most intense orgasm of her life. Her body went rigid while she stared at her shoes and slowly panted for air. She gripped his arms, her nails pressing into his flesh, and Azimuth had to fight to keep her standing.

"What's wrong with you?" he demanded.

"Absolutely nothing." Meri smiled back weakly. How had that happened?

Azimuth gave out and exasperated snarl. "No more stalling."

A moment later, he dumped her on the couch in the den of the Cabal and walked away. Meri felt his absence like a sharp, tearing sensation, but the endorphins from the orgasm lingered to lessen the pain. She was in Sheol again.

Orias approached and sat next to her. "How are you adjusting, young blood?"

Meri scowled at him, the seer of all. "I'm still not exactly sure what I'm adjusting to."

"Aren't you?"

"I intend to get my answers."

"So you shall," Orias replied, "I believe there's something you wish to ask me, and I advise you to do so now, while no one else is in earshot."

Meri scanned the room. He was right. They were alone. "Thanks for saving my life."

"Ever polite, even under duress, I do appreciate that. You're welcome."

"Can I assume when you foresaw the scene, you saw the entire scene, with clarity?" Meri said the words through grated teeth, watching Orias for his reaction.

Orias sighed, a slight frown catching on the corners of his mouth. "Indeed I did. And I presume you fear I will reveal this to Azimuth."

Anger rippled off Meri, washing away the remaining endorphins left in her system. "What's to stop you?"

"Because, Meri, I've seen the conclusion to this scenario. And I swear to you: Azimuth will not learn the truth of that day from my lips."

Meri smelled a proverbial rat. "Why? It's a juicy secret. Why wouldn't you want to tell him?"

"As I've said, I've seen how it unfolds. It's best if I don't interfere. If I do, well," a dark look passed over his features, "let's just say I've seen a few different potentials. The future is always in flux, the further out, the more possibilities. The best outcome is for you to discuss things with him on your own. Much as I'd love to assist my brother in this cause, I'd only interfere with the outcome."

Meri screwed up her face and stood to walk away. "I bet it

works out even more embarrassingly for me somehow?" she hissed.

Orias sat, and put a finger on his lips. He said in a whisper, "I won't breathe a word."

"What is this racket?" thundered Belial, striding into the room followed by Kobol and a glowering Azimuth. Meri began to pace, the sexual tension within her once again mounting with Azimuth's return.

"Meri and I were just catching up," Orias replied. He stood and walked over to the conference table, motioning for Meri to join him.

"Was she hissing at you?" Kobol asked Orias, a broad grin spreading across his face.

The others took seats around the table, and Meri reluctantly followed them but refused to sit. Azimuth's gaze drilled into her and she avoided returning it.

Orias inclined his head. "She also thanked me for my role in helping save her life. Shall we get down to business?"

"Yes," Belial replied. "It's time we plan out Meri's training and protection during her transition. And, although it may feel a bit fresh on the heels of Mahkra's defeat, we are now in a prime position to move on Saleigh's cabal, and indeed must do so before any attack can be anticipated."

"Boys," Meri said. "I hate to interrupt, but just so we're clear: I refuse to cooperate, on any level, until I receive my payment."

Belial leaned back in his chair, eyes flashing red. Apparently, the cabal leader wasn't used to being questioned or derailed.

A corner of Azimuth's mouth curled up, but just a corner.

"Am I to understand then, that once you're paid, you'll cooperate?" he asked.

"No guarantees," Meri answered with a shrug.

Azimuth slid an envelope across the table towards her, in front of an empty seat. His gaze lingered, watching her every move, and Meri's breath caught under his intense scrutiny. "Everything about your parents' murderer is in there. But for now, please, sit. There are matters regarding your survival which must be discussed."

She trusted the envelope held the name of her parent's killer, but she wouldn't open it here. Not in front of them. Meri had no idea how she'd react seeing the daemon's name, knowing the details of their death. What if she'd summoned the daemon herself, and never known? No, she needed to deal with it in private, not with an audience.

Meri pocketed the envelope but still refused to sit. Irritation swamped her senses; she'd leave now and meet Miss Ria except they had her trapped. She turned her attention back to the cabal. "From what I've gathered, I'm just some tool you've possessed with a daemon and now you've got another job for me to do? Why should I let you keep using me? How much of a fool do you think I am?"

The men, except Belial, shifted uncomfortably in their seats, faces flushed.

"Meri," Kobol spoke up, "We do each other the courtesy of not using our powers on each other without permission, and right now you need to learn to tether that Lust daemon of yours."

Meri leaned on the table, leveling him with her gaze. "And whose fault is it I'm possessed with a Lust daemon, hmm?" Kobol's eyes flashed back a brilliant green. Anger it was for his eyes, then. She looked to the others and confirmed her suspicion by their utter lack of surprise. They knew full well what they'd done to her. Mahkra was right, and if she'd had the power, she'd kill them all. Sadly, she guessed she was no match for them. "Well, you can all go fuck yourselves if you think I'm going to cooperate."

Kobol flushed crimson. "That's exactly my point. These aren't proper thoughts for a group meeting if you get my drift."

Meri pulled at her hair and screamed. In an instant Azimuth was by her side, gripping her shoulders. "You must stop fighting this and let us help you learn to control it," he spoke in firm, low tones. His contact did just the opposite, boiling her blood.

"You're not helping her," Orias growled.

Azimuth looked from Orias and back to Meri, who was now sagging in his arms, attempting to mold herself to the steel of his form.

"Let go of me," Meri said, pleading against his chest, mortified with her reaction.

Azimuth released her and, to her embarrassment, Meri let out a brief cry of pain. He pulled out the empty chair and Meri deposited herself into it without complaint. After a few moments of quiet, except for Meri's gasping breaths, he returned to his place at the table. Meri shot Orias a quick look of doom, looking down her nose, pursing her lips and narrowing her eyes while imagining he was being flayed alive, out of spite. He didn't appear surprised -- he just smiled back at her.

"You knew I'd figure it out, didn't you? That you'd infested me with Mahkra?" Meri asked.

Belial cleared his throat, his eyes still crimson. "We'd hoped you would return here shortly after the event, and we could better explain our position and the reasoning for our actions. But I'm not at all surprised you figured it out. You're intelligent, capable, and competent. I am surprised and a bit disappointed that you've already saddled yourself with another daemon, but you're to be congratulated for defending yourself without any training."

"Thanks. I think." Meri replied.

"Did you happen to acquire the daemons name? We need to keep track of the inhabitants you take on," Belial asked.

"Yeah. Trailian said I'd earned it for outsmarting her. Wait, you say that like they'll be more. There won't. My next stop is a Voodoun priestess who's going to exorcise these daemons so I can get back to my old life."

"That's what we need to discuss, Meri. Your old life, as you put it, is no longer an option. It ended well before you ever merged with Mahkra, although I daresay you were never aware how close you came to the precipice." Belial's expression was grave.

"You're not making any sense. I'm good at what I do. One of the best. I don't know anyone who's been summoning for as long as I have, at least not at my pace. I've proven my capacity as a summoner, time and time again."

"Quite the opposite, child. You'd maxed out your capacity."

Belial let the words sink in. Meri blinked long and hard. She looked around the table and was met with serious deadpan eyes from them all. "You can't be serious. Even if you are, why should I accept you at your word? You're daemons."

"How do daemon summoners die, Meri?" Kobol asked, for once without humor.

"They lose control of their charges. They summon something beyond their control. Won't pay the price, or are unable to and are consumed by the daemon. Much like my parents." A hard knot formed in her gut when she remembered the pools of blood, all she'd found of her parents after their final summoning.

"And what does the daemon ink on your skin represent?" Azimuth asked, his voice a soft whisper.

"I'm no child, so why the school lesson?" Meri snapped. Her harsh words towards Azimuth sparked a lance of pain through her mind. She bit her tongue, and the sensation abated. How did that happen?

"Let me elucidate. The daemon ink ties you to them. Do you know what other benefits this gives them?"

"They get to spend a brief time on Earth, away from Sheol."

"Because daemons are known to have such simple minded interests." Kobol's sad eyes wrenched at Meri's heart. "And the masses ate up the biggest line of hand-fed bullshit produced by the pits of hell."

"Then why would daemons answer the summons?" Meri asked.

"Because, in the ritual, you trade a little part of your soul for a little part of their essence," Belial answered. "And human souls are a succulent delicacy, much like a glass eel or puffer fish are in some areas on Earth. Some daemons become quite addicted to human souls."

Meri dropped her head into her hands, overwhelmed with a sudden, dizzy, nauseous sensation. This, she was tempted to believe. It fit the transactional nature of the summoning: a piece of daemon essence in the form of ink under the summoner's skin in trade for a slip of their soul. After a moment, when the spinning had slowed down, she looked up at the group. "I've been feeding my soul, bit by bit, to daemons?"

"And being paid quite well for it, my dear," Orias replied.

Meri turned, ready to fire off a snappy retort, and then caught the expression of dejected sadness on Orias' face. She looked back at Belial, a haze of tears threatening to break free in a torrent.

"Besides," Belial continued, "Having a soul, at a certain minimum threshold for a daemon, has definitive benefits. Teleportation access to the human realm is one of them. I'd advise against letting any more of your soul slip away, assuming you want to continue accessing the Earth plane."

Meri clutched her chest. If they were right, exactly how much soul did she have left? In the next heartbeat, she digested the second half of what he'd said -- the part about having daemon essence inside of her. "Wait. I can port?" Perhaps she could get home on her own?

"Yes. You've taken enough daemon into yourself that you can learn, but I'd advise against traveling solo for a time. Triangulation is tricky at first, and we don't want you ending up off target," Belial suggested.

Meri closed her eyes and breathed slowly, trying not to imagine herself half-embedded in the side of a building, or in the lair of some other cabal. After she'd calmed herself, Meri faced the cabal again, bristling over the assumed tone of ownership Belial was taking with her.

"I don't understand. In the early days, many summoners

died to learn the rules, to know how to summon safely. That knowledge was, in turn, passed down and carefully guarded. How were so many humans taken in by this ruse?"

Belial shot her an exasperated look. "Meri, knowledge hard-won feels real. Daemons have all the patience in the world. We'd already been to the human plane. We've already found other ways to feed on human fears and vices, but not souls. When humans offered up the dangerous summoning gamble in return for our labors, we let you set the rules. We allowed you an extraordinary complexity, with grave risks. All the better for us. A summoner fails, we consume them immediately. A summoner is competent and plays the game well; we devour them over many, many years, savoring the game. Either way, we win. As I said, daemons are patient, because daemons are, by the whole, immortal."

"And humans are simply your toys." Meri flashed Belial a look filled with rage. "And now here I sit, a human among daemons, and you tell me all this. All I wanna do is kick some daemon ass."

"Is that really what you want?" Azimuth asked.

His words slid over her skin like a silken tongue, and no, that wasn't nearly the beginning or end of what she wanted. The temperature around her rose a good twenty degrees. She wanted to be laid out on the table and pounded into until she couldn't feel the hurt in her heart anymore. She wanted to crush the daemon that had consumed the final human aspect of her parents and cradle what was left of their souls. She wanted to destroy every daemon in Sheol.

"Meri," Belial said, "eyes on me." She turned her angry eyes on him, wishing she could start with him. "Be calm, young one, I know you're overflowing with lust and retribution in equal measures, but I need your focus now. Can you do that for me?"

Meri blew out a slow, measured breath, and her temperature cooled. "You're not consuming me, Belial, so what's your devious plan now? From all you've said, your cabal doesn't fit the pattern you've described; else I'd be dead already."

Belial rose, his horns lengthening and turning an even deeper shade of ebon black. "I am not like my brethren, Meri. I do not live off human souls, not like Saleigh's cabal and their ken. This is a sickness of my kind which deserves purging because it makes us weak."

"Weak?"

"In the exchange, Meri. Daemons give to human summoners their essences as if it holds no value. Just as some humans think their souls worthless. Fools! I would sanctify our race; make us powerful again through the fiery branding of a new generation of warriors."

Meri looked around the table, at the grim faces of the cabal, and understood this small band was his chosen group. Belial had her sitting at the same table with them. The meaning sunk in through her inked skin, all the way down to her very bones, shaking her to the core. He'd artfully masterminded her possession by an Arch-daemon, and now included her with his chosen few?

She saw the proverbial fire burning in Belial's eyes, and it was something she recognized well, if not in this species. Meri had seen it with Corporate CEO's bent on power and in petroleum tycoons set on greed. Except for Belial, she'd pin it as a form of religious zealotry, and couldn't help but wonder how stable he was, or how his peers regarded him. He was set on mass destruction, and wanted her to help after betraying her 'for her own good.' What else would he do 'for her own good?'

"With all due respect, I'm no warrior, and I'm not daemon. Not like them. You're recruiting the wrong gal."

Kobol smiled, but his eyes were sad. "We weren't born daemons either, Meri, we were also turned. Belial saved us all, just as he saved you, from certain and quite unpleasant death."

Meri laughed, hearing the bordering hysterical edge to her voice. "You don't have daemon ink. None of you do."

Kobol held out his arm and pulled up his shirtsleeve. His skin flickered, and for a moment, Meri spied the intricate designs of layers of upon layers of daemon ink. Azimuth and Orias did the same. "You're human?" Daemons with varied powers were rare, and they'd all just demonstrated control over illusion, and she knew Azimuth had power over discerning the truth from others. Was he a high-level daemon, or could they be telling the truth?

"Yes. Well, we were once," Orias answered. "Also saved from a grisly death by Belial."

Meri's eyes met Azimuth's and bit her bottom lip. If what they claimed was true, and she wasn't sure it was, Azimuth was human or had been. Was it somehow less deviant to desire a human-turned-daemon, versus a full daemon? He raised an eyebrow, perhaps sensing the question in her eyes. She dropped her gaze, memories of another version of him searing kisses down her throat encompassing her thoughts. Whatever type of creature he was, Meri knew Mahkra was right: she'd wanted Azimuth from the moment she first saw him.

"So what," Meri asked Belial, trying to understand the

limits of this story. "You watch human summoners, find the good ones and turn them to your purposes before they die?"

"I save them right before they fall, when it's possible," Belial argued. "Few are willing to work with us. Few can be bargained with as you were. I find a daemon for them to kill who will initially balance out their energetic load. If it's not calculated correctly, they will flash-out during their daemonic conversion. In other words -- the daemon personality overtakes the human host, destroying whatever humanity remains in the vessel. For you, lust was a required counter balance to all the retribution and vengeance work you'd focused on during your career."

Meri thought back to her killing of Trailian, of the burning sensation she'd experienced hit home. "So that could have happened when I killed Trailian?"

"There is less and less risk of flash-out with each new daemon you absorb, assuming you don't focus on any one specialty again, or take on too many daemons in quick succession. Azimuth has proven that. He's the eldest among you, and has taken on many daemons with no ill effects, as have Orias and Kobol."

"So what do you call yourselves?" she asked. She refrained from including herself as one of 'them.' Again, this could all be smoke and mirrors, but she'd get whatever information they were willing to impart before she left. Assuming they'd allow her to go.

"Belial refers to us simply as turned daemons. I, however, have another term I've coined from mythology. The goddess Hekate of the Underworld ruled over the crossroads and all events and creatures who lingered there. The crossroads themselves were said to be a 'liminal space,' a line of transition between life and death. We stand on that line."

"To do what, precisely?" Meri asked.

"It's just my analogy, as we are in the underworld, and yet are neither here nor there. We are Liminals. Another species entirely. A hybrid, if you will," Azimuth explained.

Meri barked out a laugh. "I'll take that over daemon any day. You've turned me into a daemon, excuse me, a 'Liminal,' and now I'm a member of your cabal? Am I supposed to be grateful?" The prospect galled her, particularly since Belial had manipulated her into killing Mahkra without knowledge of the consequences.

Belial sat forward in his chair and tapped his clawed fingers on the table, his eyes tinged with crimson. "I believe you'll find the benefits to being a daemon far outweigh the death you'd soon have experienced when your unbalanced daemon ink overwhelmed your fragile human psyche. And no, I won't consider you a member of this cabal until you pledge a blood-oath of loyalty to me. That can wait until you're feeling a bit more grateful for the efforts I've expended on your behalf."

His quicksilver temper reminded her to watch her words for the time being. "This is a lot to take in, in a very short period," Meri replied, sitting ramrod-straight in her chair, hands clasped nervously in her lap. The prospect of swearing a blood-oath of loyalty to a Prince of Sheol made her palms start sweating. She practiced slow, calming breaths and focused on not freaking out.

"Why don't you take the afternoon to get settled in? We have a room prepared for you. When you're ready, you can begin your training." Belial's eyes returned to their inky pools and he forced a half-smile.

"I'll even give you the full tour," Kobol said. "The burrow is much larger than what you see here. We have a basement with a dojo area..."

Meri shot to her feet, cutting him off. "No. No no no."

"Excuse me?" Belial said.

"Belial, I'm grateful for being alive, and I will take you up on the training. After all, as you've said, I've got those daemons after me for killing Mahkra. But I'm not moving in here."

Living in the same quarters with Azimuth? She'd be driven insane with lust for him. Besides, she had to get home. Back to Miss Ria.

"That's non-negotiable. The daemons can track you on Earth. You're an easy target there and too vulnerable," Belial replied.

"It's my home. My parent's home." Meri dug in her heels. "And I'm not leaving it. I have a life there. It will help me to maintain balance and keep calm. Being here will only wind me up."

"She's telling the truth," Azimuth spoke up. "Is there another reason being here would be difficult for you?" His eyes bored into her, seeking out the smallest hint of a lie.

"Being here is hard on me. At home, I'll be more in control of myself. With less stress surely I'll be better able to gain access over my new powers more quickly." She met his gaze straight on, honest, but not in a full-disclosure sort of way.

"Being around her as she is now also adds additional stresses upon the three of us," Orias pointed out. "Taking breaks from her unfettered influence will be good for our constitutions."

"We can take turns watching her house," Kobol offered. "And train her one-on-one with our specialized skills."

Belial frowned but didn't argue further. "When she's got the basics, we'll make our move against Saleigh's cabal. Once he's bound, we will be miles ahead in this game."

"I'll take the first shift," Orias said. "I can ward her home to deter the hunters from tracking her down."

"My home's already warded from daemons," Meri replied.

Orias shot her a sly grin. "Sure it is, using human spells to ward it, which are vulnerable to high ranking daemons and Liminals like us. I've got a few tricks up my sleeve humans know nothing about. You've graduated to an entirely new class of magic, little sister."

CHAPTER 8

*H*ours later, Meri had various daemonic spell wards installed in and around her house by Orias, which only allowed herself and Belial's cabal to cross. She could have walked past her home and not have seen it from the street. Meri hoped the mail carrier would be able to find it, but Orias assured her the wards only applied to daemon ilk. No doubt she would still get her junk mail on schedule.

She had multiple calls from Miss Ria on her cell but avoided returning them. The likelihood of getting to her and away from Orias and the cabal was unlikely. Daemons were notorious for their tracking abilities.

After gorging herself on mineral water for dinner, Meri was almost ready to call it a day. She blamed her new dietary interest on her newest daemon occupant, who must crave something in the substance. Belial promised research would shed light on Trailian's proclivities and help her understand the new resident's needs. Happily, a penchant for mineral water wasn't a particularly disgusting habit.

She sat down at her mahogany desk and turned her attention to the envelope Azimuth provided, turning it over and over in her fingers, biting her lower lip. Nothing was stopping her curiosity to know about her parent's killer now except her building anxiety. Pushing through her fears, she slid a finger through the top, opened the envelope, and pulled out a single sheet of paper wrapped around another envelope nested inside. Meri unfolded it, treating it as she might a poisonous snake. Azimuth's fluid writing came into view.

Her name is Calloine. She's an Elder-Daemon Sin-Eater. In return for a successful summoning, she'll consume daemon ink from the summoners flesh, actually removing that "history" between the summoner and the other daemons. Her payment is in memories. The summoner gives her pictures of the moment they're willing to part with, covered in tears, and she'll extract that memory along with the ink, freeing up more space, and thus time for the summoner to continue their practice.

It's my understanding your parents were advanced summoners, covered in daemon ink when they sought her out and tried to use her to buy a few extra years. However, the binding failed, and Calloine consumed them both.

I caution you against attempting to contact her, but I've listed the constituents required in the envelope within below per our agreement. Please be aware, she is incredibly powerful, and even other daemons avoid her because of her appetites. This is likely why you've had such a difficult time finding her.

Make no mistake. Calloine is too powerful for you to take on at this time. I simply cannot stress this enough.

Meri huffed and set the letter to the side, rummaging through the desk, picking through the stack of her grimoires. She didn't recognize the name Calloine off the top of her head, but that didn't mean it wasn't listed somewhere in the library she'd accumulated. Going on a hunch, she started with the older books -- the ones she'd inherited from her parents.

They had to hear about her somewhere, after all. She'd searched plenty before, but never did she have a name to use while going through the dozens of books.

Forty minutes later Meri discovered a short, but definitive reference mentioning Calloine in Summoner Eric's notes. This grimoire was a relatively new acquisition for her parents, and Eric had amended his comments to the man who'd originally scribed the book, a pretentious-sounding Sir Chasen Rense. The description, to her great annoyance, correlated precisely with what Azimuth had listed in his letter. The inscription also recorded her extremely keen sense of smell, even for a daemon, as a point of note, and associated this with her taste for daemon ink on summoners.

There was a listing of ingredients for the summoning, and Sir Chasen noted it had been copied from another document and never tried personally. A picture was included in the list, fitting what she remembered from her last day with her parents.

Eric had amended in his notes that Calloine was an Elder-daemon, which he'd discovered from another summoner's grimoire, and she was not to be summoned without extreme caution.

It felt like even these other summoners, across time, didn't want her taking the risk. Meri's heart sagged within her chest. The long-sought knowledge did nothing to satiate her need for vengeance, and the Elder-daemon Calloine could squash her like a bug in a fight, tre'jor or no. She was again faced with the option of joining ranks with the cabal and biding her time before confronting the powerful daemon.

Perhaps she could sway them to aid her cause, if she took up theirs, as distasteful as the concept soured the back of her mouth.

Meri folded the contents of the envelope back up and took them to her room, placing them in the shoe box of family photos. She changed into a cami and flannel pajama pants, and then emerged, her mood a bit worse for the wear. Orias lounged, reading a large, leather-bound tome on a couch in her living room. She'd offered him her guest bedroom, but he'd politely declined, citing a reduced need for sleep.

"I'm headed to bed. Is there anything you need?"

He set the ancient book aside. "Meri, while I'm here, I'll try to impart to you a bit of my ability of insight, although it may be lost on you. I doubt you've summoned many insight daemons over the years."

"No, I'm afraid I haven't."

"There are other skills, Take the wards for example. I'm sure you'll pick those up quickly. You won't need much help with upgrading your ritual techniques and construction, so we'll breeze through those areas." He rose and walked over to her. "But even if I can't teach you foresight, I need to teach you to read the impact you have on others."

"How so?"

"Your accumulation of daemons, the Arch-daemon of lust and the many retribution daemons, evoke nonverbal and sometimes verbal reactions in others. We'll train you to dampen or control the release of these effects, but right now, they radiate off of you at full bore."

Meri shrugged. "But I don't feel a thing. I'm not trying to do it."

Orias slid a hand around her lower back and pulled her into him until their chests and hips bumped invitingly. Orias was pure muscle, and Meri knew his erection pressing against her was just the point he was trying to make.

"You see, Meri, your powers have an impact when you don't control them. Right now I want to fuck you, or slap you, or a little of both."

Meri placed both hands on his arms, pushing away, but Orias held firm. "More importantly, what do you feel right now, Meri?" His black eyes bored into her, his heat mingling with her own.

"I want you to let me go." Meri's anger grew. "You may be keyed into this 'lust' thing, but all I've got going on right now is 'pissed.'" He held on for another moment longer, and revulsion crept through Meri. She dug her nails into his biceps. "Okay, now I'm feeling disgusted."

Orias released her, his slight grin in contrast to the relief surging through her body like an electric pulse. "And now, how do you feel?"

"Relieved," Meri answered. Orias hadn't been making a pass at her; he'd been making a point. "What's your game?"

Orias rubbed his chin with his forefinger and thumb. "You're a Liminal filled with the essence of rage, retribution, and lust. Others sense these from you clear as a bell, but you don't appear in sync with your passionate aspect."

Meri thought of Azimuth, and flames shot through her core. Her cheeks flushed with heat, unable to deny her attraction to the Liminal. "What if I told you I'm in touch with it, just in a, well, limited fashion?"

"Ah, so you do know where your lust is focused. I was afraid I'd have to spell it out for you. Well, I'm glad we had this little talk. Have a nice night." Orias turned and sunk back down into the couch, picking up the tome he'd been perusing earlier.

"Wait. You've known all along?" Meri asked.

Orias put a thumb between two pages as a placeholder. "Of course. What's important is that you know."

She rolled her eyes. "You're infuriating."

"I'm simply the product of my components." He went back to reading.

She picked at the lint on her pants, and then surveyed his casual posture. "What does my focused attraction mean?"

Orias looked her straight in the eyes. "I'd advise you figure that puzzle out quickly." He flashed her a smile laced with innocence. "You appear to know the who, and the what. I doubt either of you lacks the tools or ability necessary for the job."

Meri stormed out of the room, quite clear that this work equaled spending some quality time with Azimuth. Her options included staying and pummeling Orias or leaving to fume in private.

In the relative privacy of her bedroom, she dialed Miss Ria.

"Meri?" She answered on the second ring.

"Yes, Miss Ria. Thanks for picking up."

"Where have you been? I've been waiting for you all day!"

"I was unavoidably delayed, and right now I can't get away. It wouldn't be safe for you." Even if she sneaked away, Belial's cabal would follow, or the hunters after her for Mahkra's killing might if she was to believe Azimuth. She had reason to believe him on that point, considering Trailian had already found her because of Mahkra's scent on her.

A pause on the line. "I could come to you."

"No! My house isn't safe right now. I need to figure something out."

"Be honest, summoner. Where were you when you got delayed today?" The hard edge of Miss Ria's voice cut her to the bone.

Meri didn't want to admit to being in Sheol, mostly because she feared Miss Ria would write her off immediately. "I've had problems with more daemons."

Miss Ria's drawn-out sigh reminded Meri of a balloon deflating. "They've claimed you now, haven't they? I've heard they claim summoners sometimes when they get too good and challenge them. They found you and then they claimed you, didn't they?"

That wasn't the story she'd heard from the cabal today, but 'summoners getting too good' hit a point of resonance between the two tales. Meri threw herself back onto the bed and sighed in return. "Some want to claim me, and others want me dead. I'm looking for another option."

"Tsk tsk. I'm sorry, Meri, but I don't know what I can do to help you now. If you're being hunted by that many daemons, there's no way to hide you long enough to try to get the evil out of you, and I don't want them killing me for trying."

"No, Miss Ria, I wouldn't want to put you at risk. It's why I'm not on your doorstep already."

"I'm sorry. You know I've always respected you."

Her breath caught in her throat. "I'm not giving in yet. I'll find a way through this."

"I hope you do." Her voice was gentle and kind, yet laced with doubt. "Good luck, Meri."

"Thank you, Miss Ria."

She hung up and stretched out on her bed, the last thing she wanted to do was mope. The stress of the day had wound her up, and her inability to do much about anything wore on her nerves.

Her mind drifted to Azimuth, and soon all she could think about was his sandalwood-scented flesh sliding against hers, and it wasn't long before Meri was seeking her release with her hands traveling along her breasts, lingering on her nipples, and then stroking behind the nape of her neck. She moved on to her stomach, grinding against her inner thighs. Aching for fulfillment, her mind kept drifting to specific imagery from her summoning of Mahkra, when she'd almost had the daemon she'd wanted. She could all too well remember the silky feel of his hair falling against her neck, his lips sucking and nipping at her breasts, the touch of his adept fingers right where hers were now.

The heat within and without built, but Meri came to no completion. She was blocked. Finally, in extreme frustration, she let out a strangled scream.

There was a solicitous knock at her door.

"What the fuck do you want?" Meri yelled, sitting bold upright in bed. She heard a soft chuckle.

"Are you in need of any assistance? Well, any assistance I can render?" Orias asked.

"No! And you fucking well know it!"

"Perhaps you should call someone who could help." Another chuckle.

"Over your dead body!"

She heard a horrified-sounding gasp through the door, over her ragged breathing.

"Meri! I'm appalled! Anyway, keep in mind that when you project a state of high, um, need -- to others of us who are tuned in to you, we will respond accordingly."

She was grateful she hadn't accidentally 'called' Azimuth during her efforts. "Thanks for the reminder."

"No problem," Orias answered. His footsteps faded down the hall, and Meri collapsed back onto the bed with a growl, pulling on her hair.

She wracked her brain. Why was her lust aspect infatuated with Azimuth alone? She mentally reviewed her summoning and then killing of Mahkra, and everything he'd revealed about himself while they were together. He'd said lust daemons had the power to bind a victim to a person, but he didn't say how it worked, just once it was done, his victims, once bound, couldn't sexually focus on anyone else ever again, forever. Apparently, sleeping with a lust daemon impersonated as someone must do the trick. Nice to know now, Sherlock.

Meri ground her fists into her eyes and groaned. How had she been so stupid? She'd summoned for years, and finally, a daemon had gotten the drop on her. The fact that she hadn't been attracted to Mahkra had been a hit to his ego, surely enough to warrant retribution in his book. He'd been merciful enough not to kill her outright, but he'd had his revenge by binding her to a daemon -- when he knew she'd be disgusted by the very concept. Or had he hoped, in some warped way, to prove his point to her: daemons were superior in every way to humans. She'd gotten the final blow, not that it mattered now.

Now she was bound to Azimuth, whom she found amazingly attractive sexually, but there was no way she was ever divulging the facts to him. Never. She'd rather die than give him that power over her. Sure, he might be a Liminal like herself and not the wretched daemon she'd initially assumed him to be. But if he knew the truth, he would steer her with his infallible decisions, and she'd be left unable to make any choices whatsoever.

In the meantime and as a result, she was repulsed by other men and couldn't achieve release on her own. Brilliant. Meri flopped over in bed, tucking the covers over her head. Look out world: here's one pissed off, unsated, lust daemon, coming right at ya.

*T*he next morning Orias dumped a stack of hefty tomes on Meri's dining room table. Her easy-side-up eggs jiggled in protest and the table legs groaned. She sighed, running her fingertips along the spines of the books in wonder, and then he sorted through the stack and placed all but the three largest on the floor next to her.

"These top three are critical for your understanding so study them first, and then we'll run through more of the basics of daemon ward construction today."

"Don't you need to eat breakfast first? I mean, you're part human, after all." Meri bit into a buttered bagel, savoring the crunch.

"I eat less frequently now, and things other than human food sustain me. So no, I'm not hungry yet."

Meri blinked very slowly. "Do I even want to know what you're talking about?"

"You might not," he paused, giving her a shrewd look. "But you need to know. From summoning daemons you've gathered how each one has particular appetites?"

"Certainly. It's a cause of endless study among summoners. But Belial said what they feasted upon was our souls," a sour taste formed in her mouth at the thought.

"True, on both counts, but the first is what you'll need to focus on as you take daemon occupants. Each one has an ability, or abilities, depending on the strength of the daemon, and each one has hunger that much be quenched. Their abilities can only be used at a set rate, depending on the strength of the daemon. The daemon's hunger must be fed more frequently if you utilize its abilities."

"So my sudden interest in mineral water?"

He grinned. "Blame that one on your new boarder. Now, finish eating, we've work to do."

Unable to resist the plethora of available information at her fingertips, Meri ate her breakfast and then read for a few hours, poring over the pages of the first volume Orias had designated as crucial. During her reading, he walked by and pointed out a section on weaving pure elemental energies into the spell wards, which Meri had almost missed because of the elaborate diagrams occupying the same page. She stifled a satisfied smile from his view, but he was paying attention to his text.

"Enough study," Orias said. "Come and sit across from me on the living room floor." She joined him, a bit surprised at her lack of trepidation.

"So how do we begin?" Meri crossed her legs, sitting forward on her hands.

"Back to basics for a moment. Human summoners use charcoal, oils, blood, incense, you name it, to draw out spell wards. Daemons use only their essence, or power, to cast the same wards. This makes the wards exponentially more powerful, but also limits the daemon on the number of wards they can cast at any time."

Meri chewed the inside of her lip. "What about Liminals? Don't we have more daemon essence available to use?"

He shot her a wry grin. "Some more than others, yes. However, we conserve our energy as a matter of course. Never assume you'll have an unlimited supply available. You're bound to find yourself in a situation where you run short."

She nodded. "Okay. So how do I direct this energy?"

He held up his hands, palms up, and she mirrored his

actions. "Much the same way you did when you were a summoner. With your intent. Keep in mind; this energy is more potent and volatile. It requires a stricter hand and greater focus.

A blue flame appeared in his right palm and then arced into his left, pouring like a waterfall. Meri focused and a moment later a matching flame appeared in her right palm, repeating his trick, although her fire held less cohesion and wavered while it jumped between her palms.

Shock coursed like a live wire down her spine. This was no trick, no empty claim from the cabal she had to back up with outside research. The blue fire was real, in her hands, and marginally under her control. Just like her enhanced strength when dealing with the gang members, some things the cabal said were the truth. How much, she still couldn't know.

"Not bad for a first try. As you can see this is all ephemeral, the intent is the important aspect. Now, remember the Seal of Air? This one is used for building or adding mental focus." His hands cupped together and the blue flame transformed into a translucent, white circular symbol she remembered from the pages he pointed out earlier. Wispy curlicues wove in a pattern spinning around a central, empty hub. The entire design appeared to be in motion while, in fact, remaining still.

Meri took a deep breath, cupped her hands, and then blew her breath out slowly while trying to reconstruct the pattern for herself. As a summoner, she'd always been able to draw the pattern with her hands. Sure, she'd had to imagine it in her mind's eye first, but now drawing it in her mind with the proper intention caused the ward to come to life. She got over three-quarters of the way through the symbol before the ward fell apart in her mind, and thus her hands.

"Crap! Sorry, I'm just amazed at the amount of focus this demands! It's exhausting."

He dropped his reconstruction of the air ward. "No worries. I didn't expect you to get it the first time around. Rest for a moment, and you can try it again in a minute."

"But what you did last night, with the multicolored wards all woven together. That was incredible to watch."

"Those are rather advanced forms. They can be layered together and built into complex matrices. Once you understand how to put them together, you'll be able to deconstruct and slip between poorly constructed wards as well."

It boggled Meri's mind. Hopefully one day soon she could master at least the basics to keep herself safe.

Although she wouldn't have admitted it to him, the camaraderie of working with another peer filled a space inside herself. They continued to work through until the afternoon with only a brief lunch break for Meri and by the end of the lesson; she almost had the basic elemental forms down.

"Thanks, Orias, I'll get to reading, although I may have to live a few lifetimes to get through all of these." Meri laughed at the thought.

Orias leaned back against an armchair. "I see this hasn't all sunk in for you yet. I must say, it is amusing watching your mind's gears shift slowly into place."

Meri rewound the conversation in her mind. Lifetimes. "How old are you, Orias?"

"I'm 168, but I stopped celebrating birthdays a while back. It's a rather human custom, you see."

"I see," Meri agreed with a nod, although she didn't completely understand. "What's a Liminal's life expectancy?"

He gave her a calculating look. "Daemons live to outlive, and outdo, others of their kind, and as Liminals, we inherit their power and talents. We're naturally immortal beasts, but keep in mind, that just means we are not given to the plagues of mortality. You will not face a natural death, aging, disease, or the like. However, this does not mean you are therefore invincible. You will note, rather quickly, daemons have a high mortality rate due to temperament. They kill each other as often as they can find ways to do so. In case you're wondering, the tre'jor isn't the only deadly weapon out there designed to kill immortals like daemons, turned or no. You're better off thinking of yourself less as an immortal, and more so as incredibly hard to kill."

Meri ran a hand through her hair, tugging on the ends. "Yet you all have gotten along well. Perhaps I will too."

"That's the plan." Orias' eyes took on an impish twinkle, and he stood. "Looks like your next trainer has arrived. Have a good afternoon and evening. Remember our discussions. A lust daemon needs to temper their energy on a regular basis, or they are apt to erupt unpredictably. I advise you to work out your complications sooner than later, as we discussed last night. But I forget, you're not interested in advice, are you?"

He turned on his heel and walked to her front door, oblivious to the daggers Meri stared at his back. No, Meri was sure he was quite aware of her mood. He just didn't give a damn. It was lucky he kept his counsel largely to himself, or he'd end up with a good ass kicking on a regular basis.

Orias turned, tapped a finger to his temple, and smiled. So she was right, his foreseeing abilities extended to some telepathic or empathic bleed over? Good. She flipped him off anyway. At that moment, Azimuth walked in the front door, witnessed their exchange, and frowned.

"I can see our recruit has been a joy for you to work with," he said to Orias. Meri crossed her arms and harrumphed.

"On the contrary," he replied. "I've found Meri an apt and willing pupil, and we've fallen into a comfortable and friendly rapport. I'm sure you two will do even better."

"Fuck off, Orias." Meri stalked from the room, declaring herself the self-proclaimed queen of grace and tact.

"Seriously?" Azimuth asked Orias. Meri easily overheard them from the next room of her small house.

"She's having a difficult time muting and balancing her energies. I have a feeling you'll be of particular assistance to her in this matter. After all, she's known you the longest."

"Get a move on, Orias," Meri called out.

"I do believe I've been dismissed. Good day."

Azimuth joined her in the living room. He kept his distance. She wouldn't blame him if he were wary of her mood; in fact, she hoped he would give her a wide berth. Meri avoided eye contact, but already lust uncoiled within her, begging to come out to play. As desire came to the fore-front, her anger and rage subsided, yielding to the more powerful Arch-daemon essence.

"In your opinion, how did your training with Orias go?" he asked, his velvet voice caressed her skin like a feather.

"Quite well. I can conjure a basic daemon ward on my own now. Nothing multi-layered yet." Meri half-frowned, despising how much his opinion mattered to her.

"You'll catch on with practice. Orias is a superb teacher."

"What are you here to train me on today?"

"How to mute and hide the expression of your daemon essence, so you can blend in and express just what you wish to reveal when it suits you."

"Obfuscation? So I can appear to be a human again?" Meri's hopes rose, and she made the mistake of meeting Azimuth's gaze. She forced herself to not fall headfirst into those crystalline depths.

"If you wish. However, trained humans who are suspicious and able to see through your wards may still see you for the daemon you are. You'd have to be very careful. It's best to learn to detect their wards and avoid them rather than trigger them."

Meri went into the kitchen and got herself an ice-cold glass of water, and offered one to Azimuth. He accepted, but instead of handing it to him, she left it on the counter and retreated to the far side of the kitchen, avoiding the physical contact she feared could ignite an inferno between them.

"Do you ever do it? Pretend to be human that is?" Meri downed the icy water in hopes it would cool her off, but her present company inflamed her desire too intensely.

Azimuth politely took a sip of the water. "At times, when there's information I need to know and can't get otherwise. Information gathering has always been a specialty of mine." He set down the glass and gave her a hard look. What was it about those sky-blue eyes that made her want to peel off her shirt? "How are you maintaining right now?"

Meri remembered to toe the line with him and his truth-sense. "It comes, and it goes. Right now, not very good." She flushed in embarrassment. It pained her to admit her failures to him. Damn Mahkra's bond!

Azimuth nodded as if expecting this answer. "Don't be

too hard on yourself. All of us had our tribulations. You have an Arch-daemons essence to take on as your first full melding. Moreover, taking on a lust daemon, considering your limited background in relationships cannot be easy on you. I can't imagine the challenge you're undergoing."

"You're so understanding." She'd preferred to continue believing him the straight-laced bastard, but at every turn, he was proving to be understanding and sympathetic. His protective nature stirred the heat between her thighs, spreading like wildfire across her sensitized nerves. Damn him!

"I've had time to become so. Now, you should know about your newest companion, Trailian. Belial was able to locate her name in the records quite quickly."

"And?" She took slow, calming breaths, attempting to focus on this important new information and instead of the heat erupting from her belly. She made a mental note to research the daemon independently herself as well.

"She's a mid-range succubus, known for having a minor ability to manipulate metal. I doubt you've noticed her influence much, compared to the other forces warring internally within you for control. However, once you gain the ability to harness and suppress each essence at will, you'll be able to use her skills when the time serves."

"What good will some minor ability do me? Don't we need heavy hitters?"

Azimuth's face turned grave. "We're at war with Saleigh's cabal, Meri, remember? You never know when a particular attribute will aid the cause."

Meri had no words, especially since she still hadn't signed on for the upcoming war. She wanted her life back, not some age-old never-ending conflict to appease Belial's fancy.

Meri's phone rang, and she was happy for the reprieve. She answered it, despite Azimuth's frown of disapproval.

"Hello?"

"Miss Storm," answered Ms. Ride. "I just wanted to thank you again for your swift service yesterday. I can't be happier with your work."

Meri's irritation surfaced like a familiar wave, bleeding into her tone. "You're welcome, Ms. Ride."

"And I wanted to confirm that, as agreed, I've wired the payment, plus bonus, to your account this morning," Ms. Ride replied with a stutter.

"I'm duly appreciative."

"I'd hoped you'd be. Good day, Miss Storm. I hope it's equally fruitful for you."

The line cut off, and Meri put the phone down. When she looked back at Azimuth, his eyes were full of fire.

"What?" Meri asked.

"You did a summoning yesterday?" he asked, advancing towards her.

Meri backed up, but the kitchen wasn't very large, and soon she was trapped against the counter, trembling. Whether in fear or anticipation, she couldn't say.

"Yeah. For Ms. Ride. Don't worry. Everything went fine. He was just a gleaner daemon. I've dealt with him before."

Azimuth planted a hand on either side of her hips on the counter, blocking her in. His scowl caused an uncomfortable sensation to crawl along Meri's skin, setting her teeth on edge. "You cannot summon any longer! Daemons will recognize the change in you!"

"He did sense the change. It was the weirdest summoning I'd ever tried; in fact, I'd thought I'd botched it at first. He ran off without completing the binding, and then returned ten minutes later having completed the task, quick as can be. I swear he's never been that fast on a job before -- ever! In the end, I told him not to tell anyone, and he said he'd keep his word. But, as I said, I'm not giving up my day job," Meri replied, her voice growing softer as she argued her point under the icy glare of his gaze.

Azimuth laughed bitterly, causing a lancing pain to streak through Meri's body. "Has it occurred to you that daemon promises aren't worth their salt? Or that the daemon you summoned might have been loyal to the one you've killed? Did you even think that far ahead? If the daemon recognized Mahkra's scent on you or was loyal to his faction, what do you think he'd do?"

She had no idea what cabal Penethewes called home if any. But then, she'd never heard of cabals before meeting Azimuth. He could be leading them to her now, or worse, he could have told the entire underworld what she'd done. She could be a target right now, and not even know it. The profound disappointment in his eyes hit home. She should have thought of those questions herself but asserting her independence had clouded her mind.

"This is why you demanded I return with you to the cabal right after I killed Mahkra, wasn't it? You knew they'd be out to kill me, and I wouldn't know how the rules of the game had changed."

"Yes, I feared for your life, you imbecile! Continuing to live as a summoner will get you killed. Do you understand that now?" Azimuth's usually light blue eyes filled with dark and stormy clouds on the precipice of a thunderstorm.

Pain streaked down Meri's spine in reaction to his emotional outburst, spreading outward to her fingertips and toes, but she refused to back down. "I was desperate to return to my normal life. After what happened, I didn't trust you -- you gave me no reason to! You lied by leaving out the consequences. I still don't trust any of you!"

He growled, closing the distance further between them. "Mahkra almost killed you that night, and yet we went to the trouble of keeping you alive. Doesn't that count for some level of trust?"

Meri opened her mouth to answer, but no words would form. He was always the picture of control. What was going on with him today?

"Do you trust me now?" Azimuth asked, his voice barely a whisper, his breath cool against her hot skin.

"No. I know you saved my life, and I'm grateful, but I fear it was only to keep me alive as a pawn for your cabal." Her voice was tremulous as she met his nearly ice-white eyes.

"You think we only want to use you?"

Those words from his mouth inflamed her, and she could only focus on his lush lips as she answered. "Yes." It was all she trusted herself to say.

His tongue snaked out across his lips, and Meri had to force herself not to lean in and capture them with her own, to taste him for herself. "And you think Orias, Kobol, and I are mindless pawns to Belial?" he asked.

Her eyes snapped up to his, confusion filtering through her haze of need. "Are you?"

The muscle along his jaw ticked. "We are loyal to him,

yes, but not his unthinking puppets. I can't deny he has plans for your powers, but that doesn't preclude you having your own goals and needs."

Meri thrust her chin up, her face precariously close to Azimuths. Heat from her body rolled off in waves. "I'm not on board with the cabal. I'm not sure I ever will be."

His eyes narrowed into slits, body still hovering over hers. "We'll wait you out." A corner of Azimuth's mouth slanted up in a wry grin. "We have time, after all. However, this daemon you summoned earlier? You will call out his name and interrogate him. I will find out if he's told another about Meri the Summoner turning daemon or not, and if so, who. After that, you will kill him so he can't spread the word to others."

Meri tilted her head. "I don't want any more daemons yet. I'm barely used to these two."

"This is a consequence, Meri. You've brought this one upon herself. Besides, you said he's a gleaner, and its essence won't be a heavy burden."

She nodded. "What if he has told others? Calling his name might lead his cabal here."

"Not with Orias' wards, it won't. Only he will be let through," Azimuth answered.

"Okay, let's do this," Meri replied. Azimuth remained in place, deliciously blocking her against the counter and her heartbeat fluttered in anticipation, despite his chastisement. His eyes held hers, pinning her in place more effectively than the frame of his body. His breath ran down her skin, awakening the nerve endings in her skin.

"Please, follow my directions in this matter. Your safety and the security of the entire cabal are at risk."

"I understand." She panted while he took in a deep breath

and held it for another few seconds, before he stepped back and to the side, allowing her to pass.

"There's another thing. I saw a tattooed man yesterday. They were odd, not daemon tattoos, but yellow-glowing arrow-shaped sigils. What does that mean?"

Azimuth's lips set in a grim line. "You saw a human marked with god sigils?" She nodded. "Avoid them; they're the god-touched. One with those markings no doubt bows to Jupiter, and thus why you'd never met him before. The higher-ranked god-touched never utilize summoners. Instead, they call on the gods for divine intervention. The games they play are no less deadly and have nothing to do with daemon ken. God and daemon ken don't mesh, never have."

"Okay, but if I can see what they are, can they know what I am?"

"They've never picked up on me when I've been incognito," Azimuth replied. "But it might be a different story for full-blooded daemons. Regardless, they have their powers -- given to them by whichever god they are a devotee of, and you don't want to cross them. Understood?"

"He recognized me as a summoner, but nothing more. I'll make sure to avoid them in the future."

"Now, Meri, there's no more time to lose."

She nodded and set her shoulders firm, striding from the kitchen and to her bedroom.

"What are you doing?" he asked.

"Getting dressed. Can't you see I'm still in my night-clothes? If I'm going to kill someone, I'm not gonna do it in my jammies."

Ten minutes later Meri emerged from her room in cargoes and a T-shirt. The tre'jor was on the back belt loop of her pants, and she'd taken the time to sweep her long hair up into a ponytail and wash her face. She wasn't her usual lovely self, but she was ready to off a daemon. More or less.

"Prepared now?" Azimuth asked. He leaned on the kitchen door frame, arms crossed and brow furrowed.

"Yes." Meri didn't heat under his gaze. Instead, she withered. "What do I do?"

"Speaking his name should do the trick as you're already connected."

"Right, he'd said as much to me too. Penethewes! I'd like to have a talk," Meri said.

Meri waited anxiously, but Azimuth didn't move a muscle. Within less than a minute, Penethewes ported into her living room, just a foot in front of her. He was as gangly as ever but had changed clothes and was clad now in forest green tones.

Meri smiled congenially. "Thanks for answering my call. I have need of you again."

"Of course, Miss Meri," Penethewes bowed, and then, sniffing the air, turned and eyed Azimuth. "But, who is our guest here? I'm not familiar with him."

"He's a friend of mine. We have an ongoing wager, and I thought you might be able to help us out."

Penethewes eyes lit up. "Oh? What about?"

"Well, are you sure you have time away from your cabal duties to help me out?"

Penethewes laughed. "Don't be silly, Miss Meri. I'm not with a cabal. Never have been. You join one of those, they make you fight in wars and then there's the intrigue and such. It's too much for me! I prefer living on my own, and answering to no one."

Meri laughed with him and glanced at Azimuth. He nodded. Penethewes was telling the truth. "I can't blame you for that. From what I've seen, cabals do seem to be a whole lot of trouble. I've already been courted by a few myself."

Penethewes tsked. "Stay solo, Miss Meri. You won't regret it."

Meri nodded agreement. "So, can I trust you haven't told anyone about my, um, recent change?"

Penethewes became wide-eyed in shock. "Of course not! I gave my word!"

Meri looked to Azimuth, who nodded again. Another truthful answer.

"Sorry, Penethewes, I didn't mean to offend. I've met so many liars recently. It makes a gal downright distrustful."

"You're wise to exercise caution. Now, what was this wager you wanted my help with?"

"Oh yes, over here." Meri motioned to her old mahogany desk, which was covered with papers, bills, and grimoires. Azimuth moved to the middle of the room. "There's a document here we think is a forgery, but can't quite be sure. I know you'd be able to tell in an instant." Meri found one at the far corner and made the gangly daemon lean across her to look at it.

"Well let's see here..." he began.

Meri sank the tre'jor into his back when he wasn't looking. He collapsed into a cloud of purple smoke within seconds.

Moments later, his essence poured down her throat, choking her with guilt and shame. Images of Penethewes the Gleaner's life flashed by her mind, not just his jobs, but secret moments that he snuck away between assignments. Visits to hidden forest grottos, swimming through cave-like Mayan cenotes, and the insides of cozy beaver dams were just some of the places he'd discovered on his journeys. Yes, he'd feasted on human souls, but he'd had a gentle nature and a hunger for new places. A hunger Meri now had to satisfy. Although he had been a threat to her, as Azimuth had warned, he wasn't a bad sort. He'd lived by his code, and wouldn't have turned on her, at least not until his curiosity won out. Now her safety was guaranteed, but the price sickened her.

Meri dropped the blade onto the desk and leaned with both her palms splayed out before her, panting. She was shaky, squeezed and bloated, all at the same time. Meri shut her eyes to the world, trying to ignore the sensations. She hoped they'd pass quickly.

"You did well." Azimuth's words broke through her mental fog, and with it, a languid calm passed over her frazzled nerves. He placed a hand on her shoulder. "How are you feeling?"

Meri warmed to his touch, as usual, but it was a less dramatic response this time. Less out of control. His calming energy swept over her like a cool breeze on a hot day as her pulse and breathing slowed and regulated, and her mind cleared. Meri opened her eyes and looked up at him.

"How do you do that? The healing and calming?"

"It's something I picked up from a greater incubus, I forget how long ago. He used it to ease his prey while he fed off them. I like to think I put it to better use."

Stone by stone, he was slowly breaking down her defenses. With that reflection, her temperature raised a few degrees.

Azimuth stepped away, giving her space, observing her.

Meri turned to him. "Penethewes didn't have to die. You heard him. I've seen his mind now too. He did not intend to betray me." Tears formed at the corners of her eyes, conflict warring in her heart.

"You're defending a daemon, Meri," Azimuth replied, the words soft on his lips, although his face was granite. "One who could have been taken by another, and used against you, despite his own will. We use them as tools. They are not our friends."

"Even Belial?" Meri asked.

"Even so," Azimuth agreed. "Belial affords me a method to destroy a large number of daemons, so I work with him. He's not one of us. Never forget that."

"I wouldn't have guessed," Meri began.

"What? That I'm not close friends with a crown prince of hell?" Azimuth took a step closer to Meri, and she had to look up to see into his icy eyes. "We were full-blooded humans once. If we forget what we are, and who we are, we become just like them. You can't let that happen. It's why you have to learn to rein in your daemons."

At that moment, she felt in simpatico with his goals. She'd dedicated her entire life of summoning to find and bind the daemon who'd killed her parents. Now, through Azimuth, she'd met her goal. More than that, he'd opened a doorway through which she'd be able to destroy countless others if only she could handle the process. She saw the resolution in his eyes, the determination, and knew they were more alike than she cared to admit.

"I'll get control over them, Az." Meri looked down and tugged on her ponytail, disturbed by the feeling of disappointment washing over her due to her lack of power over her daemon.

"You're making progress."

"Can I ask what's so bad about letting lust be in control? I mean, not all the time, but maybe occasionally?" Meri asked.

A whisper of a smile passed Azimuth's lips, but then he was all business again. "That's a fair question. With a daemon like Lust, it's easy to think it's innocuous or playful. Never forget, it's a daemon. I have a daemon within me that, when left to its own devices, feeds off the souls of newborns. Newborn anything. Now, I usually feed it tree seedlings, and it's satiated for decades. However, if I let it run the show, it would feed on multiple human children each day and night. Different daemon, same thirst for hunger."

"You eat newborns? That's disgusting!"

"What, you've never tried veal? Salmon roe? Chicken eggs? Lamb? Suckling pig? They're quite succulent. Honestly, Meri, your assumption I'd dine on human flesh is quite disturbing. What other upsetting conclusions have you made about my character?"

She flushed bright red, quite glad he didn't share Orias' abilities. "My apologies, I misunderstood," she answered, deflecting the question. "Of course you wouldn't eat people. But, no one gets hurt with lust, right?"

"Perhaps if you'd asked Mahkra's enslaved victims, you'd know for yourself. But remember: they don't get independent thought anymore."

"Point taken." How had she maintained her clearheaded mind despite her binding? Was it being inhabited by the daemon itself, or her hatred of the daemons and her drive keeping her from being a brainless ya-ya like the others? A shudder rippled down her spine at the thought. Regardless, she couldn't remain under the daemon's power, and she needed Azimuth's help to overcome her dependence.

Meri nodded. "Okay. Let's try it again. Touch me." Her temperature spiked as she imagined his hands cupping her breasts. She kept her expression neutral and tried to think of puppies and daisies and kittens -- anything non-sexual to shift her mood back.

Azimuth shot her a dubious look. No doubt, he'd noticed her Lust daemon gain power as he had the times before.

Meri waved him forward. "Look, you want me to improve. Yes, you'll get a rise out of the daemon, but then I'll squash it down. So go ahead, trigger me with contact." Meri didn't mention Azimuth was the one male who could get a rise out of the lust Arch-daemon within her. All that mattered was that she learned to rein it in, for both their sakes.

Azimuth gave her a quick nod. His serious expression touched Meri's heart, knowing he'd endeavor to keep things professional despite the sexual energy involved. He stepped forward, as requested, and ran a hand down the exposed flesh of Meri's arm.

For a moment, as their skin touched, a flash of sweaty, naked bodies writhing upon ice blue satin sheets stole through in her mind. A hand tracing down the outside of her thigh, a thumb toying with the inside of her hipbone.

No.

Meri winced as lightning snaked through her body after she shut out the image, willing it away. There was an instinctive magnetic pull to reach out to Azimuth right after the contact had been broken. She forced her arms to her sides, clenching her fists. It'd been there before, but she hadn't noticed the intensity at this level before so it hadn't registered in her mind. "Again."

Azimuth touched her cheek. Again, the images enticed. This time his mouth claimed hers, brooking no mercy, his fingers threading through her hair, pushing her back against a wall. Their bodies ground together, her heat licking around his corded arms.

"Meri," his voice abruptly jarred her from the delightful vision.

Meri ground her teeth through the pain threatening to shatter her bones and tear apart her skin, pushing the image from her mind and shaking off the pain. "I'm sorry, this must be challenging for you too. Do you want to keep going?" she panted.

He gave her a half-hearted smile. "I've endured far worse discomforts. Do you want to continue?"

"Yes, please. Again."

Azimuth touched her other arm. He was behind her, hard flesh pressed deep within her, holding still, not allowing her movement as he nibbled his way leisurely down her neck. She squirmed under the decadent attention of his tongue teasing her collarbone while he rocked his hips in a slow, controlled move inside her.

No!

Pain jarred her mind, exploding behind her eyes until everything went black for a moment.

Azimuth held out his hand but then hesitated, suspicion flaring in his eyes. "This causes you pain?"

Meri looked up and met his gaze, tempted to evade the

question. No, from the sweat forming on her brow, he'd figure it out soon enough.

"Yes. Do it again."

Concern flared in his eyes. "This is most unusual. The others and I all had challenges keeping our first daemons under control, fighting them for power, but never did we experience pain when we suppressed their needs. Perhaps we should wait. I can check with Belial and find out if there's a better way?"

"No, Azimuth. You were right. I need to learn control. This one causes pain when it's triggered and not appeased. It's that simple. The only way out is through. Right?"

The tension in his body relaxed, though his expression soured. "Perhaps it's because Mahkra was an Arch-daemon, but I'm still talking to Belial about it later."

Meri waved him on again. "We can argue the fine points later. This is what I need now. Trigger me again."

Azimuth shook his head in distaste and touched her.

CHAPTER 9

*S*weat ran from Meri's skin. Patches on her clothes were soaked through from the hours they'd spent antagonizing her Lust daemon. Every time he'd tried to stop and call off the exercise, she'd demanded he'd continue. Tired of watching her writhe in pain and preventing himself from swearing in reaction, Azimuth only relaxed when Kobol finally appeared to change shifts. The constant exposure to her lust daemon had nearly cracked even his toughened defenses.

"Well, this looks like an unusual training technique. What's going on?" Kobol asked, his hands set on his hips.

"He's been teaching me to control my daemons," Meri said.

"And she refused to take a break. I'm afraid she'll be useless for your scheduled sparring training now," Azimuth replied. She'd pushed herself too hard, although he did admire her for trying.

Meri frowned up at him and turned to Kobol. "I can handle more. Let's go."

Azimuth looked at the way her limbs shook with simple gestures and knew Kobol would be having a quiet evening. "I'd recommend you watch over Meri for the night, and handle sparring lessons in the morning.

"Can do," Kobol replied. "You feel like you learned a lot from Azimuth?" he asked her.

Meri looked at them both, exhaustion plain on her face. "Yeah, I learned he's less of a bastard than I thought. If you'll both excuse me, I need a shower." She wandered off to the bathroom on shaky legs.

"Well, that's a ringing endorsement." Kobol clapped him on the shoulder. "How about we skip your pointers on winning over her friendship?"

Azimuth ignored the jibe. "She's had a stressful day. I'm off to consult with Belial. I fear something is wrong with her daemon binding. Best of luck. Call us if you need assistance."

"Will do. Don't worry. I'll be okay up here with Miss Sunshine."

Azimuth ported to the burrow with a heavy heart. He'd hated to trigger Meri's daemon so intensely, but she'd been right, it was the only way to force herself to gain control over the beast. Still, watching her endure the increasing pain over hours without complaint was a testament to her integrity. In the end, he'd complimented Meri, and she'd said he wasn't the bastard she'd once proclaimed him. Progress, minimal, yet he'd count it. Azimuth couldn't help but smile.

"How did things go today?" Orias asked.

Azimuth had been so lost in his thoughts he hadn't even noticed his dark brother sitting alone on the couch.

"Fairly well. Meri works hard. She's very determined to overcome the will of the daemons."

"She has an unyielding spirit," Orias replied. "I doubt she'll give in an inch once she sets her mind to something."

"I'm sure you're right. Have you seen Belial around?"

"Yes, he's in the library, as usual. Why?"

"It's likely nothing. Good evening."

Azimuth walked off and found Belial a few levels down in the library pouring over dusty old scrolls. He leaned over a chair, preferring not to sit. "Anything new, old friend?"

"Seeking new weaknesses on Saleigh, but I may have exhausted all possible avenues of study. We need to educate Meri on the situation so she can train appropriately for the mission," Belial replied.

"I'll make sure everyone is assembled tomorrow for a briefing. However, I have a new concern for you."

Belial looked up from the ancient tomes and focused on Azimuth. He appeared reluctant to set down the scroll in his hands, despite the attention he turned towards his eldest pupil. "Is something wrong?"

"I'm not sure. I've been training Meri on controlling the expression of her daemons, but when she focuses on suppressing Mahkra, she gets a painful biofeedback loop. She fights through it, but it concerns me. What are your thoughts?"

Belial leaned back in his chair, releasing his scroll. "I did have concerns about Mahkra. Lust is demanding and difficult to rein in. In this instance, we may have to accept Meri regularly feeding the daemon to vent off the intense energy, especially in the early months. Both you and Orias have daemons you feed on an occasional basis to satiate their baser natures. This is something Meri will need to become accustomed to in time as well." Azimuth didn't miss the mild sneer that passed over Belial's features -- he suffered no such base need himself. "This would be no different, simply more frequent. Remember, she didn't start off with some low-level succubus but an Arch-daemon. Now she has two daemons inside her."

"It's three now." Azimuth broke in with a sigh. "Although the third is a low-level Incubi daemon, a Gleaner named Penethewes."

Belial sighed, and then pulled a notebook out of his robes and wrote down the details, shaking his head. "I fear we must prevent her from any further daemon influences for a time now, Azimuth. Each new daemon will make adjusting to the first one harder until it's integrated. In fact, it will begin to supersede her human life force if we're not careful."

Azimuth swore aloud. "It's that grave a risk?" He should have been the one to take Penethewes out instead of having Meri shoulder the burden. At the time, having her clean up her mess had appeared the better lesson. Or had his mind been muddled by their argument in the kitchen? Azimuth ground his teeth. He should have checked in with Belial and made sure the new addition wouldn't affect her stability.

"My new research, now that I have the benefit of seeing the full history of her summonings indicates her dynamic is more precarious than I'd originally scoped. I think it's imperative Meri find a way to vent her excess energy," Belial replied, replacing the notebook into his robes. "Otherwise, her instability will impact us all."

"What if the daemon establishes too much of a foothold over her, and she becomes lost in it?" Azimuth asked. "She'd be at risk of a flash-out. We've seen it before."

"That's what we're here for, my son. If you remember correctly, you and your brothers have had to step in and help each other out from time to time. This will be no different, in theory."

"Of course you're right. We can prevent a flash-out if it comes to that. Thanks for your counsel, Belial. I'll discuss the matter with her."

"Best of luck," Belial replied. "I hope her temper has improved for the sake of your discussion."

Azimuth laughed, one hand rubbing the tension of out the back of his neck while he stretched to his full height. "She's got the tenacity of a vepar beast, which will suit our purposes well enough in the long run, and her temper appears to be improving. She assured me I was a tad less irritating than on previous occasions."

"How charming," Belial said, his frown displaying a touch of fang. "As I said: good luck to you."

Azimuth teleported out of the library. He didn't need luck. He had sheer determination honed over lifetimes. Meri might not like taking direction from him, but he refused to lose another recruit to flash-out.

---

*A*zimuth teleported directly back to Meri's house. Meri and Kobol sat on her brown, threadbare couch, feet propped up on her faded oak coffee table and laughing riotously while eating popcorn. A lumbering group of zombies lumbered toward a pair of twenty-somethings in a hospital on the blaring television. Meri was showered and changed, no longer appearing sweaty and bedraggled as before.

"Pay attention to this next scene. Notice what the chick

picks up?" Kobol asked.

"What is that? A stand used for hanging IV bags?"

"Yeah," he answered, the glee barely contained in his voice. The actress went to work swinging the stand like a baseball bat and Kobol erupted in laughter. "So there's a lesson for you: everything is a potential weapon."

"Ugh! And look at her boyfriend, he's just whimpering in the corner!"

"Not for long." Kobol hunched over, laughing harder, as the man was attacked and bitten by a zombie who'd come up behind him. "Whoops, there goes another one! There were two lessons there: always watch your back, and if you're not fighting back, you're laying down to die."

"This is how you're training our newest recruit?" Azimuth asked. At least she appeared recuperated from their previous training. He'd worried she'd be asleep when he got here, but instead, she seemed refreshed and alert. He'd underestimated her ability to rebound.

Meri turned, startled at his arrival. Kobol, no doubt sensing him with his more trained reflexes, turned and offered a brief wave in greeting.

"Hey, you said I wasn't allowed to do any hand-to-hand tonight. Least I can do is show our girl some examples."

Azimuth furrowed his brow. "And you're doing this with movies?"

"Well, yeah, these aren't the best examples, but it's better than sitting around doing nothing. Besides, Meri likes classic movies. We did some basic porting, just within the house. She's a quick learner. Took to it naturally."

"Good. We don't have any time to lose," Azimuth replied.

"Now that Mahkra's been eliminated, Belial will want to move forward with his plans."

"I figured. I didn't think we'd see you until tomorrow?" Kobol asked, his frame tense. "Any news on Saleigh?"

"Everything's fine. I've come across additional information I need to discuss privately with Meri," Azimuth replied.

Meri's lips pursed in worry and she stopped the movie and set the popcorn aside.

"Then I suppose we'll continue your education tomorrow, Meri." Kobol rose to leave.

"By the way, we're having a meeting tomorrow on Saleigh's cabal. We'll see you there," Azimuth said.

"Will do," Kobol said. "And just so you know, your student here did very well keeping her Lust daemon in check while we were hanging out. You'd have been impressed. Your training must be paying off."

Kobol ported away, and Meri shifted uneasily on the couch.

"I'm pleased the training helped," Azimuth said. However, in response to his compliment, he noticed the energy shift around Meri and saw her aura extend, licking out towards him like a moth to the flame. However, it wasn't as out of control as before. The training had taught her to dampen her response.

"I'll need more practice," Meri replied, frowning. "What's so important it couldn't wait until tomorrow?"

Azimuth walked over and instead of selecting one of the also old and worn armchairs he took a seat next to her on the couch, but angled his body to face hers, hoping to diffuse her tension. She stiffened, most likely noticing his marked effort at a casual demeanor and interpreting it as the deliberate effort it was. She turned to face him, sitting cross-legged and with her back to the arm of the couch, as far away from him as possible.

"I took the liberty of discussing your daemons with Belial, including your newest addition, Penethewes. He's studied your current daemon makeup and shares my concerns that your present state is a bit, well, imbalanced."

"How did he know my existing 'makeup'?" Meri frowned.

"The day I inspected you in the alleyway, I smelled and cataloged your daemon essences off of you. We'd also spoken to a previous client who'd seen your ink, hypnotized them, and gotten a full accounting of your markings. We had to be very sure of our accuracy."

"That's ridiculously thorough and intrusive. You must also have an obnoxiously accurate nose." Meri's aura swirled wildly around her like a protective shield, growing dark and prickly to his attuned vision and her eyes dilated briefly, but she gave no outward signs of her emotions. He'd have to tread carefully with this conversation because she was on the defensive.

"We have to be thorough. It's important to get a good, well-balanced match between daemon and summoner for the first melding. We were lucky you were a good fit for one of our prime enemies."

"And yet, Belial says I'm imbalanced now? Is that because of a poor match? Or because I took on other daemons too soon?" Was that defeat in Meri's eyes? Or something else?

"Adding in the other daemons so quickly didn't help, but it doesn't appear they are causing the issue. I'm afraid my earlier advice to you was flawed, and for that, I apologize."

Meri's eyes grew wary, and she clasped her hands

together. Her aura retreated entirely, a clear show of her fear. "Explain, please."

Her uncharacteristic anxiety almost prompted him onto another line of questioning, but Azimuth remained on task, hoping his explanation would soothe her fears. "I'd said before that you needed to leash your daemons entirely, and not allow them to feed at all. According to Belial, your lust Arch-daemon needs to be satiated on a regular basis, or you risk losing control to it. It may even feed on your humanity if left unchecked."

Meri's eyes widened in panic, but she quickly recovered. "And you trust Belial in this? I mean, he is a full daemon, after all."

"In this, absolutely. He wants strong warriors. Pawns, as you put it. To invest time in us, then to lose one of us, would be a waste."

Meri rubbed her hands together. "Well, as long as we can rely on him in matters of efficiency, daemon combinations, and war."

"Don't be terse. This is a serious issue."

Meri crossed her arms. "Are we done with this little talk?"

"No. I need your assurance that you'll handle the situation."

Meri's face became a mask of frustration. "Yes, Az, I'll take care of it, okay?" Her lie was palpable, given away by her stiff posture, tight lips, and an aura like a second skin, wrapped so thin he couldn't even see the usual swirls of pinks and forest greens.

"I'm frankly shocked you would even try to lie to me. Why are you unwilling to deal with your daemon?"

Meri flushed and hid her face in her hands. "Why? Why do we have to have this conversation?"

"Is it because I'm a male? I know sometimes that it's easier for women to talk to other women about personal sexual issues. But I'm afraid they're no other females in the cabal to speak with about this."

"Yes," Meri continued to hide her face. "That's a large part of the equation."

"Right. I know you haven't dated recently," Azimuth said.

"Oh, you're so not helping. Can't we just end this conversation?" Meri's aura shrank into an even smaller ball of space and time.

"No. Not until we resolve the issue. Look, I don't think it's necessary for you to find a partner if you don't want to. I guess the daemon will be satisfied by your, um -- solo -- efforts. Can you commit to that?"

Meri took a deep breath, dropped her hands and looked up. She displayed little emotion on her carefully schooled features, yet her aura bubbled with suppressed energy. She was an abject example of internal dichotomy, reading like any liar on the planet. "I'll do my best, Az."

He leaned forward, wanting to reach out to her, yet sensing the precarious energy coiled in her form. "Why do you keep lying to me, Meri? You know whatever it is, I'll ferret it out sooner or later."

"Shit!" Meri exclaimed and leaped from the couch, escaping to the kitchen.

Azimuth heard running water and allowed her a moment of solitude before following. He found her in the kitchen with an empty glass of water, energetically just as shut off from him as before.

"Why won't you masturbate?" he asked. Meri put the glass down and buried her face in her hands, refusing to look at him. "I'm not saying you have to do it daily. I'm sure once or twice a week should suffice in allowing the daemon to the surface while you take your pleasure. If you don't, the daemon will slowly take over your mind. Is that what you want?"

"Of course not!" Meri spat the words out, turning to him, hands formed into fists. Irritation painted her features. "Don't you think I've tried?"

"My apologies." No wonder Meri had been so agitated lately, and here he was rubbing proverbial salt in the wound. "It should have occurred to me you'd already attempted that avenue. Have you tried with a man?"

Meri shot him a withering look. "No. As you so aptly pointed out, I don't have a posse of prospects on hand."

Azimuth ran a hand through his hair. "You need to understand, Meri. You can't not act. The consequences are dire. You have the power of a lust daemon at your command. If you unleash your energy, men will trip over themselves to spend a night with you."

Revulsion filled Meri's eyes. "Like I'd take advantage of someone like that? Like Mahkra would? Or pick up someone off the street?"

Azimuth understood her perspective, but she had to do something, or her health was at risk.

"What other options do you have, Meri?" He kept his voice gentle. "I respect you not wanting to lower yourself to his level, but we can't lose you either."

"Why?" Tears hovered at the corners of Meri's eyes, and her aura expanded again, swirled in shades of gray. "Because you've invested so much time and energy in my conversion? Or because I'm too valuable a weapon to lose?"

Her emotions seared him, and Azimuth rushed forward and took Meri in his arms, forcing her to meet his gaze. "You're not just a weapon or investment. Your soul is human, just like mine. Just like Orias and Kobol. You don't deserve to become a victim to the daemons like so many other humans they've toyed with over our existence. I refuse to let it happen."

Meri searched his eyes, and in the end, something in her aura shifted. The gray lightened, and the pinks reemerged. She sagged in his arms. "Then do something for me."

"What?"

She cast her gaze down, digging her fingers into the flesh of his chest. "Help me pacify my daemon."

Stunned by her request, he didn't respond, and Meri met his gaze, her naked desperation finally flayed open after her carefully guarded attempts to hide her desire. There was no daemon influence, simply honest female emotion. Somehow, he knew Meri would never give up, regardless of the circumstances.

"I know you're only asking this because the daemon's pressuring you intensely. An hour ago you still proclaimed me a bastard."

Her pink tongue wet her lips. "I said less of one."

"Regardless, I'd rather not take advantage of you in this state. Besides, we'll be living and be working together for potentially the next hundreds of years. Plenty of time for you to find other sexual outlets who are even less like bastards. Don't you think things will get uncomfortable when we have to see each other every day?" Azimuth asked. His excuses felt hollow in his ears. He barely knew her and had to admit she hardly knew herself and what she was becoming. When she was fully realized, would she even like him? If so, how could they put this behind them and still maintain a courteous relationship within the cabal?

He didn't bother mentioning the challenge with his powers to her, doubting she'd continue pushing the issue. Where Meri was all lusty fire, he'd go pure ice at inconveniently personal moments. What would happen if he lost control?

Meri turned away, embarrassment flushing her cheeks. "Look, you don't have to have sex with me, so you won't feel like you're crossing any lines. I have a compromise. Terms we can both agree to if you're willing."

"Explain."

"Assuming my idea works, we'll both stay fully clothed. I think minimal physical contact should be adequate to satiate my daemon's needs."

He suppressed a laugh, doubting any Lust daemon would settle for such an arrangement. "What did you have in mind?"

"Hold me closer?" Meri asked.

Azimuth cooperated, allowing Meri to slide her arms up around his neck, clasping her hands behind. He held her lightly around the waist, unsure of what she had in mind.

He noticed the moment Meri loosed the daemon, as his skin prickled with sensation and desire tingled in the small of his back. Meri laid her head on his chest, nuzzling her face towards his neck. She ran one hand down the side of his body, her fingertips drawing a near-electric pattern of energy between them. He held back a stifled groan of anticipation. He hadn't been with a woman since he was human, and her sudden onset of the Lust daemon threatened to shatter the grip on his centuries-held control.

"Az?" Meri's voice was hoarse with need.

"Yes?" He focused on remaining still, lest he give in and devour her with his pent-up desire. The temptation to fist his hands into her flesh increased by the second.

"Tell me to come."

"Pardon?"

Meri traced a hand to his chin and turned his face down to meet her desperate gaze. "Command me to orgasm. Please."

Could her daemon be controlled that easily? If so, he could hold to her terms and their agreement, and not worry about losing control to his passions.

"Come for me, Meri."

Meri's mouth opened in a silent gasp, and she buried it a moment later against his neck as her aura shimmered in waves of gold and scarlet, passing through and around him. Fingers dug into the skin of his chest and neck, and Meri threw her body against his as heat exploded from her center. Azimuth collapsed back against the kitchen counter, as Meri remained plastered against him in a most divine form of torture, her body grinding sensuously against his own.

After a few minutes, she began to cool off. "Again," she panted into his neck, her lips brushing against his pulse.

He hesitated only a moment until she moaned plaintively. His arms entwined around her shorter frame, holding her undulating curves closer to his body. "Come again, Meri."

She threw her head back, and a thin but visible circle of heat erupted from Meri's skin and shot out around her like a firecracker. Waves of moist heat knocked Meri's water glass to the floor where it shattered, and all of the appliances on the counters slammed back against the walls or toppled over.

With this remarkable woman wrapped around him, Azimuth didn't care -- his focus on her eclipsed all other thoughts. Meri had gripped her fingers in his hair, forcing him to expose his neck for the plundering of her demanding kisses and nips. She'd also managed to straddle his hips and now ground against Azimuth's very full erection.

He groaned, his left hand not just supporting but also exploring the curve of Meri's ass with abandon, while his other hand toyed with her right breast, pebbling the nipple between his fingertips.

He needed to get a better -- handle -- on this compromise before it turned into something altogether different.

"More, Az. Please," Meri begged.

Meri's half-closed eyes softened her flushed face while her lips dragged along his chin, her body moist and ripe under his touch. Her aura swirled around them both with crimson tones, and for once, he sensed no hesitation on her part emotionally -- she was fully open to him in this brief window of vulnerability. Never had he witnessed a more intoxicating sight. Azimuth brought a hand up and ran it down Meri's neck, eliciting a shiver from her fiery flesh. He brushed his lips against hers, briefly claiming her swollen lips with his own. She responded with heady need, roughly begging for more with her lips, tongue, and running her fingers under his shirt. But they'd agreed to specific terms for this encounter, and he wouldn't broach those, despite his conflicting desires.

Would she thank him for stopping or not? Azimuth stood up straight and slowly unwound Meri's legs from his hips.

"You'll regret this later." She continued nuzzling and kissing his neck, running her fingers through his hair, but her temperature decreased. He couldn't bring himself to stop her ministrations, despite the corresponding ache they produced to his groin.

"Trust me. I'm regretting it now," he ground out between clenched teeth.

"You don't have to. Please? I've changed my mind anyway," she whispered in his ear before resorting to slowly undulating against him.

Azimuth kept his arms loosely around her middle while he watched the change in Meri, lamenting the return of her inhibitions. Meri's movements slowed, and eventually, she stood still next to him, her aura pulled up tight, with the daemon completely reined in. She shivered, a thin sheen of sweat covered her skin as she continued to pant lightly.

"Let's grab you a blanket." Azimuth turned and led Meri out to the living room. He grabbed an afghan off a nearby recliner and wrapped it around her body.

"I'm sorry. I didn't think I'd get that out of control," Meri said.

"It was a trial. You can't know in advance how these things will work out. Most importantly, you managed to satiate the daemon, which should keep it easier to control for a time. Let's see how long this compromise bought you, and go from there."

"So, you'll do this again?" Meri asked, anxiety written across her face.

Had she worried the experience had been uncomfortable for him? Focusing on the concern etched around her brown eyes, it was all too tempting to pull her back into his arms and kiss away her fears. Could Meri's heat withstand his icy touch? Considering another opportunity made his shaft twitch against his leathers. But no, that wasn't to be a part of this arrangement. Not for the good of the cabal.

"I told you I'd help you, and I meant it."

"Thank you." Meri paused, looked at her feet, and then back at him. "If it's okay with you, can we not tell the others?"

Azimuth nodded, understanding her embarrassment and her need for discretion. "I can't promise Orias won't know, but I won't speak of it, other than to let Belial know you've got things handled. Now get to bed. Tomorrow will be a long day."

Meri looked up at him with the soberest look he'd seen to date on her face. "Thank you. You've saved my life more than once now. I'm in your debt." She then turned and went to bed.

Although he believed her, he sensed a depth of emotion behind her words she had once again wrapped up in the thick cloak of armor. Azimuth wished instead for the Meri he'd glimpsed just now, at her most vulnerable moment, when she'd been genuine and open with him in his arms. But what right did he have to demand a deeper relationship with her?

Therein was the problem. When he'd seen her open up, Azimuth had wanted more. Much more.

Azimuth ran a hand through his hair. He'd uphold his promise, but this compromise of Meri's was going to prove harder than he'd planned. More challenging by far.

CHAPTER 10

*M*eri slept fitfully that night. Although her daemon was momentarily appeased, the images of her encounter with Azimuth wouldn't leave her dreams. Her human mind kept extending them, elaborating, and making it all too clear to Meri that it wasn't just the daemon who'd wanted something more to happen in her kitchen yesterday.

She climbed out of bed the next morning completely worked up yet her lust daemon was fully leashed. How she was going to face Azimuth today? How did you go back to professional courtesies after... that?

Meri tried her best to maintain the status quo. She'd been living in a world without exposing her authentic emotions most of her life. How was this any different? For the first time, she wanted it to be. She was no better than a pathetic puppy begging for Azimuth's meager attentions. Damn the daemon's binding! She'd had no indication from Azimuth that he had any interest in her sexually during their encounter. Sure, he'd reacted viscerally, but the cabal had said that was to be expected when exposed to her daemon. She couldn't assume that meant anything personal. Azimuth had simply helped her out, as requested. He'd proven she could rely on him and take care of her needs, and he hadn't asked for anything in return.

She'd misjudged him. More so, since she relied on him for her future survival, Meri needed to start being, well, at least civil to him.

Gratefully, she hadn't had to divulge her secret to Azimuth, despite Orias' predictions. Friends, yes. Letting him know she was bound to him in sexual slavery? No.

Meri dressed in boots, cargoes, and a yoga shirt, assuming after the meeting today she'd be sparring with Kobol. She emerged to check on her guest and see what he had planned for the morning.

Azimuth sat on her couch, nose down in a book. What was it with daemons and books? Considering their advanced age, shouldn't they have read all of them by now?

"Did my guest bedroom treat you all right?" Meri asked, passing him on the way to her kitchen.

"Yes, thank you," he replied, joining her by leaning in the doorway. His light smile was devoid of any emotional charge. She guessed they were both playing it 'just another average day in the neighborhood,' and that was just fine with her. Then she saw the mess in the kitchen. Oh, my. Yup, I'd done that.

"You hungry?" Meri asked. Meri fixed herself eggs and toast while she set the kitchen to rights.

"I've already eaten," he replied. What had he eaten? Her gleaner reflexively began to answer, replaying in her mind an image of Azimuth taking a small, sealed flask from his jacket and carefully opening it. She immediately stifled the daemon's response, cutting off the images. Meri wasn't sure she wanted to know what had been, or was still, in that flask.

"Okay. So, I've been thinking. You said I couldn't summon, and I can't kill any other daemons for a while, right?" Meri opened a mineral water for herself, offered Azimuth one, which he declined, then continued to cook.

"That's correct. Just for a short while, until you stabilize. We wouldn't want you to flash-out."

"That means I can't take vengeance on my parent's killer yet, can I?" Meri plated her eggs and toast and began eating while standing.

"You need to be patient, Meri. Time is on your side now since you're immortal. When you face the daemon, you will have the vengeance you seek. But you need to wait until you're strong enough to face her."

Meri stabbed the eggs and nearly cracked the plate. "Patience is not my strong suit. Just how bad is this 'flash out,' anyway?"

Azimuth took a deep breath; his eyes touched with sorrow in their depths. "You'd go mad; lose yourself to the daemons inside you, to their hunger. You'd become one of them and feast on your victims unchecked, with no remorse. As you gain more daemons, you'd become an even more serious threat due to your varied appetites. I'd make it my mission to hunt you down and take you out myself."

Meri blinked into the tense silence between them and swallowed a bite of toast. Although she wouldn't mind him hunting her down, the inevitable end wasn't at all appealing.

"Why Azimuth, I never knew you cared." His pupils flashed white with anger despite her attempt at humor, and

Meri knew she needed to diffuse the topic. "Don't worry. I won't risk losing my mind. I was just curious, that's all. So, what's on tap for today?"

"A few things. First." Azimuth stepped close and brushed his hand against Meri's, his gaze trained on her, practically looking through her.

Meri welcomed the touch and felt her lust daemon stir in familiarity. Clearly, it recognized him, but she clamped it down, along with her surging emotions. Not reacting still sent an electric shock through her system. Now it was dulled, perhaps through repeated use of the punishment or the venting last night, Meri wasn't sure which.

Azimuth eyed her up and down, and then nodded. Finally, he smiled. "Your compromise worked. It reduced your Arch-daemons need, and you're able to harness it now, not the other way around. I assume you feel the difference too?"

"Yeah." Meri returned his smile.

"This is ideal. Now you'll have access to the daemon's powers. Belial will be pleased. Focus in on the essence you're controlling, and tell me what you're noticing. Don't let it overwhelm your faculties. Keep it separate, and try speaking to it, like you would another creature."

"That sounds a little schizophrenic, Az." Meri cleaned up her dishes and walked past him to the living room.

Azimuth followed Meri, but neither sat. Agitation appeared to be the unspoken word of the day.

"It's not, exactly. The daemon ceased having a separate will when the living host it used to inhabit died. In the conquest, you earned its powers and skills, including the psychic residue. These are something of an open book. It has no will of its own now, separate from yours, but you can read and question its imprint if you will."

"Having all of these 'imprints,' as you call them, inside of you. It can't be good for you," Meri replied.

"They don't remain forever. Eventually, your will overrides the previous imprint, and it disintegrates. Especially a daemon like Penethewes. You'll want to gain his knowledge quickly, for he was relatively low level and his memories will fade in a matter of weeks. Mahkra's however, because he was an Arch-daemon, may linger for a year or longer. This is why it's harder to integrate, you see. His presence won't fade quickly. You have to assert yourself more."

"Oh, I can assert myself," Meri answered.

"So I've noticed," Azimuth replied.

Meri blinked once, very slowly, and took a strong mental hold on Mahkra and shook him, just for good measure. "Okay, I have him. Now what?"

"See what you can gather from Mahkra now," Azimuth said.

Meri nodded and closed her eyes to concentrate.

---

*T*he Arch-daemon coiled and slithered under her mental grip, poised to break free, yet she held Mahkra under control and faced him down. He recognized Meri and kept the memory of their encounter fresh. He also remembered his last few days alive. Beyond that, things grew dim. She'd expected Mahkra to hate her, but at the moment he seemed content merely to mock her.

"Why did you do this to me, daemon?" Meri asked

"You offended my ego, and so I chained you to a daemon. And what sweet revenge! Then you killed me, not even knowing what would happen to you. Now you can't even use my powers because you're so distracted by the binding. It's a bit hilarious to watch from the sidelines, sweetheart."

"What do you mean? I have access to all the lust in the world!" Meri exclaimed.

"Fool, that's simply a tool for the trick. I'm sure you can shape shift, not that you've even attempted the feat. You've been too busy trying to get laid to bother, haven't you?"

"What joy, I get to have your pompous ass stuck in my head for the next year."

"I'm not happy about the situation either, trust me. What should worry you, my darling, is that you can't use my -- your -- ability to bind a lover because you are bound. It's my most remarkable ability. You have my mojo, but you can't use it."

"So what? I'd never turn anyone into a sex slave; therefore, I don't need that side of your ability anyway. But I'd love to hear more about how I can transform into other people."

"You should care about all of my mojo because everyone else thinks you can. Let that twirl around your noggin for a while. And sure, impersonations are fun and sometimes profitable, so have fun with that when you figure it out."

Great, he did not intend to help her right now, and she had no idea how to force or incite him to help her. "Will do." Meri started to pull away.

"Oh, and Meri?"

"Yeah, daemon?"

"Just a word of warning. That appetizer last night was excellent, but I'm used to full meals. Perhaps you could work

out a buffet sometime soon? My portion size is usually a bit...
larger."

"You know what, daemon?"

"Yeah, Meri?"

"You'll eat when I say you can."

A bright white light filled Meri's vision, cascading all around her. Eventually, it faded and began to register as a blanket of needle-like pain, which she'd once thought of as her skin. Meri could tell her limbs were twitching and she was lying on the floor. Her skin was numb, and she was drooling uncontrollably.

Thanks a lot, Mahkra.

When Meri's eyes fluttered open, she saw Azimuth knelt over her, an open palm over her heart, drawing out the pain.

"You can't ever do things the easy way, can you?" he said.

In her shattered, emotional state, Meri reacted to his touch instantly. Her need whipped through her mind unchecked, sending slivers of desire racing over her prone form. Her mental barriers, so carefully built, had been toppled by Mahkra's attack.

"Oh, I disagree," her words were slurred from the intense electrical shock still humming through her system. "I think that went well."

Azimuth frowned. "Did you gather any useful data of the exchange?"

"Yeah." Meri closed her eyes in pain as the numbness wore off. All of her nerves shot through with excruciating electrical fire. The Arch-daemon might be the death of her and not the other way around! "I learned I can impersonate people now."

"This is not news, Meri. You need to learn from your daemon how it's done. Not through antagonizing it."

"Whatever gave you that impression?" Meri tried a smile and forced herself to sit up.

Azimuth glowered in response, and then helped Meri to her feet. "Because you antagonize everyone. You'll need to develop a better rapport. And soon. You need full access to all of your daemon's skills. The more his skills become your own, the less of the daemon's will remains imprinted. Is that sufficient motivation for you?"

"Play nice. I get it." Meri shook out her arms and legs and cracked her neck, feeling mostly normal again except for the numbness in her fingers and toes. She'd have to ask Mahkra if the lightning was a skill or something reserved only to the binding. It would be a useful weapon in a fight.

"If you're recovered, I think we should port to the burrow. Belial is anxious to get started." Azimuth held out his hand.

"No thanks, I'd like to try it myself this time. Kobol and I spent a few hours yesterday covering the how-to's and practicing here with little jumps. Since I've been there before, and I'm not warded out, there should be no problem, right?"

"Correct. Just be clear in the exact location you're targeting. I recommend the area near the tapestry in the front room. We tend to steer clear of that section, leaving it free for porting," Azimuth answered.

"Wait, what if I do port into someone? Or something?" Meri asked, anxious again, despite all of Kobol's reassurances.

"The positive polarities in our cells work to prevent our bodies from colliding mid-teleport. Ask Belial for a full explanation sometime when you have a few hours to kill. His explanations are extensive."

"No, that's okay."

"But you will want to retain a tight focus on your location. If your mind drifts, so will your body."

"Great. Here goes nothing." Meri closed her eyes and held her breath, and imagined the burrow clearly in her mind. Then, as Kobol and she'd practiced the day before, she let go of her current location and just put herself into the new one mentally.

She knew it had worked because she suddenly heard Kobol and Belial talking at the far end of the burrow around the meeting table. Meri opened her eyes, and yes, there she was, teleported to Sheol, all on her own.

What would Mom and Dad think now of their daemon-infested daughter? Pride was not the first emotion which came to mind.

"Well, the 'closed-eyed' porting technique isn't going to win you any awards, but at least it's effective," Kobol said from across the room. "Try breathing before you pass out, genius." He laughed. Azimuth was next to her a moment later and didn't hesitate. He walked over to the meeting table and took a seat. Meri took his lead, attempting to act as nonchalant as Azimuth looked when he sat back leisurely in his chair. He ran his fingers through his hair, focusing on a piece of paper he'd picked up. She watched his hair fall back into place and remembered how those luxurious strands had slid through her fingers the night before.

Orias sauntered over to her from the kitchen. "How's your training going?"

"Good. It's all good." Meri pulled her eyes away from

Azimuth and looked at Orias, guessing he was nosing around. "Look, I've got it all worked out now."

"Oh?" He appeared genuinely surprised. "I'm glad to hear it. It's about time you came clean with the truth."

"Well, I didn't. Not entirely."

Orias tapped his lips, a silent reminder of his earlier warning. "Then I'm afraid you're out of time, my dear."

Fear gripped her stomach. "You won't..."

"Meri, my honor is not to be questioned in this matter. Besides, as I told you before, my interference wasn't an acceptable game plan." His face was deadly serious. "Come on. They're waiting for us."

Orias took Meri by the elbow and led her to the meeting table before he separated from her and went to the far end of the table while Meri sat towards the middle.

Out of time? He'd said Azimuth would learn the truth about her being bound to him from her lips. Meri's eyes flickered to Orias, who watched her like a hawk. Meri looked down at her hands and resolved to say as little as possible. Surely then nothing could accidentally slip out.

Belial sat opposite Orias at the head of the expansive table. Maps, books, and parchments covered with arcane symbols were laid out before him in disarray. Azimuth sat across from her, and Kobol was to her left. Meri noticed everyone else had books and notepads. She was the new recruit in the bunch. She reminded herself to worry less about Orias' head games and more about the cabal.

Meri watched them pore over the maps, some of which displayed topographic and geologic areas she assumed were different regions of Sheol, all of which were foreign to her.

"Do we have any better intel on Saleigh's location?" Kobol asked.

"His minions are seen hunting in the Hythrath swamps, so I took the liberty of using a scrythe to map out the area," Belial replied.

Orias laughed. "I'm surprised at the quality of the map. Those creatures are little more than eyes, teeth, and claws on wings."

"I never said it drew the map, son. I bespelled it to fly over the area and then extracted the data from its mind afterward." Belial slowly ground his claws together while he focused on the map contentedly.

Listening to the males plan, Meri considered her place in the cabal. She was stuck with Azimuth, which amounted to part and parcel of the entire group. She didn't outright despise Orias. Kobol seemed like a nice enough guy. Belial she'd still like to ditch, if at all possible. Knowing she was expected to swear a blood-oath of loyalty to the crown Prince set her teeth on edge, especially when she was certain he was a bit insane. She was stuck with this motley crew or be hunted down by their adversaries?

Meri let out a sigh. Meri wondered how she fit in the scope of their plans? When did they plan on cluing her in?

"Meri? Are you paying attention?" Belial asked, his harsh tone grating on her frayed nerves.

"Sorry, no. What were you saying?"

"I was saying that Trailian's death was a lucky blow. She and Mahkra were both in Saleigh's cabal," Belial explained.

"That's good news then?"

"Very much. Trailian's ability is related to the manipulation of metals, but I don't have further details. I'm afraid you'll have to work with the daemon yourself to discern how it functions, but you're lucky, it's a rare gift. Reshaping metal can be used to make unique arcane devices, or just unlock locks. No wonder Saleigh recruited her into his ranks."

"I've reviewed the process with her," Azimuth replied. "She's working with Mahkra. I have confidence she'll gain mastery quickly. Perhaps one of the two will even be willing to divulge the location of Saleigh's burrow, but it's doubtful at best. We know how devoted daemon essences can remain, even after death."

"This is wonderful," Belial replied. "The sooner, the better on gaining mastery over them, Meri. I cannot stress this enough, both for your health and for the next stage of our plan."

"What, exactly, is that?" Meri asked.

"To continue undermining Saleigh and bring him down. His cabal has some of the worst soul-addicts of any in the underworld. Taking out Mahkra and Trailian have left a power opening. If you can get to Cian, his third in command, it will destabilize the group enough that a direct attack will be possible for us without undue risk," Belial explained.

"You want me to kill Cian?" Meri asked. "Azimuth said I wasn't supposed to kill any more daemons for a while."

"No, no, child, you misunderstand me," Belial replied. "The plan is for Kobol to port you into a known location which Cian is known to frequent. Then, you will impersonate Kobol. Under the guise of Kobol, you'd approach Cian and bind him to Kobol, and leave the actual killing for Kobol later. Without Cian's support, Saleigh's forces will be split while Cian's underdogs fight for power. It will provide a perfect opportunity for us to attack."

Meri broke out in a cold sweat. "Wait, you expect me to be sexually intimate with Cian?"

Belial looked shocked. "Oh, mercy no! A mere kiss would do the binding justice, but you'll need more time with your daemon to master the trick, I'm sure. With your powers, you can cause a person to have an intimate encounter by binding their energy with your while still fully clothed."

Meri was disgusted by the thought of forcibly binding anyone, however practical such a power might be in fighting a war.

Meri glanced over at Orias, who continued to watch her, emotionless. How many times had this conversation played out in his mind? He'd warned her to take another path and reveal the truth of what had occurred between her and Mahkra to Azimuth in the beginning. She'd stubbornly gone the route, as it turned out, which was the most embarrassing of them all. Meri looked down at her hands, still clasped in her lap. They'd made plans contingent upon her ability. An ability she couldn't use.

"What's the timeline for this attack, overall?" Meri asked, hoping to buy time.

Belial's claws tapped in quick succession on the table. "Oh, I think it shouldn't take you more than a few weeks to get the binding ability worked out from the Lust daemon, based on other's progress in the past. I'd like to move on Cian within the month, and then, with the help of our allies, war on Saleigh's cabal in the days which follow. But I'd start calling in favors from allies, as soon as you're ready, in anticipation of success."

He had it all planned out, and it all was riding on a skill

she couldn't deliver. Meri took a deep breath. "I can't do a binding."

Belial laughed, the rumble issuing from deep in his belly. "Well, not yet, but once you've learned how from your daemon, we can move forward with our plan."

"No," Meri met his imperious gaze steadily, determined not to waver. "Mahkra bound me before I killed him. I'm unable to link with others now because of it."

Azimuth shifted forward in his chair, and Meri swore she felt his eyes burn through her flesh, but she refused to look back at him. If only last night hadn't happened. But it had. Azimuth now knew that Mahkra had bound her to him, and more importantly, how she'd deliberately kept the truth from him. The one emotion Meri hadn't expected at this moment was guilt, but there it was, pounding against her temples.

Belial sat back in his chair, mouth working yet forming no words, the claws on his fingertips slowing scraping together as he slowly digested this new development. Meri kept her eyes on him, unsure of what temper to expect from the Prince. "Well, yes, I can see how that could cause an issue," Belial replied. "Your only option to break the binding, as I recall, is to kill the one you're bound to."

Kill? Meri's heart dropped out of her chest and pain lanced through her entire body at the thought.

Orias cleared his voice. "Meri and I have discussed the situation, and she's working to resolve it."

Meri shot Orias a look of pure hatred. He shrugged in response.

"Thank you, Orias, for taking charge of the matter. I should have known you'd have foreseen this circumstance,"

Belial replied. "However, in the future, I expect you to speak to me more promptly, yes?"

"As you wish," Orias replied, inclining his head slightly.

Meri rose from her seat. "Look, I'm sorry I've mucked up the next stage of your plans. Perhaps it's best I go and keep working on communing with my daemons and this... other matter... for the time being. I'm sure you all have plenty to discuss and work out."

"Yes, child," Belial replied, his irritation thinly disguised. "But don't leave your house. One of the boys will be there soon enough to continue your lessons."

Meri ported home without saying goodbyes or looking anyone in the eye.

She looked around her calm, quiet house. She had no doubt which one of her cabal brethren would be here all too soon for her liking. If there was one thing Azimuth didn't tolerate well, it was lies. She'd managed to deliver him up a heaping platter full.

CHAPTER 11

*M*eri paced for over an hour wearing herself out. At first, she hid out in her bedroom, but that had been no good. Azimuth would seek her out no matter where she went. Besides, she still had Mahkra's hunters after her, and at home, she was warded and safe from them. She was tempted to sneak off and run regardless, just to avoid Azimuth's wrath.

Meri's Gleaner flashed an image in her mind of Azimuth, white-pupiled and framed with a cool, white glowing nimbus in her living room a mere moment before contact, but that's all the warning she got.

It all happened so fast; Meri had no time to react. She'd smelled a whiff of sandalwood and had been momentarily relieved. Then she remembered her lies and combined with the Gleaner's image panic set in, and she turned to run down the hall to her bedroom. Instead, Meri threw herself smack into Azimuth. Had he moved and placed himself into her path? Either way, it made no difference now. Somehow, he had her by the wrists, and she'd never seen him move. Meri's struggles were in vain, but she couldn't help but kick and fight despite his iron strength. Before she knew it, he had her pinned to the wall of her darkened hallway. He held her arms above her head, his thighs holding her legs in place to stop her from moving.

When she looked up, she saw an Azimuth she'd never witnessed before. In the dim hallway light, he glowed a radiant, icy white. His eyes were devoid of all color, chilling her heart. Azimuth's hair billowed out ethereally in the dark, swirling under the power of one of his daemon energies. The potent waves of icy energy rolled off and cascaded down his shoulders and onto the floor like a mist. His ghostly beautiful yet terrifyingly powerful presence awed Meri, who'd never guessed this lay under the surface of his calm, controlled demeanor. Meri wisely went limp in his arms. She would not tempt his ire further. Meri's daemon stirred but she suppressed her desires and kept a mental stranglehold on the daemon. There was no telling how Azimuth would react to her lust daemon in this state.

He looked her over, and Meri sensed the familiar awareness of Azimuth's energy melding with hers while he attuned to her energy. There was nothing gentle about his approach this time, his power pushed over and through her, a shock to her system she didn't dare fight. Instead, Meri welcomed his efforts, hoping to gain his trust. Lust battered at her inner gates, but again she held firm. The last thing she needed in this equation was another daemon with its claws drawn. The intensity of Azimuth's efforts to get under her skin left her feeling slightly light-headed.

"How are you planning to kill me, Meri?"

"I'm not, Az. I'd never try to kill you."

"So you've never wanted me dead?"

"Oh, that.Well, right after I figured out I was infested with Mahkra, I wanted to kill all of you. But, I also knew I didn't stand a chance against your cabal."

"Truth." He inclined his head. "Orias implied you had the situation 'handled.'"

"I don't know what Orias was talking about. He's a prick. An idiot. He's known about my 'situation' since the beginning and offered me no solutions."

"That's a lie." His anger flared. Icy tendrils of white light coiled and gripped painfully around her wrists. Meri refused to react.

"I don't know what Orias was talking about."

"Truth."

"I don't want you dead."

"Truth."

"He did offer me 'solutions,' but I refused them. I don't think they would have worked out any better."

"Half-truth. What did Orias offer?"

"Do we have to do this interrogation like this?" Meri looked at how he'd pinned her to the wall.

"Yes. You're much more cooperative and forthcoming. Continue."

Meri blew out a long sigh. "Orias' solution was that I come clean with you immediately. Tell you exactly what happened from day one. But I couldn't. I figured I could keep it hidden."

"That worked out well for you, didn't it?"

"Oh, very," Meri sneered.

"You're a smart girl, Meri. Too bright for a daemon to pull one over on you. How did Mahkra bind you?"

Meri dropped her head in shame. "I offended his all-powerful ego by not being attracted to him, and he bound me in retribution. I had no choice in the matter, Az. You know as well as I do when you summon a daemon and then refuse to bind them, it's lights out for you."

"The full truth, Meri."

"Isn't it enough, Az?"

He kept her pinned to the wall and with his free hand slid his finger under her chin and forced her to look up at him. "I want to know what you're afraid of."

His words sent a shiver down Meri's spine. She pressed her lips together in a grim line, silently refusing to answer.

"All right. I believe you when you say you had no choice," he replied. Meri breathed a sigh of relief. "But why'd he pick me? Did he know about your connection to our cabal?"

Meri stiffened and closed her eyes. "No. No, he didn't."

"Truth," Azimuth growled. "I can do this all day, Meri. I mean to have the full story from you."

Meri whimpered.

"Perhaps I should call Orias," Azimuth threatened.

"He won't tell you."

"You're quite convinced on that count, I see. Hmm. Perhaps Mahkra picked up a stray piece of my hair from your garments? Or picked up on the seal I'd left for you to use to summon me, in case of emergency?"

"No."

"Then how, Meri, did he know of me?"

Azimuth still held his finger under her chin. Meri stopped fighting. She was done fighting him. "He pulled your identity from my mind."

Meri watched Azimuth slowly comprehend. For once,

she didn't feel like a kid outmatched by master chess players. He dropped his hand from under her chin and placed it against the wall next to her head.

"A random person from your mind?" he asked, for once looking unsure of himself. He was like a dog with a bone, and Meri knew he wouldn't, couldn't let go. It wasn't in his nature.

"No, Az," Meri answered. He looked at her in confusion, and she stared for a moment at the ceiling, as if the heavens could help her explain. "For a successful summoning of a lust daemon, the summoner has to fall under the enthrallment of the daemon for the binding to work. I wasn't into him. So instead of killing me, out of some bizarre sense of professional courtesy, he changed into someone I was attracted to so the summoning could be completed."

Azimuth's ethereal nimbus shrank back, and his eyes regained a touch of blue as her words sank in. It was not the response he'd anticipated. At least he wasn't angry anymore. Meri sighed in relief, the tension draining from her body. He withdrew his energy as quickly as he'd overwhelmed her earlier, drawing a gasp from her lips. The sudden shift made her pulse race while Meri struggled for internal control over her lust aspect. Azimuth released her wrists and stepped away. He walked out of the hallway and into the living room, his profile to her.

Meri rubbed her wrists, which were stiff and pulsed like an electric current had been run through them.

"Did Mahkra know he'd enslaved you to a daemon?" Azimuth asked, not looking at her.

Meri remained against the wall but turned his way. "He realized almost at once that he'd transformed into another daemon's form. He even knew your name. It was a brief source of confusion to him, wondering how I'd encountered you when I didn't have your ink on me." Meri laughed bitterly. "At least he had no opportunity to spread the word."

Azimuth let out a short laugh. "You're worried about my privacy in this?"

"I was concerned he'd think I was working with your cabal. Instead, I convinced him I'd met you while on another assignment."

"That was quick thinking on your part." He ran a hand through his hair and shot her a harsh glance. "Did it ever occur to you that Mahkra may have dampened your ability to respond to him deliberately to force you into a binding? I wouldn't be surprised if he's used that trick with more than one summoner."

Meri shook her head in frustration. "The entire summoning was so bizarre. I was on edge from the beginning, more focused on the assassination than handling him. I had a difficult time keeping my wits about me once he went into full 'Lust' mode."

Azimuth crossed his arms. "No doubt with his lusty influence saturating the air you'd have had a difficult time shaking off his manipulations. Belial should have done more research on the bastard and given you ways to counteract his tricks."

"It's a bit late now. I'll ask Mahkra the next time I need an electric shock from hell."

"About that," Azimuth walked back over to her. "The pain you experience when controlling the daemon."

Meri looked up at him and knew he wasn't going to take another half-answer. "It happens when I fight the daemon's urge to be with you. When I pull away or shut you out."

Azimuth nodded, his lips set in a grim line. "No one else?"

She didn't want Az blaming himself -- hated to place any pressure on him for something which was entirely her doing. "No. You're my Achilles' heel."

"Dammit woman!" emotion filled him, causing his nimbus to pulse and his eyes to blaze white. "You had me torture you on purpose?" he asked, his voice barely audible.

Icy waves of his energy licked at her now heated skin. "Please understand, I'll do whatever I need to do to be in control over this daemon."

"Orias said you had another option. You chose pain. Why?"

"I didn't trust you enough to tell you. I didn't know if you'd take advantage of the situation. But now, as you said, I can't let the daemon run wild. I have to bring it to heel. I have to live with a compromise and learn to deal with the consequences it dishes out when I don't give in to it."

Azimuth's glow faded somewhat, but his eyes remained stormy. "There has to be another way to break the curse. You can't go on like this."

Meri reached out and laid a hand lightly on his chest. "I'm okay, Az. I don't regret what's happened between us."

Azimuth took her hand in his. "The daemon's skewed your perceptions, Meri. Don't worry. I'll find a way out of this for you."

Feeling the slide of his fingers against hers, Meri realized: she didn't want a way out.

Meri gripped Azimuth's hand and a moment later had him pinned against the opposite wall. In the back of her mind, she heard her prized teak chair rattle against the floor and the old recliner came to a sliding stop against her coffee table. In her present state, her lustful, liquid, crimson heat was blistering the wallpaper off the wall behind them.

"Meri," Azimuth said, warning clear in his voice.

Meri intertwined her fingers with his and this time pinned his arms flat to the wall. Her chest and hips aligned with his, and by the growing size of his shaft, he was reacting just like she wanted him to. For once, he wasn't fighting her.

"I regret nothing." The voice Meri replied with was not her own, but a raspy tenor which surprised both of them. She grazed her lips across his, desperate for a taste. He groaned, opening and relenting to her demands. They both gave in, exploring the contours and dimensions of their need.

Meri took a deep breath, broke off contact with languid last kiss, and then reined in the daemon who demanded more, so much more! The waves of electric shock brought her to her hands and knees. Meri crawled to the couch, each inch an agonizing chore. She fought her way back to her feet on her own a minute later. Trembling in pain, Meri faced Azimuth with her chin held high.

"I still regret nothing." Her voice had returned to normal. "Except being so stubborn and calling you a bastard all those times. Well, sort of. It was before I'd gotten to know and respect you."

Azimuth sauntered over to her, the dangerous glint in his eye tempting her to continue what they'd started. "You respect me now?"

"Yes. I do."

"And I respect your ability to control your daemon, so please don't feel the need to torture yourself with any additional displays." Azimuth ran a hand along her cheek, settling Meri's nerves.

"I need you to start listening to me. Trusting me."

"It's been a long time since I let someone past my defenses. It's going to take some adjustment for me."

Meri nuzzled his hand, and then self-consciously pulled back. "Where do we go from here?"

Azimuth pulled her close, cradling the back of her neck with his hand. He wrapped his other arm around her. Warmth flooded Meri, chasing away the rest of her trembling.

"There must be another way to break the enchantment you're under. I'll find it. One that doesn't involve our deaths, of course."

"And in the meantime?" Meri asked. She hadn't felt this vulnerable since her parents' death. She needed his help and cooperation, and for once had to will herself to trust someone else. It went beyond daunting. It was terrifying.

"It appears I have inherited the care and feeding of my little misbehaving daemon," he said, his eyes blue as sapphires.

"No, seriously, Az. You're not indebted to me. I misread your intentions when we first met. You've only looked after my best interests, despite the inconvenience to yourself. I won't ask you to commit to anything beyond the compromise we've already worked out. I know I can sustain my daemon's needs until you can find a way to break the curse."

Azimuth leaned down and whispered in her ear. "You're much more complicated than I gave you credit for. If you'd been honest with me before last night, things would have progressed in a different direction."

Meri melted against Azimuth's lean, muscular frame. She laid her forehead against his chest, exposing the tender flesh of her neck to his lips. "Oh?" Was it too much to hope for him to reciprocate her interest? Meri's breath caught in her throat, hope welling within her. She cast her hair to the side, opening herself to his touch.

He planted a soft row of rasping kisses along her jaw line. "I wouldn't have worried about taking advantage of you. I'd have worried less about damaging you when my daemons let loose. And if I'd known you were interested well before the daemon inhabited you, well, the truth of your heart makes a world of difference."

"Your interest goes beyond any obligations to my safety?"

Azimuth ran a reassuring hand up her spine, his fingers subtly drawing her body closer to his own. "You don't see what I see." His voice reverberated, taking on a deep, tonal quality. She had no doubt he was using his truth-speech on her, as she believed every word in the marrow of her bones. "I am very attracted to you, Meri, despite all of the times you've lied to me and called me a bastard. I see someone with tremendous potential and a tenacity to match my own. I won't take advantage of your binding. If you want things to continue as before, it's up to you. I'll follow your lead."

Meri's heart, once closed to the other Liminal, cracked open and shattered apart over his words. Where once she'd never imaged a place for anything other than vengeance in her life, Az had wheedled his way in, bit by bit. She regretted nothing and knew he'd never take advantage of her. The fact that he was willing to give her more, to trust her more, rocked her to the core.

Meri unbuttoned his shirt and placed a kiss on his chest. She parted her lips and flicked out her tongue, tasting his skin. He was tinged with salt and smelled of musk, sandalwood, and vanilla. She kissed a trail to his flat nipple and circled it with her tongue, and then rolled it between her teeth. Azimuth made a short, strangled sound. He reached down, scooped her up, and carried her into her bedroom. Meri hid her face in his neck.

Meri dug her fingers into his shoulders. She was desperate for him, but the anxiety crept up from her belly. She'd known that, as the first of Belial's Liminals, Azimuth must be incredibly powerful. Could she handle what she'd awoken in him?

"Could you hurt me with that cold, glowing thing you do?" Meri asked.

Azimuth's eyes flared to white, then back to blue. "Yes, if I wanted to. Can you hurt me with your fire, if you chose to?"

"Point taken," she answered. They each had deadly abilities under their skins. She couldn't even begin to guess the list of daemons he'd killed over his lifetime. They'd have to trust one another to keep their powers in check. Meri didn't have to ask why he'd avoided sexual encounters. Trust was in short supply in the daemon world.

Azimuth threw them down onto her queen-sized, unmade bed. He managed to cushion her fall and adjust Meri underneath him in the process. His full lips overwhelmed hers, and her anxieties drifted away in a sea of sensation. Every touch of his hands along her skin set off an answering fire underneath, one she could easily be consumed within.

"Meri," Azimuth whispered. She opened her eyes. His white nimbus danced with her crimson energy in the air between them. "Don't let your daemon run wild. I want to get to know you."

She nodded. The daemon fought under her strict mental control, hungry for the experience, but she was still the one in power. "Don't worry. I'm still on top."

Azimuth grinned wickedly and sat back on his haunches. "Well, of your daemon, you are."

He pulled his tailored shirt off over his head and threw it to the floor. Meri drank in the sight of his rippled abdomen and muscular shoulders. She ran her hands up his flat stomach, loving the feel of his flesh. He watched her, an odd expression coming over his face. Undeterred, she sat up, and pulled off her yoga top and bra, throwing them to the floor as well.

Azimuth studied her but didn't move. Meri went for the button and zipper on his leathers. He let her, eyes hungry yet strangely reserved. When his shaft sprang free, Meri unabashedly stroked it and then urged Azimuth out of his pants. He stood up off the bed and shucked off his boots, and then kicked the pants into a pile. She did the same and sat on her knees at the edge of the bed, waiting expectantly, skin cooling over his reluctance.

Azimuth held back, drinking her in, yet unwilling to commit.

"What's wrong?" she asked.

"It's just, you've seen all of me before. When you were with him."

Meri blew out a long breath. How could he be jealous because she'd been with his doppelganger first?

"Yeah, I saw him naked. He looked like you, sort of. He never radiated a glow as you do. He also didn't get all of the, uh, details quite right. Yes, I had relations with a simulacrum of you, take it as a compliment." Meri waved off his growing scowl. "Grow up. Besides, I almost couldn't kill him."

"Why?" he returned to the bed. He stood before her and took Meri's face in his hands. "Not that I'm complaining."

She tried to pull away, but he moved over her, caging her under him, his hair fanning out around her face. Meri reached up and traced his lips with her fingertip. "I thought it was my only opportunity to have my fantasy. I didn't want it to end."

The look in his eyes turned hungry, predatory. Meri's skin responded with both human and daemonic heat.

"I want to scour those memories from your soul. I don't want Mahkra associated with me."

"I know who you are," Meri noticed how his pupils had lost almost all of their blue. His anger was on edge, just as he'd been when he'd first arrived at her house. "Feel free to brand me as your own."

Those words were all the encouragement Azimuth needed. He descended upon her, kissing her with a passion that consumed all conscious thought. Their bodies writhed together, a desperate hunger surfacing neither could deny. Meri delighted in his intensity, daring to hope his sudden possessive streak might connect them beyond the binding.

She explored the planes of his body, discovering them to be altogether different from her previous experience with his doppelganger. The curve of his hip, the sensitivity of his ears, even the texture of his skin was finer, softer. Meri couldn't stop kissing and tasting his flesh.

He distracted her through his explorations. Nibbling down the nape of her neck. Sampling her breasts and sucking on her taut nipples until she squirmed under him. When one of his hands traveled down between her thighs, Meri cried out, arching against him in pleasure.

Azimuth pulled them up and turned her around. "Get on your hands and knees," he whispered in her ear, one hand urging her down between her shoulder blades while he held her hips with his other hand. Icy tendrils of energy licked and lightly seared her flesh from Azimuth's nimbus, but the effect was momentary against her overheated skin. Meri dropped to the mattress, shivering in expectation, barely able to think. He spread her legs wider, knocking them further apart with his own, and then slid two fingers into her slick core. He reached forward and entwined his fingers in the hair at the nape of her neck and twisted back, making Meri catch her breath. "You wanted to be branded, pet?"

"Anything you've got, I want it. Now."

Meri looked back into those icy white pupils flecked with blue. Her temperature rose another few degrees, and the cold touch of his powers snaked across her skin again.

Azimuth didn't hesitate. He entered her with such voracious intensity Meri thought she might explode. He picked a deliberate, maddening pace; driving her to a euphoric orgasm, she screamed his name throughout. As she came down from the high, he held her in place, again working her hard and fast, somehow knowing without words exactly what she needed. She drifted in the exquisite sensation of his fierce passion, crying out with unabashed abandon.

He slowed and pulled out, yet never stopped caressing her. He laid her on her back, she a compliant doll in his arms. Did he know Meri was fumbling inside her cloud of emotions? All too soon, the cravings overtook Meri again.

Azimuth sucked her nipples into pointed tips until they

pulsed with need. He kissed down her belly, spreading her thighs with his body and her delicate folds with his fingers. His touch was white-hot against her skin, and his lips descended a heartbeat later, causing Meri to shriek out his name.

Meri heard his rumble of satisfaction, but it was eclipsed by the building intensity as Azimuth licked and flicked her sensitive center. Before long waves of pleasure shattered around Meri. A crimson haze filled her vision, wiping all conscious thought from her mind.

Azimuth kissed his way back up along her body, again teasing her nipples into hard peaks before he settled upon her entirely. He captured her mouth in his and then rolled her over on top of him.

Meri straddled him, undulating provocatively over his hips. "Az, I need more of you," she begged, her steaming kisses raining down on his icy chest and shoulders.

"You redefine insatiable, temptress." Torment riddled his voice, his hands sweeping through her hair.

Her breath caught in her throat, and she paused. "I'm sorry. We can stop, I'm just feeling greedy."

He cradled the back of her neck with his powerful grip, drawing her lips to his own. "So am I." His demanding mouth overtook her own, his tongue driving home the force of his intent.

She whimpered in need, and he obliged, plunging up into her while continuing to plunder her mouth. His hands slid down her body, gripping her hips, and he picked up the pace, eliciting a sigh of delight from Meri. The cascade of her hair fell forward and created a secret grotto where they kissed delicately, in contrast to the pacing of their thrusts. Azimuth wrapped an arm firmly around her waist, controlling the pace. Her face fell next to his on the pillow, and she panted for air. Lost in each other's eyes, pulsating waves of pleasure washed over and through them as they found their release together.

When Meri saw his dark blue eyes at that moment, it stilled her soul.

They laid there for some time in the afterglow, merely stroking each other. Meri didn't push for more; for once she didn't feel driven for more satisfaction. She'd managed to satiate her lust daemon without having to give it free rein -- which was an incredible relief.

Azimuth, once he'd gotten over his reservations, had been amazing. What now? He'd made it clear he'd take care of her needs, and Meri was grateful because otherwise, she'd fall ill without his ongoing aid. He was no longer merely the cocky daemon she first met in the slums. He was her protector. Now Meri realized she'd opened her heart to him as well, and those feelings went beyond mere friendship. She wanted more from him.

Or was it just the enchantment? How could she know the difference between her real feelings and the magic?

"How are you feeling?" Azimuth asked.

"Healthier than I have for a while. The daemon is quiet for once. I bet I could even question it later."

Azimuth gave her a soft smile. "Glad to hear it. I've had another idea to break your curse." He toyed with a lock of her hair.

"Really?" Meri's heart leaped with hope, but then faltered. How would things be between them after the enchantment was broken?

"I'm going to seek out an elder today and see what she has to say on the subject."

"Is it safe?" Meri asked, a frown knitting her brows. She didn't want Azimuth taking risks on her behalf.

"She's someone I've worked with before, and we're on amicable terms. It'll be a simple discussion with perhaps some bargaining of favors down the road. It's nothing to concern yourself with."

"If you say so."

"In the meantime, you have a sparring lesson to get to with Kobol at the burrow, followed by a transformation exercise with Orias." He sat up and smacked her on the ass. "Have fun."

"Aren't you going to shower before you go?"

Azimuth stood and allowed his white nimbus to form and extend. It grew arctic cold, forming a thin, icy shell on his skin. He then retracted the energy and shook it off the ice like dew, which fell to the floor in small shards. "Fresh as a daisy. Well, mostly."

"That's cheating, you know." Meri stood and wrapped her arms around him.

Azimuth growled, but Meri saw the glint of humor in his eyes. "Others are waiting for you, and I'd be remiss to spend all day here with you. Now, go and get cleaned up. I'll be back tonight, hopefully with good news."

Meri growled right back at him, but stalked off to her shower swaying her hips the entire way, hoping he enjoyed the show.

CHAPTER 12

*A*zimuth ported into Blood from Stone, a fine, upstanding establishment in Sheol where you could find all manner of entertainment. Whether you sought a simple drink made from a wide range of bodily or ethereal fluids, or companionship of about any form imaginable, or fight matches to wager over or participate in for a nice payoff, they catered to your daemonic whims.

The fight pits were cutthroat, and the winners got not only the adoration of the crowd but also the admiration of females and honor to their cabals. Assuming, of course, they won the fight. Otherwise, the unlucky daemon might end up being served on the menu during the next evening's buffet.

The air was thick with sweat, incense, smoke from a variety of drugs, and sex. Not necessarily in that order. The décor was a mix of blackened stone walls, vibrantly colored cushions, and artful table tops with matching light fixtures of art deco melted glass. Likely the fixtures were made by the fire-breathing daemon who owned the place, Brekesh.

It was a select establishment, and this was why Azimuth

had rewarded himself before coming here so no stray element of his remaining human essence would betray him. Not that he had much left. Over the years, he'd walked a finer and finer line with his daemon boarders. Never giving up more of his human soul, but taking on so many daemons in battles that the weighted percentage was in favor of non-human. Belial had assured him that as long as he retained the remainder of his soul, he'd never fully convert. Cold comfort, relying on a Prince of Sheol.

Azimuth walked past the bar, studiously avoided looking at the buffet, and then took stock of the fighters on the board for the evening. He recognized a few of the names, most of them mid-sized daemons with sneaky or bizarre talents. They would provide an entertaining show and draw a big crowd, but none of them were from Saleigh's cabal. He'd thought about disguising his appearance, but to his knowledge, they had no idea Belial's cabal was involved with Mahkra's disappearance, or even who the members of his cabal were. If they had, there would already have been a confrontation.

The possibility of a fight in a public place was one reason he hadn't brought his tre'jor. If things got rough in the bar, he'd slide out quietly, and then port out before things got dicey. The weapon was too dangerous to let fall into the wrong hands.

Azimuth continued to the hallway in the back reserved for hookers and private business. Despite it being early in the day, business was already well underway based on the steady stream of customers. Azimuth continued to the end of the hall and knocked on an unmarked door. After a few moments, the door swung open revealing a petite woman wearing an intricate multi-layered Victorian-style dress. A matching diminutive top hat was nestled within a bouquet of bouncing, ringlet curls and framed by a dual set of dainty peach horns. Her delicate hands were covered with delicate antique lace gloves and held a period-authentic appearing fan. The dress' ruffled underskirt swept out in shades of sea foam green under a tailored and bustled velvet jacket in forest green. Arcane daemonic symbols had been embossed into the velvet jacket, making for a truly cross-cultural outfit.

Ranna rarely ever did anything halfway.

"Well, well, look what's rolled up onto Ranna's door tonight. Come on in, Azimuth, and shut it behind you. Lucky for you, my time is free at present."

"I'm grateful, ma'am," he replied, shutting the door. "May I say you look marvelous?"

"Pshaw, don't go ma'aming me! It makes me feel old! I may be your elder, but you don't have to act so stuffily. Do I act stuffy? No. Why? Because I know how to enjoy myself. That's why. You could learn a lesson from me on that point, kid." She motioned for him to take a seat in her spacious, dusty parlor filled to the brim with antiquities -- daemon and human alike -- in glass display cases.

Azimuth smiled at her predictable ribbing, knowing just how much he'd enjoyed himself today, but he refrained from sharing. He took a seat on a sky blue love seat. At least he thought that was the color. When he settled into it, a fine plume of dust arose around him.

"Nonetheless, this finery is quite a change from your last look."

"Which one? I forget, hmm? Was it the blue harem girl silks, or the skinned hide of the Elder daemon of wisdom? She had such beautiful, soft burgundy skin!"

"Yes, that was the one." He remembered it clearly in contrast to Ranna's overtly pale ivory skin. That, and the incredibly revealing way she'd worn another daemon's hide. He'd ended up cutting that visit short. "Wasn't she one of your closest friends?"

Ranna popped open her matching frilly lace fan and delicately waved it before her face. "Why yes, Lizbees was her name, the dear. Of course, I only wear her skin as an honor to her memory. I'm lucky to have inherited it after her untimely passing."

Azimuth inclined his head, pretending to understand and hoping Ranna had nothing to do with her dear friend's passing. One never did know where loyalties lie, or shifted, between daemon kin.

"But surely you didn't come by to discuss my astounding fashion sense, did you?"

"No, I'm afraid not. I have a situation, and I'd like your advice."

Ranna sat in her high-backed, black leather, overstuffed chair and rested her dainty feet, encased in high-heeled shoes to match her garb, on a matching ottoman. "Ah, yes. It's knowledge again this time. You know, not everyone appreciates my particular degree of acumen."

"Why, they are fools, my dear Ranna," Azimuth replied. He'd discovered her over a hundred years ago. She was older and had the knowledge to rival Belial's. She had less to gain from helping Azimuth, but as a free agent, she could be bought.

"I do so love how you bother to butter me up," Ranna replied, adjusting a tendril of her impeccably coiffed hair.

"Now, whatever do you need? I'm sure it's saucy. You visit so rarely."

"I need to know if an enchantment from a lust daemon can be revoked."

"Hmm, and the grade of the daemon?" she asked, adjusting in her chair, causing dust motes to swirl around her.

"Arch." Azimuth didn't hesitate to reply.

"And the victim of the enchantment is?"

"Human."

"And you care, why?" Ranna sighed, but her eyes betrayed her curiosity.

"Because the human is tied to a daemon, Ranna. I've been asked to research the matter as an issue of professional courtesy."

Ranna giggled. "Oh, my. The daemon can't stand the human, is that the issue? I mean, the obvious solution is for the daemon to kill the human. That would solve things."

"This is not the question I asked," Azimuth replied, carefully schooling his features of all traces of emotion. "Death for the human is not on the table."

Ranna pursed her lips. "A pity, because that's the easiest way out. Death for one of the two parties involved. But it sounds like you want everyone alive and healthy."

"Yes."

"You know that any Arch-daemon level or above enchantment is difficult to escape. I'm surprised you haven't thought of the solution yourself. I mean, you're one of the cleverest daemons I know, for a young'un that is. I'm not even going to charge you for this because it's so obvious."

He sighed and lifted his eyebrows in query. Something told him he wasn't going to like Ranna's "solution."

"It's the age-old trick to cheat those 'until death' curses. You kill one, or both parties involved, and then you bring them back. Either through resuscitation or resurrection spells or the like. Whichever you prefer." She waved her hand in the air as if the matter was inconsequential, but her eyes remained glued to him, watching for his response.

Azimuth was right. He didn't like her answer. "That's the best you've got?"

She snapped her fan shut and rapped it against her lips. "Sweetie, that's the only one I've got. I do wish I had something better for you." Ranna pouted, but there was a glint of a smile in her eyes. "I prefer it when you owe me. You bring the best payments."

He smiled back, but his heart wasn't up to more banter. "My thanks, Ranna. I'll try and find need of your services again soon." Azimuth stood to leave, and Ranna accompanied him to the door.

"I hope things work out for your friend. A sticky situation like that, perhaps it's best left alone? What's so bad about having an indentured slave, I always say?" Ranna raised her eyebrows and pursed her lips, shrugging her shoulders.

The part where they don't get to stop if they want to, and may not even know they want to stop. That's the sad part.

Azimuth lifted her hand to his lips and gave it a light kiss. She fluttered her fan, smiled broadly, and touched a gloved hand to her face as if she were blushing, but the calculated look never left her gaze. Azimuth opened her door and showed himself out.

The crowds at the bar had grown while he was in talking to Ranna, and Azimuth did his best to shut them out of his mind while he exited the building. Porting wasn't allowed inside to dissuade patrons from running out on tabs or gambling debts.

Azimuth knocked into some rowdy drinkers on his way out, but flashed a smile and kept on moving. Inside, he was seething, but it had nothing to do with the bar or the other daemons. He had to find an answer for Meri that didn't put her life at risk. Should he go back to the burrow or Meri's? Where was she most likely to be right now, and was he ready to share this new information with her? Azimuth wasn't sure, on any count, except he did want to see her, just not to discuss his meeting with Ranna.

He exited the bar, walked a short distance away, and breathed in the sharp smell of ozone in the region. Although there was no sun in Sheol, there was a low ambient light at all times. Ball lightning sparked through the low, rolling clouds that gave a smoky haze to the air.

A group exited the bar behind him, and others ported in arrival, but he paid them no heed. It was typical for the hour. Some sounded on the verge of a tousle, but he tried to ignore them.

What would happen to Meri, or to him, if they were to die, if only for a few minutes? They'd risk losing their daemon essences and associated abilities and return as a clean slate -- not something he was personally willing to risk. Belial had created them as unique hybrids, so he might be able to infer the outcome, but there could be no surety. There was simply no precedent. It had never happened before, so there was no way to know the costs involved. Meri might embrace that, but Azimuth didn't. He'd fought hard for all he'd gained. Would he risk deliberately killing Meri under controlled circumstances, assuming the resuscitation would work?

Fuck, no!

The risks were too high. Meri'd go right back to summoning, he was sure of it. Even knowing the costs. Even knowing she'd lost most of her soul to it. Because that was all she had before the cabal.

The hair on the back of his neck stood on end, and Azimuth braced for impact, extending his energetic nimbus and spinning to face the daemons behind him. The dozen or so in the motley group were no longer arguing among themselves but were now organized and focused on him alone. A moment before they'd been bantering about and throwing punches. He should have exited this place immediately. Now, he might not be able to evade them.

Five of the daemons attacked at once, all with energy bolts of one type or another. Fire, electricity, black void, white lightning, and energetic firecrackers hit with the combined force of multiple cannon hits. Azimuth deflected them all with a combination of shields and countered with a round of icy-white flechettes. Many struck true, bringing several daemons to their knees or screeching and howling in pain. Not all of the daemons had attacked yet. Worse, another had thrown up an energy net, preventing anyone from porting in or out. Azimuth was trapped.

He was severely drained in the assault, thanks to his previous encounter with Meri. He couldn't use too many of his powers, lest he expose himself before his enemies. He should have eaten after feeding Meri's daemon, but he'd been so focused on finding her an answer, he hadn't bothered to recharge. He hoped his mistake wouldn't turn into a deadly one.

A black lightning energy whip struck and wrapped

around his arms, cutting through his shirt and into his skin. It settled in and sucked out his energy, blood seeping out around the thick cords. In seconds, Azimuth was weakened, but he managed to short out the device with his polar opposite energy, and the whip withered and fell off, like a live animal.

While he'd been fighting off the whip, a large slogger had come up behind him and had him by the arms before he'd managed to shake off the effects of the whip. As the group converged, Azimuth was livid, causing his energetic nimbus to coalesce reflexively. He figured the behemoth behind him was enjoying the icy shards forming between them, not that he gave any sign of distress.

Front and center in the crowd stepped Cian, and Azimuth growled in equal parts frustration and anger. He knew then he wasn't porting out of this under his free will, even if he could take out the daemon handling the energy net.

Cian was a tall daemon, with horns and a serpentine pattern to his yellow skin. He lacked all body hair and his eyes glowed red. Azimuth considered it a tired, old-school look for the Arch-daemon.

"Imagine my surprise, stranger, when one of my minions runs into you in there," Cian said. "And I hear you smell like an old friend of mine."

"That's odd," Azimuth replied. "Because we're not friends. And I'm sure we don't even have any friends in common."

"Yeah, that's exactly what I was thinking." Cian smiled, but there was no humor in his eyes. "Pull off his shirt," he said to the slogger holding Azimuth.

Other daemons in his cabal stepped in and helped hold

Azimuth in place, but he didn't struggle. His shirt was shredded off him, and in moments Cian held the tattered rags. He'd been a fool not to change clothes after being with Meri. Her daemon's smell was all over him.

The slogger grabbed Azimuth's arms again, and everyone watched as Cian took a deep whiff of Azimuth's shirt. Cian's eyes glowed red as the rage poured out of him, and he walked up to Azimuth and belted him across the chin. Azimuth's neck cracked with the impact and patches of black swam in his vision.

Cian lifted his chin up and sniffed Azimuth once, then twice. "It's not you, but someone close to you. It looks like we'll be spending some good, quality time together. You're going to tell me everything I want to know about where my dear friends Mahkra and Trailian are, and then I'm going to rip you into tiny little pieces. Your parts will find their way back together, and when they do, we'll do it all over again. How does that sound?"

"Delightful," Azimuth replied through gritted teeth. He had no idea if his human body could endure that level of punishment, but, no doubt, there would be a good deal of time before Cian and Saleigh got that far. Although the daemonic strength he'd imbued his body with made him much stronger than Cian one-on-one, he wasn't alone with the Arch-daemon now. If Azimuth displayed the scope of his powers before the assembled group, they would know he'd stolen powers from other daemons and they'd tear him apart right here and now. There was always the potential for an escape later if they didn't guard him well. Not much, but maybe.

"How am I not surprised you know who I am?" Cian

replied. "Check him for weapons," he commanded, and two of his cabal-mates did just that, patting down Azimuth's pants and checking his boots for hidden objects. They found nothing.

"You came alone and unarmed?" Cian asked. "Are you a fool, or do you have a death wish?"

Azimuth didn't answer but met Cian's glare unflinchingly. He felt the blood dripping down his arms from where the whip had bitten into his flesh. When his blood landed on one of Cian's fancy black boots and sizzled in a white glow, burning a hole through the leather, Azimuth grinned in satisfaction.

It earned him another right hook, this time to the temple. Azimuth laughed when his vision began to clear. He could fight harder now, but he saved his strength. He needed time to recharge. To feed. They had no idea what he was capable of. Hopefully, his being in danger would trigger a vision from Orias, and if he saw enough, the cabal could come up with a plan to help. If not, Azimuth could at least make a serious dent in Saleigh's defenses.

Even being in Saleigh's compound would give Orias access to certain premonitions and visions they wouldn't have otherwise because of the blood-oaths between the brothers. If his powers were charged, he'd get at least one image of the inside of Saleigh's lair. The benefits to his cabal were many if Azimuth could withstand whatever Cian had planned.

Azimuth took a kick to the ribs from Cian and considered that the benefits to him were few unless he got the upper hand on this bloodthirsty cabal. Cian gave him a few more kicks to the midsection while his slogger held Azimuth in place.

"That's for ruining my boots, you piece of trash. What's your name?"

Azimuth glared in response, wheezing in pain.

"Fine, have it your way. Minions, smell his shirt. Note the essences of Mahkra and Trailian on it, but also human female. Go to Earth. Hunt the female down."

Azimuth focused on his pain and forced himself not to react. He had to believe Orias would foresee this and keep Meri safe. She'd stay inside her well-warded house where the daemons couldn't get to her. Mentally, he begged Orias to find a way to keep Meri from getting involved.

"I don't suppose you mind if we hunt her down, do you?" Cian goaded.

"Feel free." Azimuth kept his temper in check, saving his energetic reserves.

"Oh? If she means so little, perhaps you'll point us in the right direction?" Cian asked, amusement playing over his features.

"There'd be no fun in the hunt then, now would there?"

"Oh, I'd make it fun. I always get 'em to scream for me, sooner or later. Usually sooner." Cian smiled and then gave each of his best trackers a piece of Azimuth's shirt.

His sadistic smile wasn't lost on Azimuth, and he lunged, but the slogger held him firm. Meri was not ready for the horde coming after her. The minions he'd inadvertently caused to be sent. If she left her house or the burrow, she would draw them like flies to honey, and he had no way to warn or protect her.

The energy net retracted, and the minions ported away. Azimuth couldn't port without taking the slogger with him, not to mention there were plenty of others within reaching distance who would touch him and tag along if he made the slightest energy shift. There was no way he was going to lead this group to his cabal, and they'd tag along with him if he tried to run.

"Now, we go home," Cian announced, "and spend some quality time with our newest friend, who I'm sure will have much more to tell us once he's gotten to know us better."

"Don't bet on it," Azimuth replied.

"Oh, you'd be amazed at what I can teach you about your pain tolerances. I've been told I have a unique talent."

Azimuth remained silent.

Cian met his gaze. "You're not even afraid. I'm going to like working with you."

"Unlike your preferred subjects, I'm no child. I doubt I'll be as much fun as usual," Azimuth snapped back.

"You do know me. See, it's only fair I get to know you too. Isn't it? C'mon everyone, time is a-wasting!"

Please, Orias, Azimuth thought to himself as they ported to Saleigh's burrow. Find a way to keep Meri out of this.

CHAPTER 13

Meri scanned the well-lit dojo in the basement of the burrow. All of the walls and floor were padded with blue gym mats, and along one wall a vast array of weapons and body armor hung for display and use.

She fumed, wishing again that she'd been allowed to wear some of the lighter body padding. Kobol had insisted they were only doing 'light work,' although judging by how much she was sweating and breathing hard it was anything but for her.

"All of those weapons," she motioned to the wall, "will they kill daemons too?" Meri asked.

"They aren't like the tre'jor if that's what you're asking." Kobol's hands rested lightly on his hips. "But Belial has worked them to cause severe damage. We use them to incapacitate daemons, and then we move in with the tre'jor for the killing strike. From what Azimuth's told me, the tre'jor is one of Belial's newer inventions, while the other weapons he's been doing from the beginning."

"Is he always looking for new ways to kill his enemies?"

"Yeah. Are you ready for another round?" Kobol asked. She noted he was hardly winded.

"Bring it on."

He grinned and then disappeared into thin air. A second later movement whipped by her ear, telekinetically pushing her back on the mat a few feet. Meri redoubled her focus, listening carefully to her left, then her right, but she saw nothing.

"Nice power," she said but he didn't respond.

Her Gleaner stirred in reaction to her innate need for knowledge, and she tried to focus it in the moment. Gleaners were critical information gatherers, and Meri intended to learn to use this ability like a weapon. Yes, she asked, where is he? Illuminated footprints lit up across the floor, flowing in a pattern. They suddenly got brighter and moved faster, and Meri threw her arms up into a defensive block when she saw Kobol outlined in light, his arms bearing down directly over her head. He hit with quick but sure force, not for the first time that session.

Meri screeched in frustration at Kobol. "What are you trying to do, kill me?" She rubbed her wrists which had multiple bruises in evidence.

He reappeared out of thin air. "I'm not the only daemon who can make moves like these. And besides, you'll heal faster than you realize."

Meri rubbed her wrists gingerly. "Somehow when you said we'd be training in hand-to-hand combat I thought I'd be able to see my opponent!"

He shrugged, not moved by her complaints. "We did that part earlier. These are the same moves. Now you have to anticipate them by my energy signature. It'd be the same if we were in the dark, in a tunnel, or other poorly lit location. You can't rely on your eyes alone. You need to embrace your daemon skills, or your opponents will crush you." His eyes flashed green with that last sentence. She didn't know Kobol well enough to know for sure, but her gut said he wasn't referring to losing a battle just now.

"You're right, of course. My Gleaner kicked in on time with that last round, which was nice. Sorry, I think I just got a bit emotional from the pain," Meri replied.

Kobol clapped her on the shoulder. "No worries."

She surveyed all of the weapons on the wall. "With your daemonic abilities, I'm surprised you use any weapons."

He shared a devilish grin. "But that's where you catch your enemy off guard. So many daemons are purists and stick to fangs, claws, horns, and brawn alone. I have no such moral compunctions. If I can sneak up on someone invisibly with my strength and speed, pin them in place with my telekinetic tricks, and then bash their brains and body in with that war hammer over there, it doesn't much matter if they're immortal or not, does it?"

"And I bet some of them can counter an aspect or two of your gifts, or am I wrong?"

"Atta girl. That's the main reason I keep adding to my repertoire. I'm not invisible to every daemon, and the telekinesis doesn't always work. But that hammer always slows them down." He smirked. "C'mon, we've trained enough for today. Besides, if I tire you out completely, then Orias won't be able to show you his transmutation lesson, and then he'll be the one kicking my ass. Let's go."

"Wait, can I ask you something?"

"Sure."

"How old are you?"

He cocked his head. "Eighty-three, but it's only been thirty-seven years since I was turned. I was something of a late bloomer."

"Yet you're plenty spry."

"Immortality will do that to you. You get the daemons under your skin, and you'll be ageless forever."

"So, have you taken on an Elder daemon yet?"

Kobol crossed his arms and frowned slightly. "And now I know where you're going with this. No."

"Has Orias?" He'd told her he was 168--surely in all of those years?

"No."

"Seriously? What about Azimuth?"

Kobol closed the distance between them, going nose to nose with Meri. "What, you think if that old man can, you can? He's three hundred and fifty-nine. And no, he hasn't taken on an Elder either."

Meri put her hands on his chest and pushed him back. "Well, why not? All of the other daemons are fair game, right?"

He shook his head. "Look, yes, all daemons are fair game. If it's you or them in a fight, pick you. Let's be clear, on the scale; you'd never take down a Prince, they're simply too strong and wily. The Elders come second in strength and cunning. Also, there simply aren't that many of them and getting them in a vulnerable position is like catching an oiled pig. I know it's eating at you, but I don't recommend you go hunting your parents' killer down anytime soon. Give yourself time to develop and strengthen."

"That's what Azimuth's letter said too, more or less," Meri

replied, her shoulders sagging. How could she wait decades or hundreds of years? There had to be another way.

"C'mon, Orias is waiting for you."

Meri trailed after him back up the stairs, her legs aching from all the running around she'd been doing for the past two hours. Kobol, a well-oiled fighting machine, suffered none of the same exhaustion. In the kitchen, Kobol got her a mineral water, her new drink of choice due to Trailian, and went to tell Orias she was ready for him.

Orias emerged alone a few minutes later and motioned for Meri to follow him, which she did.

"How was your training?" he asked.

"Irritating." Meri rubbed her wrists.

"You didn't learn anything useful?" Orias opened the door to his chambers and walked in. Meri followed, amazed to see that his large room was as dark as Orias' skin except the far wall was covered, floor to ceiling, with mirrors. He had a black bed, black couch, black desk and chair. Even the bookcases were black. Black gauze hung down over the bookcases, obscuring their contents. Of course, the floor, walls, and ceiling, were flat black. She'd go mad if it were her room.

"Why the theme?" she asked. Looking at herself in the mirrors, she felt like a beacon of light in a sea of night.

"I do much of my scrying in here. I'll get visions on my own without much effort, but I find I can enhance the effects here, in these conditions."

She noted his attire. "Is that why you always wear all black, too?"

His lips formed a grim line. "If I keep everything dark, even my clothing, then nothing detracts from the images before me."

"It's all about the future with you."

His eyes swept the room, before settling on her. "I'm a product of my creator, just like you."

The prospect of her future blood-oath to Belial loomed heavy on her mind. "It's a bit creepy, but I find your level of dedication impressive," Meri replied.

"I'm glad you approve. It's proven useful on occasion. May I say how pleased I am that you've finally resolved things with Azimuth. Not to imply I've had any further prognostications, but after the way he left here after our meeting, and now you've returned, much refreshed, shall I say? One concludes."

Meri rolled her eyes. "I suppose you can say what you want. I'd prefer you stay out of our business from here on out if you don't mind?"

"Do me the favor of keeping out of trouble, and I will be only too happy to honor your request. It was the danger to your health which triggered my foresight, if you remember, forcing me to send Azimuth to you in the first place. Keep yourself on the straight and narrow, and you won't be hearing a word out of me again."

"Righto. I'll be a good little Arch-daemon host. Now, what's the lesson for today?" Meri asked.

"Today we're using the mirrors for your transmutation benefit."

"Okay." Meri looked at herself in the mirrors, wondering if they were imbued with some magic. "What's the point of transmutation?"

"The point of transmutation is for you to stop looking like a human. You have an established appearance and life as Meriwether Storm, daemon summoner extraordinaire.

Everyone who's anyone in Denver has heard of you, many recognize you by sight. Many daemons recognize you by smell," Orias explained.

"Of course they will," Meri replied. She'd noticed her sense of smell had improved in the past few weeks. "And they'll be able to identify me because they know what I smell like."

"This is less than ideal for you now as you step into your new role in the cabal. You've noticed that Azimuth, Kobol, and I all started as summoners. However, we no longer display our old human appearances. This was accomplished by sublimating our human natures and allowing our daemon essences to emanate through."

Understanding dawned on Meri. "That's how I never guessed Azimuth was human. Can other daemons smell the trace of human on you?"

"Not usually. If they do, they assume we've recently eaten or otherwise interacted with one," Orias smiled. "There's enough time spent between humans and daemons to have some excuse for a passing smell, and we rarely linger for long among other daemons."

"I've never seen the three of you in human form. Except for the one glimpse of daemon ink you all showed me."

"We don't do it anymore. I haven't found a reason to shift to human form for decades. It's too risky letting another daemon get to know my true scent. Besides, maintaining my present state takes little energy. Once the form is released and set, it tends to gel. It's the shifting back and forth that costs you energy," Orias explained.

"You know I don't plan on living here. I plan on staying at my home."

Orias shrugged. "We can discuss that later as a group, or you can talk about it with Azimuth if you'd like." He smiled, evidently of an opinion on how that conversation would work out. "Your safety is of the utmost importance. I'm sure you realize that."

"And I'm sure you realize I'm not ready to give up my life either," Meri replied.

"Even though you can no longer summon?" Orias asked. "Any daemon you call upon will know you as one of them. The gig, as they say, is up, Meri."

"I'm not about to hand over full control of my life to the cabal, all right? I need time."

"And yet you've committed to this involvement with Azimuth," Orias replied.

Meri flushed. "I don't think 'commit' is the right term. Not for his or my part. At least not yet."

"Fair enough. However, be warned: no daemon can discover you've turned or your cover is blown. And by blown, I mean they might just set fire to your house to toss you out."

"Seriously?"

"Daemons may visit the human realm, but they don't fancy others of their kind taking up permanent residence there. It puts their ability to travel at will at risk of being discovered," Orias explained.

"Great. Just, great. So, how do I do this transmutation stuff?"

Orias walked over to the mirrors. "Come a little closer and get a good look at yourself. Specifically, look at your exposed skin."

"Okay." Meri came to stand a few feet from the mirrors and looked at her reflection. She had on a tank top, so the daemon ink on her arms and across her clavicles and breast-bone was visible. Turning around she could see the ink on her upper back from where it emerged at the nape of her neck to where it disappeared under the black shirt. Each of those markings represented a different daemon, the mixture of colors and designs blanketing her skin -- and how much of her soul had they cost her?

"When we transmute we allow all of these markings to flow and mingle, in effect, creating a new outer shell for us to live within. A daemon one," Orias explained.

"So I'll have a new, tough, daemon outer coating, and a yummy soft human center hidden away?"

"Don't forget the daemons you're hosting. Think of them as the ephemeral binding agent."

"I'll be the daemon-human equivalent of an M&M," Meri said, raising an eyebrow.

"More or less," Orias laughed. "The trick to transmutation is learning to let the connections to the daemons you've summoned flow."

"How's that possible? They're each grounded to a different part of my body."

"Come now, you know that's not true. I'm sure you've seen one shift before, yes? When it makes room for another one in an adjacent space?" Orias asked.

Meri nodded, but she wasn't convinced. "Well, yeah, now that you mention it I have seen them shift. But never by more than an inch or so."

"This is similar but on a much grander scale. I want you to focus on one, whichever you like. Set it loose under your skin," Orias said.

Meri frowned in disbelief, but then selected a large,

yellow ink in a spiral pattern on her left arm from multiple encounters with the luck daemon Sprauge. She focused on the marking and noticed things, as a daemon, she'd never noticed as a human before. Under her skin, it was rooted to her flesh in a single spot like a weed. Meri watched in the mirror as she mentally picked at the spot and the entire patch of ink swayed under her skin as if underwater. She mentally dug it out, and the marking floated free, bouncing around, bumping into other ink in the area.

"This is disturbing," Meri stated, bile rising in her throat.

"Only because you've grown used to your skin looking a particular way. You've taken comfort in certain changes over the years. Soon you will have a new image to take comfort in. Release them all."

"All?"

"You'll need them all for your new shell," he explained. "Besides, any remaining ones would be evidence of your human life as a summoner."

"Which I'm not giving up yet," Meri pointed out.

"You'll be able to display your old appearance at will. It'll be easy for you with Mahkra's impersonation gift. The transmutation will cloak your human scent with those of the daemons. Now release the rest of the daemon ink."

Meri sighed, hating her lack of options. "Fine." She went to work, uprooting ink after ink. Soon all of her exposed skin swam in overlapping colors and designs. It made her dizzy.

Orias went to his closet, returned with a black robe, and handed it to her.

"What's this for?" Meri asked.

"You'll want to remove your pants and shirt. I'll turn

around. Be sure to get them all or we'll have to do the last part again."

"Right." Meri took the robe, and once Orias turned away, she stripped off her clothes, donned the robe, and went back to work, hiding from his view. Not that she needed to worry, every time she checked, he was turned the other way.

It took nearly an hour, but Meri got them all floating, even the pink, sparkly one on her foot she'd gotten after glamoring kids at summer camp. "Okay, what now?" Meri tied the robe closed.

"Watch them in the mirror. Visualize them thinning out, each one spreading out as flat and wide and far as it can go. Let them merge, overlap, and mingle. As you push, the transformation will pull of its own accord. Don't fight it," Orias advised, then turned away to give her privacy.

Meri opened her robe and followed his directions. The moving daemon inks understood her will, thinning and spreading out, overlapping but also lightening somehow, although she wasn't sure why that was the case. She kept pushing and prodding at the ink patterns. At some point, her occupant daemons took notice of the shift, coiling within her, preparing for something, but she didn't know what.

"My daemons. They're getting antsy," Meri told Orias.

"That's normal. Don't worry. They won't do anything. At least they shouldn't. Just keep doing what you're doing. I can sense you're close to completion."

"What? How?" Meri watched the patterns continue to form and shift.

"I can sense the energy shifting in you. Stay calm," he replied.

Meri took a deep breath, and the patterns began shifting

on their own, just as Orias had said they would. Her skin rippled, contracted, expanded, and heated, all in reaction to the change within. Stay calm.

All at once, as if a chemical switch was thrown, a shock wave traveled through her skin, leaving her feeling raw and tender on the outside. The force of the blow knocked her to her knees and left her trembling, arms curled up around her middle.

"You did great. How do you feel?" Orias asked.

"Like I got run over by a Mack truck," Meri answered, and then caught her reflection in the mirror and gasped. She barely recognized herself. "My skin. It's creamy white."

There was not a drop of daemon ink in sight. She closed the robe since Orias was looking at her. Meri stood and her legs, arms, and neck, nothing had any ink.

"It's weird, isn't it? The marks are still a part of you. As I said, you can reveal the old patterns at will, but this is your new skin."

"But, this isn't even my normal skin tone! I had a natural tan. Now I look pale and anemic. I mean, I look Irish!" Meri turned and caught a glimpse of her ponytail in the mirror. "Oh no!" She worked the band out of her hair, and it cascaded to her shoulders in deep shades of crimson. "You have got to be kidding me! Can I dye this back to brown?"

Orias' eyes glinted with amusement. "Do you think I've always had black hair? Things change when you become a daemon. Skin, hair, eyes. Just be glad you didn't grow horns or a tail."

"I could have grown horns or a tail?" Meri yelled.

Orias' laughed in earnest. "No, not likely. I mean, none of us have so far, but we are a relatively small sample size. So far, we've kept very humanoid appearances with minor surface variations. I'm just trying to put things in perspective for you. You can deal with these little things."

"Wait, eyes?" Meri took a closer look in the mirrors. Sure enough, what were once brown eyes now matched the deep crimson of her hair. "That's. Just. Dandy. I look like a freak!"

"Calm yourself, Meri. You stood out before in the human world, but you won't stand out in the daemon world at all. In fact, you make a rather attractive, modern, and human-like daemon. Some daemon males and females for that matter go for that look. I wouldn't worry. Besides, we have bigger issues to deal with. Now check yourself for any ink you might have missed and then get dressed, please."

Orias turned his back to her, and she checked herself over and found no errant ink. She dressed, lost in her thoughts. Orias was right. She didn't look horrible, just quite a bit different. It was just that she'd once again had no choice in the change, even though it was self-inflicted. Meri stuck her hair tie in her pocket and turned to apologize to Orias. After all, it wasn't his fault she was in this situation. The cabal had, helped her, so far, albeit to their own ends.

Orias was bent over, silently clutching his hands to his head, a dark miasma shrouding his form.

"Orias? Are you all right?" He didn't answer and an uneasy sensation formed in Meri's gut as the room chilled. Soon she could see the breath in front of her face.

"No, I don't think you are," Meri whispered. She ran to the door and threw it open. "Kobol! Belial! Come quick! Something's happening to Orias!"

She remained in the room and watched awestruck as the miasma expanded and clung to the mirrors, rolling down it like smoke over a river. In it, amorphous forms slipped and glided. The images took color and shape, and Orias stood before them fearlessly, like some grand composer over a play. Somehow, she knew her mere glimpses were but a shadow where he delved deeply and saw things with exquisite clarity.

Kobol ran into the room. "What's wrong?" He looked around the chamber, and then at Orias. "Oh, it's just a vision, Meri. C'mon, leave him to work it out in peace." He whispered, grabbing her by the arm. Meri allowed him to pull her along, mesmerized by the forms taking shape in Orias' mirrors.

That was until she saw Azimuth, beaten and bleeding, with a yellow-skinned, horned daemon hovering over him delivering more blows. Upset and unwilling to leave, Meri protested and kicked when Kobol slammed a hand like a vise over her mouth and picked her up like a generous bag of flour. He hauled her out of there with no apology and shut the door behind them. Kobol didn't release her until they were back in the main area. He threw her down on the main couch and swiped his hand across the air in front of her, his eyes flaring dark green with anger.

"Never, and I mean never interrupt Orias when he has a vision."

Meri tried to sit forward and was immediately blocked by his invisible barrier. Meri had never seen Kobol angry before, and it shocked her. "I'm sorry. I saw Azimuth and just reacted. I didn't know."

Kobol paced back and forth, throwing punches so fast she heard the air snap as he pulled his fists back towards his body as he worked to calm himself down. Meri was glad she didn't have to go up against him in a fight. She'd never have guessed there could be this much intensity to Kobol's rage. "If Orias is interrupted the vision is lost forever. There's no getting it back. And I guess we'll want that entire one."

She settled into the couch, confident Kobol wouldn't contain her there indefinitely. Fear shook Meri, remembering how badly beaten Azimuth had appeared. For someone who healed others so easily, the presence of so many open wounds and flowing blood on Azimuth terrified Meri. They must regularly be re-injuring him to keep the skin from closing, Meri realized.

"I'm sorry. I didn't know. You don't think I messed him up, do you?" Panic twisted within her and her Gleaner aspect responded, replaying the last few moments she'd been in the room with Orias and Kobol within her mind. She was able to remember where she'd walked in the room compared with Orias and apparently her aura hadn't come into contact with Orias' after his vision had begun. "Never mind, I didn't."

"Nicely done," Belial said, walking in from the library. "It's good you're getting a handle on your daemons. And your transmutation looks good on you, as well."

"Thanks," Meri frowned, "I'd prefer to be a bit more discreet." She motioned to her hair.

"Dress a little Goth or punk, and you'll blend right into the human scene," Kobol replied, his eyes back to normal now. "Someone might even think you're in a band. And you're completely rocking that hair."

"Have you picked out your daemon name yet? One to match your new look?" Belial asked.

Meri gave him a withering look. "You're joking, right? After what we saw in there? That was Azimuth, beaten and bloody."

Belial's face turned grim, but he said nothing. Kobol shrugged. "That vision could be next week, or month, or in two years. There are certain probability ratios to these things, which Orias hasn't explained to you yet. You need to relax until he delivers his interpretation. 'We'", he pointed at the three of them, "are not qualified to guess at the meaning or timing of his foresight. Get it?"

"I got it," Meri replied in a huff. "Where is Azimuth, anyway? Shouldn't he be here to hear what Orias has to say?"

There was an uncomfortable silence.

"We last saw him during the planning meeting this morning," Belial said. "He left for your place afterward, to help train you on communing with your daemon tenants, which he did admirably, by all appearances."

Meri gave a half smile. She wasn't about to tell them how things had worked out.

"Yes, and he left my place a few hours later, about the time I came here to train with Kobol. He said he had an errand to run, but I didn't ask what, and he didn't offer," Meri explained.

"So he's been MIA a total of four hours?" Kobol replied, the muscles of his jaw working. "That's no reason to panic."

Orias half walked, half stumbled into the room looking drained and hollow. Kobol waved a hand in her direction, and the invisible barrier holding her down dissipated. Meri rose to her feet, not trusting the way Orias looked at Belial and Kobol but not at her.

"We have a situation," he announced. "Cian captured Azimuth and has him at his cabal's burrow. According to my vision, we need to move on Saleigh's compound in the next three days or Azimuth will die."

Belial's horns lengthened and glowed red, matching the crimson of his eyes. "This forces my hand, but I was tired of waiting for the perfect moment. We have contingency plans for such an emergency. Now's the time to call in our allies, destroy Saleigh, and wipe the memory of all who stand with him from the annals of time."

"Three days, Belial. That's all the time we have," Orias warned, his voice weak.

"We'll use all the resources at our disposal," Belial replied. "I'll begin contacting my allies. I have several blood-oaths to call in."

"Can you recall the interior of his burrow accurately?" Kobol grabbed fresh sheets of vellum and prepared to draw out a map. All humor had faded from Kobol, and every movement had become precise and measured. Meri sensed ruthlessness in him at that moment she'd never before glimpsed.

"Yes. But first, we send Meri home," Orias said.

Meri gaped. "What? Why? Because I'm the new girl?"

Orias walked right up to her and faced her down. "Yes, because you're the new girl. Because you don't know how to handle what little powers you have, and because, most of all, if you go along on this mission with us you'll get yourself, and others, killed. Do you understand me?"

Meri met his eyes and understood what he wasn't saying. If she went with them, Azimuth would die. "But, I thought you needed me in this war? It was in your plans!"

"Plans change," Orias replied, his features grave. "We no longer need you to bind Cian to Kobol, as we'd initially planned, and you couldn't do that now anyway, could you? No, this situation, this vision, changes everything. I'm sorry, Meri."

"In these matters, I rely on Orias' foresight above all. If he says things will turn out better without your involvement, then that's final," Belial said.

"No, by all means," Meri replied, her heart beating hollow in her chest. "I don't want to make anything worse."

"Kobol, can you escort Meri home?" Orias asked. Kobol nodded, no compassion whatsoever in his eyes. "And Meri, do not leave your home. Under any circumstances." His eyes were grave, and the look sent a shiver up Meri's spine.

"Okay," she replied.

"If this isn't worked out by the fourth day, well... We'll speak again by the fourth day," Orias said.

Kobol escorted Meri home to a quiet house. She was unable to get the images of Azimuth being tortured out of her mind. She had so many questions, but what good would asking them do?

Meri sank into her couch and cried in frustration.

CHAPTER 14

*H*aving nothing else better to do, Meri spent the evening cleaning her house. She had arcane manuals on warding to read but didn't have the patience for it. She also had no idea how to fix the bubbled up wallpaper in her living room, but she found herself staring at it for a long while.

There was no way she was sitting still in her house for three days straight.

The hair on the back of her neck stood on end as a presence manifested behind her, and she spun on her heel.

Orias' face was grim. "You need to understand something, Meri. There are hunters out there with your scent. If they catch you, you'll be in a worse position than Azimuth is. They're only using him to get to you. You can't let them win. They'll kill Azimuth once they have you. They'll use his death to break you, and once you're broken, they'll tear you apart." Shadows drifted in the murky depths of his eyes.

Meri didn't doubt he'd seen each of those images. "And

I'm useless in this fight?" Tears welled at the corners of her eyes as frustration tore apart her insides.

"There's nothing you can do to help us," Orias said.

"I can't just sit around here. I'll go crazy." Meri threw her hands up in the air. She didn't care what he thought. Her building panic wouldn't settle.

"I'm sure you've stayed alone at home for extended periods of time before."

"This is not the same!" Meri yelled.

"Why?" Orias asked, calm as ever.

"Perhaps it's the binding," Meri answered.

"Does the lust daemon hunger?" Orias asked, a look of concern on his face.

Meri checked in with the Arch-daemon, but it was passive and well sated. "Well, no. That's not it. But if something happens to Azimuth..."

"Then you'd be free of the binding, wouldn't you?" Orias broke in. "And free to do as you wished without this enchantment hanging over your head. Isn't that what you want?"

"You're implying I'd rather have him dead than be bound to him?" Meri clenched her fists. "Don't be ridiculous. Everything's fine the way things are. If that changes, he and I can work it out later. I'd never let something hurt him for my benefit."

Orias rubbed his fingertips against his forehead. "And why not?"

"Because I care. There, I said it. Happy now? He's watched over me, and I'd like to return the favor. Please. Let me help."

Orias took a deep breath and shook his head. "I'm sorry, but no. I'm glad to hear of your motivations, but if you come with us, you'll both die. I'm sorry, but my visions are never wrong. You need to stay here. Will you give me your word, Meri?"

Meri growled in frustration. "I hate this."

"I know, but he begged me," Orias replied.

"What?" Meri whispered, startled by his newest revelation.

"In my vision, Azimuth begged me not to let you get involved. I did anyway, and then you died. So please your word, Meri."

"It's a guarantee? If I come along on your mission, I die?" Meri asked.

"Yes. Regardless of what precautions we take, if you're with us, you die."

"And you'll get Azimuth out fine?"

Orias' eyes flicked to the floor and back. "Foresight isn't a science, you know. There are many factors in play to know for sure. Too many for me to give you a guarantee."

"But his odds?" She heard the strain in her pitched voice.

"Not great, but we'll do our best." Tension played over his dark features.

Meri winced. "Does he always die if I come along?"

Orias ran a hand through his hair. "I never played you for the martyr, Meri."

"Just answer the fucking question, Orias." Meri keyed into her Gleaner aspect and soon mapped out Orias' body posture, his surface temperature, his heart rate, breathing, and every movement. She was aiming for lie detection -- a not uncommon trick for the Gleaner, if a bit unreliable.

The Gleaner clued her in that Orias knew precisely what she was doing.

"That's not polite, Meri," Orias wagged a finger at her. "But I'll answer your question. No, he doesn't die, but he blames himself for your destruction. Happy now?"

"No. You're holding something back." Meri didn't know how she knew it, but the Gleaner was confident.

Orias shook his head with sadness in his eyes. "I'm holding a lot back. I always do. If I didn't, I'd be intolerable."

"You're not now?"

"He'll blame himself if you don't listen now. To him. To me. You'll be safe here. Do you understand?" He shook her by her shoulders to get her full attention.

"I do," Meri heard her voice crack with emotion, and she couldn't hold Orias' gaze. "I'll leave you guys alone since it's what he wants." The knife twisted in her chest as she spoke the words.

"I'll see you in four days, Meri."

His heartbeat skipped a beat, and her gleaner skills lit up like a torch, mapping out a network of deceit. "See! Right there! You don't believe what you're saying. Are you going to be all right?" Meri asked.

Orias held up four fingers in front of her face. "Four days. Your word?"

Meri sighed. This was a battle she couldn't win. "Yeah. I'll leave the cabal alone. But you can go right back to Sheol with your secrets, Orias."

He inclined his head in acceptance and then ported away without another word.

*M*eri awoke from a fitful sleep, unable to get the conversation with Orias out of her head. The images from his mirrors and snippets from the conversation kept replaying in her mind, like pieces of a puzzle she just couldn't put down. She lay in bed for some time but then got up and began pacing the house. A part of her mind recognized this was the Gleaner at work, as this new detective behavior was completely unlike her. Or perhaps she should think of it as 'her gleaner skills' instead of something separate? They'd been the easiest to deal with, and her gut told her that's because he was the least powerful and the most amiable. In combination that worked out for an easier-to-use tool.

Well, it was a theory at least. She'd have to wait until she could run it by the cabal to know.

In the meantime, her gleaner skills kept tripping over certain things Orias had said. She didn't like how Azimuth had known Orias would have a vision of him and then communicated with him via the foresight how he didn't want Meri there.

Of course, he didn't. He was protecting her, which was his way. Azimuth would blame himself if something bad happened to her. However, Azimuth didn't get a basic, simple fact.

Meri had to choose her fate. Being 'protected for her own good' riled her up. How did Orias not know she'd react this way?

That's when it dawned on Meri the gleaner. Orias did know she would get involved. Orias always knew. Because Orias played everyone.

Meri just had to figure out how he was playing her now. For instance, why not just tell her what he wanted her to do? Wouldn't that be easier?

Then again, Meri had to admit she wasn't exactly an easy person to manage.

In her conversations with Orias, he'd made her swear to not go along with them. But he hadn't said a thing about her going on her own. He'd told me she wasn't supposed to leave her house because of the daemon hunters, so she had to avoid them. She'd have to work out a way to go to Sheol, but she knew of no places in Sheol other than Belial's burrow. Meri didn't know where Saleigh's lair was located.

However, Mahkra and Trailian did, didn't they? But how could she coax it out of them?

The location was step one. How she'd contribute was another matter entirely, especially not knowing what the rest of the group was doing or who else they had helping them. But she had three days to figure it out. She had three days to intervene and save Azimuth's life, regardless of whether or not the others wanted her help.

Meri took a deep breath and tried to stay calm. What other resources did she have available?

Annamie. Annamie would bring her any supplies she asked for. She was the most powerful spell caster in town and mostly on Meri's side. Mostly. Well, she could be talked into it. Another point in her favor.

What else did she have?

Wait. She had objects from Azimuth himself. One was a clay disk he'd given her to break and summon him after Mahkra's summoning, which she'd never used. Another was the envelope containing the information on her parent's killer. The last was the packet of "insurance" he'd given her on their second meeting, should she ever need to summon him. She realized it wouldn't work to invoke the part-human Azimuth, and was at a loss how it would help her now.

Meri ran to get the items. With her gleaner skills, she identified the ward around the clay disk that teemed with Azimuth's energetic patterns. To Meri's surprise, she also noted the envelope also was infused with a similar ward that she hadn't noticed before Orias' training, but it was evident now.

Both objects would summon him unless wards were holding him in place preventing it. Was it too much to hope for? Meri tore open the envelope, and the ward's spell matrix crackled as it sprung open releasing the magic. It traveled outward into the ether and dissipated. Meri waited, but nothing happened. She was left with an envelope which Azimuth didn't want her opening without his counsel, and yet she'd done it anyway. She waited for the binding to kick in with a little retribution for defying his will, but nothing happened. Perhaps since Azimuth had only requested she not open the letter, versus demanded it, Meri hadn't triggered the binding? She let out a sigh of relief and skipped to the part detailing the necessary constituents required to summon the Elder-daemon Calloine.

Orias had said she didn't have the power necessary to help them -- to save Azimuth -- in this battle. Certainly, this daemon would tip the scales in her favor; assuming Meri could kill her and not be devoured like her parents.

Meri planned to appear like a summoner to the Elder-daemon for as long as possible, so she made a list of everything she didn't already have readily available. She laid the letter down, knowing if Azimuth had had his way, he'd be here, right now, talking her down from running headlong off this cliff.

But he wasn't. It was just her and her fresh grief and her fear of losing someone else she cared about, again.

Meri looked at the clock. It was five a.m. Meri called Soul Paths and left an extended message for Annamie including all of the ingredients she needed. She requested that Annamie deliver the package as soon as possible, and how she needed to beg a few favors, one last time.

Then Meri settled down into a meditative squat on her couch to have a heart-to-heart with her lust and metal daemons.

"*L*et's start at the beginning, shall we?" Cian asked.

Azimuth looked up at him but didn't deign to glorify his rhetoric with an answer. It wasn't that he couldn't speak. No, Cian's torturous methods had avoided all contact with his mouth and throat. Cian was a consummate professional in the trade. He was also a psychopath.

By the way Cian had him stretched out naked on the slatted metal rack, Azimuth could only wonder what surprise was in store for him this time. He'd learned Cian liked to draw out the anticipation before using his various devices. Fear elicits responses more quickly.

Cian underestimated his resolve. Then, almost everyone did.

Azimuth had been under Cian's ministrations for only a day, and he already had all of his bones broken at least once.

He knew that was just the beginning. It was Cian's little welcoming method of warming up his new "guests," as he liked to put it. He hadn't even asked questions during the initial beating.

The constant beatings meant all of Azimuth's energy went into regenerating his body. He wasn't anywhere as robust as the daemons thought he was. At this grueling pace, he could barely stay conscious.

The prospect of escape was slim at best. Cian was with him at least eighteen hours a day, and he kept a dozen minions in attendance to witness and assist.

From the discussions he'd overheard, the disappearance of Mahkra and Trailian had upset the inner workings of Saleigh's cabal deeply. Unfortunately for Azimuth, Cian had taken things personally.

The only upside was Azimuth's ability to feed off other's disgust. All he had to do was breathe it in and swallow the bitter emotions. It wasn't something he ate frequently, but these daemons were so disgusted with Cian's inability to break him, it gave him a boost where little was to be found.

A blade pricked his skin, bringing him back to the present. He saw his nimbus flare in response. Cian leered.

"Did that get your attention, mystery daemon?" Cian taunted.

A trickle of black blood ran down his chest. Azimuth now noticed the bundle of piercing blades in Cian's hand and bit back a groan. He forced himself not to struggle in the bonds. It wouldn't help. Cian was a demented sadist and the bonds were warded to prevent his escape. Any encouragement would only serve to inflame and feed Cian's appetite.

Azimuth held his tongue.

"All right," Cian continued. "I'll make this easy on you. I'm going to ask some simple questions, and you're going to answer me. When you don't, I'll be driving one of these," he held up one of the needle-like blades in front of Azimuth's face, "straight through you. Mind you; it's not fair if you pass out on me. Besides, I've learned you regenerate. I'll just wait around for you to come to, and then we'll keep right at it. You clear on the rules?"

Azimuth glowered at Cian, and his nimbus flared out with his temper, freezing the metal rack underneath him. At least he was immune to the effects of extreme cold due to his present constitution. However, he did hear the frame creak in complaint from the temperature shift.

Cian gave a rough laugh, his eyes glistening with joy. "I'll take that as a yes. Now, first question, and it's an easy one. Your name and cabal leader."

"You can't even count," Azimuth scoffed. "That's two questions."

Cian flicked a tongue over his sharp teeth. "You're right." He traced the blade across Azimuth's skin, drawing a thin trail of fresh blood in its wake. "Your answer?"

"I'm afraid it's slipped my mind," Azimuth replied.

"That's unfortunate," Cian replied. "But I have to admit; I'd hoped you'd say that." Without hesitation, he drove a blade through Azimuth's left shoulder and then down through his right calf.

Pain flared through the wounds. Azimuth could tell Cian was watching, and waiting for him to reach a breaking point. They both knew he was nowhere near it.

More questions followed. Did he have any idea where Mahkra and Trailian were? Where was his burrow located?

What were his powers? How was Mahkra overpowered? What was the connection of the human female to Mahkra's disappearance? How was Mahkra being kept against his will? What were his cabal's plans for Mahkra? Was Mahkra in good health? Azimuth couldn't keep track of all the questions; he merely refused to answer them.

The questions were repeated cyclically until Azimuth's body was a pincushion riddled with Cian's fancy blades. Azimuth could hear his blood hitting the floor with regularity. Not just spatters, but a steady stream gushed forth down the table legs.

Could he die from blood loss? He didn't know. Or would they replenish him, simply to begin again? Azimuth suspected the latter. The only side benefit from the exsanguination was the dulling of the pain.

A knock at the door interrupted Cian from delivering yet another blade thrust. Instead, he threw the knife against the wall and motioned for one of his lackeys to answer it.

Through the sweat and tears clouding his vision, Azimuth watched Ranna walk into the crypt. She eyed the space with great distaste. When she settled her eyes on Azimuth, the flash of recognition and pity was not lost on him. Nor did Cian miss the exchange.

"Thanks for coming, Ranna," Cian said, rubbing the blood on his hands off on a towel.

Ranna turned to him, her pristine Victorian silks and velvet in sharp contrast to the filthy torture chambers. "I came as a favor to Saleigh and am under blood oath to parley. Mind you don't cross the line with me, or I'll be bound no longer, Cian."

Cian shot her a wary look. "I mean you no harm and no offense, Elder."

She glanced towards Azimuth. "Your blood sport causes me pause."

"Ah, yes," Cian replied. "This troublemaker is the reason we asked you here. He's harmed one of our cabal, thus the treatment. Showing him to you in this state was never meant to be taken as a threat. My humble apologies."

Ranna looked Cian over and harrumphed. "Then be clear, Cian. Don't drag your explanation through the depths. Get on with it!"

"Saleigh asked you here for your expertise, Ranna. We need to identify him. With your resources, we thought you might know him or might recognize him from Blood and Stone, as you work there, and that's where we picked him up. We're willing to pay any price you name," Cian said. His face was brutally desperate, eyes flashing a brilliant red.

Ranna walked over to the table and looked down at Azimuth, an unreadable expression on her face. "You said he'd caused you some trouble?"

Ice spread through his limbs. Was that from the torture or his doubts around Ranna's ability to be bought? In his present position, there was no way he could counter Saleigh's price.

"We've connected him to the disappearance of our cabal-mate Mahkra. Perhaps you knew him?" Cian asked.

Ranna's gaze held Azimuth's, and her eyes sparkled with curiosity. "I'm familiar. He's an Arch-daemon of Lust, correct?"

Cian nodded, his eyes narrowing. "Did you know him?"

"I can't say I ever had the pleasure."

Cian frowned, but then shrugged off her question. "He's

missing, and when we ran into this trash at Blood and Stone, he reeked of him and some human woman. We've sent hunters after the human, but in the meantime, I'm trying to get information from him on his cabal. We figure they must be holding Mahkra."

"Is that so?" Ranna's lip lifted in the slightest hint of a grin, but then her expression turned imperious, and she shifted to face Cian. "Well, I'm afraid I can't help you."

Azimuth didn't know why Ranna would defend him, but he promised to gift her extravagantly if he made it out of this situation alive, which he intended to do.

Cian let out an exasperated breath and hung his hands on his hips. "That's unfortunate. It would have helped us out if you knew him."

"Oh, I never said I didn't know him," Ranna replied with a genuine smile. "I said I couldn't help you."

Cian growled, his skin flushing an unusually dark shade of yellow. "Explain."

Ranna waved her hand at him. "Don't threaten me, Cian. I could flash you to cinders in a heartbeat, and, if you war on an Elder, what position would that put your cabal in?"

"Apologies," Cian replied. He took a few deep breaths and his color normalized. "Can you please explain?"

"I'm happy to. His sire is a Prince, and this trash is a favored son. I took a blood-oath not to betray his sire, oh, an epoch or two ago. I'd be hard pressed to remember the exact date, but you understand my hands are tied in this. To betray his lineage would break my oath to his sire and render my life forfeit," Ranna replied.

Azimuth had no idea Ranna was under a blood-oath not to betray Belial. Yes, Belial had technically "created" him, and was thus his sire, but she creatively stretched the limits of convention to protect him. Didn't she? By his blood-oath to Belial, he'd sworn fealty as his lineage, did such words make it true?

"This is most unfortunate. But I suppose it's more information than I had before," Cian said.

"I suppose it is." Ranna smiled politely.

"Can I trust that you won't betray us to his sire, despite your oath?" Cian asked, his voice deadly calm.

Ranna walked up to Azimuth's head and peered down at his face. Her emotions remained unreadable to him, and he, in turn, kept his expression blank.

"My oath to Saleigh stands," Ranna replied. "I cannot break it without consequence either, now can I?" A bitter tone tinged her words. "I will keep your secrets, as in doing so does not betray his sire. But know now, I will never swear another oath with your cabal again."

Cian spat on the ground. "Never is a long time, Ranna."

"For some of us, more than others, child," She replied. "I was here well before you, and I can promise, I'll be here long after that." Then she leaned over Azimuth and kissed him on the forehead. "Farewell, my favorite clockwork child," she whispered. A wisp of a smile played on her lips. "I hope next time we meet it'll be under less precarious circumstances?"

Azimuth opened his mouth to speak, but she turned and swept out of the crypt without a backward glance.

A second later Cian's face replaced hers. "What did she mean!" he demanded. "Is 'clockwork' a key to your powers, or your lineage?"

"I'm not sure, Cian. She's never called me that before. I'm as surprised by her loyalty as you are," Azimuth replied.

Cian's eyes flared bright red, and his skin flushed dark yellow. Azimuth waited for his anger to unleash in any one of a million ways.

Cian threw back his head and laughed. "You've answered a question for me. Nicely done. The first of many, I'm sure. All it takes is one to put a chink in the armor."

Azimuth wanted to rip the self-satisfied smile off of Cian's face and then keep on shredding, but the daemon was right. He'd made an error answering anything.

"Someone pull those things out of him, rinse him off with some salt water, feed him up, and I'll be back in an hour," Cian said. "I think it's time to break all his bones again before we have another little talk."

Azimuth heard Cian's throaty laughter ringing down the corridors as the blades were ripped from his flesh, one by one.

CHAPTER 15

"*L*ook, we understand what you're asking for, and for my part, I'm happy to show you whatever you'd like to know about metal manipulation," Trailian said.

"Just as I'm now willing to show you some of the more advanced moves where it comes to my impersonation techniques," Mahkra said. "But please, Meri, be reasonable. You can't expect us to do anything to send you into Saleigh's burrow? Can't you see it from our perspective?"

"Sure, you won't betray him. I get it." Meri stretched her back out. She'd been at this for hours now with little progress.

"It's just, going in there on your own. You'll be killed, and then where will we be?" Trailian asked.

Meri had no answer. She was roused from her conversation by the sound of a small rock hitting the front door. On the upside, she was negotiating well with them both. On the downside, she wasn't getting clear images of Saleigh's burrow from either. Neither was willing to divulge secrets and betray their previous alliances.

She couldn't blame her demons. Meri needed to come up

with a better incentive plan for them, but what?

Another rock hit her front window and Meri jumped up to answer the door. She checked to see who it was and relaxed when she saw Annamie and Drew out front. Remembering the cabal's warning not to let any humans see her in her Liminal state, Meri focused on the illusion of appearing as her old appearance and the image shifted to her will, just as Mahkra had described and -- voilà! There she was, brunette and covered in daemon ink again. The sensation strained her senses, and her skin pulled tight, feeling unnatural.

Meri opened the door and came out onto the porch, which was also warded along with the rest of the house. Meri brought with her a bag containing some things she'd prepared, assuming Annamie accepted her pleas for help.

"Thanks for coming, Annamie," Meri said. Annamie stood on the sidewalk leading up to the porch, which didn't surprise her. The spell caster stood just outside of the range of the daemonic wards, certainly aware of where the magical effect ended. Drew stood close by her side, one arm tight around Annamie's waist. Meri doubted they wanted to linger, and she didn't blame them. If they knew the full truth, would they go running or stay and help? What would Meri do if she was in their shoes? She sighed.

"I told you I would keep filling your orders, and your message was desperate." Annamie's eyes danced over her body, and Meri guessed she was trying to read her aura. They'd left the bag full of her order ingredients on the porch, for which she was very grateful.

Her gleaner side rankled at the intrusion. Yeah, you like learning everyone else's secrets, but you can't handle anyone poking around yours, eh? Meri, however, would welcome any advice Annamie had to offer.

"I can see you're not looking much better." Annamie frowned and shook her head.

"On the contrary, Annamie. I'm starting to improve. I may not be where you'd like me to be, but I'm where my decisions led me, and I'm at peace with it now. You don't have to like me like this, but there are good things I can accomplish, and I mean to do them."

Annamie squinted, her skepticism plain on her face. Drew looked back and forth between the two of them, appearing confused.

"Okay. If you're content with your fate, so be it. What did you drag me out here for?" Annamie asked.

Meri took a big breath. "I need a huge favor. Well, a few favors." She held up the bag she'd brought out and pulled out a zip-locked baggie with an item of clothing in it. "First, I need these planted around the city. In unoccupied areas away from human traffic."

"What is it?" Drew asked.

"My dirty laundry," Meri answered. "Also, bespell the bags, so my scent isn't on the outside. I don't want whoever is carrying the bags to get tagged as smelling like me."

"You have daemons tracking you?" Annamie replied, understanding at once. Panic flooded Drew's face.

"Don't worry. This house is warded. But I can't stay here. I have to go somewhere safe where I can summon, and the hunters can't get to me."

"You think summoning more daemons is the answer?" Annamie asked, flushing red with anger. "Why not stay here where you're safe?"

"Because if I stay here, my friend will die. He'll die because of me, Annamie. But if I go, this there's a chance I can save him. I have to try," Meri begged.

Annamie looked tired. "And where will you go? Your regular summoning spots have likely all already been overrun by the hunters if they're going off your scent."

"That's what I figured as well. This is why I need a recommendation for you to get me into the Flesh Playhouse Burner Enclave up north. I know they're warded like Fort Knox against daemons. All the enclaves are. You're on good terms with the leader. She'll listen to you."

Annamie laughed. "You're serious? You want me to ask them to allow you, possessed as you are, into their haven? Knowing you want to summon a daemon there? It would ruin all credibility I have with them!"

"I swear to you, Annamie, I'm no danger to them. And the only reason I want to summon it." She had to motivate them to trust her somehow.

"What Meri? What can this daemon possibly tell you that's worth endangering the enclave?"

"Nothing. This is why I'm going to kill it. Then I'll be able to kill the others holding my friend." At least Meri hoped she could kill the Elder daemon before it realized she was a Liminal. It wouldn't be easy.

Annamie and Drew exchanged glances, and then looked at her in disbelief. "You can kill them?" Annamie asked. "Tell me truly, Meri."

"I have, Annamie, and I will again. However, I can't do it here. I'd destroy my home, or at the least expose it to other daemons. I need an open space protected from the daemon hunters."

"And killing this one daemon, how does that help you?" Annamie asked.

"It's very influential. Once it's dead, infiltrating the place my friend is being held will be much easier for me."

"All right," Annamie answered, "I don't think you're being honest with me, but I do believe you about killing daemons. I never liked you working as a summoner. I like the title 'daemon hunter' even less."

Meri gave a mirthless laugh. "It's not on the top of my list either. So, will you talk to the Burners for me?"

"I will, Meri, but it's up to them. I can't predict what they'll say. But they may be tempted by your offer because it's so unusual. Take care. They despise everything daemon-tainted. If they find out you're possessed, well, there's no telling how they'll react."

"Right. I'll keep that under wraps. Thank you, Annamie. For everything."

"I hope you're able to help your friend, Meri. I'll let you know what they say." She turned to Drew. "Grab the bag for me, will you, dear?"

Drew climbed the steps to get Meri's bag of dirty laundry. Meri stepped back, not wanting to come too close to Drew, just in case her scent might rub off on him.

"There's cash in the bag for the supplies you brought," Meri told him.

"Thanks, Meri. Good luck," he replied and took the bag. Annamie chanted under her breath when he returned to her and then she swept him down with her palms and then swept the bag as well, presumably to get Meri's scent off. When she was done, she wiped her hands off on the ground like they'd been covered with some sticky sludge.

"You'll be traveling by car?" Annamie asked.

"That was my plan," Meri replied. "It's in the garage."

"Let me sweep your scent off it too. Then you can ward it before you travel. It should help to keep the hunters off your trail, wherever you go."

Meri nodded. "Thanks, good thinking." She went inside and activated the garage door, and then waited while Annamie finished her spell.

"You'll hear from me soon." Annamie went to get into her car. "When will you know about your friend?"

"Three or four days." Meri's head ached, disbelieving her own words.

"I'll expect to hear from you then," Annamie replied.

Meri nodded. "I'll call to let you know it all worked out okay."

There was a tense moment where the unsaid remained unsaid, and then Annamie and Drew got in their car and left. Meri closed her garage door, went back inside her house, and returned to her preparations.

She shook off the false image of her daemon ink as it had begun to chafe. How odd; looking like a daemon feels more comfortable.

As she waited for a response from the Burners, Meri debated the best way to surprise, and thus kill, a Sin-Eating Elder-daemon.

---

*M*eri used her best warding knowledge on her car. It wasn't a multi-leveled matrix like Orias could do, but it would have to serve. Trailian even showed her a neat trick with grounding the pattern into the metallic structures in the car, which added another layer of buffer to the wards.

In theory, Meri only had to be in her car for about an hour, which was how long it would take to get up north to the Burner Enclave. If she'd been there before, Meri could port up based on memory recall, but she'd only heard of the location and never been there herself. Plus, she was taking her summoning supplies with her and wanted to have a place to keep her things while she was gone, assuming the summoning went well. She hoped that she would be porting directly from there to Sheol afterward, assuming she could figure out where she was going.

One thing at a time, Meri. Just continue onward like it'll all work out, right? She put all her faith in Orias' predictions.

Meri packed up her car with all of her summoning gear including the new supplies plus some of her emergency stash cash she always kept at home. You never knew when the banks were going to "close down" for a few days, or weeks when things got rough politically locally or abroad with the Corporations. Then she packed her camping gear too, assuming the Burners wouldn't let her use their space. She didn't want to sleep in their homes, or yurts, or whatever they used, and get her scent everywhere. She knew they were warded, but it was better not to have daemons hounding them at their boundary line.

Just when Meri thought she'd burst from the tension of waiting, her phone chimed.

Annamie.

"What's the verdict?"

"I talked to Jackie. She says you've got a conditional yes."

Meri's heart pounded at a hundred miles an hour. "Conditional?"

"Yes. It means you can enter the Enclave, meet with her, and describe how it is you can kill daemons. If she believes you, you can attempt it. If you fail or endanger her people in any way, she reserves the right to use whatever force necessary to remove you and whatever you've summoned."

Meri breathed out a sigh of relief. "I can live with that. Thanks, Annamie."

"You might not. But you're welcome, and good luck. You know how to find the place right? You take the Firestone exit."

"Yeah, I know that much. I won't have a problem finding it." Gleaning was becoming second nature to her now, so finding a 'hidden encampment' of about a thousand people would be easy.

"If you say so. I have my people planting your scent bags all along the Front Range, even one down in the Springs. You'd better get moving now."

"Will do. Thanks, Annamie."

"Thank me in four days."

The line disconnected and Meri slid her phone into her pants pocket.

Looking every bit the daemon, Meri focused and roused her daemon occupants. Happy to be let out to play, her daemons responded to her will and rose to the surface of her mind and skin, infusing her body inside and out, from head to toe, overpowering all lingering human scent. Their powers and consciousnesses vied with her own, but it was a small price to pay. Meri tightened her focus, determined not to let them get the upper hand. Happily, none of the strong-willed tenants were hungry at the moment, so they settled without complaint.

Meri changed into a fresh set of clothing from the laundry. It would have to be enough. Satisfied she'd done all she could to hide her human scent, Meri climbed into the car and headed for the Burner Enclave. She hoped that no hunter would catch her tail in the next hour she'd be away from the strength of her home's wards.

W ith the help of her gleaner aspect, Meri located the hidden Burner Enclave by following the well-worn sets of tire tracks visible to her daemonic senses. It was easier to see with her daemons so forward and present in her mind, and yet they became harder to keep under control with each passing moment.

Her car headlights lit up the old road ahead of her in the fading daylight. From its condition, she suspected that only cattle used it now. She drove slowly so she wouldn't blow out a tire on a prairie dog hole or yucca plant.

All the way up the hillside, Meri debated how to present herself to the Burners. Meri had the advantage since the Burner's had never met her and thus had no idea what she looked like. She had her long, cowled robe on hand to aid in her disguise from the Burners, while her pants and long sleeved shirt already covered most of her body. The only exposed parts were her face, hands, and neck. Meri wasn't sure she'd be able to maintain the illusion of her human self for an extended period in front of so many. How would they react if she slipped up?

No, it was better to play the con artist with the Burners and only show her human side when summoning the daemon. She'd have to play it that way. With great effort, Meri reined in the daemons and tamped them down, as deep within her consciousness as she could muster. Mahkra fought tooth and nail, searing her mind with tempting images of Azimuth's lips trailing up her thigh, yet the yearnings only made her grieve, not give over. The daemon had underestimated the outcome of his gambit. Now they were well below the surface for when she passed through the Enclave's wards. She could only hope her superior daemonic wards would keep them at bay.

When she came around the final turn before the enclave, Meri was amazed at the level of security on the gates. A natural, hilly barrier surrounded the entire compound, or had it been bulldozed into that shape? It was hard to be sure. Curls of razor wire covered the top of the hill, sending a clear message that the Burner Enclave drew a hard and definite line in the sand with the outside. The front gates were thick and wooden, and an armed sentry stood watch in a small building made from cinder blocks painted earth tones to blend into the surrounding landscape.

Meri pulled up to the gate and felt her daemons recoil from the wards surrounding the Enclave. Hopefully, the hunters would have a similar problem.

Meri rolled down her window to talk to the sentry who approached.

"Hi, I'm Meriwether Storm. You should be expecting me."

The sentry was dressed in jeans, a flannel shirt over a simple t-shirt, and work boots. He kept a rifle slung over his shoulder, apparently not expecting trouble from the little woman in the sedan.

"You don't look like the description I was given for a 'Miss Meri.'"

Her hands gripped the steering wheel as she mentally sifted through a list of lies he might buy. "Well, you may be aware I'm on the run and, as such, I dyed my hair. You know, women do that to look different," Meri replied.

"But aren't you supposed to pick a less-conspicuous color when you're on the run?"

Meri sighed. "Yeah, I guess I made a bad call on that one, didn't I?"

"The ladies might be able to help you out with a different look. I'll let them know you're here. Just so you know, Jackie has said you can come in, but only so far as the first turn off to your right. You'll see where to park. She'll meet you there. Don't go wandering about. You don't have free run here. Got me?"

Meri nodded.

"I'm glad we understand each other." He turned and strode off to the gate and opened one panel wide. Meri drove through and watched the Enclave's wards dance against, and repel, those encircling her vehicle. Immediately her three daemon boarders wailed, moaned, and roared in such agony Meri could scarce hear another sound, in pain just from the proximity. If they could have fled her body willingly, she had no doubt they would have, but the option was beyond them. Once inside the gates, they quieted again, but they sniveled in pain like they'd been dragged through a meat grinder.

She'd experienced none of their corresponding pain, much to her relief. Somehow, their consciousnesses, or whatever remained, were isolated from her own within her human body.

Meri drove a couple of miles before locating the turn off the sentry spoke of. Meri parked a quarter mile off the main road in an area that looked like a park rest area. She got out and checked her watch. Six o'clock. Never had the hours of the day passed so quickly for her, knowing that each hour spent was an hour in pain for Azimuth.

No one was there waiting for her, so Meri scouted the immediate area. There were basic camping facilities that perhaps they used for visiting groups of other Burners? She simply wasn't privy to their cultural idiosyncrasies to know for sure. A short distance from the parking area stood a large meditation circle marked by stones and natural greenery, which grew in patterns around the outer edge. It was delineated with a series of differently colored pebbles forming swirls of color but no particular design or pattern. Standing at the rim of the circle, Meri's gleaner aspect could tell the space was sanctified and had been used for various ritual purposes, but she didn't ask for specifics. It didn't feel like her business to know.

Meri turned to the sound of bicycles crunching on gravel and saw five riders approaching, three men and two women. Meri left the circle and returned to her car, pulling her cloak up around her neck to hide her exposed skin.

The Burners appearance didn't surprise Meri. They wore a mixture of flamboyant tie-dyed and natural clothing, some of which appeared made of things they'd knitted or woven themselves. The Burners lived off the grid and away from the Corporations as much as possible.

Meri didn't blame them. She had been able to live outside

the rules within the city, but only because people feared her and thus no one dared to question her. Few others had the luxury of thumbing their noses at the Corporations.

One of the Burners stepped forward. It was impossible not to notice how the others deferred to her. She was short, stocky, and looked ready to take on any challenge despite her whimsical pigtails. Meri assumed this was 'the' Jackie. By the look in Jackie's eyes, if Meri took even one step out of place or looked crosswise at any of her people, Meri would be marched out of there quicker than she could blink.

Jackie also didn't look convinced that she liked what she was seeing.

"You look different than how Annamie described you." She stood with her arms crossed.

"I'm well aware," Meri replied.

A man stepped up next to Jackie and removed his helmet. Meri spied daemon ink on his neck and exposed arms. Another summoner. He walked up to her and grimaced. "You smell like crap."

Meri ran a hand through her hair and sighed, knowing he wasn't talking about her choice of body wash. "Yeah, I'm aware of that too. Let me explain."

"She's tainted, Jackie," the summoner revealed. "I can't explain how. I've never seen it before, but I wouldn't trust anything she says."

Determination fired within Meri's veins. "Annamie vouched for me. I am Meriwether Storm. I came here to summon a daemon and kill it."

The man shook his head and went to stand next to Jackie. "I've never heard of someone killing a daemon. How do you propose to do so?"

Meri reached to the sheath tucked at the small of her back and Jackie was pulled behind three of the Burners protectively while the summoner drew a blade on Meri. The atmosphere had shifted from tenuous to icy in a millisecond.

Meri froze and shook her head. "Look, my bad there. I'd like to show you the weapon I use to kill daemons. Okay?"

Everyone took a collective breath. The summoner was ready to dance with that knife of his.

"I'd like to see this thing," Jackie replied, pushing her way forward.

"I don't rec..." the summoner began.

"Show me," Jackie ordered.

The summoner kept his position flanking Jackie while Meri withdrew the blade. She held it out, allowing the last rays of dusk to fall upon the handle length. Light reflected from the handle but not from the blade itself. Instead, the metal absorbed all light; consuming it with the same hunger it did daemon flesh.

"This blade is the only thing that will kill them. Now, before you think of taking it and using it yourselves, know that I pay a hefty price for wielding it. Unless you want to be tainted like I am, you won't even touch it."

"This is why I stay out of all your crazy city bullshit," Jackie replied. "I go soft for a moment, and where does it get me? Trying to figure out if Annamie's been hoodwinked, which would be a rare thing indeed. What do you think, Martin?"

The summoner next to Jackie nodded. "What you're claiming you can do is unknown to us. If you let loose a daemon on our compound, we're the ones who have to pay the price. That's an impressive little dagger you've got there, but you've hidden all your skin. I can't even see your ink. How do we know you can handle daemons?"

Meri sheathed the tre'jor. "That's a fair question." Meri peeled off her robe and outer shirt, tossing them onto the trunk of her car.

Martin snorted and turned to the other three who Meri presumed were the backup muscle in case she was difficult and didn't want to leave when asked. "I'm not seeing any ink. Perhaps it's time you go now and not embarrass yourself further, novice."

"How about you promise not to freak the fuck out on me, all right?" Meri asked. Should she be doing this? How could she not? The alternative at this point was leaving and she couldn't, wouldn't back down.

"I'm not promising you shit," Jackie replied, looking more pissed by the second.

"All right, just don't shoot me." Meri took a deep breath, concentrated, and shook off her daemon appearance like a bird shakes off water after the rain. Her hair and eyes shifted back to brown, and her skin darkened to her old olive tone and revealed etching upon etching of daemon ink.

Immediately one of the burners backed up a few paces, tripped over his bike, and then fell on his ass.

"Holy shit!" Martin said.

Jackie looked her up and down with a mildly surprised, "Huh."

Meri lifted up her tank top and showed her stomach and then turned and showed her lower back and upper back to them. She didn't bother with her legs. The amount of daemon ink displayed should be well enough sufficient to prove her point.

"At least now you fit the description Annamie gave us," Jackie said.

Meri nodded and allowed the image to slip away. "But as Martin said, I'm tainted, and it's from my fights with the daemons. This next kill will help me save my friend. It's the only reason I'm here."

"And what will you do if the daemon wins the fight?" Martin asked.

Meri swallowed, hard. "The daemon will be constrained to the summoning space, so if I fail and die, it will be forced to depart, leaving your Enclave peacefully."

This assumed the Elder-daemon wasn't a soul-eater and thus couldn't teleport on her own, which Meri had no way of knowing. Just how confident was she in her ability to take down the Elder, or in Orias' predictions? If she were wrong, the Burners would pay -- but she didn't let a shred of doubt show on her face.

"You're in this game all or nothing?" Jackie asked. Hands on her hips she walked towards Meri, intimidating despite her diminutive stature.

"I'm in it to the end," Meri answered. "If I can't do the summoning here, I'll go back out there and kill off the hunters who are after me and then summon the one I'm after. That's assuming I can kill the other hunters, who I know nothing about. I'd hope I could deal with them one-on-one because I'm betting their fighting skills outmatch mine. It'd be much harder, and take more time, which is frankly the one thing I don't have right now."

She stared Jackie down for a few moments, and then Jackie shook her head.

"Sarah, George, Ben, you head back to the main camp.

Tell everyone there's a curfew tonight. I don't want anyone running around. If I find anyone down on this end of the Enclave, I am biting his or her head off myself. Got it?"

"We'll spread the word," Sarah replied. The three got on their bikes and left, leaving Martin, Jackie, and Meri alone.

"I want to be crystal clear with you, Meri. I'm only doing this because I owe Annamie, big time. She supported our Enclave from the beginning, and over the years has gotten us cash and medical supplies when no one else was willing to make the drives under the Corporate radar. Also, I can't wait to watch you skewer this piece of crap," Jackie said.

Meri was uplifted by the revelation about her long-time friend but then realized what Jackie had planned. "Wait. No. I don't want you two here. I can't endanger you like that," she shook her head.

"My Enclave, summoner. I call the shots. Martin's here to clean up afterward in case you fail. I'm here to witness from a distance and see you leave in the morning, assuming you're successful. We're here to help you prep and get this thing happening as quickly as possible. Got it?" Jackie replied.

Meri couldn't help but smile at Jackie's no-nonsense take on the situation. "I assume I'll be using the existing circle?"

"Yes. Building your summoning space inside of it should help reinforce the integrity of your sigils because of the residual magic," Martin replied.

"Agreed," Meri said. She opened her car and started toting supplies out and to the circle space. "Here we go."

CHAPTER 16

*I*t was well past dusk when the summoning space was prepared, and Meri's nerves were frazzled. Azimuth had warned her not to take on the Sin-Eater, but in her gut, she knew the Elder's strength would make her unstoppable against Saleigh's cabal. Also, Calloine's heightened sense of smell could aid her hunt for Azimuth in unknown territory. Meri couldn't deny wanting to settle the score with the Elder-daemon as well but considered this an opportunity of convenience, nothing more.

She had many reasons, many excuses to want Calloine dead. If she was honest with herself, vengeance still drove her hard.

Assuming she could overpower the daemon, which was a large assumption. Azimuth and Kobol had both assured her she was much too young, too weak, to handle Calloine, but what other choice did she have? If she went, Azimuth's life would be spared. She tried not to think of what would happen to her in the depths of Saleigh's burrow.

"I want both of you clear of the summoning space. And whatever you see, don't get involved," Meri said.

"I can't wait to see how you use this dagger of yours," Martin replied.

"So how does it work, anyway? Does it slice the daemon to ribbons?" Jackie asked.

"You'll see soon enough," Meri hoped.

"Well, good luck," Jackie replied.

"Thanks," Meri replied, surprised at the show of concern.

"Aw, I just don't want to be cleaning up Meri parts all day tomorrow. I've got better things to do," Jackie replied.

"Yeah." Meri rolled her eyes. "Thanks anyway."

Jackie and Martin remained by the car and bikes, a safe distance away but close enough to watch what was happening. This made Meri uneasy. She'd have preferred they never understood the workings of the tre'jor, but you don't always get everything you want.

Meri prodded her daemons and forced them to the surface of her mind and skin, allowing them to saturate her awareness. Her senses expanded, vision growing sharper with her gleaner's skills, her awareness of everyone around her heightening with her lust aspect, and her metal skills made the tre'jor's weight even surer in her grasp. She hoped that Calloine wouldn't be able to sense them over her humanity and her daemon ink shell. Meri had added the unnecessary skunk-smelling asafetida to her anointing oils, hoping its inherent, pungent stench would help mask her daemon scent. Lastly, Meri held the tre'jor in the palm of her hand, hidden only by the robe. She was taking no chances having to reach for it.

Meri walked through the aspects of the nighttime

summoning. Candles provided the only light, and skunky incense hung thick in the air. She felt the walls of the spectral space hold while the wind kicked up, swaying tree branches high overhead. Time and space didn't matter to the summoning nor the daemon, only the will of the summoner mattered.

Meri stood confidently. Her daemons had no fears about Calloine. They had all been in battles before. Meri had no exact plan how to kill the Elder daemon. She just wanted to be as opportunistic as she'd been with the first three. After all, no daemon suspected she'd have a tre'jor. It was her ace in the hole, and Calloine had to touch her to do the Sin-Eating bit. It all depended on how determined Calloine was for another meal, and how distractible she would be.

"Get on with it!" Jackie yelled from the sidelines. Meri heard Martin say something to her, but not what, and Jackie quieted down. Meri had to admit: she was dawdling.

Meri bent down and touched the sigil. It flared with unearthly light, illuminating the forest. Meri performed the incantations given to her by Azimuth, word for word, in the singsong voice as the directions instructed. If she hadn't known better, she'd have been singing a nursery rhyme about lost children and ships lost at sea, but knowing this was no doubt how her parents last moments had played out dampened her potentially playful refrains. Moments later Calloine rose up from Sheol, an apparition through the thin void rendered permeable via the summoning's sigil.

She was a thin, ghostly figure for a daemon. Calloine floated above the ground, clad in scraps of white fabric. Her eyes and long, wispy hair were a pale gray color. The overall effect made her look a fragile, weak thing. If you'd met her on the street, your first instinct would be to take her in, wrap her in a warm blanket, and feed her something that would put some weight on her.

"Why have you summoned me?" Calloine asked, her tiny plaintive voice sounding so tired that for a moment Meri felt sorry for her.

Meri lifted her right arm. The robe fell away, revealing the daemon ink underneath. "I need to rewind time. I understand you can do this for me. Take away some of my history." She dropped her arm and the robe settled back into place.

Calloine smiled, revealing two rows of very sharp, long teeth. "I can. Are you willing to pay the price?"

"Yes," Meri replied. With her right hand, she withdrew a picture of herself on a swing set pushed by her father -- a happy time before she'd ever learned of daemons -- from a pocket in her robe and held it out. "From my childhood. My memories, covered in my tears."

Calloine approached and plucked the picture from Meri's grasp, balled it up, and ate it like a bon-bon without even looking at the image. "As I consume your memories, you'll feel them slipping away. If you try and hold onto them..." She left the threat hanging.

"I won't," Meri replied.

Calloine grinned from ear to ear, revealing far too many teeth. "That's what they all say." She motioned for Meri to give over her arm, and Meri did. Calloine's icy touch slid up Meri's arm pushing the robe out of the way.

"You reek, summoner."

"Sorry," Meri shrugged, fear tugging at her gut. "Too many summonings this week. Thus why I require your services."

Calloine laughed. "If you want, I could take more." She looked up, her hungry eyes questioning.

"I wouldn't mind," Meri replied. "As you can see, there's a lot I need to clean out."

"Let's see if you can endure through my first bite, shall we? Then we can negotiate further, perhaps?" Her eyes roved Meri's skin. Was she picking out the particular ink she wanted to sample?

"Perhaps," Meri replied. Trailian pointed out how hunger-drunk the Elder was already, and Meri felt the blade descend a few inches towards her target. Mahkra wanted to see the Sin-Eater brought low. He'd heard tales of her voracious appetite, and hovered on the edge of adding his full potency to the attack.

Calloine held Meri's right arm in her left hand like a vice and wrapped her right arm around Meri's body as one might a lover, pulling her in close. If Meri hadn't had the tre'jor, she'd be in full panic right now instead of on the verge, and then Trailian's will melded with hers, and they waited for the vulnerable moment together. All of the centuries bending metal to Trailian's will, including weapons, flashed into Meri's mind in an instant. Trailian's skill with blades was formidable, but would it be enough?

The Arch-daemon spread her jaws wide, saliva dripping from her long rows of razor-sharp teeth. Meri didn't flinch. She needed Calloine committed and engaged before she struck, just as she had with Mahkra, to lower the risks of the daemon attacking her during the struggle.

However, she didn't anticipate the searing pain of Calloine's teeth tearing into her flesh, the blood welling around the daemons maw. The physical pain was eclipsed by mental anguish as her mind blurred and sadness welled within her. The childhood image from her photograph, of her on a swing set being pushed by her father, filled her mind. Just as quickly, it was ripped away and torn apart as if it had never existed. Meri tried to remember what she'd been thinking of and stared at Calloine feasting on the daemon ink on her arm.

Trailian railed in a fury, grasping the tre'jor in her left hand, primed to act. Tears ran down Meri's face. The pain in her arm was nothing. She'd lost something. Something important, but she couldn't remember what it was. If she could just remember.

A shot rang out in the night and Meri watched while Calloine grunted after being hit with a rifle round. It shocked Meri out of her stupor, and Calloine started to shudder. Meri realized Martin fired the shot. Perhaps he'd sensed Meri was floundering.

Calloine didn't release her grip. If anything, she dug in deeper.

Clear-headed, Meri swung the tre'jor into Calloine's back. Calloine, retaining her grip on Meri, swung her to the ground and Meri felt her head crack hard enough that her ears rung. The Sin-eater released her jaw's grip on Meri's arm and instead closed her jaw around Meri's neck. Her blood rushed out and soaked the ground beneath her, and she heard footsteps running despite the pounding in her ears. The blade was lodged in Calloine's back, but Meri managed to dig it deeper with Trailian's metal-moving assistance.

"Don't step into the circle!" Meri croaked out and then heard feet grind into the loose rocks of the forest floor. Pain washed through her. Meri dropped her human guise, hoping to mitigate the blood loss, letting her daemon essence rise to the surface. Calloine noticed and roared like a beast, clawing and biting at Meri, furious at the guise.

Meri heard another rifle shot, and then another, and yet still Calloine's gruesome attack continued. Meri didn't dare try to move Calloine off of her. She couldn't allow the blade to leave the daemon's flesh. Her daemons fortified her strength, but her consciousness was fading as her blood rushed out onto the forest floor below.

Calloine's flesh turned from ghostly pale to charcoal black, and she howled like a wind through a long-dead forest before collapsing in upon herself.

Martin swore, and Jackie screamed, but then they were both by her side, pressing torn scraps of shirts to Meri's throat and arm to stop the bleeding. Meri watched Calloine's spirit gather and roll in the air around her.

"Back away, now!" Meri said though it came out broken and hoarse. She pointed to the space above her.

When Martin and Jackie saw the amorphous cloud of gray mist hovering above Meri, they obeyed. Ten seconds later, Calloine's essence descended onto Meri like a cloud of black ash, first wrapping itself around her body, and then forcing itself down her nose and throat. Even in death, the Elder-daemon appeared to resist the process, clogging Meri's throat until spots formed in her vision from the lack of oxygen. Meri's back arched in pain and near asphyxiation while the last of Calloine eased itself inside of her before she slumped down and gasped for breath. The body shakes started as the pain, inside and out, hit Meri.

"You are one crazy-ass bitch," announced Jackie, kneeling down and applying pressure to Meri's still-bleeding wounds.

"Now I understand how she's tainted," Martin said. "But I'm not sure she'll live through these wounds."

"If I die," Meri croaked out. "I don't know what happens to the daemons inside of me."

Jackie and Martin shared a look. "Then you're not gonna die. At least, not in my Enclave," Jackie replied. "There's no way I want that bitch freed up."

"Let's get her to the car. We can treat her better at the community center," Martin said.

Meri passed out from the pain when they lifted her body.

Sometime later Meri awoke, bleary-eyed and aching all over. Her neck felt like tenderized meat, and her right arm was on fire. Would she heal more quickly with the daemon hosts? Meri could only hope so. She didn't have time to recover right now. She heard people moving in the room around her, but no one was hovering nearby. Meri took the opportunity for an internal self-check.

Everything felt off kilter. Meri felt stretched to the gills and wrong inside. Calloine's presence was undeniable and much more pronounced than Mahkra's ever had been. Her energy was a ruthless slimy substance. She was enraged over being caught, and now that Meri was awake, memories began to filter through her consciousness.

Memories of her parents and their death at Calloine's teeth.

At that moment, Meri realized this new boarder was a vindictive creature and tried to pull away in a panic, but there was nowhere to go from the massive force suddenly occupying vast regions of her mind. Calloine picked through her consciousness, tossing away today's motivations and pouncing upon Meri's vengeance for killing her parents, and she was gleefully happy to show Meri how they died in exquisite detail.

Meri had no defense. She knew how to get a handle on her other daemons, but this new Arch-daemon was so new and so powerful, she couldn't hold back the images before they poured out in gruesome detail.

The old, gutted house her parents used for summonings. Her parents covered in daemon ink, doing a dual summoning, holding multiple pictures at the ready for offerings to the Sin-Eater. Calloine, appearing to her parents just as she had to Meri.

Her mother, Bethany, went first, and Meri could sense her trepidation. Her father, Gary, reassured her he'd watch over her. They'd always done that, watched each other's backs and handled the daemons together. It had proven a good strategy.

Meri watched her mother offer up her arm for Calloine to feed on. Calloine set into her, and despite the pain, her mother didn't pull away. She allowed the transaction even as her chosen memories began to strip away. Bethany never fought back. She did everything right.

So what went wrong?

The images kept playing through Meri's mind. Calloine finished feeding on Bethany, and when the daemon licked her open wound, it closed, leaving a scar in its wake on the pristine skin. Calloine released her, and Bethany wilted and fell to the ground, listless. Gary tried to rouse his wife, but she was too foggy from the experience. He became at first concerned, and then irate.

Calloine indicated it was Gary's turn. He looked at her with distrust and hate.

To Meri, it was the apparent beginning of the end. She wanted to turn away, but inside her mind, there was nowhere to turn. She tried again to compel the Elder-daemon to stop, but it did no good.

Gary denied Calloine her due, convinced she'd injured his wife. Calloine, in all her ethereal charm, couldn't have appeared more pleased by his insults and repudiations. The Elder-daemon seemed to take his attitude with a healthy dose of glee, not at all upset by Gary's distress over his wife's condition.

"Again, do you refuse to follow through on your side of the summoning?" Calloine had asked.

"You bet I'm refusing you!" He exclaimed. "You haven't abided by yours!" He began chanting a devocation spell meant to send Calloine back to Sheol, but such things were tricky at best, and as an Elder daemon she resisted him.

"No, summoner, I will take what is my due," Calloine replied. Her mother was curled on the floor, a weak groan escaping her lips. She didn't see Calloine set upon Gary in a blur of speed. Nor did she see his throat ripped open, ear to ear. But Meri watched as blood poured down her father's chest and spattered upon her mother's face, rousing her from her daemon-induced fugue.

Her father crumpled to the ground next to her mother, and Calloine feasted upon Meri's dad's flesh, organs, and bone. The ongoing sounds furthered Bethany's awakening, and soon she opened her eyes and took in the sight of her half-eaten husband sprawled next to her while she laid in an ever-widening pool of his blood.

Her revulsion and pain were something Meri shared equally. Silently Meri pleaded with her mother to do nothing, to lie there and be safe. Calloine was done with her, and when she had finished consuming her father, she would depart.

Bethany was unable to control her emotions, and it broke Meri's heart all over again. Her mother valiantly, if feebly, began chanting devocations while also launching herself upon Calloine, pushing with all her might. But her mother was taxed, and her efforts only served to break her bond with the Elder-daemon who looked up at her with a wide, bloody grin.

"Can't live without him, Bethany?"

To her credit, her mother never stopped chanting the devocations until her voice box was torn clean from her body. At that point, Meri gagged and vomited. Someone helped her, but she was lost to the visions and couldn't see them or respond coherently. The images continued to play out in her mind until the entirety of her parents were consumed and Calloine left for Sheol.

The house was just as she remembered finding it. She saw again the pools of blood, hand prints, and footprints showing a struggle, a few scraps of clothing, evidence of the summoning, and nothing else. Meri vomited again, and this time someone was there to wash her face.

Nothing could wash away her newfound anger towards her parents. She'd always thought of her parents as innocent victims and pro summoners. From what Calloine had shown her, her father had refused the terms of the binding, sealing his death warrant. She had more sympathy for her mother who was reacting in shock, but their decisions had left her an orphan.

Meri hated Calloine and her parents for her years spent seeking retribution.

Her other daemon occupants rallied with her to gain control over Calloine. Evidently, they didn't like the Elder daemon being in charge either. Meri was emotionally ripped apart, and all of her anger and rage came to the forefront. She reached again to suppress Calloine as she'd done with the others, and bit by bit gained power over the wily beast. But it took all of her control, and she sensed the balance was tenuous, at best.

Meri finally opened her eyes. Jackie, Martin, and a male nurse stood next to her. Calloine bucked in her grip, wanting a taste of Martin, but Meri and her daemons held firm.

"You look like shit. How're ya feeling?" Jackie asked.

Based on how she felt, she didn't doubt it. Her shirt was torn to bits and covered in blackened blood. Was her blood black now? Meri stared in shock. Of course, the daemons taint. The blanket they'd thrown over her was also soaked in vomit, and her head pounded in time to an unseen drum. "Like Sheol," Meri answered. She lifted her right arm and saw the bandage there. "Can you take that off so I can see it?"

"I don't recommend it," the male in charge of medical responded. "It's already infected."

"Do it," Meri replied. "Please," she said to Jackie.

Jackie shrugged and carefully removed the bandaging. Meri looked at the wound and fought the urge to gag. Where she had expected on her forearm to see holes matching those perfect rows of Calloine's predatory teeth, instead the skin was ripped loose in two large jagged semi-circles, puffed up and oozing copious amounts of green and yellow pus. She'd mild infections before from cuts, and this went well beyond slapping a little antibiotic ointment on the problem.

Then she remembered how Calloine had fixed her mother's wounds by licking them shut. Perhaps the disease was also the cure?

Help me fix this, or you'll be feeling my pain soon enough, bitch. Meri threatened Calloine. This is your home now. Deal with it.

Calloine rebuffed her, effortlessly slipping away underneath her mental hold, as difficult to control as before, but less primed for retribution. Help me. Meri demanded, holding her bloody flesh in front of her face.

She sensed the Elder-daemon capitulate, although she wasn't sure why, and then Meri's salivary glands at once dripped with a sickly sweet-tasting substance she wanted to spit out. She remembered the scenes Calloine had shown her and how she'd healed her mother's arm. Meri went to work licking her torn up flesh, pushing the disgusting and putrid tastes in her mouth to the back of her mind.

"Woah! I wouldn't do that!" the nurse reached out to grab her arm away, but Martin held him off.

Although the daemon-enhanced spit was painful on contact, the reforming of the flesh happened seamlessly, leaving minimal scarring. However the bruising remained. Can't win them all. Meri reached for the bandages at her neck, and Jackie moved in to assist, detaching the tape.

Once it was removed, Meri spat on both of her hands and rubbed her saliva across her palms. She applied it to the bites on her neck and the cuts everywhere else she could find them. She repeated the process numerous times, and although Martin and Jackie could handle it, the nurse had to walk away at one point, a sheen of sweat covering his pale skin.

"This is the single most amazingly disgusting thing I've ever seen," Jackie said.

"You've got that right. But at least we know you'll live," Martin replied.

Meri could tell when the cuts were closed because the skin was smooth, but she still felt the muscle tenderness and bruising. She sat up, and wooziness struck her hard.

"Careful. We couldn't give you a transfusion," Martin explained. "Not only do we not know your blood type, but you're also, well, bit different."

Meri tried not to laugh.

"That's okay. I didn't intend to tax your resources. I brought plenty of money with me. It's in my car, and you're welcome to it all for your aid." Meri rubbed her head, which had an enormous bruise on the back where she'd cracked it on the ground. A minor injury. It hurt less than her heart.

"It'll help us out," Jackie replied. "We're always in need of cash. My thanks."

"Thank you for not having Martin shoot me along with Calloine out there," Meri croaked out, her voice still rough. With the mention of the Elder daemon's name, Calloine bucked, and Meri hunkered down, gripping the bed while she mentally grasped at the daemon's reins.

Calloine overpowered Meri's will and stepped into the lead, imbuing Meri's skin and thoughts with her own. Her hunger was ever-present, an insatiable need, and before her stood Martin, filled with a handful of tasty hors d'oeuvres in the form of daemon ink, which she'd be only too happy to take off his hands. Calloine sensed he didn't want them anyway, not that it mattered. Her hunger drove her, guided her, had never failed her.

Meri stood, eyes glued to Martin. A step forward had the IV tugging on her left arm. She pulled it out and licked the wound shut, allowing herself to refocus on her quarry.

Her transformation wasn't lost on either Jackie or Martin. They shared a dark look. Meri took a single step forward, and Jackie pulled a revolver seemingly out of thin air and leveled it between Meri's eyes.

"You may heal wounds with your spit," Jackie said, "but I don't think you can cure a bullet to your brain, so how 'bout you settle the crazy outta you real fast now?"

Meri didn't move, but Calloine assured her she was quick enough to take Jackie. She eyed Martin's exposed ink, such tasty little morsels. He didn't have a firearm on him. She scanned the room. Was the guard at the door armed? He had a radio and could call for backup, which would certainly cut her feeding short.

"Hey! Meri!" Jackie waved the gun in her face. "Eyes on me."

Meri returned her focus to the short woman, waiting for her to drop her guard. "Do you remember why you came here?"

Meri stared at her and smiled. Jackie swore.

"The daemon's in control, Jackie," Martin said. "Meri's not in charge anymore. She's lost it. Shoot her now before she's gone over the edge."

Meri cocked her head at Martin and frowned. Someone

had said that to her once, but who? Something about not taking on another daemon. There was some risk?

Calloine wrestled with her mind, and Meri forced herself not to scream, hands over her ears, eyes closed. When she reopened her eyes, she was panting, focused on Martin's right wrist. A scrap of loathing daemon was lodged in ink there. It was a rare one, to be sure. Quite a delicacy. She'd get the entire story of it when she lifted it from him.

"Meri!" Jackie screamed her name, gun still aimed at her head.

It was painful to hold her attention on Jackie, but she managed it. "What?" she yelled back.

"Isn't there somewhere you need to go now?" Jackie asked in a raised voice.

Meri worked to focus her mind on the question, but the hunger kept driving her thoughts away. "Where?" Meri asked, lost to all but the need.

"You said you had a friend who needed your help. That's why you came here. You did this crazy shit for your friend," Jackie explained. The gun never wavered. "And now you're acting like one of them."

Meri stared at Jackie, and a cold sweat broke out on her skin.

Friend. She had to save her friend.

Azimuth.

Calloine had killed her parents. She'd been warned by Azimuth not to kill any other daemons. He'd said her system couldn't handle it yet.

She was flashing out. Now she understood. Her personality was being burned to bits by the Elder-daemon.

"I can't let that happen," she said to Jackie and her inner daemons.

"Damn straight," Jackie replied, nodding support, but she didn't lower the revolver. "Pull your shit together!"

Orias knew. "He foresaw I could do this, and he's never wrong." The notion gave Meri a mental fortitude and belief in herself she'd lacked. When she reached out to enforce her will over Calloine this time, it stuck like glue. Gone was her previous, slippery façade. Meri had her hold, and she wasn't letting go.

Meri forced Calloine down like the others, proving she would not allow her mind to be overrun. This time the Elder-daemon screamed in frustration, but no one heard except her cellmates. In minutes, Meri was calmly herself again.

"I'm sorry about that, Jackie, Martin. It won't happen again," Meri said. She leaned up against the bed and took a drink of water from a glass on the bedside table.

Jackie kept the gun leveled. "You sure you're done with the bat shit?"

She nodded. "Soon I'll be leaving to help that friend of mine."

Jackie sighed and holstered her gun. "What the hell was that crap?"

"I couldn't handle her for a bit there. But I've got her leashed, and it won't be an issue going forward. It's just the initial shift in energy. Thanks for talking me down, Jackie."

"No problem," she replied with a half-smile. "I'm willing to hold a gun to your head anytime. By the way, your car is all packed up and ready whenever you are."

Time. "What time is it?" Meri asked, anxious.

"'Two o'clock," Martin answered. "How soon do you need to leave?"

Meri groaned. It was already the afternoon of the second day, she had lost hours of precious time recuperating, and she was still a mess. But she thought she knew why Orias did what he did.

Meri could smell all the daemon essences off Martin. Every single one. Although Calloine had almost killed her and caused her to flash-out, she now grinned as she realized the daemon's skills. Yes, she was insatiably hungry, but more importantly, Calloine also could smell other daemon's abilities like a bloodhound could track a scent.

Meri scented the daemon Martin had summoned multiple times to heal a friend's daughter of a terminal illness in exchange for blood payments. She doubted the Burners would approve, but it wasn't her place to disclose his secrets.

Once in Saleigh's burrow, just how close would she have to get to Azimuth to allow this new nose of hers to scent him out? Her lust Arch-daemon stirred, savoring the idea of a hunt. She also noticed it was hungry.

They all were.

"I need to leave now," Meri replied.

"I can show you to your car," Martin offered.

Meri looked back and forth between the two of them. "Yeah, um, I'm not taking my car this time. You all mind if I pick it up in say, two days?"

CHAPTER 17

eri stood in the meditation circle under cover of darkness, once again flanked by Martin and Jackie. Meri had changed into her all-black, heavy-duty camo gear she'd brought along for her trip to Saleigh's burrow, assuming she'd gotten this far. After all, if it was good enough for the military, it was good enough for Sheol. Her pants and vest pockets were filled to the brim with a flashlight, snack bars, a water bottle, other blades Kobol had given her to practice with, and of course her trusty tre'jor -- assuming she didn't die within two minutes of arrival.

Wanting to remain connected in some way to these people who had helped her, and perhaps be able to return the favor someday, Meri picked up a flat, polished piece of hematite from the ground around the meditation circle. Trailian recognized the iron ore in it at once, aware it was practically pure metal. Forming an upraised "M" on the surface was nothing for her daemon occupant with metal-manipulation skills. A mere parlor trick, but it served her purpose. Meri then focused her will on creating a ward around the stone, similar to the ones Azimuth had used, but this time meant to invoke herself. It needed a few tries, but she was finally satisfied with the results. A light tapping on the upraised M attuned her senses, much like a chime going off in her mind.

Meri smiled and held out the stone to Jackie, who was none too eager to take it. "Go on, it won't bite you," Meri said." Instead, Martin took it, jolting in surprise upon contact with the stone. "It's a present," Meri explained.

"You've placed daemon wards on it," Martin replied, yet he held it in his hand, studying and poking at it.

Each poke chimed in Meri's mind, bringing a distinct image of Martin's face to mind, the one who was currently invoking the ward. "Momma always told me to use what I've got. And stop that, mister. That's my calling card you're using!"

"Oh." He looked at her and then at the stone again, stroking the lines of power she'd imbued around it.

"Look, I figure I owe you. If you need me, use that to call me. I'll come by as soon as I'm able," Meri said.

Jackie swiped up the hematite from Martin and pocketed it. "We'll keep it in a safe place. I wouldn't want you to get called by someone other than me and arrive thinking you were among friends," Jackie replied. "And thanks. Not that I imagine we'll ever need your help, but it's good to know you're on our side. The alternative wouldn't be pleasant."

Meri couldn't help the smirk that formed on her lips. "I understand." She turned to Martin and gave him a serious look. "You don't summon anymore, do you?"

He shook his head, his dark hair hiding his downcast eyes. When he looked up, Meri saw the conflict he tried to hide. "I maintain the wards on the compound, to keep the suckers out. But I'd be lying if I said I wasn't tempted to take a job to earn the Enclave some cash."

"Well, don't," Meri replied, looking at his skin, smelling the daemon essence he'd exposed himself to. "Never again. Each time you do, you lose a part of your soul to them. I got lucky." Meri heard the sarcasm in her voice in those final words and saw the reflecting pity in his gaze as he looked at her anew.

He held out his hand, and Meri took it. "My word, Meri. Never again. Not for any reason. I'll spread the word about the consequences. Not everyone will listen or care. But some will heed the warning."

He let go of her hand, but relief washed through her. She'd saved one. Perhaps more would follow. It would have to do.

"Thank you, Martin. Now, if you'll excuse me, I'll be on my way."

"For the record, you don't look ready to take on shit," Jackie replied, tugging on one of her braids.

Meri loved Jackie for her brutal honesty. She was very likely right. "It's day two. Tomorrow my friend will die if I do nothing. If I do something, he might live."

"And you?" Jackie asked.

"I'll look and feel about this bad off if I wait until tomorrow," Meri answered.

"You know that's not what I meant." Jackie cast her a withering glance.

"Yeah, I know. Thanks again for your help," Meri said to them both. She turned and walked into the forest.

Essentially, Meri was alone with her inner daemons.

The moon was low in the sky, but it was plenty of light for her to see. She leaned against a boulder at the edge of a small clearing and took in the beauty of the summer night. Everything was so still and quiet; colors reduced without the light of day into stark contrasts. Not entirely black and white, but almost.

Sometimes she thought of her daemons by their names, sometimes by their abilities. The gleaner was already a faded personality, his skills left behind in easy fashion. He'd been a low-level daemon and one who'd been under her skin before. It had made for an easy transition.

Calloine had almost flamed her out, and Meri feared dealing with her power again, especially her hunger. She was gambling on Calloine being able to sniff out Azimuth, but how could Meri keep her focused?

Meri focused on Mahkra and Trailian and roused them both. Neither was eager to talk, but they waited to see what Meri would do.

"Where is Saleigh's burrow located? Both of you know. Show me a safe location inside or out to port into," Meri commanded.

The daemons hesitated. "We feel this is an unwise course of action," Mahkra replied.

"You bound me to the daemon that's held there. As I'm sure you've noticed, I'm in need. The discomfort I feel will only worsen, and you will share in it with me."

"I've heard your talk and your thoughts," Mahkra replied. "If you go to Saleigh's burrow, you will die. If you cease to exist, what do you think will happen to me?"

"I don't know. You'll float off and find another host?"

"Idiot summoner. The blade you used to kill me forced

the transaction. If you die, I will cease to exist along with you. And although what existence I have here is paltry, at best, I'll take it over nothing," Mahkra replied.

"I agree. Why should I help you in this way?" Trailian added. "You soon will have the best of me, and I will fade into nothingness as Penethewes did. I gain nothing."

"By not going to the one I'm bound to, I will suffer, and so will you," Meri reminded them.

"Orias said Azimuth would be dead by tomorrow," Mahkra replied. "Then the enchantment will be broken, and you can work off your needs on any available body you find convenient. You will. It's inevitable."

Meri's heart skipped a beat. They were right. She had nothing to entice them to comply, and they had every reason to refuse her. She could port to the burrow and try to convince her cabal to let her tag along, but Orias had already said Azimuth would surely die in that combination of events.

"What can I do that will make you give me what I want?" Meri asked.

Both daemons warmed to her, pressing their essences invitingly against her mind. The effect was stifling, and for a moment, she fought to draw breath.

"Now that you mention it, summoner, there is one thing," Mahkra replied.

Meri's gut tightened. "What?"

"You see, for all those millennia I lived under Saleigh's rule, I could never stand the bastard."

"Right." Meri did not like where this was going.

"If you're willing to change your focus towards retribution, then we'd be only too happy to help you out," Mahkra explained. "In the end, you'd win Saleigh's burrow and all the spoils therein. Including your little friend, Azimuth."

Kill Saleigh?

"I'm nowhere near strong enough to manage what you're asking, Mahkra."

She heard laughter inside her head. Mahkra's, Trailian's, and now Calloine's.

"Calloine is ancient. The combined might of an Elder and an Arch-daemon should be enough to take him down despite his more aggressive powers," Mahkra replied.

I could flash-out. Lose control and leave them in charge of my body. Saleigh's burrow would have a new, more terrifying leader.

But Orias had put his faith in her. Meri looked at the options and saw no other path forward.

"All right. We'll go after Saleigh, using Calloine," Meri replied. The Sin-Eater rejoiced, slithering around inside Meri's mind, digging painfully at the recesses of her past with her claws.

I'll be damned if I'm letting them call the shots. I got her under control once, and I can do it again.

"Go ahead," Mahkra replied. "Hand her the reins, and we'll share the most advantageous position to port into."

"And I can trust you on this?" Meri asked.

"Think about it, Meri. We all get what we want," Mahkra replied.

Meri held back a snarky retort. Stopping now equaled failure. She refused to fail. Putting Calloine in charge was in no way what Meri wanted.

Meri reached for the now-cooperative Calloine and invited her into the forefront of her consciousness. The other daemons didn't back off, if anything, they crowded in, allowing all of Meri's abilities to manifest at the fullest. It was disorienting and painful to manage.

Meri pulled out the insurance packet Azimuth had given her on their second meeting. It contained a cutting of his hair, fingernail, and most importantly, a small thimbleful of his blood. "Will this aid you in tracking him?" she asked Calloine.

Her eyes caught upon the thimbleful container of blood in the packet. "Yes. Give me the blood," Calloine demanded, reverent tones fighting her eagerness. Meri's mouth watered in anticipation.

Meri ripped open the package and retrieved the vial, trying not to think of the inevitable next step. She tucked the remainder of the bag back into her pocket.

Calloine shook the vial, popped it open, and downed it without hesitation. Meri expected to gag, but to her disgrace, Azimuth's blood tasted like a fine liquor. Calloine reflexively began to tally Azimuth's plethora of daemons, but Meri snarled in response.

"Stop it. Now! Was that enough to track him?" Meri asked.

"I'm an expert tracker, and his scent is distinctive. Let's hunt," Calloine replied.

"Wonderful," Mahkra purred. "And now that we have that taken care of, here's the location for you ladies."

Images flashed through her mind almost too quickly to process until she realized he was giving her an extensive view of the entire burrow. It was segmented, unlike Belial's, with gates and guards between the different wards. Mahkra's area had been one. Cian had his own, as did Saleigh. Unlike Belial's burrow, Saleigh's wasn't cozy and built to accommodate Liminals. This place was dark and filled with secret chambers and passageways, all of which Mahkra had been privy to while alive. Mahkra didn't reveal a section where prisoners were kept, but Meri knew it was there. Mahkra must be saving the location of the crypts for after Saleigh's demise, and Meri didn't blame him. After all, if she knew where Azimuth was being kept, would she keep her word and go after Saleigh first?

Likely not.

Most of Saleigh's lair was warded, making it impossible to port into directly. A smart move on his part for just this sort of situation. Mahkra knew what tunnels led into the lair from the outside where porting was allowed.

Meri wasted no time. Her anxiety was eclipsed by the haze and hunger filling her mind. She knew she had to act now or lose the opportunity to save Azimuth forever.

Meri closed her eyes, pictured the outside of the hidden tunnel to Saleigh's lair, and ported.

---

*M*eri opened her eyes to a grim, dark landscape filled with blackened rock and rolling fog. The distinct taint of a swamp assaulted her senses, but there was no sound or sight of water. She stood against a rough rock wall stretching as far as the eye could see in the night and out from the mists, sounds of something being chewed upon caught and held Meri's attention. The noise echoed into the distance and Meri gathered she was in some grand, cavernous structure. Calloine didn't scent the creature as a daemon but a lower life form roaming the wastes, feasting on something unseen. All of this was bizarre and new to Meri, but to her daemons, it was banal and held no interest. She tried to shut out her fears over the oddities and stay present in the moment.

Meri turned her gleaner's attention away from the beast and hunted for the burrow instead. At first, she couldn't see the tunnel opening, but Mahkra and Trailian remembered it well enough, having once called this place home. When she looked closely, she saw faint evidence of foot and hoof prints leading in and out of a nearby crevice in an otherwise unremarkable wall, so she knew she'd found it.

Meri tiptoed along the edge of the wall when a new scent drifted her way. Calloine licked her lips in anticipation, identifying the scent of a lurking envy daemon. Meri swore. The tunnel was guarded. Of course, it was. What else had she expected?

Calloine was not in the least deterred. If anything, she was pulled forward by the smell.

"Did you have a cabal, Calloine?" Meri asked.

"Never," Calloine's voice saturated Meri's essence, filled her, as they continued this internal conversation. "I came from a time before such petty groupings. Back when our bloodlines were pure and vigorous. We each stood alone. Those who were weak fell. It's how things should have remained."

"But I, a mere human, took you down. How do you feel about that?" Meri asked. Infused with Calloine, her thoughts were emotionally wild yet focused with hunger. She moved to the tunnel entrance.

"You are no mere human. You had the might of an Archdaemon and two others within you. You also had a weapon without equal and a willingness to sacrifice everything to accomplish your goals. There is nothing 'mere' about you, human. You are also as vicious as I am, if you'd only admit it to yourself. Now with my ancient power harnessed, you will see just how far you can go."

Not pausing in her stride, Meri rounded the corner and came upon the envy daemon unawares. The small-but-muscular purple beast leaped at her, but Calloine's addition had made Meri potent despite her injuries. Meri grabbed the daemon by the throat in mid-air, spinning and throwing it against the far wall. It hit with a satisfying crunch, and Meri closed in, her fingers growing claws. She straddled the beast, more of a dog than a human-like form, and sliced through its neck. Ebony blood flowed freely, and Calloine urged her to drink.

"Is this the same as when I use the dagger?" Meri asked.

"No, you won't take on its spirit. I need this to survive and gain strength. If you want me to fight, this is necessary. This is a cost of harboring my essence, Meri," Calloine explained, the hunger evident in her words.

Meri was committed. She let her mind drift and allowed Calloine her due. She consumed the daemon's blood greedily, but Meri sensed she fed not simply on the liquid itself but also on the remaining life essence. The daemon's blood and skin had a unique taste and flavor, as well as a particular intensity unique to its power level. When she was done, all that remained was a dried husk. It was cleaner than consuming a human, yet the blood on her hands and the corpse still marked it as death, albeit daemon. Meri felt alive with a vibrancy she couldn't express.

"Another two or three of those and Saleigh won't stand a chance," Calloine said.

Meri shuddered. How often would she have to satisfy this new hunger? She knew how demanding Lust was, and it was only at an Arch-level. Would she have to eat daemons daily to survive?

She shook off the morose thoughts and cleared her mind. Now was not the time. If she survived, there would be plenty of time to worry about the details of her day-to-day life later.

Together they rose and checked their surroundings. Mahkra confirmed the tunnel led into the heart of the compound, straight into Saleigh's innermost chambers. Still, Meri was wary, having encountered only one guard on duty.

"It doesn't matter," Calloine replied, her bloodthirsty interests no secret. "We continue regardless. Even if there had been ten. Yes?"

"Yes," Meri replied, but she couldn't shake her anxiety.

The tunnel was filled with switchbacks and stairs leading up, then down. There was no rhyme or reason to the flow, and the stairs felt endless. She'd grown irritable with the never-ending passage into the depths of unfriendly territory when the smell of fresh meat presented itself.

Or better put--fresh daemon. Calloine cloaked Meri's smell as a trained hunter would when nearing her prey, dampening her natural scent and exuding a scent that mimicked the dank and muddy scent of the tunnel behind them, hiding from detection while she scented out the four daemons in the next room. One was a lowly succubus, while the others were all daemons with an actual tang to their scent: jealousy, rage, and fear defined their abilities.

According to Mahkra, this was Saleigh's parlor, located

outside his bedchamber. The tunnel opening was hidden behind a decorative wall tapestry, and Meri could hear the conversation in the room despite the steady thump of music they were listening to.

"Are any of these Saleigh or Cian?" she asked her internal confidants.

"No, but one is Namae. She is the most human-looking of them all. She has golden eyes. Saleigh beds her often, so she is likely to know where he is," Trailian answered.

"I scent no others in adjacent spaces," Calloine said. "We must move on these now. We'll hide the bodies here in the tunnel afterward. Give over to me, Meri."

"Do it, but remember we must question Namae," Meri replied, surrendering full control.

Calloine moved her body faster than Meri thought possible, sliding out from behind the tapestry. Three of the daemons were sitting around, talking, while the fourth, Namae, was getting herself a drink. Calloine pursued the four daemons like a mountain lion descending upon unsuspecting hikers. She broke the neck of the first daemon before any of them even noticed her and attacked the second daemon while watching his stunned expression as his neck cracked before the third even reacted.

He, at least, jumped up with a start. Calloine met him face-to-face, but he was half-drunk. She ripped his throat out and showed it to him.

Meri watched from the sidelines inside herself, reflecting on the persistent focus Calloine had with throats, and how she kept their deaths in tempo with the beats of the raucous music. The sound of the third daemon's body crumpling to the floor drew Namae's attention.

"What's up with the quiet, boys?" she said as she turned back around. "Nothing to say?"

Her eyes fixed on Meri, still holding a bloody, dripping trachea in her hand, and then spotted the bodies of her dead companions. She spilled her drink, the crystal tumbler shattering on the stone floor. Meri dropped the trachea on the body, not bothering to wipe her hands clean before grabbing her blade.

Calloine leaped over to the shell-shocked Namae, claws around her neck while Meri held the tre'jor in her other hand, a millimeter from Namae's belly. She didn't want to use the blade again, but knowing she was Saleigh's special girl meant she might be privy to critical information.

"We can do this the easy way or the excruciating way," Meri explained. "Either way, you tell us where Saleigh is, and you tell us now. I'm not going to negotiate with you."

Meri saw the conflict play across Namae's features, in her golden eyes. She was beautiful yet tough, and she struggled for a moment in Meri's grip, testing her strength. Meri touched the dagger to Namae's skin and watched panic alight in her features as she felt its odd, disturbing energy. "Now, Namae."

Namae shook her head. "Never."

Meri allowed Calloine's essence into the foreground, and her scent enveloped Namae, whose eyes widened like a doe's when she feels the mountain lion's teeth sink into her hide.

"Sin-Eater!" she cried out, even as her body went eerily still, and tears poured down her cheeks.

"Tell me what the combination is, and we'll work something out. I might even let you go." Calloine dangled hope on a false string.

Her eyes held the sorrow of the already dead. "I can't betray him. Blood-oath."

Meri met her gaze, cringing inwardly at the mention of the oath. "I shouldn't be surprised." She plunged the tre'jor deep into Namae's belly and watched emotionless as the look of horror crossed her face. Soon enough, she'd know everything Namae had known. Namae burst into a fine golden powder in mere seconds.

Moments later Namae's essence filled Meri, and her mind was lost to incorporating the sensations. If she'd felt stretched with Calloine, Namae cracked her at the seams. It wasn't by much, but Meri sensed it was enough. Too much.

Once Meri was able to walk again, Calloine focused on moving the three dead daemons into the tunnel. Calloine wasted no time by feeding on her kills, slicing them open with her sharp claws and teeth and gorging on her succulent blood and essences. She wasn't a fastidious eater and coated Meri's face and arms in ebony blood.

Meri did her best to shut it out, instead working with Mahkra on garnering relevant information from Namae. Daemonic multitasking had never been so efficient.

She discovered Namae was a minor succubus who fed off impure thoughts.

How convenient; now I not only generate lust in others, I can now sustain myself on it as well. At least she wouldn't have to go out of her way to feed this new daemon.

Meri made a mental note to ask Azimuth after they got out of this particular subset of hell if he kept a notebook on the care and feeding of all of his daemons needs. Surely, after so many years the time involved in maintaining them had to become laborious. Or, perhaps, over the years they each fed less frequently. Meri realized she needed to know, sooner rather than later.

Next, she discovered Saleigh and Cian were off torturing Azimuth in the crypts. Also, Saleigh always returned here at night to sleep with her, his favorite pet. She also divulged the combination code to the lock on his bedroom door.

The desire to go now and stop them from torturing Azimuth almost brought Meri to her knees. How much time did he have left? Was it down to mere hours now?

"We can find them. Wipe them all out," Calloine said.

"Lie in wait in his chambers," Mahkra replied.

"Move like the ghost you are," Trailian urged. "Take them out one by one, huntress."

"I will not help you further," Namae spoke quietly.

"You've done enough," Meri replied.

Meri took the newcomer by the reins and flattened her up against a wall in her mind, grinding out every element of the newcomer's personality beyond retrieval. Her skills might remain, but Meri had no interest in a heart-to-heart with the lover of the man who was torturing her lover, Azimuth.

There was a pause of inner silence.

"Well done," Calloine stated. "You are indeed my match, cruel sister. Do we lie in wait, or seek them out?"

The power pumping through Meri via Calloine's feedings and the recent addition of Namae was heady. Meri drifted in a sea of rushing blood punctuated by each staccato heartbeat. Nothing would taste, or feel, so sweet than to allow Calloine her freedom to dance uninterrupted through these halls. Focusing was difficult, but Meri kept her goals in sight.

"If we hunt him down, we could be overtaken. He's likely in a group at this hour. If we lie in wait, Azimuth's time may run out. We near the end of day two and Orias said he wasn't due to die until day three. Namae claims Saleigh's due in his chambers with her every night. Perhaps we would make a worthy substitute for Namae tonight? I'd hate for him to get lonely."

"And then?" Calloine asked.

"Then, sister, we mow through every daemon between us and the crypts."

Calloine took control of Meri's body and swept through the room. First, she washed up in the kitchen, and then she cleaned up the broken glass, wiped the blood up off the floor, and then entered the secret combination code to the bedroom door. It swung wide, and Meri closed and locked it behind her. She waited on a daemon she'd never have considered summoning, but now had just added to her late-night dinner menu.

CHAPTER 18

$\mathcal{M}$eri waited in Saleigh's bathroom and drew a bath in the large natural rock tub. She left the water running, creating an ever-thickening cloud of mist. Calloine allowed Namae's scent to exude from herself, mixing with the steam in the chamber, wanting to draw Saleigh in unawares.

An hour passed. More. Meri grew restless, but Calloine the Huntress enforced her nature with a state of silent and ready watchfulness.

When the door clicked open, Calloine unfurled. For the first time, Meri sensed her true power and held her in wonder.

Although she couldn't see the daemon, his scent was familiar to Mahkra and Trailian: Saleigh had arrived at last.

He strode around his chambers. She heard items land on the bed.

Calloine smelled daemons he'd been in contact with. Mahkra identified Cian while Trailian picked out some others of note. Meri didn't care because she recognized

Azimuth's sandalwood musk in the fresh-spilled blood on him. Her rage blossomed, spiked by a flash of need to go to Azimuth and then an accompanying spike of pain after denying her need.

"You're worked up tonight, Namae?" Saleigh asked. "Looks like you have the water hot enough to singe the skin right off of you." He laughed, and Meri could hear him kicking off his boots, peeling off clothing. "Keep the hot water flowing. No matter how many times we flay his flesh and turn his bones to dust that bastard just won't crack. Now I need to work out my aggression another way. But I know you can take what I dish out, pet."

He rounded the corner and came face to face with Meri in the thick steam. He'd stripped down to his pants, and she'd taken him by surprise. Any weapons he'd left behind in the other room. He was a full head taller than she was, but Meri was not intimidated. His bulk, thick red skin, and matching dark red horns marked him for the Arch-daemon of hate he was. His shape was reminiscent of Engetheus, who used to induce a healthy dose of fear in Meri's mind. Calloine had faced larger and more deadly foes. She wasn't impressed.

It was a mark of her time among daemons that his appearance no longer surprised Meri. It was simply something to catalog.

"Yeah, I think I can," Meri answered, before decking him full-on in the face with such force Saleigh was pushed back against the wall. In a heartbeat, her claws were out, and Calloine was slashing his resilient, exposed flesh. His blackened blood oozed out slowly. She would have preferred rivulets running down his flesh.

Saleigh recovered from his initial shock and scanned the

room, ignoring her attack. "Where is Namae? What have you done with her?"

Calloine smiled fiendishly, taking advantage of his shock to pin his arms to his sides next to his shoulders. "She's right here, sweetheart."

Saleigh's gaze darkened. "You consumed her?"

Calloine shrugged, and when he fought against her, pinned him with her entire body. "And guess who my next course is?"

"No, I've met the cannibal Calloine, and you're not her!" he yelled.

"I'm right here, Saleigh. Let's just say I got a makeover. Doesn't change anything," Calloine licked at the blood on his chest and began to feed, keeping her eyes trained on Saleigh. His essence slid down her throat, burning with its heat and hate.

"Who sent you after me? Tell me at least that much," Saleigh asked, struggling under her grip.

"Let me give you a hint," Calloine replied. She let out Mahkra's scent only because she wanted to rub his nose in the loss of his cabal-mate. Perhaps his anger was already affecting her.

Saleigh went wild, roaring and fighting until he managed to buck off Calloine despite her amped-up strength. Then he threw her onto the floor and straddled her, pinning down her wrists and preventing Meri from using either her claws or the tre'jor.

"What do you know of Mahkra? Tell me now!" he demanded. "And how can you produce these scents at will? I will know! Tell me!"

Hate and frustration poured from him in equal amounts,

and Meri laid there at his mercy, but she also held all the answers he desired: particularly everything he wanted to know about Mahkra.

Meri felt the rush of blood between each heartbeat. "You want to know what happened to Mahkra?" She panted, feeling the daemons shifting within her. "You wonder where he is now? You'd like to speak with him, perhaps?"

Saleigh understood Meri was playing him and his anger cascaded into pure rage. He stood and grasped Meri by her bruised throat and pulled her up, dragged her to his bed, and tossed her upon it like a piece of meat.

Calloine laughed, half splayed on the gargantuan bed the hate daemon spent his nights. "Do you want to, or not, Saleigh?"

Meri couldn't say why they offered him this opportunity. Why they teased him. The pleasure Calloine derived from the act was a visceral thing. The line between them was so blurred Meri no longer cared to seek it out.

Saleigh towered over her, pacing back and forth while Meri lay sprawled. He crouched over her, horns all threatening, and demanded. "Get him."

"Your wish is my command," Meri answered with a sly smile. She slipped around him off the bed and stood. Calloine stayed at the ready while Mahkra rose up, permeating every pore in Meri's body. The room filled with lusty potency and Meri's heart longed for Azimuth, sparking the familiar denial feedback loop of punishment. It didn't hurt her this time, not with Calloine's influence pumping through her system.

Saleigh took a deep breath, confusion, and anger evident on his features. "What is the meaning of this?"

"You wanted to speak to me," Mahkra replied. "So talk, old friend."

Saleigh growled deep in his throat. "I don't believe you're my late partner in there. What trick is this?" He grabbed her hair and pulled her close, sniffing Meri's head and then throat.

Meri took the opportunity to palm the tre'jor from the sheath at her back. She knew Calloine wasn't going to be able to take him out. Meri had to use the blade. There was no other way.

"You want proof of things only I would know, old friend?" Mahkra replied. "I'm the one who helped you overthrow Kalil when he encroached on your territory a few thousand years ago; it's when you made me your second. I'm the one who introduced you to Cian, and I'm the one who knows where you store your secret stash of Bloudroot liquor, so no one else gets a hold of it."

"No. No, how can this be?" Saleigh exclaimed. He grabbed Meri by the shoulders. "What dark magic has caused this?"

Meri leaned into him. She reached up and grabbed his right forearm with her right hand, hiding her left hand, and drew her body closer.

"Would you help me, if you could?" Mahkra asked.

"If it were possible, I'd be oath bound to do so," Saleigh replied, although he looked unsure.

"I knew I could count on you," Meri replied, flashing him a wide smile. A simple flick of the wrist brought the tre'jor into contact with the bare skin of his belly, and a slight upward thrust embedded the short blade to the hilt.

Saleigh roared and burst into fighting mode. He released

her shoulders only to begin punching at her in an attempt to throw her off. Calloine extended the claws on her right hand, forced her arm around his waist, and bit down on his shoulder as she snaked around him for a grip, holding on with all of her strength. Blood flooded her mouth, and with it, Saleigh's essence. They had him on two fronts now. Would it be enough?

If the blade didn't remain in, the likelihood of getting another go at him was slim to none. Despite his heavy, consistent rain of blows and string of curses, Meri wouldn't give up.

They all hung on despite the punches and kicks. Meri's ribs cracked and skin tore. Blood ran down the side of her face, and she couldn't see out of her left eye. Was that her right shoulder dislocating? Meri ignored the pain. She knew the only reason she was still hanging on was the might of the daemons she'd hijacked. Calloine bit down harder, and she swallowed more blood. Trailian twisted the knife deeper with her skills. Mahkra poured his determination and vengeance into her, bolstering her strength.

They all aided her, each for their own reasons.

Minutes passed, and Saleigh slowed. Calloine strengthened, but she was the only one, propping the rest of them up. Meri didn't know for sure who'd win.

Saleigh wavered and fell to the floor, taking Meri with him. When he finally burst into a red fog, a sob of relief issued from Meri's throat. Meri dropped the icy tre'jor and curled into a ball on the floor, merely watching the miasma of Saleigh coalesce around her.

Meri shut her eyes. When the daemon of hate slammed into her, shoving down her throat, Meri's body was an inferno he burned through. She knew taking on another Arch-daemon was madness. She'd run out of options today, but at least he'd been removed from the equation.

Now Saleigh would never kill Azimuth.

However, that didn't lessen her pain now. His anger revolved through her in waves, racking her frame in uncontrollable jerks and spasms. All Meri could do was lie there and wait it out, knowing the melding would happen. After all, she hadn't saved Azimuth, so whatever was happening inside her body likely wouldn't kill her. At least, not yet.

When she remembered back over his parting words to her, Orias had said Azimuth came out alive if she helped, but there was no guarantee Meri would. She tried not to dwell on that possibility.

Besides, Meri couldn't doubt her assumptions now. Lying on the floor of Belial's nemesis' bedchamber having just inhaled Saleigh's essence, it was too late for second guesses. Meri hoped it wasn't too late for her sanity either.

After what must have been nearly an hour, Meri's body finally calmed. Together with Calloine, she was able to rein in Saleigh, despite his predictably volatile state.

Mahkra, true to his word, shared a clear mental image of the fastest route to the crypts, just like looking at a map with him. Except his had doors, possible guard locations, and false turns to avoid.

Saleigh roared in impotent rage, their plan revealed to him now, but there was little he could do to stop them.

"I need to feed on the way," Calloine demanded. "I expended most of my energy keeping your body from the worst of his blows."

That was amusing to Meri, considering the damage she sustained. She didn't bother to look in the bathroom mirrors, knowing she'd look like she'd been run over by a truck. More like a train. Her right arm was barely mobile. Nonetheless, she made sure she still had Kobol's daggers and slipped them into her belt for easier access. Perhaps she could use them with her left hand, or Trailian's skills, if the need arose.

"Fine," Meri replied, knowing as Calloine ate, she'd heal. "You find it; you can eat it. Let's move."

---

*M*eri navigated the labyrinthine complex of Saleigh's burrow, encountering no one for some time. The halls had been deserted, causing Meri to wonder where everyone had been drawn.

She smelled the signature sage and diesel of Cian mere moments before encountering him rounding a corner. Trailian had the presence of mind to pull one of Kobol's daggers. Calloine picked up the presence of two more daemons mere paces behind him, sending Meri's adrenaline through the roof. All stank of blood and battle and Cian reeked of Azimuth's blood, flaring her temper.

When they came face to face with the scaly, yellow-skinned, and red-eyed daemon, Meri's claws were out, and her teeth were sharp as the dagger in her left hand.

Her voice, however, rang out in Mahkra's deep baritone. "Hold! Come no further!"

She heard Cian's two companions stop around the corner, likely confused not only by the command but also by hearing it in Mahkra's voice. The disbelief was mirrored in Cian's face, marked in bruises and blood. Their seconds of hesitation would gain her an advantage.

She sunk the dagger into Cian's chest, Trailian aiding her by guiding the metal with her skills deeper by the second. Blood gushed out around her hand and out his mouth, but her grip remained firm. Calloine wasted no time and sunk her teeth into his neck, ripping his throat fully open and soaking the front of them both in ebony blood. She then buried her face in the free-flowing stream, inhaling his potent power.

Cian struggled against her, and then a sudden, sharp, shooting pain lanced through her thigh. The fire burned through her, but Meri knew better than to relent. Her gleaner skills clued her in that he'd buried his short sword into her, for all the good it did at this moment. If she could tolerate Saleigh's brutal attack, a single piece of steel wouldn't be her undoing.

She felt Cian's life essence draining, being consumed into her own, healing her shoulder via Calloine's transference. She noticed Azimuth's blood spattered all over his clothes, and Calloine ripped apart his throat with renewed furor. Then Meri observed that blood on the blade he'd embedded in her thigh belonged to Azimuth. The bastard hadn't even bothered to wipe off his blade after torturing Azimuth with it.

Meri's only regret was feeling Cian's heart stop beating and knowing she could cause him no further pain. When what was left of his body fell lifeless to the ground, Meri held onto the dagger and the short sword, which was still embedded in her right thigh. Trailian helped her guide the blade out, but the pain seared through every inch. Meri felt the blood gushing out of the wound, and spat upon her fingers, which she worked into the slit in her pants. In a few seconds, the flesh around the cut knit back together, although the area was swelling badly.

"Cian! Mahkra! What's going on? May we proceed?" The calls of Cian's daemons down the corridor jarred her back into focus.

Calloine was re-energized from the feeding, and her shoulder was almost back to normal. She gripped the dagger and short sword each in one hand and flew around the corner.

The daemons weren't prepared, to say the least. Trailian embedded a blade in each of their skulls before either could mount a defense. They fell to the ground, immortal, yes, but twitching in shock and immobile. Calloine feasted on them while they lay helpless and groaning in pain.

Calloine also sensed the captured essences of human souls slip away as she fed. The Elder feasted on the daemon essence, not the newer human souls within, but she was keen enough to scent the difference. Their presence registered like fragments of emotions and thoughts, and once released took off like puffs of smoke on the wind. Where would those go after the daemons perished? Back to the humans, if they still lived, or to some form of afterlife? Yet another question for Belial and her cabal, after she got out of this predicament.

After this feeding Meri could see out of her left eye again, although it was still very swollen and bruised. Meri's ribs were still a lost cause. Looking down at the two desiccated husks that used to be daemons, Meri felt it was a fair trade.

She retrieved the blades and continued towards the crypts. A few corridors further and the familiar smell of Orias, Kobol, and Belial hung in the air. Meri sighed with relief, tears welling in the corners of her eyes. However, they were nowhere to be seen. Only the hint of their passing lay in the air. Meri listened and gleaned her surroundings carefully, but the burrow had gone quiet. Perhaps her cabal had taken out the majority of the remaining threats?

She encountered no one else along the way. Azimuth's scent was easy to pick up once she reached the lower level and Meri ran to the dungeon proper despite her injuries. The outer door was barred and lacked any guard, which didn't fit the images Mahkra had relayed earlier. Something had drawn the guard away. She lifted the locking mechanism, left the door wide open, and walked in, again scenting no one other than Azimuth.

When she saw him, she nearly cried out. Meri managed to clasp a hand over her mouth to prevent any sound from escaping, wary of sound echoing through the catacomb complex.

Azimuth was suspended from a low alcove, clad only in blood and filth. His head hung low, and by his complete lack of responsiveness and slack frame, Meri guessed he was unconscious. Spiral-shaped wires ran from the walls and into his flesh, penetrating deeply. Dozens of these wires held him aloft, and fresh blood seeped from his open, gaping wounds. Breath barely moved in his chest.

"I helped design this device. The metal is venomed with a daemon's poison of remorse and regret. In a human it's so profound it kills, in a daemon, the suffering is simply unbearable and never-ending," Trailian explained. "Each movement from the victim only draws the venomed spirals in deeper. I can unwind them with my powers, but he's going to get more venom on the way out. And we have to hold him up, or delicate organs and tissues will tear as we get down to the last few wires."

Meri found a chair, placed it in front of Azimuth, and then climbed to face him. Saleigh's smugness over a job well done washed through her and she locked him away in the corner of her mind with images of cute kittens shoved in his face. She slid her arm around Azimuth, avoiding touching the wires herself, and shouldered his weight on her left arm. Even with her daemon-infused strength, it was just barely possible.

Meri loosed Trailian to the telekinetic task, and soon enough the wires were unthreading their way through Azimuth's flesh. As she freed each wire, they retracted into the wall by unseen spindles and weights. Each one took time, and the effort was all-engrossing. His arms flopped down to her sides, adding to the dead weight, but Meri was grateful for each step towards his freedom. When she reached the ones bound through his lungs, Azimuth moaned in pain.

"Shh, be quiet. Just a little bit longer now." She doubted he even recognized she was there. He hadn't yet opened his eyes, but at least he continued to breathe. Hope flared in her heart, warming the cool skin between them.

Another set of coiled wires spun and hit the wall, and his legs moved free and then soon enough his back and chest had the last of the dreadful devices out when another round of pings collided with the alcove wall around them. All of his weight hit Meri and getting gracefully down off the chair was questionable at best. She hopped down and landed hard, going to her knees and eliciting a groan from them both. Meri laid him out on the dirt covered, rocky floor, well aware his wounds were worsening in their bleeding.

Meri drew upon Calloine's gifts and tended to Azimuth's weeping cuts, licking them and watching them seal up. The foul taste on her tongue was rancid for a moment but then numbed because of the venom. She worked on the worst cuts on his back first, hating to see such glorious skin marred. It eased her heart to watch his skin slowly smooth back over, despite the bruising her ministrations wouldn't treat. Meri alternated licking the wounds closed with spitting out dirt and grit. Notwithstanding the numbness in her tongue, she took her time, loving the feel of his flesh against her own. Her temperature heated solely by being in his presence.

She grasped the least-damaged areas on Azimuths arms to hold him by, trying not to hurt him further and failed, unable to locate an area his captors hadn't already damaged. When she flipped him back over to deal with the gouges on his front, Meri noticed extensive bruising on his belly and worried about his internal injuries. He'd always had a gift at healing. Perhaps if she could help him, Azimuth could do the rest.

Meri continued her ministrations over his front, trying not to focus on his unclothed state and failing miserably. Being this close to him stoked her suppressed hunger. If sex with Azimuth had been wondrous, the taste of his blood licked off his muscular flesh intoxicated her. It'd been three days since Meri had last seen him, and her body craved him in every way. Running her tongue all over him, albeit for healing purposes, caused her to respond, raising her temperature several degrees. She'd continue, as long as it took until he was revived if it meant they could share a single kiss. A caress. More...

In the back of her mind, Calloine remarked on the

daemon abilities Azimuth had picked up over the years. "He's got three different daemons with regenerator skills. I can feel him beginning to regenerate. Go more slowly on his wounds," she urged, and Meri complied, lost with the heady intensity of his blood in her throat, her hot body draped over his cool flesh, her nails scraping the rock floor rhythmically. "Yes, see, he'll be just fine. Oh look, he's got over a hundred in here. Rare ones even I've never seen before. Take this truth-seeker you know of. It's an emotional calibrator. You see it checks to see if your emotions are in check with the words you speak and all of your bio stats at the same time. It's remarkable and quite delicious."

Meri moved on to the next wound on Azimuth's shoulder. She'd nearly gotten them all, and sighed in disappointment.

A moment later, she was flying through the air, only to slam into the alcove wall with tremendous force. Dozens of venomous corkscrew wires dug into her back, arms, and legs, and Meri roared in pain, as Saleigh broke free, appalled at being put on his own ingenious torture device. Trailian tried to retract them, but there was nowhere for them to go. The wires were already flush against the wall.

When the crimson pain bled from her eyesight, Meri looked upon her captors: her cabal-mates. They appeared battered, blood-stained and worn. So, they'd finally found Azimuth? A little late is better than never.

"What the hell!" Meri demanded. "Let me down! I was helping him!"

A livid Kobol held his hand up in her direction, immobilizing her with ease. The venom began to work into her system, and Meri's body began to shake.

Orias bent over Azimuth, obscuring his face from her view.

"You were supposed to sit this one out, Meri," Kobol stated, his eyes blazing green.

"I interpreted things differently!" Meri replied. "Let me down! This wall is trapped and venomed! I was removing them from Azimuth when you got here!" The shaking got worse as the poison ate into her thoughts, eroding the links between conscious thought.

Belial nodded to Kobol, and he dropped Meri to the ground where she landed on her hands and knees. However, the damnable wires traveled with her, having embedded themselves in her skin. With each movement, they inched deeper, spreading more venom and gaining a greater foothold.

Saleigh roared.

"You're different," Belial stated, his voice imperious as ever.

Meri raised her head met his accusing gaze and threw it right back at him. "No shit, Sherlock." Trailian began working the wires out although it hurt like, well, hell. The buggers managed to leave more venom on the way out than in.

"Let's help her get those out," Kobol said to Orias.

"Stay back," Trailian replied through her mouth. "This is my specialty."

Meri, lost in her inner world of venomous pain, didn't notice for a moment how Belial, Kobol, and Orias turned and leveled their attention on her. Nor did she care. She wanted to scratch out Kobol's eyes for throwing her against the torture device in the first place.

Quickly enough, Trailian had the wires freed, and

Calloine produced her healing saliva, which Meri spat upon her hands and rubbed under her clothing on the wounds. Each point of contact doused a separate flame, and eventually, Meri could begin to think straight again.

"How's Azimuth doing? Any chance he'll awaken soon?" Meri asked.

"Time will tell," Orias answered, still crouched over Azimuth.

Her defensive hackles rose, not at all liking the way they were looking at her. "My saliva closed his wounds, counteracting the venom. I'm not sure how much internal bleeding is left, but his regenerating abilities should keep up with that, right?"

Again, the three males looked at her oddly, as Meri finished up her self-care. What were they bothered about?

Orias walked over to Meri and stood to face her. She looked at Azimuth. He appeared paler than usual, and Belial bent down to scoop him up and carry him, cradling him like a child.

"He'll be all right now? I got here in time, didn't I? Meri asked Orias.

Orias' face was sad. "Yes, you did." He ran a hand down her arm. "We almost didn't get here in time."

Meri's gaze flickered to Azimuth's prone form, paler than usual. He appeared smaller in some way, but she couldn't put her finger on it.

"You're not making sense, Orias," she replied. His expression didn't change.

"Discussion's for later. We need to leave, now," Kobol said. His free hand was balled into a fist, while the one carrying the war hammer swung it in a lazy arc. "The front gate will have reinforcements gathering, and although we've wiped out the bulk of Saleigh's forces we've been separated from our allies. We're a bit short on time to escape."

"I can lead you out the back. There's a hidden tunnel outside via Saleigh's quarters where the porting blocks aren't in effect," Meri replied.

"We don't have time to fight that battle today," Belial said. "Saleigh and Cian are still out there. We weren't able to find them."

"I killed them." Meri held her chin high despite their shocked faces. "And there's no one left alive down that route. We can exit quickly."

Orias said nothing, yet continued to look morose. Meri wanted to kick and rail against him. Wanted to scream 'This is what you wanted!' at the top of her lungs right at him. He rubbed his temple, receiving the message loud and clear. He smiled and then nodded his head.

"I do not want this story right now, let's just get gone," Kobol replied. "Meri, you lead the way."

"Happy to." Meri set to retracing her footsteps back to the tunnel. Calloine cast her scent tracings as far ahead as she could, yet nothing triggered, so they were able to maintain a fast pace. As promised, they encountered nothing alive on their journey to the tunnel, and the cabal was either diplomatic enough not mention the desiccated corpses they encountered along the way, or they simply didn't want to know the details. Meri suspected the later.

When they reached the outside of the tunnel and the relatively "fresh" air of the swamplands, Kobol took Meri firmly by the arm and ported her to the cabal's burrow, not that she minded. Her intention was to stay with Azimuth and make sure he recovered.

"See to her," Belial said to Kobol, and then rushed Azimuth off to the library, Orias close on his heels.

Meri tried to follow, but Kobol kept his grip. "No, leave them to it. You need rest. Let me show you to your room." The hard lines in his body and the grim set to his mouth made it clear he wasn't taking no for an answer.

"I'd like to help them," Meri replied. "Besides, what kind of medical treatment can you do in a library?"

"The alchemical kind," Kobol avoided meeting her eyes. "His body isn't the problem, you saw to that yourself. Now, come on. How long have you been running straight, without sleep?"

Meri shrugged. "Two days, maybe three? But with the daemons, I haven't needed it."

He stretched his jaw until it made an uncomfortable pop. "Your human body still needs it. C'mon," he said, giving her a gentle push.

He led her down the hallway to the training room but then took a turn at the end and kept going. "We wanted you to have some privacy," He explained.

"Thanks." Still, she didn't feel tired, just worried about Azimuth. Why had he been so pale? She worked it over in her head and anxiety began to roll around in the pit of her stomach.

They reached a small studio room with a doorway, but no door and Meri walked in, laughing. "Uh, for privacy, this isn't exactly working for me."

Kobol remained outside and lifted his hand, swiping it across the broad opening with finality. "Works for the rest of us just fine, little sister," he replied in a suddenly brusque tone.

Meri spun around and returned to the doorway, knowing what she would find even as she tested it. Although she could see through it, it was now hard as a rock. Kobol had telekinetically blocked it, locking her in.

"Why?" she asked, anxiety cresting like a wave over her head, sucking her underwater.

The accusatory look in his flashing green eyes nearly felled her. "Don't take this personally, Meri," Kobol said. "You're not the first summoner who's flashed out. It happens. Belial will see if you can be fixed. He'll do his best, all right?" Kobol turned to go.

"Wait!" Meri yelled, pounding her hands on the unseen barrier, anxious and angry in equal amounts. "I haven't flashed out! I mean, there have been moments, but I'm in control of the daemons!"

Kobol returned, stood right in her face, only inches taller than Meri, but nearly double her width and for or the first time since they'd met, his size intimidated her. His face was calm, but fury rode hard in his stormy eyes. "In control? That's why you let them speak through you. Your scent flipping back and forth like a light switch?"

"So what? I direct them!" Meri replied.

"So what?" He shouted, shaking his head with distaste. He spat to one side. "Did you also direct Calloine to feed on Azimuth?" His words shattered her nerves and ran ice water through her veins.

"I... she... no... We were healing his wounds from the venom."

Meri remembered Calloine's rapt descriptions of

Azimuth's collection of daemon abilities. And how they were delicious.

Meri clutched her stomach, threw a hand up over her mouth, and looked up at Kobol in horror as her body bent in pain.

"Like I said. You've flashed out." Kobol's words were emotionless, hard. "And this is where we keep the flashers. If Belial thinks you can be fixed, he'll do it. He'd rather keep you if you're salvageable. We're all his investments, after all."

Meri hardly heard his words. She fell to the floor, her binding to Azimuth dealing out blow after incessant blow of electrical current upon her body as she realized the damage she'd inflicted upon him.

She wept, because if Azimuth didn't recover from his torture, it wouldn't be because of anything Saleigh had done to him. It'd be Meri who'd killed him. Plain and simple.

CHAPTER 19

*M*eri awoke sometime later on the floor, eyes crusted over with tears, her body worn, bruised, beaten, and exhausted. She sat up and examined the tiny room, wiping crusty tears from her eyes. Four unadorned stone walls stared back at her in isolation. A small recess across from the open doorway she assumed led to the bathroom. The spare furnishings included a bed with unadorned sheets and blankets, and a small bedside set of drawers, all made of wood.

A tray of food had been left near the doorway for her while she slept, not that she was in a mood to eat it. A quick check confirmed that her tre'jor had been removed from the sheath behind her back. She supposed that shouldn't have come as a shock, but it spoke to her new status as an outcast from the cabal more clearly than being stuck in a cool-down room did. Tears threatened the corners of her eyes again, but Meri forced the emotion aside, reminding herself she hadn't wanted to be a part of their cabal in the first place anyway.

Meri stood and moved on shaky legs to the recessed area,

turned to the right and located the toilet. The small space also had a sink and a shower stall. While there was no door, it had the privacy of no direct view from the front door of her cell. Mercifully, there was no mirror here or elsewhere to see the various injuries on her body. In the gray-tones of shade, she only now noticed there was no overhead light. All of her light came from the hallway outside. Things were perpetually dim. Much like her outlook on getting out of this cell.

Meri stripped off her clothes, placed them in a folded pile there, except for her tank top and undies, and crawled under the covers. Meri tried not to look at her body during the process, but the purple and red bruises drew her gaze despite her best efforts to ignore them.

Her daemons were restless, hungry, and eager to act. Meri wanted to disappear. Unfortunately, that wasn't a skill she or her cadre of daemons possessed.

Meri fell into the bed, curled into a ball. Food untouched.

*W*hen Meri awoke, there was a stack of fresh clothing and personal toiletries from home, including her shampoo, conditioner, toothpaste, but no razor for shaving, stacked next to a new tray of food by the pseudo-open door. She poked at the plate of pancakes, the eggs, bacon. Meri salivated when she saw the bottle of mineral water, and the coffee smelled divine. Somehow, they were watching her, monitoring when she slept, and then only visiting when she was not likely to give them trouble.

Meri didn't blame them. She picked up the clothes and smelled Orias on them. Her heart sank, hoping it would have been Azimuth going through her things instead. Was he up and moving yet? Was he even still alive?

How much time had passed? She supposed it didn't matter.

Meri showered and assessed the current state of her injuries, which, despite her occupant daemons and superior strength and supposed quick-healing abilities, were still quite plentiful. She could feel the bruising around her throat, likely from both Calloine and Saleigh's attacks. Her left eye had full motion again, so the swelling must not be too bad, but she had no idea how discolored it was. Although she'd treated the cuts from the venomed wires, there was bruising around the entry sites. Her head continued to ache from where Calloine had banged her into the ground, and now, without her adrenaline running a thousand miles an hour, the ribs Saleigh had broken made every breath ache. Her right shoulder was about back to normal, much to her amazement.

Meri pulled on a pair of soft yoga pants and a loose t-shirt and decided to ignore the epic bruising mottling her skin. Meri wasn't even going to ask for ibuprofen. After what she'd allowed Calloine to do to Azimuth, Meri planned to rot in this pathetic cell.

She didn't bother putting on shoes. After all, where was she going? She left her bloodstained and torn clothes by the door in a pile. Hopefully, the others would take them and burn them.

Meri ignored the food.

She lay on the bed, her daemons grating inside her mind.

Calloine railed to her defense. "I did nothing serious to him. It was just a taste, a mere sample during the healing. It couldn't be helped. Besides, he's a regenerator. He'll be fine."

"Be quiet, or I'll find a way to cause you pain," Meri growled.

Meri wanted nothing to do with any of them.

Trailian offered avenues of escape. With her ability to bend and manipulate metal she could undo parts from the fixture in the sink or shower and carve out a hole in the earthen wall.

"We're being watched," Meri pointed out.

Trailian fumed, and within moments found the hidden camera in the corner of the room. "I can disable it," she replied.

"Do that, and they'll be in here in a jiffy. No."

That was the last she heard from Trailian. She continued to be irate, but lost mental airtime to the big whiners, Mahkra, Calloine, and Saleigh.

Meri slept and woke intermittently, lost to a mental circus of Lust and Hate, who, oddly enough, tolerated each other well, but both despised the Cannibal, who despised everyone else. She kept time by the food trays the cabal delivered, which she continued to ignore.

Another two days of her captivity a note on the food tray read: You will eat, or you will be force-fed.

Meri ate, but only part of the meals that they brought. She drew little, indecent caricatures of herself flipping them all off on the note. They weren't particularly good drawings, but she thought they'd get the general gist of the message. Some days she wouldn't change her clothes, although they provided her with new ones on a regular basis along with the food. There just wasn't much point.

Time passed slowly. She marked days in food tray deliveries. She slept more than average, so she knew tracking by sleep cycles wouldn't be entirely correct. Meri worked internally to suppress the daemons as Azimuth had originally taught her. Rein them in and flatten them out. Within another week or more, Trailian's personality had faded to dust. Then she was left with the unholy triad of an Elder and two Arch-daemons.

Each day their hunger grew, and Arch-daemons were not used to dieting. Worse yet, her enchantment binding her to Azimuth began to cause her constant, irritating pain, much akin to being regularly jolted by a low-level bug zapper. The only upside of the enchantment still being in effect was Meri's knowledge that Azimuth must have survived Calloine's feeding.

As she watched her skin slowly regain its pale, transmutated shade, Meri remembered the day with Orias when he'd taught her to shift forms. He'd also mentioned taking a daemonic name, and she hadn't given it much thought since. She did now, wondering if she'd ever get to claim it within the cabal.

Meri slept longer and longer each day, sometimes lying in a half-awake state, often replaying her parents final moments in her mind. Had she brought them vengeance? Did they deserve it? She didn't know anymore. She tried for some sense of peace, but after her betrayal of Azimuth, Meri was sure she was beyond redemption.

Since she'd eliminated Trailian, at least another week had passed according to her count of food trays. Perhaps they were just waiting for her to implode to save themselves the trouble of making a decision?

Meri ate little, dealt with the ever-growing pain, slept, listened to the infernal internal bickering, and reined in her unholy trinity. It passed the time, which Meri had plenty of.

The buttery fragrance of blueberry pancakes roused her from sleep, but this time she didn't awaken with a smile dancing across her lips. Meri sat up in bed, the naked soles of her teenage body cool on the hardwood floor beneath her. She looked towards her bedroom door, a vice clamping over her heart.

Sunlight didn't fill the house. Instead, the shadows of dusk crept around every corner, twisting everything dark in a heartbeat.

She didn't want to go out there, but that's how the dream always played out, so she went.

Shuffling down the hall, she was overcome with the gruesome smell of blood. When she entered the living room, her toes caught the edge of the coagulated puddle, littered with scraps of clothing on the far end. Reflexively she backed up and into the wall.

There'd been so much blood.

"Do you come back here often?" Meri looked up to see the waifish girl form of Calloine standing on the other side of the desk; her face was impassive, yet curious.

She didn't want to speak to the daemon, hated her for invading the sanctum of her dreams. "What you did still haunts me."

"Me? Don't be ridiculous. I showed you everything. They made choices. All summoners live and die by them."

"You didn't have to eat them!"

Calloine crossed her arms and tapped her nose with one finger. "Well no, I didn't. But I'm a daemon. Well, I was. Can you blame me for acting in my nature?"

Meri bent over and picked up a picture of her mother and father together off the desk, one of them at a picnic. It was of a time before she'd been born, and she'd always wondered, why this one? Why the one of Mom walking the dog they'd only had for a year? Or Dad with that ridiculous goatee? Why not others? What were you using these for?

Now she knew. There were some memories you could live without. None of these pictures included her. At least they weren't willing to trade away any of their memories of their daughter. It was a small consolation.

"No, I don't blame you for being a daemon or acting like one. Mom and dad knew the risks, they knew them every single day, but they kept doing it. Their choice is why I'm an orphan now."

Calloine glided around the desk, nodding. "Do you still blame me?" Curiosity glinted in her eyes.

"No." Meri returned her focus to the pictures.

"Good, because I think we make an excellent team," Calloine replied, placing a hand on Meri's arm.

Meri shook it off and faced the daemon. "There is no 'we.' I do not like you. I will use you, and then I will throw you away when I am done with you."

The waif transformed into the beast, full of teeth, and launched herself upon Meri. Calloine's jaws widened and then fixed upon her throat. Pain shot through her body, and she beat at the daemon, but it was no use.

Then her feet slipped, and she was falling backward, landing with a splat in her parent's blood.

*M*eri sat bolt upright in bed, clutching her throat and gasping for breath, checking her neck. There was no damage, unlike the last time she'd fought Calloine. It wasn't the first nightmare she'd had here, but it might have been the most visceral.

Deep within, Calloine laughed at her.

Meri turned over, pulled the covers up higher, and shivered.

*M*eri awakened to the most incredible smell, the smell of sandalwood and musk, a balm to her very soul. For a moment, she wanted to drift back off to sleep, for the pain had lessened, and she was at ease.

Hunger got the better of her and her eyes trained on the dark form leaning against the wall on the far end of the room. She'd fallen asleep on top of the covers in her clothes again, and Meri sat up in bed and inched herself as far away from him as she could with her back against the wall, knees to her chest. Meri wrapped her arms around her legs and balled her hands into fists, willing her fingernails to not erupt into claws. The temperature around her flared and sweat immediately rolled down between her shoulder blades.

"Azimuth," Meri said, her voice sounding odd after days of disuse. "Are you okay?"

He didn't move a muscle, yet observed her. "I've recovered." The silken chords of his voice washed over her, and she luxuriated in his return for a moment.

His reserved tone made her nervous. His mere presence made her want to explode out of her skin.

"Any, um, lasting effects? Did I hurt you?" Meri dropped her chin to her knees. The hunger of multiple daemons ate at her, shaking her to her core.

Azimuth's gaze penetrated her, and Meri had no doubt he knew what she was going through.

"No, Meri. It took me a few days to recover, but nothing you did was permanent."

"Thank the gods," Meri replied, burying her face in her hands. Calloine was quick to rise to her own defense, but Meri cut at her mentally, vocally hissing, and the Elder-daemon wisely retreated.

"Meri?" Azimuth asked. "How are you?"

Meri wiped tears from her eyes and looked up to meet his gaze. He was giving her "that" look, the one that saw straight through her. Is that why they'd sent him in here to interview her, because of his ability to discern the truth? Of course, that was all it meant.

"I'm about as you'd expect, Az. Thanks for checking in on me. You'd better go now. And please send someone else next time." Meri began to tremble, and she held herself more tightly, anticipating the painful shocks that would return when Azimuth left. It'd be worse, at first, since they'd let up while he was here. Meri steeled herself.

"What is wrong with you? I've had pets smarter than you!" Saleigh screamed inside her head. "At least they'd avoid me after I kicked them around a bit. You just keep going back for more."

Meri ignored Hate. He was a whiny bitch when it came to pain.

"Is that what you want?" Azimuth tilted his head. "For me to leave?"

Meri took a deep breath. "I need you to go. Yes."

Azimuth took a step closer to Meri. She pushed herself harder into the wall behind her, and he stopped in place.

"I need you to go away, Az. Now."

He shook his head slightly. "You're not sleeping. You're in pain. I came to relieve your suffering. Don't you want that?"

Meri laughed bitterly. "I don't have a right to ask anything from you. I tried to eat you. If your friends didn't show up when they did, I'd have sucked your corpse dry and then chewed on the husk. Oh wait, I forget you're a Liminal. I'd have ripped you open and dined on your organs. You owe me nothing. Not even common courtesy. Please, just go."

Azimuth walked closer. "You don't know how far you'd have gone without their interference."

"I'm glad I didn't find out," Meri spat back at him. "Do you have a death wish or something? Get. Away. From. Me."

Azimuth stopped when he reached the bed. "I'm back to full strength, and I'm not afraid of you. I am afraid for you and what will happen if your pain threshold goes any higher."

"I'm healing," Meri said.

"Your physical healing is progressing," Azimuth replied. "I doubt your ribs are cracked anymore, and most of the bruising has faded. But we both know I wasn't talking about that kind of pain."

"What's Belial going to do with me, anyway?" Meri asked, changing the subject. At this proximity, his scent calmed her nerves yet heightened her desire. Meri avoided meeting his gaze.

"That depends on you. Can you work past the flash-out, or not?"

Meri threw her head back, unable to avoid looking at him any longer. His scent wasn't just a balm; it was an intoxicant. "I'm trying, Az. But I've got these three daemons who won't stop hounding me."

"The others aren't an issue?"

"No, Penethewes, Trailian, and Namae are all silenced now."

"Namae?" he asked.

"Some minor succubus. Namae fed on impure thoughts. Whatever," Meri explained, waving off the detail with her hand.

"I'm surprised you're that far along," he said. "You're down to the heavy hitters already. I'm impressed."

Meri warmed throughout over Azimuth's compliment. She couldn't tear her eyes away from his. "Please, Az," Meri begged.

"What, Meri? What do you need?" His features had softened, and Meri knew he'd stay with her if she only asked.

But she couldn't.

"Go. Keep yourself safe." Still, Meri couldn't look away. She panted with need, but wouldn't endanger him.

"I'm perfectly safe in this room, Meri." Azimuth sat down on the bed, inches away. "I don't blame you for what happened. You were never supposed to be there. I told Orias to keep you out of it."

"He said the odds weren't good," Meri replied. "In Orias' visions, if I hadn't been involved, you most likely would have died." Her voice broke, unable to go further.

"I've lived a long time, Meri. Although I prefer to keep

doing so, it wasn't your job to keep me alive. He should never have laid it upon your shoulders."

Meri's temper heated in anger. "I would never sit by and let you die! Besides, Orias didn't tell me what to do, but he sent me on the path if you know what I mean."

Azimuth glowered, his eyes turned dangerous with an icy internal fire. "Oh, I know exactly. He and I have had many discussions on the topic. Yes, you flashed out, but you wouldn't be fighting this battle if you hadn't come after me. I owe you my life." He reached out and ran his fingers through Meri's hair, drawing a sigh of contentment from her lips. "I like your new look, by the way. Scarlet looks superb on you."

Meri gave an exasperated sigh. Before, she'd shaken with fear of the anticipatory onslaught of pain. Now she shook with raw, sexual need from a single touch. It was unfair. She needed him too much, and he was so close after too long apart. Meri wanted to fuck, consume, and destroy him, all in the same heartbeat.

Meri looked into the depths of resolution in his blue eyes and knew she had to prove her point. She was about to pounce when the creases around his eyes contracted imperceptibly, and a ghost of a smile haunted his lips.

Meri launched herself at him anyway, claws extended, aimed right at his throat. She nicked him on the collarbone, but he caught her by the wrists and flipped her onto her back before she could counterattack. He pinned her under his legs while he tied her by the wrists to the headboard with a length of rope he just happened to have in his back pocket.

"You planned for this!" Meri sputtered.

"I wasn't sure how bad off you'd be," Azimuth replied.

"You can try slicing through the rope with your claws, but it's warded especially for you."

He finished tying her wrists and then pulled her body lower onto the bed. He left no slack in the lines for her to move against and then pinned an arm over her hips. Yeah, she'd done an impressive job proving just how dangerous she was to him.

The scent of his blood made her salivate, and Meri couldn't help but stare at the line of blood trickling down his neck and soaking into his shirt.

Azimuth held out his hand in front of her face. "Lick my fingers."

Meri did so, hesitantly, loving the salt and sandalwood taste of his skin. He took her saliva and rubbed it over the claw mark on his collarbone, and it instantly closed.

"Sorry," Meri said.

He cocked an eyebrow. "You didn't even intend to hurt me."

"Yes, I did." Meri wriggled her fingers. "Claws."

Azimuth climbed over her, straddling her hips. He leaned forward until his hair brushed her face. "You little liar. You forget I can tell."

Meri struggled under him, which only managed to scratch all the right itches, so she stopped moving. Mostly. "Besides, the binding would have caused you horrible pain if you'd been trying to hurt me. We both know you were just putting on a show." A sly smile graced his lips, and Meri couldn't help but imagine those lips on her own.

Meri retracted her claws in defeat. "You can let me go now. You've made your point."

"Have I? I haven't accomplished what I came here to do.

Besides, you're much more receptive like this. It reminds me of another time you didn't want to talk."

The skin of her face burned with heat. "I still want you to leave," Meri replied, turning her face away. "It's safer for you."

Azimuth nuzzled her exposed nape up to her ear, playfully nipping her earlobe. "Liar." He gripped her hair with his fingers while he plied the curve of her neck with his lips. "Until you're able to be honest with me, I'm assuming our agreement still stands."

"What agreement?" Meri turned to face him, and Azimuth captured her lips in his, and she drowned under his touch, swept away as their tongues probed and teased. Meri writhed under him, desperate for his touch. When he pulled away, Meri moaned in complaint.

"As I figure it, I'm still responsible for your care and feeding, pet." He teased her with the offer of a kiss but pulled back at the last second. "I tried to find you a way out, but I failed. There's no breaking the curse." The disappointment on his face was apparent.

"Not until one of us dies, right?" Meri asked.

Azimuth raised his eyebrows. "I don't know about you, but that's a less than appealing prospect."

"Perhaps we'll find another way, later."

"Until then," Azimuth finally delivered on the teasing kiss, claiming her mouth with such intensity and raw hunger Meri could have sworn he was the one living with the Lust daemon, not her. "I have my pet to take care of, unless, of course, she keeps insisting I leave?"

Meri was well past fighting Azimuth or her own needs. If he left now, she would explode or wish she had.

"Stay, Az."

He smiled wolfishly and descended, laying a trail of kisses down her chest while he unbuttoned her shirt, revealing the swell of her breasts.

"Untie me," Meri asked.

He pulled her bra aside and captured a nipple with his tongue. He rolled it around between his teeth, ignoring her plea.

"Please?"

Instead of answering her, he lavished attention on her breasts. Nuzzling, kissing, nibbling and licking until she was struggling under him. "I'm not sure, Meri. Will I be safe?" he asked, gently teasing, then his mouth captured a taut nipple, and for a time, Meri forgot his question entirely.

"I don't want to hurt you, Az. I'll do my best. Please?"

Azimuth returned to hover over her lips for a moment, and then reached up and untied her wrists. "That's my girl."

My girl. Something in Meri shifted and opened, and her fear crumbled away.

Meri brought her arms down and laced them around Azimuth's neck.

"Your eyes. I've never seen them like this before. They remind me of the indigo depths of the Arctic seas."

"And what do you think it means? What do your instincts tell you?" His lips curved in a smile while his hands traced along her outer thighs.

She shook her head, fingers running through his hair. "No, I'm not gleaning my way out of this one. Now I know when your eyes go white, you feel angry, threatened, or betrayed, right?"

He shrugged. "'You've pinned me." He kneaded her calf

while running kisses along her breastbone, gaze caught on hers.

"Oh no, rather you've got me pinned at the moment," she cast a heated look up at him. "Tell me, Az. What does the indigo mean?"

He reached up and cupped her cheek. "I'm not sure it's happened before, so I think we're in uncharted territory. But I can tell you I trust and feel safe with you, and I feel a connection to you I haven't felt with anyone else before."

She gasped, awed by his revelation. "I do too." The words didn't go far enough to encompass her feelings, but her emotions choked out anything else from coming out. Meri didn't know how she'd managed to earn his trust, but she'd do anything to keep it.

"Your actions have spoken much louder than any words could have."

His words pushed her over the edge, and she pulled him down into her lips, wanting nothing more than to lose herself in this moment. Need surged within, and Meri went to work on the buttons of his shirt.

"No one's watching us, right?" Meri looked at the camera, ready to disable it in a heartbeat.

Azimuth sat up and slipped his shirt off over his head. "No. Rest assured, I was most convincing."

His toned abs drew Meri's hands, and she ran her fingers across them, delighting in the slight electric charge between the two of them. "I can only imagine." Meri pulled him down beside her on the bed and rolled on top of him. She quickly removed her top and bra, while Azimuth's hands guided her hips atop his own. She groaned in delight, feeling the firm pressure of his straining erection against the juncture of her thighs.

Her daemons shifted with disquiet within her, but she blocked them out, channeling a touch more lust to overcome her anxiety.

The effect wasn't lost on Azimuth whose energetic white nimbus flared in response. He stripped them both of their pants in record time. Meri kissed a path down his tight abdomen, desperate for a taste of him. She held his engorged manhood firmly in her hands while she snaked her tongue out and around the bulbous tip. Azimuth groaned and bucked in response, and Meri slid him into her mouth, tonguing the underside of his shaft on the way down.

Meri lost herself in the sleek sensation of his skin until she felt Calloine stir and buck within. Meri immediately pulled away from Azimuth in fright.

He reacted with preternatural speed, sitting up and grabbing her by the arms before Meri could escape the bed. His eyes were sapphire-blue and locked on hers. "Despite how wonderful that felt, perhaps we need to skip that activity for now?"

"I'm sorry," Meri murmured.

"I'm not." Azimuth smiled irreverently and drew her down into a kiss. He plundered the depths of her mouth relentlessly, and the discomfort soon fled her mind.

Meri forced him back down onto the bed. She straddled him and slammed his shaft into her, unable to draw out the foreplay any longer. In three swift strokes, Meri arched her back and crested her first waves of pleasure.

When the first wave abated, Meri rolled forward onto Azimuth's chest. She gasped for air in the now-radiant heat of the room. They were both slightly slick with a thin sheen of sweat, but he was cool to the touch.

Meri reached up for the headboard; her need already peaking again. Azimuth understood and gripped her hips and set a fast, rough pace, urged on through her sighs and whimpers. Meri was soon lost in another round of cascading ecstasy, and Azimuth rolled her over onto her back.

He captured her hands above her head with one hand and proceeded at a deliberately slow rhythm into her core. Azimuth relentlessly teased the ripe buds of her nipples with his mouth and lazily circled her most sensitive spot with his thumb. Meri squirmed underneath his luscious torture, which only heightened her pleasure.

"Azimuth," she cried out his name while pleasure shattered all around her and he growled in pleasure into her ear.

The air around Meri cooled, and she opened her eyes to the sapphire gems that penetrated right through her. He knew all her secrets and yet hadn't turned away. He kept coming back, despite it all. There was a history to Azimuth she didn't know and didn't need to know right now. He'd proven himself to her when it mattered.

"There you are," he whispered, nipping lightly at her lips. "Now your daemon is satisfied, and I get you all to myself." Azimuth thrust into her with renewed intensity. Meri caught her breath and ran her hands down his back, urging him on.

"If you kept better care of your pet, you wouldn't have this problem," Meri replied. She nibbled and licked her way along his shoulder.

Azimuth grabbed her hair by the nape of her neck and breathed hotly into her ear. "So, if I fuck my pet more regularly, I could fuck her more often?" He laid a series of sharp bites in a line down her throat, punctuated by harder and deeper thrusts.

Meri's smile turned into an open-mouthed groan. "More," she demanded.

He growled into her ear. "Of course, pet." He slid his hands under her hips and angled her so she could take him more deeply, and then moved within her with an agonizing slowness meant to torment the most pleasure out of each moment.

She dug her fingers into his hips, trying to force his motion to quicken, yet he only laughed at her distress. "Damn you," she wriggled underneath him, but he held her tight.

"No, pet. Let it happen. Give over."

She stared up at him and relaxed, frustrated but undeniably enjoying his passions. Lost again in the depths of his azure eyes, her body felt him pulsate within her, and she followed, breathlessly pushed over the cliff of passion yet again.

When Meri's eyes started to flutter closed, Azimuth rearranged them on the bed, spoon-like, and drew the covers up around them.

"Are you sure you should sleep here?" Meri asked, doubt again gnawing at her gut.

"I told you, I'm safe." His breath on her shoulder was so calming Meri had a hard time staying awake.

"I can't believe you'll trust me enough to sleep next to me."

"You'd be surprised what I'd do for you now, Meri."

His words, so protective, shocked her a little. "But the others? Will they approve?"

"It's not their decision," he answered. "As I said, you're my responsibility."

Awed by his faith, Meri turned to him. "I swear to you; I'll be better. I'll be good. You don't need to worry about me flashing out again."

Azimuth's laugh echoed off the hollow walls of the chamber, but he cupped her cheek tenderly. "I'm not worried about you flashing out. Not at this point. My instincts say that danger has passed. But 'good?' I think you need to come to terms with your nature, pet."

Meri's brow knit. "I don't understand. This cabal recruited me to hunt down daemons. How is this not a good thing?"

Pity flashed through Azimuth's eyes, but it was quickly replaced by compassion. "Yes, we hunt other daemons, but you forget the bigger picture, sweet. Belial's raison d'être is to rid Sheol of daemons who've tainted the sacred bloodline by indulging on human souls, and we're essentially his avatars. Yes, this happens to protect a few humans as a consequence along the way, but it's a side effect, not his purpose. In the meantime, do you honestly think summoners will cease in their efforts? Or, that Belial would encourage them to do so? After all, he is constantly watching for more recruits. Did you, for example, step in and save Reverend George when you had the opportunity?"

So Azimuth had been watching then? How was she not surprised? "No. I wasn't willing to bargain with the daemon for his life. He wasn't my responsibility. He brought that fate upon himself." Perspective was everything. Guilt overshadowed the memory, but she didn't regret her choice.

"Exactly. Over the years, you've learned to pick your battles. So has Belial, and so have I."

Bile rose up in her throat as Meri realized the truth of his words. "And so you work with him. Aid him."

Azimuth shrugged. "The enemy of my enemy is at times, my ally. Belial is an incredible resource and will do nothing to kill me, or any of us. We're too valuable to him. We're his constructs."

Meri didn't miss the bitter note in Azimuth's voice at that term. He'd come to terms long ago with the arrangement he had with Belial.

"But always remember," Azimuth continued, "his purposes are not yours. You are a human with a scrap of a soul left to your name, and on an ongoing basis, you'll be tasked with harboring new and challenging daemons and conquering their essences lest you lose your sanity. In the midst of this, you need to find your purpose. No one else can give it to you. Orias, Kobol and I each have our hobbies, our research. It helps while we wait for Belial's next set of orders, when he targets the next 'blasphemers' who imbibe human souls, and he will, soon enough."

"He's off the rails, isn't he?" Meri asked, voicing her long-held fears.

Azimuth sighed. "I've learned from talking to some Elders in Sheol that he's a bit of an extremist. On Earth, he'd be the equivalent of a Nazi in his views. It doesn't change the fact that he's our maker."

"I can't ever walk away from the cabal, can I?" Meri's voice trembled. Belial's never-ending blood feud scared her. How long could she endure?

Azimuth studied her for some time, running a reassuring hand along her face and neck. "There's more danger to you on your own than with us, but I understand your fears. Didn't Orias warn you not to get involved?"

Meri smirked. "Sort of. He said, more or less, not to go with the cabal. I took creative liberties."

Azimuth's gaze pierced her. "Belial warned you about the dangers of taking on more daemons. You did anyway."

"If I hadn't, I would never have gotten to you. Besides, Orias was wrong on his premonition. We both came out alive."

Azimuth frowned, his brows drawn together. "That's part of what worries me. His premonitions are never wrong."

Meri yawned. "But he was wrong because here we are." Meri curled back into the safety of his arms and drifted off to sleep.

CHAPTER 20

The most delectable taste filled her mouth, and for a moment, Meri had a difficult time placing descriptors to its perfection. Salty, savory, potent, healing, musky, sandalwood.

Meri's eyes shot open and saw her teeth sunk into Azimuth's arm, tasted his blood in her mouth and sliding down her throat, and gagged. Calloine snaked around in her mind, controlling her body with ease, feeding on her lover while they both slept. The hideous cannibal had no qualms and never would.

Meri swallowed hard, forcing the blood into her mouth, down her throat. He lay curled up behind her, cradling her body against his own. She spat on her fingers and spread her saliva on Azimuth's open wounds, closing them, hoping he'd sleep through her indiscretion.

The sound of someone clapping drew her attention to the open doorway. Kobol, watched, his expression filled with disgust. He stopped clapping and crossed his arms. "I think this proves you're not ready to come out of the flash tank."

"On the contrary," Azimuth answered, and Meri nearly jumped out of her skin in shock. "She recognized the daemon's actions and stopped early into the feeding."

"You were awake the entire time?" Meri asked, looking over her shoulder at him. His eyes had lingered on her lips before he answered. There must still be blood on her lips, she realized. Meri craved it, yet resisted licking her lips. She was not Calloine.

"Yes." There was no accusation in his voice and only compassion in his eyes.

"So this was a test?" Meri asked, recognizing the truth of it in Azimuth's gaze.

"Not the entire night," he whispered, sliding a finger across her cheek.

"It's time you come with me, Azimuth," Kobol said. "Belial will want your report."

"I'm on my way," Azimuth replied.

The men shared a look, and then Kobol made an exasperated sound and left.

"Why didn't you stop me?" Meri asked. "I could have hurt you. You don't know what Calloine does to bodies. She desiccates daemons and devours humans whole. That could have been you!"

"Yes, Calloine would do that. I trusted that you would not. Now tell me. Why did you stop?"

Meri blushed. "I recognized your taste."

He smiled. "Calloine figured she could slip one by you if you weren't paying attention, but she was wrong. Your will is too strong for her. You did well."

Azimuth kissed her lightly, and, enjoyable as it was, it did little to settle her nerves because she still tasted his blood in her mouth and on her lips.

"I'm going to go speak with Belial. He'll be pleased with your progress." Azimuth got up and dressed while Meri curled into the blankets, not feeling anything near pleased.

Azimuth bent over her and rubbed Meri's neck gently. "Don't worry. I won't be gone long."

"I'll be fine," Meri replied, hunching up in the blankets.

Azimuth shook his head. "Little liar." He walked out of the room, and Meri was left alone with her daemons.

Was the invisible door in place? It didn't matter. Certainly, they were monitoring her, and if she left the room, they'd just come after her.

Meri got up, grabbed some fresh clothing, and took a shower, seething the entire time. Azimuth had spun the whole incident in an upbeat fashion, but it didn't change anything from Meri's perspective. Calloine had just proved to Meri her infatuation with Azimuth's plethora of daemons would never end. Eventually, the Elder-daemon would go too far. That or Meri would be stuck in this cell until Calloine finally faded away, which could take what? Months? A year? More?

Another day might prove to be too much time.

No. Meri was done. She remembered how she'd crumbled Namae's personality to bits. How hard could it be for an Elder-daemon? By the time she'd towel dried her hair and pulled on her clothes, Meri was resolved. If she was to have any future with Azimuth, Calloine had to be put down.

The second she made up her mind, pain rattled Meri's entire frame, bringing her to her hands and knees on the floor of the bathroom. Certainly, Calloine disagreed with her plan.

Her retaliation wasn't much of a surprise, but Meri wasn't daunted in the least. Mahkra had regularly dealt out worse.

Meri, fury flowing through her veins, reined in Calloine. The Elder countered, becoming slippery and defensive in her mental grip, evading Meri's thoughts and sending more slivers of pain radiating throughout her body. Meri collapsed into a heap on the floor, but she didn't care. This fiendish horror had reveled in the memories of her parent's death, never wasting those emotions to manipulate Meri.

Calloine had devoured her parents over their mistakes. Their lack of judgment on that fateful day would always haunt her, but Meri didn't have to follow their footsteps and let the Elder own her too.

"Fine," she said, "You've got me down, but I have you by the tail, and I'm not letting go until you're a forgotten pile of ash."

Calloine's defiant screams echoed through in the small flash-out chamber and down the hallway. Meri didn't care who heard. She was resolved to end this daemon.

She held on, fighting tooth and nail until Calloine's real shape emerged. Not as the ethereal, ghostly form she preferred to present to all, but instead as a giant, scaly, eel-like serpent. Meri beat and kicked her with mental fists and feet. With each passing heartbeat, she watched microscopic particles break away from Calloine's flesh, floating away into the mass of her consciousness. The daemon howled, cursed, and fought, but couldn't break free as Meri continued her relentless assault.

After a time Meri was aware of others around her. She was no longer on the floor but had been moved to something softer. Someone begged her to stop. Blue eyes fleetingly swept past her vision, but she wouldn't stop fighting Calloine long enough to let them in. She knew if she released her grip on Calloine to respond, the daemon would recover fully in time. So Meri wouldn't give up. Not at any cost. The only way out was through. She shut out the voices. Everything but her internal struggle.

Meri redoubled her efforts, beating Calloine ferociously as the daemon howled in terror. She fueled her rage by remembering when the daemon had attacked Azimuth after he'd been tortured. Anger spilled from her, and before Meri knew it, she was tapping into Saleigh's dark energy. Massive chunks of psychic debris flew off Calloine's pale flesh while sniveling pleas fell on Meri's deaf ears.

In a sea of ashes and elation, she witnessed the end of Calloine, once the formidable Elder. Meri spaced out, drifting within her mind, finally free of the cannibal's influence. Meri almost wept in relief. She'd never be free of the hunger, but at least Calloine's obsessions would no longer rule her body.

Predictably, her focus turned to Mahkra, and a need for retribution for tricking her into the enchantment boiled in her blood. She was so pumped up on Saleigh's anger, and Mahkra was sated from her time with Azimuth he'd barely paid attention to her destruction of Calloine. Meri wasted no time and grabbed Mahkra, stripping his awareness to ribbons while he gasped in shock. In truth, Mahkra was still too lust-drunk from last night's festivities to defend himself. Midway through Meri's assault Saleigh rose, shrouded in bitterness, and joined in the fight. Mahkra's wails of pain ended moments later.

Saleigh retreated, coiling into the depths of Meri's mind.

He alone was her single internal adversary. However, despite his savagery, she didn't fear him as she had the others. She'd dealt out retribution and vengeance for many years in service to the Corporations. Having an Anger Arch-daemon that would slowly waste away within her for the next few months was the least of her concerns.

The other daemon powers were entirely under her control now. The binding still loomed over her head, of course, but she could live with that.

As Meri's focus returned to the world around her, she realized others were in the room with her, quarreling. Did they have to be so loud? Her head felt like someone had taken a gigantic hammer to it, throbbing with the beat of their percussive staccato argumentative points. She floated, disconnected and larger than her body until a hand brushed through her hair and smoothed down the side of her face, cupping the side of her cheek. Azimuth grounded her instantly with his healing touch. How long had he been by her side? Knowing him, likely the whole time.

"Can you ask them to shut up?" Meri asked, opening her eyes. Azimuth appeared concerned, irritated, and relieved, all at the same time.

The others quieted, all the same, turning their focus on Meri. Everyone in the cabal was present in the little chamber, arguing over... what?

"What did you do, Meri?" Orias asked.

Meri struggled to sit up. Azimuth tried to keep her flat, but she pushed back and got herself upright despite the ache in her noggin.

"You mean to tell me there's something the all-knowing Orias doesn't know?" Meri gaped at him in mock horror.

Orias glared in response. "I don't get images on the present, or of events unfolding directly in front of me."

"That's a definite lack in your skill set," Meri replied.

"Answer the question, Meri. Because from what we just saw, it looked like you just went nuclear," Kobol said.

Was Kobol the calm one in the bunch today? That set off Meri's warning bells and sobered her into a grave mood faster than a knock to the head.

Belial stood silent, sadness permeating his features. He held a special-looking dagger in his right hand. Not a tre'jor, but no doubt just as deadly for human summoners who'd flashed out, if her gleaner skills were right on the money, and she had no reason to doubt them. Saleigh raised his energy, poised for defense, but Meri forced him back down. Now was not the time, and there was no way she could fight her cabal off.

Meri took a deep breath. She glanced at Azimuth and gave him a reassuring smile. "Look," she said, "I appreciate how serious everyone is right about now. I was busy destroying Calloine and Mahkra. It was just something that couldn't wait. I didn't know you all were out here, freaking out and getting ready to slice and dice me. Are we cool now?"

"It's not possible," Kobol replied, eyes flashing green. "The others didn't recover."

Meri groaned and turned to Azimuth. "I beat the personalities of Calloine and Mahkra to cinders. I only have Saleigh left in here now. Period. Truth. No more flash-outs. Let's all get out of this tiny-ass room now, okay?"

Azimuth frowned. "Meri's truthful. The others are incorporated, although I have no idea how she managed it."

Meri stood, a little shaky on her feet, but determined to

prove she was all right and walked to the center of the room. "Perhaps girls are simply tougher than you boys? You ever consider that?"

"Saleigh must have given you an edge over the others," Belial replied. "I'll have to research your methodology. It may be helpful to save others in the future." He slid the blade into a pocket inside his robes and relief swept through Meri. "The quick incorporation may have some side effects, but generally once the personalities have disintegrated, the risk of flash-out has passed entirely. Still, this is very unusual. You are full of surprises." Belial rubbed his claws together on his left hand, lost in his thoughts.

"Then it appears it's time for a group discussion," Azimuth said.

"Okay," Kobol replied. "What's on your mind?"

"Let's go to the meeting table," Azimuth replied, wrapping an arm around Meri's waist. "We're done in here."

"I'm not sure I agree," Kobol replied. "Belial said there could be side effects."

"I'm assuming responsibility," Azimuth replied. "Come on."

Azimuth and Meri led the way to the main floor; arms twined around the other's waists.

"Now appears an opportune time to discuss your living accommodations, Meri," Belial said, sitting at his usual station at the head of the meeting table. "We have a room for you here in anticipation for your transition." He cleared his throat. "And your blood oath, of course."

Everyone had his usual seat, except Azimuth who'd taken a seat next to her this time. Kobol had broken out some beers for everyone except Belial, who'd declined. Meri didn't think alcohol was a standard for cabal meetings, but she wasn't complaining. At the reminder of the blood oath, she took a long pull from her beer.

The tension had lessened somewhat, but that didn't make what Meri had to say any easier. "Right, and that's very kind. I'll be using it part of the time. However, I'm planning to return to my home. In Denver."

Kobol hung his head in his hands, and Orias took a swig from his bottle. Azimuth looked at her as if he was trying to work out a series of mathematical formulas, and failed.

Belial was the one to respond. "I can't allow this. Your life as a summoner is over. You've got to accept this." For an immense, blue, horned daemon, he sure looked ridiculous when befuddled, Meri mused.

"I know I can't summon anymore. I get that. However, you've told me there are daemons which regularly port into the human realm, feeding on humans at will. We need someone on that side, finding them and their hideouts. The burrow is a great safe house in Sheol, but we need more. We need an operating space on the other side," Meri said.

Kobol nodded along with her argument. "She's got a point. But you don't need to live there. Just use it as a front. Pop in on occasion, seek and destroy, get out."

Meri shook her head. "No. I'm willing to stay here part-time, but I need to have a presence there. People need to remember me as a summoner. Request my services. I can even deliver the goods, so to speak, on select jobs. They'll never know how I did it. I've never allowed anyone to watch my summonings before so it's not like this would be anything new."

"And as you age," Orias asked. "You'll just appear to be an older summoner Meri?"

"Right, it'll be easy enough with Mahkra's ability. I can also hide my daemon scent with the cannibal's stealth ability. Again, I won't be seen in public often, just enough to maintain the assumption that I still exist. The rest of the time I'll be seeking out daemon lairs or back here."

"You've given this a good deal of thought," Azimuth replied. He ran his hand down the outside of her arm, his touch instantly comforting.

"I've had some recent quiet time to myself. It helped me sort out what I could contribute. Look, I have ties to many of the large Corporations in the Front Range area. They're usually the ones hiring the daemons. I'm in a perfect position to hear about current summoning interests. Secondly, I've inherited this, literally, killer nose. It'd be a shame not to put me to use."

"I find I'm loath to put someone so new to us in such a vulnerable position," Belial replied. "You're barely trained and just recovered from a brush with flashing out. I'm not entirely comfortable with the risks you're proposing."

"That's utter crap, Belial," Meri replied. She could feel Saleigh was itching for a beat down, but she told him to stuff it. "I'm a tool and a well-crafted one at that. All of you have had a hand in what I've become." She looked at each of them in turn, meeting unflinching gazes. "We all share a common goal: destroying those nasty soul-eating daemons. That's what makes us a cabal. Am I getting this right?"

"You are," Belial growled in response.

"So you either use me, or you might as well throw me away. The best use is to let me question my resources for any and all data on what daemons are running around right now and to put my nose on the street. Hiding me away in here for a few months or years for additional training is a waste of resources."

"We could continue your training in the field," Azimuth offered. "You'd be fighting for us while also information gathering in your spare time. I don't see a downside."

"You support this?" Belial asked, voice rising in shock.

"Why not?" Azimuth replied. "At least for the short term. We can mine Meri's old life resources, as she says, there are valuable contacts there. If there's a problem that arises, we can always move her here."

"I'm sure Orias would foresee any such crisis in time for us to act. Isn't that what you're best at, All Knowing One?" Meri added with a smirk.

"I caution you against relying too heavily on my talents," Orias replied. "I've told you before my gifts aren't foolproof."

"Sure thing. I'll take it easy out there," Meri replied.

Belial harrumphed. "You will act as a scout, Meri, and bring any intelligence gathered back to us. Understand? No more daemon assassinations without my explicit go ahead. I need to monitor your makeup much more closely going forward. This random hodge-podge you've gathered so far needs my examination and retrospection. I must determine how best to keep you stable and prevent further problems for your own good."

Meri smiled. Belial had just agreed to her plan despite her fears that he'd be immovable on the subject. "All for the good of the cabal," Meri answered. "Of course, I'll defer to your judgment and limit my activities to reconnaissance only, mainly among the humans. I'll defend myself if necessary, but I won't go seeking trouble. Promise."

"Somehow, I think trouble will find you," Kobol said, pointing his hand like a gun at her and then firing a mock bullet. She felt a slight ping of air hit her square in the chest.

Meri frowned at him, and he blew air across the top of his finger as if a gunslinger would do with the barrel of a pistol. Meri rolled her eyes.

"Defend yourself as necessary," Belial replied. "But call in reinforcements at the first sign of trouble, agreed?"

"Agreed." Meri relaxed in her chair.

"Have you chosen your daemon name yet?" Orias asked.

"Pardon me?" Meri asked.

"You can't continue using your old human name when using your assumed daemon form or while in Sheol," Belial explained. "Daemons aren't stupid and are likely to connect your new form to the old human one if you're using the same name. It'd blow the cover you're using and hoping to protect."

"Right. I've given that some thought recently too. I've chosen Nadir."

"Why that name?" Azimuth asked.

"I've hit bottom, a few times, recently. It's a reminder that I've found my greatest strength when I've been at my lowest," she answered.

The table got very quiet.

"That's a beautiful choice," Orias replied.

"Thank you."

"Is there anything else we need to discuss?" Kobol asked.

"Only the cleanup effort on the rest of Saleigh's petty minions," Orias replied.

"There were some remaining? The place looked pretty cleaned out when we left," Nadir said.

"Not everyone was home when we hit," Kobol replied. "Our priority was getting Azimuth out safe. We managed to take out most of Saleigh and Cian's top guard. Still, there are a few petty daemons we hear are still hiding out. We need to make another pass of the place."

"Okay," she put her elbows on the table. "When are we going in?"

"'We' aren't all going," Orias replied. "You'll be sitting this one out, Nadir."

She slumped back in her chair. "You don't think I can handle it?"

"You've been through quite a bit lately," Azimuth replied, his voice low. "Besides, you're harboring Saleigh, which could be a benefit to us, but if he acts out, you could also be quite dangerous to us in his burrow."

"Okay, I wouldn't want to endanger anything you've got planned. This is an excellent opportunity for me to go back home and put things in order there. My car is still at the Burner Enclave, and I need to pay some bills and stuff at home. It'd be good to reconnect with my usual connections and let them know I'm not dead. By the time you're done, I'll be back in touch with what's going on and be able to report back."

"Do nothing that will put you at risk. Understood?" Azimuth said.

"Of course not. I'll walk the straight and narrow. Well, you know, for a daemon hunter who's not actively hunting. I'll be going now," Nadir stood, and Azimuth followed. "But I'll pop back in every, what, three days?"

"Two days," Belial replied. "And plan on staying here three days per week so we can maintain your training schedule."

"Whatever you feel is best," she stood to leave. Belial also rose, striding over to her and closing the distance between them.

He towered above her, holding his head with an air of superiority. She noticed the others had risen as well for this moment of formality. "Nadir, present your hand to me, of your own free will."

"Which one?"

"It's inconsequential."

She took a deep breath and held out her right hand, palm up. He cradled her small hand in his large, blue, clawed hand. "Do you swear fealty and allegiance to me and your cabal, from this moment forward, above all others?"

Nadir didn't hesitate. She wasn't sure about Belial, but she was already bound to Azimuth, both by magic and in her heart. Staying with one meant accepting both.

"I do."

The blade cut sure and true across both of their palms, and then their fingers intertwined, and the blood mingled, sealing the oath for eternity.

Now she was cabal.

"Welcome, child. Now, if you don't mind, we have business to attend to." The triumphant look on Belial's face before he turned away gave her pause, but there were so many things she didn't adore about her new patriarch, Nadir didn't know where to begin.

She spat in her palm, and the wound closed over. "Have fun storming the burrow again, boys," she walked away only to get hit in the back with another fake air bullet by Kobol. She threw him a frown over her shoulder and kept right on walking.

Azimuth walked with her to the far end of the room near to the tapestry where they all usually ported.

"Keep yourself safe," He kissed her on the forehead and then handed her a sheathed tre'jor. "Just in case. But remember; use it only as a last resort."

"Will do." She gazed up into Azimuth's sapphire-blue eyes. Leaving him was the last thing on her mind. By the way his lip curled, he knew it too. She was tempted to make a fool of herself in front of everyone but thought better of it. "I'll see you guys soon."

She ported to the Burner Enclave, aware she was just a tad behind schedule.

CHAPTER 21

*N*adir stood next to her car in the bright sunlight of a brand new day. It was covered in dirt and next to it stood a small collection of candles, flowers, and sundry offerings. She remained in her daemonic form, as that's how the Burners' had seen her last.

A memorial? How touching.

She'd told Jackie she'd contact them in three days. How long had it been, anyway? She suspected weeks.

It was sweet, really, especially considering she hadn't left on the best of terms.

A scent on the air changed. Someone was coming. She tripped over a ward; likely one Martin had left, and grinned with approval. Breathing deep, she recognized the scents of Jackie, Martin, and other humans approaching. Nadir climbed atop the trunk of her car and calmly awaited her visitors.

Minutes later, the Burners rolled up on their bicycles, all of them displaying differing degrees of surprise.

She waved. "How's everyone on this fine summer day?"

"Shit, girl," Jackie replied with a grin. "You certainly gave us a scare. Where you been all this time?" She parked her bike and walked over.

"Unavoidably delayed," Nadir answered.

"That all you got?" Martin parked his bike and came over to lean against the car. "It's been nearly three weeks, not three days."

"I had to storm a castle and then work through some deep personal issues."

"You went to therapy?" Jackie laughed, shaking her head.

"You could put it that way. I'm feeling much less stabby and likely to bite your head off now," Nadir answered.

"I like the sound of that, Jackie," Martin said.

"No complaints here," Jackie replied. "Think fast." She threw Nadir her car keys which she caught with near preternatural speed. Jackie was quick to wipe the look of shock off her face. The others weren't.

"Thanks. Hey, could we talk privately for a moment?" She looked to the other Burners.

"Sure thing," Jackie replied. "Y'all head back to the camp. Nothing to see here. Move along now."

They dutifully obeyed their leader, and soon Nadir had the private ear of both Jackie and Martin. She slid off the trunk of her car, absently toying with the keys in her hand.

"Just so you're aware, when you use that stone I left for you, I'll appear in my daemon state. Please address me as Nadir during those encounters."

"A secret identity?" Martin asked, cocking an eyebrow.

"Yeah, I know it's a little odd, but I need to maintain my old life and contacts as much as possible. I can hunt more efficiently if Nadir is simply a daemon who's known to be at Summoner Meri's beck and call. Think of her as my pet."

"You got it," Jackie replied.

"My thanks. Now, if you don't mind, I need to get going. I'm guessing my public service bill is overdue."

"You know, if you lived up here off the grid with us, you wouldn't owe those bloodsuckers a penny," Jackie replied.

"I envy you that, but I have other reasons for remaining plugged in for now. Say, can I buy into your food co-op?" she asked.

"What, I doubt Summoner Meri would ever do something so disreputable!" Martin said, grinning ear to ear.

"Of course not." She grinned right back. "And I'm obviously all about propriety. Sign me up. I think you know how to contact me for pickups?"

Jackie held up the stone, grinning. "Just wait until Steve finds out we've got a pet daemon coming to pick up veggies and eggs every week. I can't wait to see him piss himself!"

*N*adir pulled her car into her garage a little over an hour later, shaking off the human illusion she'd maintained for the car ride now that she was home. She unloaded the car and got the mail, entering the house assaulted her acute senses. The smell of the mold on the dishes in the sink, the piles of undone laundry, even the rotting trash in the kitchen overwhelmed the simple but omnipresent odor of must. Despite having to fight her urge to gag, within two hours the house looked livable again, except for a desperately needed dusting. Perhaps she'd acquire a spell for that one. She hated dusting.

She'd plugged in her cell phone on arrival. It had completely run out of charge sitting in the car while she'd been away. She listened to the long list of messages she'd missed, wincing as the list grew longer and longer. Many were from an increasingly distraught Annamie, so she picked up the phone at once.

"Hello, Soul Paths, this is Stephanie. How may I help you?"

"Hello. Are either Annamie or Drew available?"

"No, I'm sorry. They're not in right now. Can I take a message?"

"Yes, please. This is Meri. Tell them I've returned from my trip from out of town, and although it took longer than I'd planned, everything is fine."

"Got it. Do you need to leave a number?"

"No, they know how to get ahold of me. Thanks!"

She hung up relieved, assured her old friend would no longer worry she'd perished.

Many of the messages were requests for work. She'd have to review those and see who'd already found alternate summoners to do the job. Also, all new customer quotes would include her new, increased fee schedule, which should slow down her requests and keep only the truly high-powered players calling.

Nadir had a plan. Foremost in her mind was getting her life back in order. Now that the house was livable she headed to her warehouses with a few large duffel bags in the trunk of her car. She wouldn't be using them to summon anymore, but she had a lot of gear there, and she didn't intend to leave them full of things someone else could pilfer and use after a break-in. Especially since she wouldn't be returning on a regular basis, she wouldn't know if someone got past her security.

Before she left Nadir took the amulet Azimuth had given her to summon him for extra security. She was confident she could summon him mentally, but just in case, she was cautious. Just as the cabal had demanded.

She was impressed how simple it was for her to maintain the human illusion throughout the drive over to the warehouse, just in case someone recognized her car. Nadir had to admit it was uncomfortable to sustain for extended periods of time, despite it being an innate talent from Mahkra. She pulled into the parking lot outside of the primary warehouse. Everything looked par for the course. Typical abandoned building upstairs, typical false doorway to the basement, and then her high-security door with thumbprint access lock, which failed to admit her. Confused, she tried again, and again. Nadir sighed, switched to her guise as Meri, and tried again. The lock slid open, and she opened the door.

She looked around, scenting the air deeply. There were some homeless folks in neighboring buildings, but no one in the immediate facility. She shut the doors behind her and headed down the stairs.

Nadir looked around at the mess she'd left after Mahkra's summoning, but seeing it again didn't make her feel any better. All that pink oil on the floor and the stench of roses had somehow gone rancid. Could it be from the dove's bone marrow she'd mixed in with the charcoal to draw out the sigils?

Lovely. What a time for an enhanced sense of smell.

She threw her duffel bags on the bed and went about

examining the room for reusable items. The brazier was a keeper. That had been in her family since she was three. The curios in the corner held a diverse selection of oils and unguents, which she put into a special padded case and then into her duffel bag. The scents of earthy cassia, sweet pink lotus, and pungent osmanthus wafted past her nose, despite the tight wrappings. Candle holders, chalks made with various flowers, bones, and tree sap mixed with the ash, even the custom-ordered charcoal. She gathered them all and carefully stored them for transport.

The kitchenware and toiletries? She could care less. The homeless could feel free to have them.

Nadir was wrapping up her prized collection of ritual sacrificial daggers when she caught the barest scent of four unfamiliar daemons, their sudden arrival sending her instincts on high alert.

Saleigh, typically quiet, surfaced and was the happiest she had ever sensed him.

"Ah, my old friends have come for a visit. I can't say you'll enjoy this, but I know I will," he said.

"Shut up, you bastard." Of course, the daemons were familiar to him: they were from his cabal.

"Cian's hunters are most impressive." Saleigh's essence swirled around the depths of her mind.

They were the ones Cian had sent to hunt her down for her involvement with Mahkra's disappearance. Now they'd finally found her. Persistent daemons.

Well, shit.

"Azimuth!" She mentally called out at precisely the same time as her reinforced steel security door became much less secure. It was kicked down flat as a pancake with no preamble. Nadir reached into her side pocket, broke Azimuth's amulet, sensing the summoning ward shimmer, and reverberate outward.

In through the door swept four daemons, all appearing humanoid. They proceeded to circle her in a predatory fashion. There was only one door, and they blocked it. She attempted to port, but couldn't.

The daemon female with long, beautiful blond hair and bright green eyes pouted, one hand casually hooked on her hip. "Anything wrong, darling?"

Nadir focused on her skills, and although she'd absorbed six daemons in total, two of them Arch-daemons and one an Elder, defending against four daemons at once was going to be a tall order. Sure, she was much stronger than any one of them individually. Saleigh railed against her mind, making it difficult to concentrate by screaming and forcing her to use a portion of her focus to keep him under control.

He wanted her to lose. Even knowing it meant the end of his consciousness. He won by exacting retribution on his killer: Nadir. In a way, she appreciated his tenacity.

All the hunters saw and smelled was Meriwether Storm, a human Daemon Summoner. Obfuscating her abilities was a critical ruse.

"You've been hiding out a long, long time, Summoner," a daemon with short, jet-black hair and a scar running the length of his face said. What type of injury would leave a daemon with a permanent scar? By his smell, she guessed he specialized in thought control or dream manipulation. What kind of attacks could she expect?

The female flexed her hands, revealing blades attached to her index and middle fingers shaped like cats claws and she was suddenly glad of the razor-sharp sacrificial blades she had in her own hands.

"We've been back to our lair to check in, Summoner, and what do you know? Our bosses have gone missing." A daemon with punked-out green hair and a nose ring said. He didn't have visible weapons but had more piercings than she would have thought possible. By his scent, she determined he was able to bend space. Could that be right? If only Saleigh would be quiet!

"That's a shame," Nadir replied. "I'm sure it must be sad to have to give up on your quarry."

The daemons chuckled, laughed, or scowled, to her comment.

The fourth daemon, a squirrelly fellow with greased down red hair and a tailored suit that fit just a tad too tight, stepped up closer to her, breaking formation. "Oh, now see, we never give up on a hunt. Not unless it's called off nice and proper. Cian gave us the order, and now he's a mite bit indisposed, you see."

Yeah, she remembered. Intimately. She shifted uncomfortably under tailored suit's gaze. The daemon looked like a serial killer. Who was she kidding? He was. Then again, who was she to judge?

"I see."

"I feel that you do, Summoner. I must say I adore the fear emanating from you right now. It's such a glorious symphony of darkness I could almost bathe in it."

Nadir felt like a fool. She would never have left the house if she'd known the hunters were still out here looking for her. She'd thought they'd likely been killed in the fray at Saleigh's burrow as well, or at the very least, their hunt for her called off with Cian's death.

"Yes, you should feel that way. Do you think those little blades will make a difference against us? We were formerly ordered to bring you to our master. Now he's dead; we'll simply carry out the questioning and dispatching he'd have done, were he still with us."

"It's only proper," the Blond chimed in, sliding her blades together with an unnerving, grinding sound.

"What I can't quite work out," said the pierced, green-haired one, "Is why she reeks of Saleigh? The scent of Mahkra's not there as it was on the trace, and now here, she smells like our leader who's been dead for two weeks. I can't quite figure that one."

"I can pull it out of her," said the thought manipulator with the jet-black hair.

Saleigh laughed. "It won't be much longer now, girl." Nadir panicked. Where was Azimuth? As soon as these daemons saw through her human illusion, there would be a real fight on her hands.

"Well, well, well," came Kobol's voice from the stairwell. "No one told me you were having a party, Meri. Is there room for more?"

She almost cried out in relief as Kobol, Azimuth, and then Orias strode into the warehouse cellar, each carrying their weapons of choice. Azimuth had two short swords, Kobol a blunt war hammer, and Orias a curved scimitar. All their weapons were already stained with ebony blood. Saleigh screamed inside her head because he knew exactly where they'd been. She almost smiled at his displeasure. Almost.

"It looks like you have your own party to attend to, brothers. I can assure you, this doesn't interest you," the tailored suit said.

"We have varied interests, and we like to keep busy," Orias replied. Azimuth's eyes were pure white, and she watched the three fan out, each pairing off against a daemon.

Which left Nadir paired to tailored suit and his ability to easily discern her emotions. She allowed Saleigh's hate to pour through her, eclipsing all other feelings. It floated on the surface, shielding her. She needed to incapacitate him, and her metal manipulation gift was one of the few offensive gifts she had.

Tailored suit turned back to her, ignoring his brethren, and smiled garishly. "What's got you so angry, Meri? Worried what the other daemons will do to you if we lose to them?"

"It's on my mind," she answered. Her gleaner gift identified every metal button, ring, and zipper on the daemon's body and Nadir struck without hesitation. She pulled the metal free of the clothing and embedded it deep into his flesh, elongating and twisting the metal as it wound under his skin. The look of horror on his face was gratifying while he dug at the embedded shards, trying to free himself from the pain. Blood erupted from his flesh at each entrance wound, each a jagged entry. She didn't stop the passage of the metal until they were bound deep into his internal organs, lacerating and binding them into shards. In his frustration, he ran blood-soaked, shaking fingers across his skin, digging at the entry points, attempting to pull out the metal, which was bound and wound through his flesh.

She was vaguely aware of motion in other quarters of the room, but she didn't let up. Panic flooded her system, but she gleaned it was counter-attack and set her emotions aside. Her enemy had no idea how much practice she'd had defending herself from internal emotional turmoil. He couldn't begin to compete.

Next from her hands flew four of her precious sacrificial blades straight into his ribcage. Nadir drove the thin knives below, again twisting and curving the metal along the way. Tailored suit screamed in horror and fell to his knees clutching his chest as she worked the metal deeper, immune to his pleas. Soon enough the knives bent and constricted around his heart, preventing it from beating.

There were no longer any halfway points in her mind.

Nadir shook off her human disguise and stepped forth, extending her claws. She bent over the tailored suit, sliced open his throat, and then drank in his essence greedily. In moments, his struggles ceased.

While she fed, she surveyed the activity in the room. She'd dispatched the suit so quickly; everyone else was just beginning to get engaged in his or her battles. Everything was happening at once, but with her heightened daemonic senses, Nadir had no problems following it.

Orias fought with the punk, who appeared able to dodge his attacks with his space-bending skills. However, the punk's strikes fared no better; Orias anticipated his every move. In the end, the punk materialized on top of Orias' scimitar and then collapsed in a daze when his entrails poured out in front of him.

Kobol took on the dream manipulator with the jet-black hair, who moved almost as quickly as he did. Unfortunately, he couldn't go invisible as Kobol could. Nadir watched an invisible hammer smash the dreamer into the black wall. His bloody, cracked skull stuck for the briefest of moments and then slid down, the whole of him crumpled into an unconscious pile.

Azimuth had taken on the steel-clawed blond, who looked none too happy with her odds against his blades. She managed some impressive parries with her claws, but the first time Azimuth's blade pierced flesh, a streak of white light trailed along it and shot into the gash in her flesh. His energy, once past her simple barrier, froze her where she stood. When he pulled out his blade, her body toppled unceremoniously to the ground.

Once all of the other daemon hunters were incapacitated, her cabal-mates turned to watch her eat while they cleaned their weapons. Their expressions ran the gamut of emotions. Kobol's face was grim, no doubt remembering her feeding on Azimuth. Orias' gaze was stormy and filled with sorrow. No doubt, he blamed himself for her physical hunger, despite the necessity.

Was she the only one who required feeding on daemonic flesh to maintain her abilities? Despite her curiosity, now was not the time to ask.

Azimuth's expression held no judgment, only compassion. She wondered if he made himself watch out of a feeling of misplaced responsibility, perhaps to witness what saving him had cost her.

Nadir held his gaze, not regretting a thing she'd done to save him. Emotions rolled through her like a thunderstorm, and for a moment, she couldn't breathe because of their intensity. Her love for him, and her commitment to stand by his side solidified in her heart at that moment, even if it meant eating raw daemon flesh and being tied to a Prince of Sheol.

Azimuth reacted viscerally. Although she wasn't speaking, he was still attuned to her energy and her feelings. No, he wouldn't have caught her thoughts, but he couldn't miss the intensity and focus she had trained on him. His eyes deepened from white to azure-blue in hue, and he took in a sharp intake of breath. Without speaking, he nodded once in understanding. Only then did she drop her gaze.

When she finished with the tailored suit, Nadir washed up in the bathroom and then returned to the group. "The blond can block others porting by some fashion. The black haired one practices thought control or dream state manipulation, I'm not exactly sure, and the pierced one bends space somehow. Sorry, I'd have gotten a better read on them, but Saleigh was throwing a fit trying to distract me."

"What about the one you ate?" Azimuth asked.

"He read emotions," Nadir answered. "Sorry if you wanted that one."

"Nah, no worries," Kobol replied. "There is the matter of the body."

"I could set fire to the warehouse." she replied.

"No, we'll port it back with us to Saleigh's burrow," Orias answered. "It's a less risky proposition. You know, before you, we had to take the daemons we captured back to the flash-out chamber and keep them unconscious until Belial could identify their gifts and know how to best match them up with our existing powers before we'd take their abilities. Now we know who does what right away. This is much more convenient."

Nadir frowned. "I'm glad my cannibalistic tendencies are finally paying off for everyone."

Orias laughed, but the dark humor was still stormy in his

eyes. "Anyway, I'm calling the thought control." He pulled out his tre'jor and pegged the black-haired daemon.

"I'm going with bending space. Somehow," Kobol stabbed the punk.

Azimuth smiled up at her. "Which leaves me with the blond. No hard feelings?"

"Stab away, sweetie," She shook her head.

It was an odd thing watching others imbibe daemon essences, especially knowing they each harbored dozens to nearly a hundred each. Assuredly, it grew easier in time because all three coughed a time or two and then went back to putting their weapons to rights and acting as if nothing had happened. A far cry from her most recent experiences.

Azimuth walked over to her, casting an evaluating glance around the room along the way.

"You came here to clean things out?"

Nadir shrugged. "I didn't want to leave all of this expensive, and frankly, dangerous equipment here. Figured if I had it at home or the burrow, I might get some use out of it."

"A wise move." Azimuth ran a surprisingly clean hand down her cheek. Had he done that aura-dirt cleaning thing to his hand so that he could touch her? "Sorry, it took us a few minutes to get here. We were, of course, at Saleigh's burrow on cleanup duty. We'll head back now if you're okay?"

"I'm fine. Saleigh said they stated that they were the only hunters and he's furious as all get out over their failure, so I doubt I'm in any particular danger now. Just back to my 'normal' risk levels." she laughed.

Azimuth frowned. "Perhaps we should escort you home?"

"No. Seriously. Go back to your hack-and-slash fun. I have my cleanup to do."

"Okay. But if you need to, send for me again." He chucked a finger under her chin. "I heard you loud and clear when you called my name. You didn't need the amulet."

His blue gaze filled her heart, from the top of her head to the tips of her toes. Her temperature elevated slightly. "Go now. Before I kick the boys out."

He grinned wickedly. "I'll check in on you tonight. Just to make sure you're doing all right."

"Uh huh. Sure thing," she answered, pulling away before she allowed herself to get too ramped up. "Have fun boys!"

They ported out a moment later, taking the desiccated husk of the tailored suit with them.

Nadir refocused on wrapping her remaining sacrificial blades in blessed linen and then stowed them in a duffel bag. Now, what else couldn't she live without?

CHAPTER 22

The alternate warehouse cleaned out much more quickly and easily with no drama whatsoever. After which Nadir, once again in human form, headed home and unloaded her copious wares. Where she'd store them might prove to be a challenge. Perhaps her new room at the burrow would get more use after all?

She changed into more relaxed evening wear, just a cami and loose, light flannels, and ate a light dinner of frozen left-over lasagna and a glass of merlot.

She felt normal for the first time since she'd accepted the Lust daemon summoning. This was her life back. It wasn't amazing, but it was hers. Sure, Saleigh continued to grumble away, but a girl couldn't have everything, could she?

The doorbell rang, and she looked to her front door like it was possessed. Next, a knock came from the door. Nadir shook off her state of shock at having a visitor who didn't port inside and went to answer.

She opened the door to reveal Annamie and Drew, for once willing to brave the daemonic wards to stand on her porch. Nadir's jaw almost hit the floor. Although the wards posed them no threat, her longtime friend had always preferred not to expose her energy to such magics.

Annamie got that far-away look in her eyes and studied Nadir's aura carefully. Drew's face was cautious, his brows drawn in concern. She considered inviting them in until Saleigh reacted to something in Annamie, which gave her pause.

Her old friend frowned in disappointment, and Saleigh could taste the raw disgust on her, resonating with him like a fly to honey. He tasted it, savored it, and appreciated as an aficionado would a fine wine.

"I got your message," Annamie said. "I had to come and see for myself if it was really you." Annamie shifted uncomfortably on the porch. "What's happened to you?" Bitterness laced her words in silent accusation.

"Perhaps you'd like to take a walk and talk with me? The night's warm out," Nadir offered, knowing her friend didn't like the feel of the daemon wards.

"Thanks, I'd prefer that."

Nadir grabbed a sweat jacket and shoes, and they ambled down the sidewalk on the quiet neighborhood street.

"I'm sorry I didn't contact you sooner," she said. "I got pretty sick and wasn't in a position to call."

"It appears you're improved since the last time I saw you," Annamie replied. "However, you're still walking down this new path? You're set on it?"

Nadir nodded. "I've become a hunter, Annamie. I work with others like me. I'm not alone. They protect me when I need it."

"Like when you were recently sick?" she asked.

"Exactly. Or backup in fights."

"Sounds dangerous, but I suppose no more so than what you're used to," Annamie replied.

"I guess it does," she replied. "But I can hold my own, and I'll only get stronger."

"So this new occupation of yours. I take it you're not broadcasting it?"

"No, I'm telling you in confidence, Annamie." She stopped walking and turned to her old, if-now-dubious friend. "I need you to keep an eye out for me and filter me news of daemon activity. You've always told me what you hear. Can you keep doing so despite my change?"

Annamie held her index finger to her lips. "I'm torn, Meri. You're one of them now."

Nadir tilted her head. "I'm not entirely one of them, Annamie. I'm out there taking out the ones who have the ability to roam our streets at will. Does that make you feel any better?"

Annamie's eyes widened. "That's impossible! They can't come through without being summoned."

"They can, since they've been feasting on summoner souls, and you can be assured they are, however quietly. I need your cooperation in feeding me the latest gossip on what daemon-related attacks are going down. That's all. Nothing to put you in harm's way, just keep sharing what you hear. It'll be like old times, except I'm a wee bit different now."

Annamie's face had changed, brows now knit with right-eous indignation and mouth agape with horror while Nadir explained. Now Annamie held her hands on her hips resolutely. "Well now, that's another story altogether. Why didn't you say so!"

She smiled at Annamie's righteous indignation. "I've been trying to tell you."

"Next time hold me still and shout, for goodness sake! All right, I'll get you your gossip. There's a series of attacks down south of the city in Lone Tree that's not sitting right with me. I'll call you with more details in the morning."

"Lone Tree? That's about as peaceful a suburb as you can get!" Nadir exclaimed.

"That's why it's stuck in my mind. I'll call you with the addresses, and not the ones the media are citing. The actual ones."

"Thank you, Annamie," she replied. "Whatever it is, I'll get it cleaned up."

Annamie shivered from head to toe. "Let's leave those details out of our future discussions, shall we?"

"No worries," Nadir grinned. "I wouldn't want to talk about it anyway."

Annamie's sad frown touched her heart. Although they weren't back to hugging status, it was the closest their friendship had been since Nadir had taken the job saddling her with her first daemon.

They said quick goodbyes and Drew even gave her a one-handed shoulder pat before the couple walked back to their car and left. She watched them drive off and then strolled back towards her house.

Under a clear, moonlit sky, Nadir breathed in the crisp night air. Her parents were finally avenged, but it was bitter-sweet in her heart. She still harbored resentment towards them over how they'd messed up Calloine's failed summoning and left her alone, but she had plenty of time to heal now. Her life was finally back under control, as far as she could make it under the circumstances. She feared living under Belial's allegiance might one day cause her problems, but at least she wouldn't be alone if it happened. She had her cabal-mates to rely upon now.

Besides, she had a budding relationship with another daemon. No, Liminal.

Nadir was so caught up in her thoughts she didn't notice the shadow rising in front of her until it eclipsed the view of her home two houses down. Adrenaline shot through her veins, and she backed up reflexively, but it soon surrounded her, blackness incarnate.

It had no smell, made no sound, and set off none of her daemon warning bells. It was no daemon. It was only a shadow.

Saleigh, however, sang out joyfully, as he expanded and fought for dominance within her.

Azimuth! She called out mentally.

"It's too late now," Saleigh's voice mocked as he opened up to her and embraced the shadow descending upon them both.

"What is this thing?" she croaked out, choking through the darkness.

This time, his energy gripped hers, anger pouring through her every cell. "This is my shadow. My darkness. You pathetic, naïve, little creature! There were things even I couldn't abide in my long life, so I had them torn from me, magically, and stored in a canopic chest, freeing me. But your friends must have opened it, looking for my secrets. Now my past has come home to roost and will free us both, eternally. It looks like I'll win this gambit, after all."

Unimaginable darkness oozed into Nadir, bringing her to her knees. Her illusion of humanity flashed away, along with her dinner, into the gutter. She shook in pain, gasping for breath that never came. The pounding of her heart slowed, churning not blood but instead some brackish, ebony substance.

"The sorcerers who worked the magic told me," Saleigh whispered to her, "that if I ever rejoined with my darkness, I would surely perish. You forced this binding to me, you bitch. Now I'm quite sure we're not going to survive this." He laughed the chess player who'd declared checkmate. "Tell me. Is it as excruciating a process as I'd feared?"

Nadir tried to speak, to scream. Instead, she curled to the ground in a fetal position, tears streaming from her eyes. Again, she called out to Azimuth and looked up at the moon, watching as it too faded to black.

All she could hear beyond the pain was the sound of Saleigh's triumphant laughter.

---

*S*he sucked in the air, aware of an extreme pounding sensation in her ears and a fire that burning every nerve so she couldn't think straight. Hands held her down, and she kicked and punched them away. She screamed, and then coughed, phlegm stuck to her sore throat.

The pain continued to burn through her, touching every cell, every nerve. She curled into a ball, vaguely aware of voices around her.

"I have no idea what happened," said one. "When I found her on the street with no heartbeat I feared the worst."

"Well, she's revived now," said another. "We'll have to wait and see how she recuperates in the long term. I've never seen anything like it before. It's unprecedented."

"Our little group is unprecedented, Belial," said a third. "This little lady has already shown us to expect the unexpected, in more than one way."

Their words scraped on her mind, cutting against the exposed raw epicenter of her world.

"SHUT UP!" she screamed.

Finally, silence. Or near to it. There was a shuffling of feet and quiet murmurs. She forced her hands over her ears, shutting out the noise the others wouldn't cease making. Didn't they understand?

Everything hurt.

She smelled so much. Too much. Her body reeked of the bloody iron of pain and the lighting-sharp tang of death. The others in the room. There were four. Why were they here? Why did they continue their incessant murmuring?

"GO AWAY!" she screamed.

Silence. Blessed silence.

"You'll keep her here?" asked another.

"Yes. Go," said the one.

Feet shuffled, and a door closed softly.

She still smelled the one. Her irritation was only overshadowed by pain.

Why did everything hurt so much?

She didn't remember why.

Coughs racked her chest. Her throat was sore and dry.

Footsteps neared, and she instinctively drew back. What had happened to her? Panic flared and grew within her.

A hand touched her bare arm, and she slapped it. The hand withdrew.

"Be calm, Nadir," said the one. His voice flowed like silk over her and her muscles relaxed, but the pain remained.

"Nadir?" she croaked, her voice was broken, wrong. She hid her face in her hands, curled back up, and shivered in pain.

His hand touched her arm again, and this time she flinched but didn't fight him off. After a moment, a languid sensation suffused her limbs, her heart rate slowed, and the pain dulled.

She sighed in relief and lowered her hands from her face. She opened her eyes, but it was too bright, and she cried out from the blinding pain of the light.

"Dammit, hold on." He left and in his brief absence, the pain intensified. When he returned, he replaced his hand on her arm. "It's alright," he said in a whisper, "the light's darker now."

She opened her eyes again, and this time they only stung and watered. He crouched over her, his deep blue eyes full of concern under a halo of silvery-blond hair. He ran his fingers gently down her cheek.

"I'm confused," she said. The words came out more easily although her voice was still cracked and dry.

"Hold on," he said. He reached for a glass of water with a straw in it. "Drink."

She accepted the water and drank greedily. When she was done, he started stroking her hair, which both unsettled her and yet stirred something inside of her.

"What happened to me?" she asked.

A sad look clouded his eyes. "We were hoping you could clue us in a bit. You called me. I came and found you lying on the street outside your house. You weren't breathing, and your heart wasn't beating either. I ported you here. We did CPR while Belial did a resurrection spell, just to be safe. We covered all the bases. After a while, you came around. Then I brought you in here."

She looked around; her pain abated to the point where it no longer prevented motion. She lay on a large bed covered in black linens. The room was big and had some bookshelves and a pair of overstuffed, high-backed armchairs on either end of a plush couch on the far end. Everything was in coordinating dark green tones. A door led off to what appeared to be a bathroom and another perhaps to a closet. Everything was simple, yet spoke of refinement.

"And 'here' is?" she asked.

"My bedroom," he explained.

"Right," she answered. She looked to where he touched her and again noted how calm she felt and how the pain continued to fade. "Are you stopping the pain?"

A look of alarm passed over his face but he hid it quickly. "Yes, of course."

"Thank you." She looked up at him and the look of caring in his eyes. Why was he helping her?

"What's my name?" His hand on her arm stroked her tenderly, but tension lay just under the surface of his voice.

Nadir. Is my name Nadir?

Somehow, that didn't sit right with her. It felt incomplete.

He said she'd called him and then he'd helped her, and now she lay in his bed. Unmistakably, she knew him. What was his name?

Something stirred within her, and an ancient knowledge supplied the word "Azimuth" to her. She didn't comprehend it, but it was simply there.

"Azimuth," she answered.

The muscles around his eyes tightened slightly. "You have memory loss, don't you?"

Her ancient knowledge stirred again, and she knew Azimuth could discern whether she told the truth or lies. Interesting. "I knew your name," she replied.

"True, but now you're going off your gleaner's advice, not memory. You don't usually call me Azimuth in private." He cupped the nape of her neck with his hand. "Don't worry; you're among friends. You're safe. And, most likely, your memory will soon return in full."

He said these words with such power she believed him completely. It struck her as some gift he had of convincing others, and the inner knowing inside her head agreed.

"How long?" Her lower lip trembled from the fear of never regaining who she'd been.

Azimuth shook his head. "Most likely this is only short term."

She calmed a bit, eased by the feel of Azimuth's touch on her arm. He massaged the back and side of her neck, comforting her with his contact. She stretched into his touch, no longer fearing him. As the pain faded, she could breathe fully again. The heady smell of his scent filled her lungs. She closed her eyes and vanilla, musk, and sandalwood pulled her into a dream, another world for a moment, and she was lost to the pleasure of the smell, stirring a need she didn't know she'd forgotten. Her temperature rose a few degrees, heating the air around her noticeably.

Her eyes snapped open. "What's happening?" she demanded, but Azimuth didn't appear disturbed in the least. In fact, a sly hint of a smile graced his lips.

"You are imbued with many different talents. This is just one of them manifesting. There's nothing wrong," he answered.

His smile, although smug, left her unable to look anywhere but his deliciously full lips for a moment. Now, why had she done that?

"Then why do you look so amused with yourself?" Nadir asked. Her temperature continued to rise, and she had no idea how to make it stop. Azimuth withdrew his hands and stood up, appearing uncomfortable, but no less pleased by the grin on his face. She sat up and watched her red hair billowing out around her.

"I'd only thought, with your death -- brief though it was -- when it severed the enchantment you were under, that perhaps your inclinations might have changed. It appears I am happily incorrect," he said.

While he talked, she couldn't concentrate. She was flooded with images of what his chest would look like with his nicely tailored shirt off, or what he might look like out of those leather pants and black boots. Nadir smiled when she glimpsed the outline of his erection pressing against his pants.

"You're not hearing a thing I'm saying, are you? Nadir. Eyes here!" He pointed to his face. His commanding tone irritated her beyond reason, so she got up from the bed and stalked towards Azimuth, her eyes locked on his.

"I see your amnesia caused you to lose your ability to modulate your talents. And I am not taking advantage of you when you don't have your full faculties," he said, wagging his finger like a schoolteacher.

"Perhaps I'll take advantage of you? Thanks to you, I feel perfectly fine now. You're welcome to check me out for yourself," she offered, stepping ever closer. She could taste him in her mouth, and she swallowed hard, imagining the musky tang of his skin on her tongue.

"What we need to do is trigger your memories, or otherwise wait them out." Azimuth stood with his hands on his hips.

"Waiting's not what I had in mind," she replied, a pout playing across her lips.

"So I gathered." Azimuth stood his ground near the couch.

She closed the distance, pressed her body against his, and ran her hands over his chest. He groaned but didn't move in response.

"This isn't so bad, is it?" The air sizzled between them as droplets of sweat formed on their skin. Nadir couldn't help but reach up and slip a hand through the silken strands of his hair. She closed her eyes, savoring the sensation, and did it again, and again.

"I should take you home," he said.

She pulled her hand back with a jerk. "Is it safe for me there?" She searched his face. "You said that's where I got hurt."

He took her hands in his. "You were outside your house, outside the safety of your protective wards. Inside, you'll be safe and surrounded by reminders of who you are."

"You'll come too?" she asked.

"I won't leave you alone, Nadir, not in this state."

"What state?" she smiled and leaned into him, which he dodged, keeping her at bay with his suddenly firm grip on her wrists. Nadir struggled playfully, whining when he wouldn't let go.

"Your amnesiac state, pet," he replied. "Come on."

Azimuth dragged her by the wrist out of his room and down a hallway. When they entered a large room, the others quieted their discussion immediately. Nadir recognized their scents from earlier, and now matched faces to the smells. The big blue one stunk like burning fire, the dark one oddly like cloves and sugar, and the redheaded one like pine and orris root -- not overpowering, yet each distinct in their own way.

"I'm taking her home," Azimuth said. "She's got amnesia from whatever happened. Hopefully, something around her home will trigger her memory."

The dark one with the black eyes walked over to them, but he stopped a few feet away. "The enchantment broke upon her death." He looked to Azimuth.

"Yes, but she's having a difficult time controlling all of her abilities right now. I think it's a simple matter of not remembering her past," Azimuth explained. "At least if I take Nadir to her home, she'll benefit from the triggers, and you all won't be exposed to her unmodulated energies."

The other two, one of whom was taller and had dark blue skin and horns, joined them.

The one with curly brown hair laughed. "She's not bugging me, brother. Nadir may not be able to control her output, but she's got you pegged."

Azimuth turned to her, an eyebrow raised and his smug grin had returned. "So you're able to direct your abilities, but not control the response?"

She frowned, unclear what he was asking.

The dark one walked up to her and lifted her chin with his index finger. "Even while touching you, you don't direct your abilities at me. Fascinating. It's amazing control for someone who's struggled so much." He backed off, his thoughtful eyes kind.

"Thanks?" Nadir replied, unsure of the context of the conversation.

"We should go now. The sooner, the better," Azimuth said.

"Are you sure someone else wouldn't be a better choice to accompany Nadir home?" the blue one asked.

"No," Nadir and Azimuth replied loudly in unison, drawing a smirk from Orias and stifled laughter from Kobol.

"It'll be okay, Belial," replied the dark one. "Let them work this out on their own."

The blue one grumbled a deep, gravelly sound. "I don't like relying on your foretellings, Orias."

The dark one smiled sardonically. "Then you shouldn't have built me this way, no? Besides, this is no foretelling, simply instinct on my part."

"Have fun bantering," Azimuth said. He pulled Nadir to him, and they were gone.

CHAPTER 23

One second they were in the cave, and the next they were in a small, cozy living room in a comfortable smelling house.

"How did you do that?" she asked, pulling away from Azimuth.

He leaned back against a wall where the wallpaper had shriveled and warped. "It's teleporting. You can do it too. You just don't remember how to right now."

"Uh huh. And that wall, what happened there?" she asked.

A mischievous glint gleamed in his eyes. "You did it, proving a point to me about your control."

Nadir took another look at the wallpaper. It looked like she'd tried to melt it off the wall. "Oh."

"Yes. 'Oh.'"

He laughed and shook his head, all the while she was hyper aware of the heat pouring off her body. She could generate enough heat to melt the walls. Hopefully, she wouldn't burn the house down too.

"Why don't you take a look around?" Azimuth said. "It's why we're here, after all."

She did and had to admit the place felt familiar, but not exactly her style. She felt like it belonged to another era. The couch was a dingy brown and the accompanying armchairs a faded, threadbare yellow with colorful afghans thrown over them to hide their age. The end and coffee tables were well-used oak. The drapes hanging on the windows were white eyelet cotton in front of wide slatted blinds that did the real work. The newer electronics spoke to what she thought must be her sensibilities. Beside the large front window, a mahogany desk sat covered in papers. Some were written in English, some were bills, and some were in a variety of arcane tongues. This space she identified with even if she didn't remember it.

"'This place is due for a makeover. Why do I live with this old crap?" she asked.

"It belonged to your parents," Azimuth answered.

He said nothing else. She looked at him and then back at the room, and the mantle over the hearth covered in pictures of herself with, presumably, her parents. She drew close. In none of them was she older than a teenager. Nadir understood without words. This house was her memorial after they'd died. The memory wasn't there, but the conviction sat firm.

"I need to let go. I can let go now, can't I?" she looked to Azimuth for confirmation.

He nodded. "It's time for a remodel. You could certainly buy a new place if you wanted."

"No," she said. "I don't think I should. This is mine. My territory."

"Even without your memories," Azimuth chuckled. "How am I not surprised?"

The smells of lightning and iron of her clothing disturbed her again, reminding Nadir of her recent brush with death. "I need to change."

She walked down the hallway to her bedroom and pulled out a fresh set of pjs. She stripped off her clothes and kicked them into the corner, mentally marking them for future incineration. Nadir realized her skin stank of death too, so she carried her pj's with her to the bathroom and showered. After she pulled on the new clothes and towel-dried her hair, she emerged refreshed and somewhat cooled down.

Azimuth hadn't moved. He remained casually leaning against the wallpaper she'd damaged, looking sleek and refined compared to the old-fashioned interior of her home. Nadir's internal temperature cranked back up a notch.

"You realize you knew where your bedroom and bathroom were, don't you?" he said.

She paused mid-step. "I didn't even think about it. It just flowed naturally."

A cell phone rang, buzzing away on the desk, and Nadir jumped. For a moment, she simply stared at it, and then she rushed to answer it.

"Hello?"

"Meri, this is Annamie. I have the information on the location in Lone Tree for you. Do you have a pen handy?"

She paused, processing the familiar names, and then caught back up with the stream of the conversation. "Just a moment." She grabbed a pen and paper off the desk. "Okay, go."

Annamie rattled off three addresses, and Nadir wrote

them down. "From what I hear there was someone killed at the last one just last night, and the others have all had deaths in the past week. The cops were rattled because the bodies were missing their internal organs but otherwise completely intact. I've never heard daemons doing this before, have you?"

"No, I agree, that's very odd," Nadir replied, for lack of a better response, lost to the deeper meaning of Annamie's words. She wrote 'daemons' and 'humans missing internal organs' on the piece of paper under the addresses. Azimuth stood, watching over her shoulder, which was both comforting and distracting.

"I hope that's what you wanted to know when we talked earlier."

"Yes," she replied, although she had no context whatsoever for their entire conversation. "That's exactly what I needed. Thanks, Annamie."

"You're welcome. Let me know how it works out."

"Okay."

"Goodnight, Meri."

"Goodnight."

The line went dead, and Nadir put the phone down.

"Well, that was interesting," she said, turning to face Azimuth. She was suddenly exceptionally aware of her breathing and felt like the walls were too close.

"Enlightening," he replied. "So you talked with your friend Annamie earlier about giving you leads on daemon infestations in the area, and she agreed. She's been a valuable resource for you in the past. She knew you as 'Meri,' but you likely figured that out already. From what you've said of Annamie's leanings towards daemons, I guess you wouldn't have talked inside the house, because it's protected by daemon wards, right?"

"I don't... I'm not sure," Nadir replied. She looked at her arms, and they flickered with images of flashing swirls and splashes of color where none had been before. The ink-covered skin felt more authentic and real, disturbing her.

"I need a drink of water," she said.

She pushed Azimuth out of her way and bolted into the kitchen. She grabbed a glass out of the cupboard and filled it from the tap. Nadir downed it in a series of gulps without breathing, and then gulped in air.

The sound of maniacal laughter rippled at the corners of her mind, but she pushed it away. She turned, and Azimuth stood leaning against the counter. Something about that was altogether too familiar. She grabbed another glass.

"Do you need a drink?" she asked, frowning. She went ahead and poured it, not waiting for an answer.

She'd been here before, with him. She'd done all of this before. She held out the glass and the memories, everything she'd lost when she died, cascaded through her mind like a giant, unforgiving waterfall. She dropped the glass in shock. Azimuth caught it, placed it on the counter, and then caught Nadir, whose knees gave out.

"We were here, before." She looked up into his eyes, embarrassment flushing her skin as she remembered what they'd done in her kitchen. Desperate need for him filled her and battered at the inner walls of her heart. At least this time she hadn't trashed her kitchen, hadn't broken yet another glass.

"Yes," his voice was hushed, his eyes searching hers. "Is that a question, or are you remembering?"

Nadir recalled wrapping herself around his muscular frame, practically climbing up him right here, just a few days, or was it weeks, earlier. How long had it been? She looked up into his aquamarine eyes and blushed. She forcibly calmed herself, reining in her abilities. Her need for him.

"Remembering it is, then," Azimuth ran a hand through her hair and tucked it behind her ear. "How much? Do you remember earlier tonight? After you met with Annamie?"

Saleigh's laughter haunted her, and Nadir trembled. "Everything. It all just crashed through like a wave. But it doesn't make sense. Saleigh is gone now and so is his essence," she explained.

Azimuth's brows narrowed, and he kept her close, which she loved but also wondered over.

Mahkra's enchantment had been broken with her death -- and the truth hit her like a fist to the gut. There was no need for him to protect her, watch over her, or otherwise see to her needs. He and the others had mentioned it earlier, and she hadn't understood or cared at the time what they were talking about. What would it mean to their relationship? Enchantment or no, she'd given her heart to him, despite the short time and odd circumstances.

"I believe you," he said. "Tell me more of what happened after Annamie left."

Right, Azimuth was always about business first. She described her encounter with the shadow and how Saleigh had described it as his parts he'd had secreted away in some part of the burrow.

"There was an unadorned, heavily warded chest Kobol found in Saleigh's chambers. He was convinced it might hold some unique weapon. We broke into it, but it contained only shadows," Azimuth explained.

"That must have been his canopic chest where he kept all the parts of himself he couldn't live with anymore. He said if he ever recombined with the shadows, he'd be destroyed," Nadir replied. She pulled away from Azimuth and poured herself another glass of water and then settled against the opposite counter.

"And so he was, along with his shadows." Azimuth's face grew pained.

"He never stopped wanting revenge towards me, so he waited and hoped someone would come upon that chest and open it, just as you did," she continued. "He laughed the entire time as I struggled to breathe. It was Orias' prediction come true after all, just with different timing."

"I warned you Orias is never wrong. Saleigh did succeed in killing you. If I'd been any later, we wouldn't have been able to revive you. That daemon nearly fried your entire nervous system out during his death throes. It explains the damage I healed earlier. Are you sure the pain is fully resolved?"

Nadir shivered at the thought of Orias' premonition finally resolving, and aware just how close she'd come to death. "Yes, thanks. It feels weird having him gone. Not that I wanted him in the first place, but I feel weaker overall. Perhaps it's just residual damage from his passing." She took another drink of water and crossed her arms in front of herself protectively. Whether it was from the memory of her close brush with mortality, or her feelings for the daemon across from her, she'd be hard pressed to pick.

Azimuth closed the space between them and placed a

hand on the counter next to her. "You don't have to feel guilty for how you feel. We take these killers out, and they hitch a ride inside us until they fade away over the next weeks to months. During that time, we have to put up with their personalities and yet still learn the finesse of their talents, making them our own. With Saleigh's death, you lost an opportunity to gain knowledge from him on how to use his skills and suffered damage. Give yourself time to heal. I'm sure you're drained on multiple fronts."

She kept a tight rein on all of her abilities, especially Lust. "Now that my memory is back, I should probably get some rest." She drained the rest of the water in her glass, set it on the counter, and then slid past Azimuth and into the living room.

"That's one option," Azimuth replied, following her. "Unless you need a recharge."

Nadir stopped and turned to him, gathering her thoughts. She'd never been one to run from a difficult situation. "I don't want you feeling obligated to me, Azimuth. You're free now."

"I was free before." Azimuth's walked toward her in slow, deliberate steps.

"You were free, sure," Nadir replied. "You didn't have to help me. But you knew I'd suffer if you chose not to, and you're too honorable not to have helped me."

Azimuth's eyes raked over her body in a way that made her temperature fluctuate despite her best efforts. "It's amusing. When you were first healed, you had a very definite idea what you wanted." His gaze challenged her.

"The enchantment is broken. I know I have to sustain my daemon essences, but it's not your job anymore to be stuck to me. I can find other ways now."

"You're saying you don't want me now that your memory has returned?" Azimuth backed her up into the back of the couch. His legs pinned hers in place. The look in his eyes was demanding. Dangerous. The air around him sparked like lightning, glowing radiant white.

"This isn't just about what I want, Azimuth. It's about your needs. Don't you see? You had a life before I came along. A long one. I hijacked it. You have a right to have it back."

Azimuth stroked a hand down her arm, light as a feather. "Are you saying you'd let me go, and move on if I didn't want this?"

"Yes," Nadir replied. I'll have to.

"Little liar," he replied with a chuckle and slid a hand up to grasp the nape of her neck and another around her waist and drew her close. "How about I make this easier on you, pet? I'm glad the enchantment is gone. It served an undue burden on us both. Instead of choosing to be together, our hand was forced."

"Exactly," she broke in and was quickly silenced by Azimuth's lips lightly brushing against hers.

"To be clear," he continued. "My interest in you remains quite focused. I do believe I need some time to explore just why I'm so mesmerized by you." Azimuth bent his head down and kissed along her jaw line, and then nibbled her ear.

"How long are you planning this interest to last?" she asked, panting. She remained in tight control of her abilities. Her temperature remained normal, despite the distraction of his hand working over her backside. Nadir reciprocated by pulling his soft, white shirt out of his leather pants.

Azimuth groaned in satisfaction when she slid her hands up his bare chest under his shirt.

"I hadn't picked out a specific timeframe. With your new lease on life, the decades will fly by. Trust me on that. But, no pressure, we can just take it one day at a time," he replied.

Nadir laughed aloud, and Azimuth caught her face in his hands. "What's so funny?" His azure eyes sparkled in the dim light of the room.

Her breath caught in her throat. "A month ago I didn't think I'd live out the year. Certainly not a decade. Immortality. I can't wrap my mind around it. Give me time."

"You'll see it, and more. So much more."

He bent in and captured her lips with his. She opened to him, and he languidly explored her mouth with his tongue, sweeping and probing her depths in a teasing play. His fingers danced down her arms, and then brushed back up her chest, teasing her breasts through her thin cami top. Nadir wound her fingers through his hair and whimpered. Azimuth pulled her top off over her head and soon turned his attention to her sensitive nipples.

When his mouth returned to hers, Nadir was demanding, grasping at his shirt. He immediately pulled the fabric off over his head. The feel of his bare skin on hers sent a primeval sigh issuing from her lips. She dug her fingers into his back, wild for more contact.

"I need you, Az. All of you."

He growled in reply, every inch the predator again with her. He stripped her pj bottoms off and lifted her up onto the couch. Azimuth bit a line of possessive bite marks in a line down her neck. Then he spent a moment nibbling and teasing her nipples before he crouched down and kissed her inner thighs delicately while slowly parting her folds with his fingers.

"You're going to kill me, Az," she moaned, running fingers through his silken hair.

He grumbled in laughter before locking his mouth onto her already throbbing core with a hunter's intensity. Nadir could barely breathe when his fingers slid inside of her, deepening the sensation while he sucked gently on her swollen nub. Her feet sought purchase on his shoulders while she trembled with waves of pleasure, surprised at the immediacy of her orgasm.

Azimuth lingered for a moment, tonguing her folds, but she speared him with a glance. "Oh no, you don't. Up here."

He pulled away and stood, glowing with a faint white charge. He dropped his pants and kicked them off, all the while holding her gaze. Once he was naked, she slid off the couch and pounced on him, pressing him against the wall with the melted wallpaper, kissing him urgently.

She reached between them and stroked his firm shaft. "If I want a taste of you, will you stop me this time?"

"I didn't stop you the last time, pet," he replied. "But I must admit, I'll be a bit less cautious now." A corner of his mouth curled up in a smile, and then he captured her mouth and kissed her, claiming her. Nadir almost forgot her purpose, except she felt his manhood continue to pulsate within her grip.

When she pulled away, breathless, she dropped to her knees, his throbbing erection still in her hands. Azimuth's nimbus glowed brighter, as if on reflex. She drew her tongue along the length of his smooth flesh before circling his engorged mushroom tip. When she finally wrapped her lips around him and slid his swollen flesh deep into her mouth, Azimuth groaned in pleasure.

Nadir continued her strokes, taking her cue from his reactions, and looked up into Azimuth's lust-drunk gaze. He fisted his hands in her hair, gripping firmly, and set her pace.

He let out a growl. "Enough. Up. Now."

She rose and smiled at the look in his eyes, which bore the barest hint of self-control. For once, she wasn't the one on edge.

He picked her up easily, spun around, and pressed her against the wall, her legs slung over his arms. When he drove home inside her, she cried out. She'd been too long unfulfilled. He completed her in a way she'd never known before.

Nadir wrapped herself around Azimuth in a passionate embrace, lost in the sensation of his skin covering hers. His scent shifted, taking on the slight hint of clove. She licked and nibbled along Azimuth's shoulder, loving the musky flavor of his skin. He caught her jaw with his hand and turned her to face him, slowing his pace.

She frowned. "What, did you think I was going to bite you again?" she laughed, and he lifted an eyebrow. "I can if you want," Nadir offered, digging her fingers into his backside and urging him to resume his earlier pace.

"I doubt you would, pet, but just for safety's sake." Azimuth grinned. He picked her up, still kissing her fervently while he disentangled them. He stood her up, spun Nadir around, and bent her over the old sofa.

Azimuth ran his fingers lightly up her sides, sending shivers down her spine. His lips rasped against her ear, his hot breath on her neck.

"You certainly couldn't bite me now," he whispered, digging his fingers into her hair, pulling her head back firmly.

He teased her mercilessly by rubbing his throbbing erection between her thighs.

"You know I wouldn't," Nadir managed to gasp out. She tried to press back onto his straining masculinity but lacked all leverage in this position. She was completely at his mercy.

Azimuth pressed into her slowly, and then stopped part way. Nadir squirmed for more, and then she felt his smile against her ear.

"You sure I'm not going to push you over the edge?" he asked. He slid inside a little deeper.

"I'm begging you, Az," she replied. It was all she could do to hold herself up with her arms, her toes not touching the floor. Nadir shook with need. Burned with it.

He buried himself deep inside her, and she cried out in delight. Azimuth plunged into her with increasing intensity, filling her as she strained under him.

"I've managed to push the woman over the edge this time," he whispered, sounding very pleased with himself.

Their passion had been driven to new heights and untamed in a way she'd never experienced before. Her daemonic lust hadn't emerged until those moments of her completion when it fed upon her orgasmic waves and then subsided at this lull, retreating within her psyche.

Nadir was satiated, in her body, heart, and mind. When Azimuth picked her up and carried her off to the bedroom, by the look in his eyes, sleep was not yet on his mind.

She smiled and snuggled her nose against his neck, savoring his sandalwood musk.

*T*hey spent the remainder of the night and the following day together, entwined, asleep, or eating. That evening, Nadir insisted they contact the others about the situation in Lone Tree.

"I've had enough recuperation time, Az," she said, pulling on her shirt while studiously ignoring the way he watched her every move. She didn't need the encouragement. "Besides, according to Annamie's call, the daemons there are taking someone out every two to three days. They're due again tonight."

"We have a few hours left until then, pet." His heated gaze lingered over her hips as Nadir pulled up her underwear. "Plenty of time to prepare. Come back to bed."

"No," she replied, and then cringed reflexively, but no enchantment punished her for denying his directives. Those days had passed along with Saleigh and her brief death.

He smiled sympathetically. "Soon enough those memories will pass."

She sighed. "I hope so. I feel a bit Pavlovian-trained right about now. Gods help Belial if he suggests me using my lust binding on anyone! I'm still disgusted by the thought. I swear I'll deck him before he finishes his request." She finished pulling on her pants and looked up to see Azimuth fighting back laughter. "What?"

"You have my word," he said, suddenly solemn. "I'll try and steer him clear of using that particular gift of yours."

"Damn skippy," Nadir replied with a huff. "Now we should go, yes?"

"You're right, of course." He sighed dramatically and then stood and dressed quickly.

She couldn't help but watch with rapt attention, fascinated with his lithe movements. Suddenly his suggestion to wait a while longer didn't seem all that unreasonable after all. "Surely this won't take the entire night?"

"We can't know for sure," he replied, frowning slightly. He brushed a finger across her lips, heating her blood infinitesimally, and then held out his hand. "Let's get the others. We'll make short work of it."

Nadir took his hand. "We don't even know what we're getting into."

"This is not unusual. But we know who we're going with, and that's all we need to know."

THE END

Want more? Sign up now for updates and I'll send you a newsletter exclusive extra!

GLOSSARY

- Arch-Daemons -- These daemons command armies of daemons, immense wealth, vast power, and the like. Often they have waged and won countless battles, assuming it suits their disposition. It does.
- Burners -- The Burner community of artisans started in 1986 around a festival known as 'Burning Man' and grew through the early 20th century, with a number of self-reliant enclaves springing up through the 21st century. By the time The Fall occurred in the 22nd century many fled to these off-the-grid communes to escape the Corporate-imposed rule.
- Cabal -- A group of aligned daemons in Sheol. They are always under blood-oath to a leader (determined by age, power, ruthlessness, or all of the above).
- Cambions -- (Daemon/human hybrids) These

happen very, very rarely, and only live on earth when they do survive the initial gestation. Always the progeny of a daemon and a human woman and rarely do they realize they are a hybrid. Abilities manifest in their teens and cambions often end up in an insane asylum or prison, depending on how their abilities manifest.

- Daemon -- A denizen of Sheol and descendant of Hades. The power of the daemon depends on how close his or her blood ties lie to the god, and the expression of power varies widely. Your average mid-level daemons who have lived for under a thousand years and are just now getting their wits about them. Generally, they are coming into their power and forming alliances, assuming they've survived enough battles to gain a reputation for their name. The numbers of daemons are countless and never ending.

- Daemon Summoner -- A human who uses arcane means (oils, herbs, unguents, symbols, incantations, etc.) to summon a daemon and bind them to their will. This transactional cost is different for each daemon, often related to daemon's power. Once bound, the daemon's ink sets into the summoner's skin, and the daemon will then complete a single task for the summoner before returning to Sheol. Multiple bindings with the same daemon will increase the size and complexity of the given daemon's ink on the summoner's skin. Summoning is a very dangerous business, as failed bindings leave the daemon free to attack the summoner.

- Elder-Daemons -- Of which there are thousands. These daemons sometimes command by age alone, with others too afraid to challenge them. Alternatively, they may be loners and choose not to align to any cabal, not needing the strength of others to withstand threats. Elders are formidable enemies, and invaluable allies.

- God-Touched -- A human devotee of a god, always marked with sigils (specific to the deity they revere), although they have the ability to hide the sigils from non-supernatural beings. They avoid others who use magical influence, because they feel their choice of dealing with the divine directly as the superior one.

- Hades -- God of the Underworld.

- Liminals -- A species of supernatural hybrids overseen by the goddess Hekate of the Underworld, who rules over crossroads and all events and creatures who linger there. Liminals hold the crossroads -- the line of transition between the living and the dead.

- Princes (daemons) -- Of which there are dozens. This is determined by birthright under the direct lineage of Hades himself. They are plentiful enough few feel particular value in the title. Few challenge their strength.

- Sheol -- The daemonic plane exists in close proximity to Earth. Made up of various regions, pits, and sections in a vast network constructed over aeon's, possibly only Hades himself understands its entire history, terrain, or inhabitants.

- Sigil -- A symbol used to summon and bind daemons or other entity to a summoner's will by referencing the elements related to the daemon's true essence. The original sigils date back to The Lesser Key of Solomon, but other, more modern sources exist, many in private collections among summoner's grimoires.

- Succubi/Incubi -- Very minor daemons, still deadly to humans but inconsequential within daemon politics. There are lesser and greater forms within these classes.

- Teleportation -- (aka Porting) Done via simple visualization and requires an elemental tie before a being may port into a plane of existence. I.e. daemonic essence to port to Sheol, human soul to port to Earth, etc.

- The Fall -- In the years 2035-2045 the American and EU governments became financially inviable and step-by-step privatized functions to Corporate bidders in order to remain solvent. The intention of a temporary fix turned permanent. Eventually, the government did so little the Corporations moved to disband them. There was no recourse to stop them. Now, instead of political parties jockeying for power, Corporations vie for territories.

- Tre'jor -- A blade fabricated by Belial to eradicate daemons, capturing their essences and transferring them into the human hosts of his cabal.

AUTHOR'S NOTE

If you loved the book and have a minute to spare, I would really appreciate a short review on the page or site where you bought the book. Your help in spreading the word is greatly appreciated. Reviews from readers like you make a huge difference to helping new readers find similar stories.

Thank you so much for reading and supporting my work!
Candice

P.S. If you'd like to know when my next book comes out and want to receive occasional updates from me, then you can sign up for my newsletter at candicebundy.com. I promise I will never sell your email to the daemonic marketing hordes.

ALSO BY CANDICE BUNDY

The Stolen Legacy Series

Forbidden Fates

Entangled Essence

Hidden Hearts

The Shadow Series

Shadow in the City, A prequel novella

Twinned Shadow

Poisoned Shadow

Shadow Underground

Caught Between Worlds Series

Smoke and Daemons

(*previously published as Daemon Whisperer*)

Other Works

Ripples, a novella

Open Rack, a contemporary short

WRITING AS CR BUNDY

The Depths of Memory Series

The Dream Sifter

Dreams Manifest

For a list of my full catalog of available titles, visit my Amazon Author Central page.

ACKNOWLEDGMENTS

No book happens in a vacuum. I've been blessed with fabulous support by loving, smart, and talented people, and this made all the difference in completing my journey. I want to take a moment to mention these wonderful people, and I hope you'll take the time to appreciate them with me.

First, I want to thank my family, who've not only gotten used to my daily writing routine but embraced it, managing to tolerate my writing despite the time I've devoted to the cause. And no, I'm sorry son, I have yet to write something suitable for you to read. It's on my list, sweetie.

A wave of adoration to my beta readers: Nancy, Morgan, Isha, and Brian. Your feedback helped me mold this universe when I hit my initial potholes and aided my nitpicks on the end run. You're also some of the fastest readers I know. And you're mine, all mine!

To my Twitter posse, filled with crunchy goodness, daily inspiration, oxford commas, and enough humor to keep me laughing no matter how much hair I've pulled out in a day. Amber West, Keri Lake, Kiersten Fay -- I'm lucky to have found you and have your support. Alan Edwards -- We'll always have whale sharks. Jen Kirchner -- Thanks to you I didn't commit homicide. I, and my family are forever grateful. K.M. Cambion -- You helped encouraged my daemons in devious ways. This surprises no one. Steven Montano: You're a solid rock of crack coffee. Don't ever change.

A huge group hug to my family and friends for their ongoing love and support. You've been fantastic.

Thanks to Zippy Wizard Redaction for their editing and proofreading services. You're fabulous!

Lastly, to my mom and your sage words of advice. I'll continue to write with freedom.

ABOUT THE AUTHOR

Candice lives in Denver, Colorado with her son and their cat Newt. A professional hedonist, rabble-rouser, winemaker, and goat-herder, she adores archeology and mythology. Candice focuses on habit hacking to meet minimalist, health, productivity, and positive mojo goals, and sometimes even blogs about it. An unrepentant epicurean, she grows heirloom tomatoes and ferments a variety of sauerkraut, sourdough, kombucha, pickles, and water kefir.

If you would like to know when she has new books out, please sign up for her newsletter at candicebundy.com. Or, email her at candice@candicebundy.com if the mood strikes you.